SILKWIN'S QUEST
A Sequel to Silkwin's Edge

By Harvey Bateman
and Judy Schwinkendorf

Strategic Book Publishing and Rights Co.

Strategic Book Publishing and Rights Co., LLC
USA I Singapore

For information about special discounts for bulk purchases,
please contact Strategic Book Publishing and Rights Co.
Special Sales, at bookorder@sbpra.net.

ISBN: 978-1-63135-974-3

Book Design: Suzanne Kelly

DEDICATION

S ilkwin's Edge and Silkwin's Quest have been dedicated to Virginia Bateman, wife and mother, and grandmother. She passed away August 9, 2007 after a year long struggle with cancer. Her support and encouragement helped make these novels possible. She is the one who suggested the name "Silkwin" for the family name and the Title of both novels..

ACKNOWLEDGEMENT

I would like to thank my family for their support and encouragement, especially my son, Gary Bateman and my daughter Judy Schwinkendorf. I also would like to thank my grandson Joshua and his wife Erika who were instrumental in coming up with the concept and design of the cover. A special thanks to a special friend Jean Steck for her encouragement and advice.

CHAPTER ONE

Eric Silkwin stood at the foot of his best friend's grave. The midday sun cast flickering shadows on the monument.

JASON CORKLAND 1929 – 1948.

Vivid memories flashed through his mind with sudden clarity. It seemed impossible a year had passed since escorting Jason's body back to his hometown of Wyler, Illinois.

Eric sent out a silent prayer for the easygoing redhead, who had been more like a brother than just a friend. The pleasant spring weather failed to help Eric overcome the sudden depression he felt.

"It's going to start raining soon," Maxine Tyler Quinlin said softly. A gentle breeze brought in patches of gray clouds, which battled the sun for control. Tyler and Eric watched Cindy, Jason's girlfriend arrange the flowers on his grave.

"It's the best I can do," Cindy said, as she brushed away her tears, and stared at the light gray monument. "I wonder if he really knows we're here."

"He's with us. I feel his presence," Eric said. Eric thought about Cindy, and how she had reacted at Jason's funeral. He could still see—as if it was yesterday—her clawing away at his casket. Eric could almost hear the conversation he had with Jason that last night they were on a pass.

"Jason, just a little less than a month to go, tonight, that seems so far away."

"You'll make it," Eric. "Pour on the gym workouts," Jason had responded.

"Eric, remember when I told you about my dad meeting someone. I'm gonna ask if they'd agree to a double

ceremony with Cindy and I. Wouldn't that be something? A father and son wedding?"

"*That would be great, Jason. You'd like that, wouldn't you?"*

"*More than you know, Eric. I'm glad my dad found someone. Oh, by the way, I'm going camping Monday, so I'll see you Tuesday."*

"*Maybe one last Camel, you know, to wrap up the evening."*

The following day, Jason drowned. Eric tried to force that painful memory from his mind. It started to rain. Tyler, Cindy, and Eric rushed back to the car.

"I think we better head back," Eric said. Everyone seemed quiet on the ride back to Bedford. Eric thought of the last ten months since his discharge. He was gradually taking over his father's shoe repair shop. Colleen, his daughter, and the most important thing in his life, would soon be a year old. His attraction to Tyler seemed to be growing stronger.

Her inner strength, mixed with just enough shyness, was one of the things Eric liked most about her. In some ways she reminded him of Alice, his wife, who died after the birth of their daughter, Colleen, almost a year ago.

"Eric! You're drifting off again," Tyler said.

"Sorry girls, I guess I just have a lot on my mind"

"Let me off anywhere in town," Cindy said. You could tell Cindy had been crying; her eyes were red. "It meant so much having you two with me," she added softly. Eric pulled over to the curb. The rain had stopped, bringing freshness in the air.

"Cindy, if you need someone to talk to; call me," Eric said. "When are we gonna meet this new guy of yours?"

"Soon, I hope. I think you'll like him."

"I'm sure we will," Eric said.

"She's quite a girl," Tyler said. "Fighting her way back after all she's been through."

"Cindy's determined, that's for sure," Eric said. "She told me she hasn't had a drink in three months."

"That takes a lot of guts," Tyler blurted out.

2

Eric grinned. At times, her unexpected comments surprised him. "You're quite a girl yourself," he said. Eric pulled in front of the Quinlin farmhouse. He put his arm around Tyler and looked into her eyes. "Sometimes at night, I find myself reaching for you," Eric said.

"I know you have certain . . . er . . . feelings," Tyler said and grinned. They walked slowly toward the house.

"Don't you two get enough of that hand holding stuff?" Patsy, Tyler's ten-year-old sister yelled.

"Patsy, why don't you give Eric a break?" Mrs. Quinlin asked.

"I will if he'll answer some questions. I've gotta do a school paper and describe someone that's not in the family." As Patsy smiled, you couldn't help but notice her freckles and front missing tooth. "How about you, Eric? Tyler told me you're one quarter Cheyenne Indian."

"That's true," Eric said.

She wrote in her notebook, and then looked carefully at him. "You have dark eyes, short dark brown hair. Can you tell me anything else about yourself?"

"I'm five foot eleven and half, and one hundred and seventy pounds."

"Well, that's not very much, but I guess it will have to do," Patsy sighed.

"I certainly hope so," Eric said.

After supper, everyone listened to the radio. "Patsy, it's getting late," Mrs. Quinlin said. "I think you better get ready for bed.

Patsy ginned. "Eric, you describe Tyler for me, and I promise I'll go to bed."

Tyler's eyes met Eric's. "Well, she's tall, pretty, has long black hair and big brown eyes. The first thing I noticed was those incredible dimples."

"She's skinny too, Eric," Patsy said.

"I thought you were going to bed," Tyler interrupted.

"I'm going," Patsy said.

"I think it's time for us to turn in too," Mrs. Quinlin said.

Tyler changed the radio to music.

Eric took her in his arms and whispered, "I love you, Tyler Quinlin." Her lack of response bothered him. He tried to ignore the feeling of separation. After the music ended, he led her to the couch.

"Easy Eric, I . . . ."

"What're you two doing?" Patsy asked. She laughed when they jumped. "I thought a glass of milk would help me sleep," she said

"We were dancing and . . . ."

"It didn't look like dancing to me," Patsy said.

Eric got up from the couch. "I've gotta be going anyway."

"I'll walk you to the door," Tyler said. She glanced toward the kitchen. "Things were getting outta hand anyway."

He kissed her. Eric grinned as he walked to the car. It was the first time he had that kind of physical feeling since Alice died.

When Eric walked in the door, his mother looked up and yawned. "Colleen fell asleep a few minutes ago. Ellen and Johnny were here, she misses Colleen so."

Ellen, Eric's sister, and her husband Johnny, had moved into their own apartment after he received his discharge. Johnny opened his own radio shop under the GI Bill.

Eric glanced at the familiar Bible beside his mother's chair. "Colleen's growing so fast," Martha, Eric's mother, said. "She's jabbering all the time."

The next morning Eric was up early, feeding Colleen. His father came in the kitchen, and slumped in his chair. "Seems like that girl is always eating," he growled, failing to hide the pride in his eyes.

The phone rang, so Eric handed Colleen to his father. "All right Frank, I'll see you at six." He laughed and hung up. "It sounds like Karen and Frank have their hands full."

"It's no wonder," his mother said, "With two little ones less than a year apart. You'd think they would have planned a little better."

Howard, Eric's father, laughed. "Sometimes you make a mistake."

Eric remembered when his best friend Frank and his cousin Karen told him and Alice about their situation, and that they had to get married.

Eric saw the weariness on his father's face. "Why don't you take off today and help take care of Colleen?"

"Maybe 'til noon," he sighed. He lifted Colleen over his head and she screamed with laughter. Eric decided to walk the eight blocks to the shop, so he could enjoy the warm weather. He grabbed the phone the minute he opened the shop and dialled Tyler's number. "Hello, Tyler."

"Hi Eric, how are you this morning?"

"Fine, except I miss you," he said as he leaned back in his father's old swivel chair. "You know we're invited to Karen and Frank's tonight."

"Great. I'm feeling a little feisty this morning," Tyler said.

"Does it have anything to do with me?" Eric heard her laugh as he looked up to see Linda Maynard enter the shop. Linda was that special girl that a guy could never really get out of his mind. She still looked terrific. It was as if nature wouldn't have it any other way.

"I thought I'd drop off my mother's shoes," Linda said. "I gave my two-weeks notice today. I'm going out east. Bill has asked me to marry him. Mother and Walter Blanchard have agreed to a double ceremony. Isn't that something?"

"That's great," Eric said. "I remember a father and son wedding that didn't quite make it," thinking of Jason and his father.

"I have to hurry," Linda said. "I've got so much to do. Kiss your daughter for me, Eric."

"Glad to—you still look lovely, lady."

"Oh Eric, you're always saying things like that."

That evening Tyler met Eric at the door. He leaned over to kiss her and she ducked away. "Can you believe it? I'm ready. Aren't you going to say anything about my hair?"

"It's different," Eric said. She had it up in kind of a sweep he'd never seen before. "You get caught in a wind storm?"

Her smile turned to a pout. "You don't like it?"

"It's nice. You just look a little different," Eric said. She didn't say another word until they arrived at Karen and Frank's. Her moods changed so often lately.

Frank opened the door. "Hi Eric. Tyler, is that really you?" Tyler face turned red as Karen came rushing out of the kitchen.

"Tyler, I like your hair—don't mind these guys. You can help me in the kitchen."

"Hey Eric, I've got some news. I got a chance for a real promotion," Frank said. "The company wants me to move to Glenville, Ohio. Karen and I are driving there Tuesday morning." He grinned and added, "Her folks don't know it yet."

"That's great Frank, if that's what you really want, but are you sure you're ready to make a move like that, especially with a new baby"

"Supper's ready," Karen called.

"The timing isn't very good, I admit, but you have to grab the opportunity when it comes along," Frank said.

The conversations went on through the evening, first the excitement, then the moody silence that followed. "How do you two feel about going to the cabin?" Eric asked.

Frank stared at him, "This is the first time I've heard you mention the cabin in months."

"I thought it might be a good weekend just to get away," Eric said, ". . . and I think now, I'll be able to deal with the memories there."

Tyler just looked at Karen, but didn't say anything.

The drive to back to Tyler's house was quiet, except for music from the car radio. A song about an enchanted evening somehow seemed out of place.

Tyler stopped Eric at the front door, "I'm not going to ask you in. You can kiss me goodnight here," she said.

Eric felt the warmth transmitted from her slender body,

"Maybe I should . . . ."

"Not tonight Eric. I got a lot on my mind."

Eric could not help but feel the tension between Tyler and himself.

As Eric walked into the kitchen the next morning, he saw his mother getting ready to feed Colleen. "There's some oatmeal on the stove if you want some."

Eric grabbed a cup of coffee, waving off breakfast. "No time, I've got to go. I'm running late, I have to pick up Tyler, Karen, and Frank. We're going to the cabin. You think Dad can handle the shop today?"

"I'm sure he'll be fine. You've been carrying the load for a long time, and he feels he owes you. Don't worry."

Eric pulled up in front of Karen and Frank's house. Frank opened the car door. Karen pushed him in the back seat. "Karen was up early bugging me," Frank said. "I guess it's the chance to get away for a while . . ."

"You got that right," Karen interrupted. The early morning breeze blew through her strawberry blonde hair. Their boys, Bruce and Barry were staying with Karen's folks. It wasn't often that she had time to just enjoy the day.

Strangely enough, the drive to the cabin and lake was quiet. They walked along the lake enjoying the view. "Frank, you seem to have a lot on your mind," Eric said.

"The job opportunity and leaving Benford. I'm not sure about this move," Frank said. "I have mixed feelings."

"You'll figure it out, Frank."

It was a beautiful day, until suddenly a breeze from the lake sent the leaves rustling overhead. The weather was changing into a chilly, depressing evening as the trees captured the rays of the sun. Tyler shivered and Eric put his arm around her.

"Why don't we head back to the cabin," Karen said.

They went inside the cabin and the feeling Eric was afraid of overtook him. Alice's words flashed through his mind. *"I know you're watching me cause you can't keep your eyes off of me — your hands either."*

He walked to the couch near the fireplace. He could see her big blue eyes full of mischief, her red pajamas, which had come alive from the glow of the fire. *"If you want me, you're going to have to peel me like an orange."* The words seemed to echo through the stillness of the cabin.

"Eric, are you alright?" Tyler asked.

Eric didn't answer. Karen and Frank watched Eric's actions carefully. He waited a few minutes, before looking into the little bedroom Alice had called a room full of sunshine.

Eric turned toward Karen and Frank, "I think we better go."

Tyler was silent until they arrived at her house. "Call me, Eric," she said and rushed in the house. Eric drove to Karen and Frank's apartment to drop them off.

"We'll see you when we get back," Karen said. "Tomorrow will be a busy day for us."

"It didn't turn out exactly like I thought it would," Eric said.

"Eric, you can't blame Tyler."

"You both need more time," Frank added.

"Maybe you're right," Eric said. "Good luck with your trip."

When Eric arrived home, Johnny's car was in the driveway. He took a deep breath and opened the door.

"Look what I have," Ellen said. "Isn't she just gorgeous?"

"She's a cute one," Eric said. "How are you doing, Johnny?"

"Great. I can't keep Ellen away from Colleen—at least until she gets her own."

Ellen's smile gave her away before she could say anything.

"Ellen, is that what the special news is?" her mother asked.

"She wouldn't say anything until you got here Eric. I'm going to be a grandfather again," Eric's father said. "Now for a little wine."

"Congratulations to both of you," Eric said.

"Thanks, Johnny and I are pretty excited. The baby is due the middle of October. It's getting late. We've been here quite a while—I think we better get going," Ellen said.

It was Sunday morning. The service was about to start when they walked in church. Eric saw his cousin Bryan, with his girl Liza. He had the feeling Bryan was avoiding him. After services, he shook hands with Reverend Langtree.

"Thanks for coming Eric," Reverend Langtree said, "As for Colleen—what can I say, Eric? She's beautiful. Are you still giving healings?"

Eric thought it was strange Reverend Langtree would ask him that. He did not answer at first. He hadn't mentioned anything about his healing gift the last few months, which seemed to help stop the telephone calls, and other forms of harassment directed at him. Even Karen and Frank seemed closer to him because there was less stress. Even though Eric still had dreams occasionally about his healing gift, he didn't bring up the subject—although deep inside, he felt there was something special in store for him in the future.

"I'm sorry reverend, I got lost in my thoughts for a moment," Eric said. "I haven't really been involved with healing for quite a while."

"I'm sorry, maybe I shouldn't have brought the subject up," Rev. Langtree said.

"That's okay, Reverend."

Tuesday morning Karen and Frank came in the shop. "Hi cousin," Karen yelled. "We have some news to tell you. You better tell him, Frank."

"Eric, I've decided on taking that position," Frank said, with that familiar grin. "I really feel it's the right thing to do."

Eric didn't know what to say, except, "Congratulations, Frank. I hope everything works out for you."

"I hope so too, Eric."

"We just stopped in for a moment," Karen said. "We wanted you to know first, Eric." She grabbed Frank's hand, "We have to be going, there's a lot to do. We'll see you later."

After a few moments, Eric decided to call Tyler, but hung up the phone when he heard her voice.

"You look like you're sleep-walking," Eric heard his father say as he walked up from the back of the shop. "You called Maxine, I'd guess, from the expression on your face." His father was the only one who called Tyler Maxine.

"Karen and Frank are back in town, they were just here," Eric said. "Frank's taking the position he was offered."

Eric's father grinned, "I just hope it isn't the position that's taking Frank. Anything you want to talk about?"

"Things are changing so fast. Frank and Karen are leaving. Tyler and I are . . . drifting apart. There seems to be some kind of barrier between us."

"That doesn't surprise me, Eric. You're not ready for a serious relationship. Why don't you take off? Your mind's not here anyway."

"I think your right."

Eric was thinking, *I'm going to have to make Tyler understand my feelings for Alice don't change how I feel about her, and what she means to me.*

CHAPTER TWO

Eric heard laughter coming from the bathroom. He peeked around the doorway to see Colleen yell and splash water, her dark curly hair plastered down on her head. "You're a mess, little one!" Eric said. Colleen saw her daddy and tried to reach out for him.

"How she loves her bath," Eric's mother said, wrapping Colleen in a big towel. "She's such a joy. You better get cleaned up, Eric. It won't be long before supper is ready. Besides, I don't want you spoiling her. Maybe I do a little, but you and your father are worse," she added quickly. "Eric, do you think you should call her little one?"

I haven't thought about it, but I don't think it's that serious," Eric said. "Oh, by the way, I won't be home for supper; I'm going over to Tyler's house. I have to leave in a few minutes."

The sky was cloudy and overcast. It began to rain. Eric pulled his car close to the Quinlin house. Patsy stood in the doorway laughing. "You're gonna get wet."

"You are right, young lady." He wiped his feet on a rug and winked at her.

"Tyler isn't ready as usual." Her grin revealed mischief. "Tyler's old boyfriend, Jerry Yount, and his folks were here last night."

Tyler suddenly appeared out of the hallway. "Patsy, you talk too much. How are you, Eric, other than all wet?"

"I'm fine. You look very pretty tonight Tyler."

"Thanks—Patsy, you behave yourself until Mom and Dad gets back."

"Watch her Eric, she's a real grouch," Patsy said. "I don't know what's wrong."

After they drove off, Tyler didn't say anything. She stared out the window. Eric decided he'd waited long enough. "Is it something I've done?" he asked.

"No it's . . . ." She avoided looking in his eyes. "I didn't mean for it to be this way."

"Something has changed in the last few days. What's wrong with you?" Eric asked. When she refused to answer, he pulled off on a side road and stopped. The sounds of the night turned into silence.

"People are going to think . . . ."

"They'd be wrong, wouldn't they," Eric said

"I want us to stop seeing each other—at least for a while," Tyler said. She faced him. "Sometimes I need the kind of security Jerry gives me. I'm closer to him than I realized . . . ."

Eric could only add, "I guess you've said it all."

"Eric, I told you about the son I gave up for adoption—the adoption agency called me. His parents were killed in an auto accident."

Eric responded, "That explains part of it, but me and you . . . ."

Tyler interrupted, "Eric, you can't seem to let Alice go . . . You're just not ready for a relationship. The other day at the cabin only confirmed what I've known all along." She said it so softly he barely heard her. "I can't ignore it any longer. It really scares me!"

Eric didn't answer. It was like he was in a dream and he would wake up any moment.

"I have a lot on my mind," Tyler continued. "My parents are upset and Patsy doesn't know about my son." Her voice broke, "You're not *ready* to be in love with anyone!"

Depression closed in on Eric like a fog. He started the car. "It seem like you're the one not ready to be in love, or maybe it's just not me your ready to be in love with. I think we better just call it an evening," Eric said. "If you ever need someone to talk too or whatever—call me—promise me that much!" he said.

13

"I promise," Tyler said softly. It was the last thing she said to him.

The following week, Eric tried to keep his mind on his work, but he kept thinking about Tyler's five-year-old son. Late in the afternoon, the phone rang. He was surprised and pleased to hear Tyler's voice.

"Hi Eric, I've been thinking and I feel I owe you more of an explanation than I gave you the other night. I thought maybe we could have a hamburger at Cookie's Drive-in and talk."

"Okay Tyler, I'll be at your house a little after five."

"I'll be ready," she whispered.

The moment he walked in the Quinlin's house, Patsy took Eric aside and whispered, "There's something going on around here and nobody will tell me what it is."

"What makes you think so?" Eric asked.

"Tyler, Mother, and Dad are keeping something from me. I know it, Eric. I'm not dumb," Patsy said, just before Tyler walked in the room.

The minute they stepped out the door, Tyler said, "I felt I had to talk to you," She did not say anything else until they finished eating at Cookies. Suddenly her voice rose to a fever pitch. "I'm going to adopt my son Evan!"

"I understand. I'm on your side, Tyler—remember?" It was as if she hadn't heard a word.

"How am I going to explain a five-year-old son to Patsy?" Tyler asked.

Eric looked into Tyler's eyes. "Don't underestimate Patsy. Just come out and tell her. She'll understand more than you think."

"I want you to help me explain this to Patsy. I admit I had this in mind when I called you. There's something else . . ." She hesitated a moment, then blurted out, "Would you like to make love to me? Eric?"

Eric had just taken a drag off his Camel and started choking.

"Eric! You all right?" Tyler yelled.

He put his hand up, trying to catch his breath . . .

"You're laughing at me. I didn't realize it was so funny," Tyler snapped.

"Sorry. You caught me off guard," Eric said, finally bringing himself under control. "I've wanted to make love to you for a long time, why ask me now?"

"I feel I owe you that much," Tyler blurted out.

He grabbed her by the shoulders and pulled her to him, "You *owe* me! What in the *hell* are you talking about?"

"Don't swear Eric."

The impulse to laugh was so overwhelming it was ridiculous. Here was a girl, torn between a struggle to adopt her son, and her willingness to make love for an obligation she felt she owed him.

"Are you laughing at me?" Tyler asked, and pulled away from Eric. "I'll have you know it wasn't easy for me to ask such a thing."

"I know. It's not easy for me either," Eric said. "I've always wanted you, but under the right circumstances."

"I can no longer compete with another girl, especially one who's . . . I think we'd better go," Tyler said.

Eric didn't answer. When Eric pulled into the Quinlin driveway, he noticed the back porch light was on.

Tyler's parents met Eric and Tyler at the door. They couldn't help but notice the strain on their faces. The four of them sat around the kitchen table sipping coffee, waiting for Patsy.

"I'll be out in a minute, Eric," Patsy yelled from the hallway, then appeared a few moments later. "I get to stay up later tonight; we're all supposed to have a special talk."

"That's great," Eric said. "Sometimes it's important to talk about things."

Her freckled face became puzzled. "Huh?"

"Patsy," Tyler said suddenly, "There is something I need to tell you. I have a five-year-old son."

Her face revealed complete confusion. Patsy looked to her parents, to Eric, and finally to Tyler. "I don't understand."

"Remember when I stayed with Aunt Lenore, almost six years ago?"

"I remember. Is that when you had your baby?"

"Yes," Tyler said. She brushed back her long, dark hair and added, "I had a baby boy that I gave up for adoption, He's five years old, and I want to bring him home."

"Why did you give him away?" Patsy asked, still puzzled.

Eric could hear the pressure mounting in Tyler's voice "I was young, and in school. Now I think we need each other. The people who adopted him were killed in an automobile accident and he is all alone now.'

"Is Jerry the daddy?" Patsy asked. "Is that why he asked you to marry him?"

Eric just looked at Tyler.

Tyler lost control. Her face reddened and her voice broke. "Patsy, I'm going to ask you to trust me, and I'll explain later."

The look on her face turned from confusion to a big grin, "All right—when you gonna bring him home?"

"Soon," Tyler said. "His name is Evan."

"Patsy, there are many changes coming," Eric said, "and I know you'll help Tyler and Evan through these changes."

Patsy walked over to Eric, and put her hand on his shoulder. "I will. I've got so much to think about," she said. "Are you and Tyler gonna get married?"

"No," Eric said, trying to keep his own voice steady.

Patsy turned to Tyler, "I'll help you as much as I can."

"I know you will, honey," Tyler said with tears in her eyes.

"Good night everybody," Patsy said. She looked confused and excited at the same time.

Mrs. Quinlin sighed, "It went better than I expected. I guess we underestimated Patsy."

"Yes, I guess we have," Tyler said. "Eric, I really appreciate you being here for me. That thing about Jerry asking me to . . . ."

Eric interrupted her, "If you need a friend, I'll be around." He then left.

The month of May passed quickly. In two days, Colleen would have her first birthday. That same day a year ago, his whole life fell apart when he lost Alice. A feeling of hopelessness came over him. He needed something to numb the pain he felt. Eric walked to Daily's Tavern. The place was crowded, as usual, with conversations and music from the jukebox drowning each other out. Eric ordered a drink and lit a cigarette, trying to fight off the thoughts of a year ago.

"Hello Eric." He snapped out of his daydream to see Liza, Johnny's sister, standing beside him.

"Hello Liza, I haven't seen you for a while—Bryan either, for that matter."

"I don't want to intrude, but I happened to see you come in here and was wondering if I could talk to you."

"Sure Liza, what's going on?"

She sat down on the bar stool next to Eric and looked him straight in the eye. "Is there something wrong with me?" she blurted out. "Maybe I should explain: Bryan and I have split up."

"Why would you think something like that?" Eric asked.

Her big, dark eyes watched him carefully. "He never made a pass at me. Maybe I shouldn't say this, but it's my way of coming to the point, if you know what I mean."

"You mean . . . ." Eric hesitated a moment.

"Yeah. You know the usual things guys do," Liza said. "I think there's something wrong with somebody." Her reputation for bluntness was well known, but this surprised even Eric.

"It is unusual," Eric said, feeling awkward. "You have been together quite a while."

"That's just the point. I just don't feel right with him," Liza said. "You always seemed so easy to talk too. I think I'm embarrassing you." Her dark eyes bore into Eric's. "He's probably seeing another girl."

Eric knew Bryan was avoiding him, and wasn't sure how to respond to Liza's accusations. "Did you trying talking to Bryan?"

"I tried talking to him, but he gets upset. He's been so moody lately—even more than usual. Last week we broke up and he had tears in his eyes." Liza continued. "It's strange. It was as if we really didn't know each other at all—unbelievable . . . Maybe you'd better forget I'm telling you this."

Eric looked into her dark eyes. "What are you doing tonight?"

Her eyes widened, "What do you mean?"

"Cindy and her boyfriend are coming over tonight," Eric said. "How would you like to join us and be my date? I know it's sudden, but why not? Maybe it will give Bryan something to think about."

"What would people think?"

"Because you're my sister's husband's sister?" Eric asked. "That's quite a mouthful."

"Yes, it is." She joined him in laughter. "Come to think of it—why shouldn't I?"

"I have to head back," Eric said. "I'll call you when they get in town. Maybe it will give both of us a much needed lift."

Liza smiled, her dark eyes looking into his with complete attention. "Sounds great." She stared at the man at the bar, whose attention seemed focused on her, and added with her voice rising, "It would be my pleasure, *Eric Silkwin.*"

Later that evening, after calling Liza, Eric played with Colleen. "Listen to her laugh," Ellen said. "Just think; she'll be a year old in two days."

"My cute, little, chubby year old daughter." Eric said. He feigned shock when Colleen grabbed his nose and handed her to Ellen. "I've gotta shower and shave; Cindy and her boyfriend are coming over later."

"Got a date with Tyler?" Ellen asked.

"No, Liza," Eric said with a grin, enjoying the expression on Ellen's and his mother's faces. He turned to Johnny, "I hope you don't mind?"

"Of course not. In a way, it doesn't surprise me," Johnny said.

"How does Tyler feel about that?" asked Ellen.

"I really don't know how Tyler feels—I never bothered to ask her."

Ellen and her mother just looked at each other. Eric went to his bedroom after showering and took Alice's book of poems out of the closet for the first time since she passed away. He glanced at them quickly and put them back. He would look at them later . . . *much later*.

"Your friends are here," his mother called from the hallway.

"Hello Eric," Cindy said. She looked radiant. She turned to the tall, blond guy next to her. "I'd like you to meet Stuart Praust."

They shook hands. "Call me Stu."

"Nice to meet you Stu," Eric said. "Cindy, you look great. Stu wouldn't have anything to do with that, would he?"

Cindy just smiled.

We'd better go," Eric said. "I hope you don't mind, but I asked a friend of mine named Liza to join us."

A little later, they pulled in front of Liza's aunt's house. Eric felt a little strange and at the same time excited. He knocked and Liza opened the door. Her dark eyes sparkled, surrounded by her short, dark wavy hair.

"You look very pretty," Eric said. The red dress with a white belt only added to her attraction.

She laughed. "I'll figure out how to answer that later."

Liza and Eric crawled in the back. Cindy turned to Liza. "I know you from somewhere."

"New Years party at the cabin. I was Bryan's date—Eric's cousin."

"I remember now," Cindy said.

Morgan's was Benford's only dance-hall/restaurant combination. A family dining area separated the larger section, consisting of a bar along one wall. Tables for four surrounded the oval-shaped dance floor. Booths, along with the orchestra section, filled the remaining area. Although it was early, the place was crowded. "A table with candlelight, how nice," Cindy said.

The walls above the booths displayed murals of scenic mid western landscapes framed against a dark, textured background of wood panelling. Lights mounted on suspended wagon-wheels seemed to create just the right atmosphere.

As the lights dimmed, the music cut into the surrounding intimate conversations. After giving the waitress their orders, Stuart and Eric led the girls to the dance floor. In a few moments, Liza was in Eric's arms, humming along to the music with her head buried in his shoulder.

After a couple dances Stuart, Eric, and the girls returned to their table. The conversation shifted to Eric. "What do you do for a living, Stuart?"

"I have been a truck driver, construction worker, anything outside, you name it." Stuart's actions reminded Eric of Jason. Stuart gave the impression he would stand by what he believed in. "Eric, I don't know what your politics are, but I feel that this guy Truman is a straight shooter and I think . . . ." He glanced at Cindy, and said, "I promised Cindy I wouldn't mention this stuff."

"I don't mind that much," Cindy said. "It's just that when I read about Russia testing an atomic bomb . . . Well, just all that kind of talk upsets me."

"I don't think about that stuff too much," Liza added. "I admit it's a little frightening, but what can you do? You can't change things anyway."

"Maybe that's the way to look at it," Stuart said. "Oh, by the way . . ." he grinned, ". . . I've asked Cindy to marry me."

"Of course I said yes." Cindy smiled, and added, "I've told Stuart about Alice and Jason, he knows what Eric and I have been through."

"We are survivors, aren't we Cindy?" Eric asked.

"It wasn't easy," she said, seeming to drift off a moment. "The thing I learned is when you hit bottom, the only way is up."

After a few more dances, and pleasant conversation, the evening faded away. Cindy and Stu drove Liza and Eric to Eric's house. "I had a wonderful time. We must do this again soon," Cindy said just before they left.

"It's been nice," Liza said to Eric, "but I do wish you'd forget, at least for tonight, that I'm Johnny's little sister."

"I'm trying to, believe me. Would you like to get something to eat?" Eric asked.

"I'm really not hungry, but it is a beautiful night." They drove to the lake and parked. It was a calm and peaceful evening, with a few other cars in the distance. The music from the radio drifted through as Liza gazed at the star filled sky. After a few restless moments, Eric instincts took over.

He put his arm around Liza. He felt a little uneasy, until she moved closer to him. Eric kissed her, she responded and he kissed harder. He felt his hand tremble as he placed it on her knee. Liza didn't move. Her only reaction was her low-pitched laugh. Eric pulled her to him and slowly moved his hand along her leg, ignoring the dryness in his throat.

"Eric, it's all right," she whispered.

The feeling of uncontrollable desire swept over him. "Let's get in the back seat," Eric whispered, surprised at the sound of his own voice. Liza pulled away and in an instant, her long slender legs crawled over the seat.

"Ow," Eric yelled, grabbing his leg.

"What's the matter?" Liza whispered.

"Cramp in my leg," Eric yelled. He forced himself over the seat.

"Let me," Liz whispered, massaging his leg with fingers that felt like magic. Moments later, her movements met his. Soon after their encounter, they both relaxed with breathless sighs, her fingers again working her form of magic on his leg.

Eric whispered, "I couldn't control myself." He stared at this slim, dark-eyed girl, who suddenly took on the appearance of a little girl.

Liza's voice became soft, followed by a low laugh, and her usual bluntness. "Don't blame yourself, I wanted you as much as you wanted me."

"You look so deceiving," Eric sighed.

Her laughter rang out into the night. "I think you had better get me home." On the way back to town, she hummed along with the radio, until he pulled in front of her house. "Don't worry Eric," Liza said in that, low throaty laugh. "It happened and I am glad. Why do you find that so hard to understand? The expression on your face defies description."

Suddenly Eric joined her in laughter, feeling better than he had in a long time. He kissed her. Liza pulled away, and added, "We've already said goodnight."

"Liza, Colleen's birthday party is tomorrow and I would like you to come," Eric said.

"We'll see," Liza said. Her laughter was the last thing he heard as she ran to the door.

CHAPTER THREE

Colleen's birthday party got under way about one-thirty. Liza, looking bright-eyed, and pretty as ever came with Bryan, Ellen and Johnny. A short time later, Karen and Frank came. "I'm glad to see you, Liza. It's good to see you too, Bryan," Eric said. "It's been awhile."

"I wouldn't miss Colleen's first birthday party," Bryan said. "It's too bad it's the same tragic day Alice died."

"Bryan, let's just focus on Colleen's birthday party," Liza said.

Eric didn't respond. Eric's mother and father seemed excited, the pride in their eyes made it all worthwhile. Colleen watched the glow of the candle with wide-eyed fascination as everyone sang *Happy Birthday* to her. Colleen tried to open her presents. At times, she was more interested in the wrapping paper than the gift. Everyone had cake. It seemed Colleen had more cake on her than she got in her. Everyone seemed to be enjoying themselves.

"Hey Eric—Cleveland won the World Series—I told you they would," Frank said.

"I thought for sure Boston would take it," Eric rebutted.

Frank grinned. "I know. You're just upset because your idol is retiring."

"Yeah. There'll never be another boxer like him. He was the greatest." Eric said. "Twenty-five title defences. It's depressing. With Babe Ruth gone and Joe Louis retiring—what's this world coming to?"

Liza came over to join in the conversation. It wasn't long before Ellen followed her. Ellen watched Eric carefully, noticing how his attention seemed to be focused on Liza.

"Liza, Eric tells me you and he went out," Ellen said. "From the expressions on your faces, you both evidently had a big evening."

"Very nice," Liza replied. "He was a gentleman, and his friends are tops."

Eric looked straight into Liza's eyes. "I'm glad you enjoyed it. It was an evening we both needed . . . I think I'll see how Karen's doing," Eric said, "She's been pretty quiet." As Eric approached Karen, he noticed she seemed distant. "Hi Karen, how are things going?"

Karen's voice fought for control as tears appeared in her eyes. Frank put his arm around her. "Okay, I guess," she responded.

"Are you leaving tomorrow?" Eric asked.

"Yes, tomorrow we leave," Karen said. "I know it's a new beginning, and I'm sure everything will work out alright," seemingly trying to convince herself, "We'll miss you, Eric." Karen hugged him. Frank and Eric shook hands.

"Well, I guess this is it. I hope we're doing the right thing," Frank said. "I guess there's no way knowing, unless you take a chance."

"I'm really going to miss you, too," Eric said. "Remember, keep in touch."

"It was a nice party," Ellen said, "and I'm crazy about the birthday girl, but I think it's time for us to go."

"Thanks for coming, Liza," Eric said. For a moment, they looked in each other's eyes.

"Come on Liza, I'll walk you home," Bryan said. He turned to Eric. "I've missed our talks. I got the impression you resented my feelings against your healing business."

"It's not a business, Bryan," Liza said.

"I don't resent you, Bryan," Eric said, "Your opinions are your own."

Bryan's smile faded. "I've got some problems to work out," Bryan said.

Eric thought for an instant that he saw fear in Bryan's eyes. Finally, everyone said their goodbyes and left. Colleen played on the floor with the wrapping paper and ribbons. Eric's father grabbed her hand. "Don't put that in your mouth," Howard said. He handed her a toy dog. Colleen stared at him and put the dog's ear in her mouth. "This girl is just determined to eat," Howard said with laughter. Eric smiled.

"I think I'll go to the cemetery," Eric said. "Maybe next year I'll take Colleen with me."

The late evening sun cast shadows through the trees, across the familiar ground as he walked up the slope. He put flowers on Alice's grave and stared at the monument. His eyes followed her name, carved in stone, as if somehow a contact could be made.

"I brought you roses, Alice—your favorite." Eric's voice echoed through the silence. He felt emotion rising within him. "I see more of you in Colleen every day. What I can't help wondering is why this healing power didn't help you."

The sudden feeling of guilt swept over him. "Maybe someday I'll understand." The sun settled behind the trees, bringing a chilly breeze with the shadows. Eric bowed his head. "I'm taking off now. Colleen and I will be praying for you." The walk back to the car wasn't any easier than before. He felt it was going to be this way for a long time.

"We were wondering about you, it's getting dark and . . . ." His mother looked at him and didn't say another word. Eric went to Colleen's room. She stood up in her crib and reached for him. "I'll bet you need changing and naturally you're hungry," Eric said.

"I'll feed her," Howard said, "I know how to handle her. Eric, I wish I could help you. It just takes time—there's no other way."

"Any idea how long?" Erik asked.

"No. I wish I knew," his father said.

"Eric, I'm worried about you," his mother said. "You haven't been yourself lately. I know it's only been a year since Alice left us, and your life was turned upside down. I also know I could never begin to understand what you're going through. In the Bible, Proverbs 3:6 says, 'In all thy ways acknowledge him, and he shall direct thy paths.' Eric, God has given you a great gift of healing to help others and maybe even help yourself. Just think about what I said."

Eric lay in bed staring at the ceiling, when a brilliant white light spread over his consciousness. He felt a sudden feeling of peace for a few moments. Tawnya, the little girl in his dreams suddenly appeared. *"Have faith and be prepared for the road ahead. Know that we are with you, and we will help you as much as we can."* The vision vanished as quickly as it came. He felt a power through his body just before falling into a deep sleep.

The next morning when Eric woke up, he felt very uneasy. The dream he had seemed very real, but didn't make any sense. He was trying to put together pieces of the dream that he could remember. It seemed Bryan was trying to communicate with him, but he couldn't understand what Bryan was trying to tell him. Then all of a sudden, Bryan was gone. Liza walked over, handed him a letter of some kind, and had tears in her eyes.

Several months passed with routine. The thought of Tyler and her son, Evan, entered Eric's mind occasionally. He saw Liza and Bryan now and then, but it seemed Bryan intentionally avoided him.

"You need to go out more," his father said one evening. "You've shut yourself away long enough."

"I'm all right," Eric said. "I've taken Liza to the movies a couple times. I don't know if Bryan cares. At certain times he acts a little strange."

"You mean he's more moody than usual," his father said.

"It's hard to explain, but it seems so at certain times."

"How does Liza feel about Bryan?" his father asked.

26

"She wants to be with him, but she told me she's confused about their relationship. She doesn't think things are right between them."

"Sometimes Bryan's hard to understand," Howard said. Colleen was playing with her food and jabbering as if to join in on the conversation. "Colleen's almost a year and a half. Shouldn't she be saying a few words?" Howard asked.

"She's only seventeen months," Martha countered, "Give her some time. She'll talk when she's ready.

"We better get ready for church," Howard said. "We don't want to be late."

Ellen and Johnny joined the family for the usual Sunday dinner. Ellen looked like she might have the baby any minute. "You haven't said much Eric," Ellen said, "All during dinner you seemed to be somewhere else."

"I've just got a lot on my mind," Eric said.

"Have you heard anything from Karen and Frank?" Ellen asked.

"Not much. I don't think things are going as well as they expected," Eric replied.

"That was a big decision to make, I hope everything works out for them," Ellen said.

"Liza mentions you often," Johnny said. "I think you've impressed her."

Eric grinned, "I like her too—she's quite a girl."

"I think we'd better be going," Ellen said. "I hate to leave this little bundle, when she's so close to talking, but it's getting late. We'll see you later."

Eric put Colleen, who had fallen asleep, to bed. "I'm going for a walk." The late evening sun settled behind the large oak trees that lined the street. The ground was covered with leaves; the weather was mild for late October. It was a calm, peaceful evening, with the exception of kids playing football across the street and a couple dogs barking off in the distance.

Eric decided to walk to the diner. He walked and took a seat at the counter. He thought about his first encounter with Rita, when he attempted to make love to her on the school fire-escape. He could still hear her say, *"What you lack in experience you sure make up in enthusiasm, but let's face it—I'm almost, notice I said almost, old enough to be your mother."*

"Well, look who's here," Rita said. "I haven't seen you in a long time."

"I just had to get away from things for a while," Eric said

"Closing in on you, huh? I know the feeling sometimes," Rita said.

Rita and her husband had recently bought the diner and they were remodelling. They bought an adjoining dress shop that closed and were in the process of combining it into a first class restaurant. She joined him at the counter, trying to ignore the workmen who were installing a double doorway between the two buildings. She laughed over the noise. "Paul and I are really stepping out on a limb, but it's been our dream for a long time."

"You'll make it, that's what dreams are for," Eric said. "The food'll make it a success."

"That's what we're counting on. It's a gamble," Rita said. "We haven't really decided on a name yet, but it will come to us. The look in your eyes tells me there's something on your mind." She took a sip of coffee and grinned, "I haven't seen you in church lately." Eric could always count on Rita to help him understand and see things as they really were. "I haven't seen you with Tyler either," Rita said.

"Tyler and I have split up," Eric stated.

"Her last name's Quinlin—right?" She leaned closer to him, "The one with a five-year-old child."

"She's the one." Eric looked at the few customers willing to put up with the construction.

"Could that be one of your problems, Eric?" Rita asked.

Eric didn't answer.

"Maybe we should change the subject," Rita said. "How's Colleen?"

"Great, jabbering, and eating all the time."

"That sounds normal enough to me," Rita said.

"That's one of the few normal things in my life," Eric responded.

"You just hang in their Eric," Rita said. "Everything will work out."

"Eric, Johnny called—he's at the hospital with Ellen," his mother said. "I guess the baby's here or close to it. You get dressed and I'll fix you a cup of coffee. I already woke up your father. He's getting dressed."

He looked at the darkness outside the window and glanced at the clock. It was almost two a.m. His mother rushed out of his bedroom. Eric got dressed and hurried into the kitchen.

"You don't have to go, Mother, with your cold it would be silly. Why don't you and Dad come later," Eric said. She didn't argue. She nodded and pulled her shawl tighter around her shoulders. Eric downed his coffee and rushed out to the car.

The cold rain had suddenly turned into snow flurries. The ground started to turn white and the wind seemed sharper.

When Eric got to the hospital, he saw Johnny in the hallway. "Mom and Dad will be coming later; Mother wasn't feeling well this morning."

"Ellen's fine," Johnny said quickly. "I'm about to become a father." He looked tired, but happy.

"Mr. Bowers," the smiling nurse said, "You have a seven pound three ounce daughter. Both mother and daughter are doing fine; you can see them in a few minutes." Later, Eric and Johnny stood beside Ellen's bed, when they brought in this beautiful baby girl and placed her in Ellen's arms. "I'd like you to meet Elizabeth Bowers."

"My pleasure," Eric said. "What a beautiful addition to our family. Congratulations to both of you. I know Mom and Dad will be anxious to hear all the details, so I better get going. It's snowing pretty hard. We will be back later."

Eric's mother was dozing in her chair, but suddenly woke up when she heard Eric at the door anxiously waiting to hear what he had to say. After hearing Ellen and the baby were fine and all the details, she took a sip of tea, closed her eyes and drifted back to sleep

The next morning Eric's mother's woke him, "Eric, telephone—it's long distance." He sat up, wondering if he wasn't dreaming. "Eric!" she shouted, "It's long distance!"

"Hello . . . Ted? I can't believe it! Where are you?"

"Home. Just got in today," he said with laughter. "Marie's here with me—wait a minute."

"Hello Eric, how are you?" Marie asked.

"About the same, I guess. You still as cute as ever?"

"You haven't changed a bit—wait a minute, I'm putting Ted back on," Marie said.

"Eric, this is me again. Listen, we have to hurry, my folks are taking us out to breakfast. If you're not busy, we thought we'd drive over about six Friday night."

"Sounds great," Eric said. "I'll be looking forward to it. It's good to hear your voices again." Eric hung up, suddenly feeling much better. "Marie and Ted are home on furlough. They're coming Friday night." Eric's mind drifted back to Ted and Marie's wedding and how happy they both were. He also thought about boot camp—about how inseparable he, Ted, and Jason were. How he and Ted felt when they heard Jason had drowned the day before. They both wondered what their future held for them.

The next day about four-thirty the phone rang. "Hello Eric," Tyler's unmistakable voice said softly.

"Hello," Eric answered in shock.

"Eric, you're probably surprised to hear from me. I would like to take you up on your offer for help, if you still mean it. Can you come for supper tonight? Evan is with us. You said if I needed someone to talk to, to let you know."

"I'll be there," Eric said. He held the phone for a minute after she hung up, hoping it wasn't desperation in her voice. "Tyler called. I'm going to the Quinlins' for supper tonight."

"It's been awhile since you two got together," his father said.

"It's not what you think," Eric said. He wondered if he should mention Evan, then decided against it.

He turned to Colleen in her high chair, "What do you think, little one?"

"Dada," she yelled, "Dada."

"Finally some words." Eric laughed. "It's about time."

When Eric arrived at the Quinlins', Patsy greeted him with a big smile. The long-legged, freckle-faced girl took his hand. "I've been waiting for you."

Eric entered the house. The first thing he noticed was the expression on Tyler's face.

"Eric, I'm glad you could come. I'd like you to meet my son Evan."

The Quinlins watched carefully. Tension showed in their faces, but they still managed a smile. Eric extended his hand and the boy shook it with a trace of a smile. "I'm happy to meet you, Evan."

"Me too," he said. The blond-headed boy with big, green eyes turned to Tyler. Eric couldn't help but wonder how hard it must have been for Evan to lose the only parents he ever knew.

"What do you think of him?" Patsy asked.

"Patsy!" Tyler shouted. Suddenly her face turned red at her outburst.

"What'd I say wrong?" Patsy yelled, close to tears.

"Nothing—I'm sorry Patsy, for yelling at you," Tyler said.

Eric watched the boy closely, and suddenly felt awkward. He searched for words to overcome his feeling of helplessness. Later, everyone ate in almost complete silence, Eric waited for someone to lead the conversation. "How's that daughter of yours?" Mr. Quinlin finally asked.

"Fine. Colleen's been jabbering for some time," Eric said. "This morning she actually put a couple words together."

Mr. Quinlin laughed. The tension was gradually fading. "You wait a few days and she'll be talking all the time. Right, Patsy?"

"Oh, you mean me?" Her smile broke through. "I guess so."

Eric turned to Evan, "I have a little girl who is about a year and a half old."

"Does she have a mommy?"

"No," Eric said. *What could he say*? He could see the look in the boy's eyes searching for something more. Something he didn't have.

After Patsy and Evan went outside, Tyler turned to face Eric. "Have you heard anything about Evan in town?"

"As a matter of fact, Rita mentioned Evan's name a couple days ago," Eric said.

"That means it's all over town," Tyler mumbled

"It bound to come out, honey," her father said. "Remember, we talked about this. You have to deal with it."

"I know, people will always talk, right Eric?" Tyler said.

"Yes, people will talk, but it doesn't make any difference what people are saying," Eric said. "Evan is the important thing.

He's a very sensitive little boy who's gonna need all the support he can get."

"I guess you're right, Eric," Tyler agreed.

"Eric, I've also heard rumours about you," Tyler said.

Eric couldn't help but grin. "People have to have something to talk about. Maybe it's their way of coping with their everyday boring existence."

Patsy and Evan ran into the house. "Jerry's here."

"I didn't know he was coming," Tyler said to Eric.

"It doesn't matter."

"Hello everybody," Jerry said. "Eric, I thought that was your car. Evan, look what I have." The little boy shyly moved closer, then smiled as he reached for the bright red truck Jerry had brought him.

"Thank you," he said and ran outside.

Eric wondered why he hadn't thought of bringing the boy something. He felt disgusted with himself. The idea of seeing Tyler had taken over his thoughts.

"I've always known about Evan," Jerry said. He put his arm around Tyler, "I've asked Tyler to marry me."

"Eric, I . . . ." Tyler's voice broke off.

"Tyler's happiness is more important to me than anything," Eric said. Eric realized there was nothing else to say. He thanked the Quinlins for supper and left.

He drove to the familiar, winding road, leading through the cemetery. Eric stared at the faded, scattered roses on Alice's grave and whispered, "Forgive me Alice. Seems like every time I have to face something, I come running to you. I was expecting you to put the pieces together for me. I'm gonna have to learn to deal with things myself. It's just gonna take a little longer."

Sleep eluded him. He still loved Tyler but could live with it, as long as she was happy. He heard Colleen cry and rushed to her room. After changing and feeding her, he rocked her to sleep. "Can you handle it, little one? All the things they're probably gonna say about your old man?" He kissed her softly and put her back in bed.

The following day Eric walked to Grover's drugstore. It was almost deserted, except for a few people in the back. The guys at the jukebox were Dexter and Idlers; they worked with Bryan and seemed to make a habit out of terrorizing him. Eric remembered when he had his own confrontation with both of them. The last thing he needed was more trouble. He turned back toward the front just as Bryan entered and sat on the stool next to him.

"Hi Eric, you look like you've got a lot on your mind . . . You heard from Tyler?"

"It's over. Sometimes I wonder if anything really existed."

"The same with Liza and me. We tried. It just isn't meant to be."

"You and I seem to have our share of girl trouble." Eric glanced at his watch, "That's the way it goes sometimes. Sorry Bryan, I gotta take off."

"Hey Bryan, how you doin'?" Idlers asked. He and Dexter stopped for a moment, and then laughed before going out the door.

"Don't pay any attention to 'em," Eric said. He paid his check and added. "It's probably one of the highlights of their day. Bryan, sometime, we're going to have to talk about what's really on your mind." Bryan blushed and looked away.

CHAPTER FOUR

Friday seemed to drag on forever, until the phone rang. "Eric, this is Ted. We'll see you about six—how's that grab you?"

"Great. I'm taking you to Morgan's for a late dinner."

"We appreciate it, but you don't have to take us out."

"My pleasure. See you soon."

Eric dialed a familiar number. "Hello Liza, my friends from Cutler City are coming over tonight." The thought of her excited him. "I thought maybe . . . I need you."

Her laughter made him feel even better. "Sound good Eric. I think I need you, too."

"How about dinner at Morgan's . . . Say about seven? I've missed you."

"Morgan's? This calls for my new dress. I've missed you, too. Seven's great

Later that evening, there was a knock at the door. "I'll get it," Eric said, "It's probably Marie and Ted. It's so great to see you two again," Eric said. "It's been too long." He shook Ted's hand and kissed Marie on the cheek.

She smiled with the same cute expression. She hadn't changed at all. Eric stepped back, and looked Ted over. He had put on weight, at least ten pounds and it looked good on him. "Sergeant Ted Faulkland," Eric said with a smile.

"Ted, nice to see you again," Eric's mother said, "And this pretty thing has to be Marie."

"Nice to meet you, Mrs. Silkwin," Marie said.

"Colleen just woke up," Eric's mother said. "I'll bring her out just as soon as I get her changed."

"What are you doing now Ted?"

"Clerk typist. Real gravy job, but I'm really looking forward to getting out . . . ."

"You going to tell him, honey, or you want me to?" Marie asked, and then added quickly, "All right—Ted and I are gonna have a baby in late May."

"Congratulations," Eric said. "I'm happy for you both."

Eric's mother joined them with a wide-eyed Colleen. She looked at Eric and yelled, "Daddy, Daddy." He took her in his arms, hugged her, and handed her to Marie. Colleen stared at her, then laughed, and buried her face in Marie's shoulder.

"I just adore her!" Marie said.

"She's a real beauty," Ted added. "Look at those big blue eyes."

"Alice's eyes. I'm just crazy about her," Eric said. He glanced at his watch, "I told Liza we would pick her up about seven; we should get going."

They arrived at Liza's house a little while later. Eric knocked. When Liza opened the door, he realized how much he had missed her.

After an awkward moment, she said, "Eric, aren't you going to introduce me?"

"Sorry, I got carried away for a moment. Ted, Marie, I'd like you to meet Liza."

"Nice to meet you too," Liza said.

Marie and Liza hit it off as if they had known each other for years. They laughed, glancing at both Ted and Eric. Later in the bar, Ted stared at Eric. "You look strained."

"Good days and bad. I've got a lot on my mind." Eric said. He explained the healing and breakup with Tyler. He found himself talking about the deepest feelings that drove him. Ted listened carefully.

"What are you men talking about?" Marie asked. Her eyes were bright as the wine.

Ted laughed. "Man talk," he said, then took Marie's hand. The way they looked at each other hadn't changed. Liza watched Eric, her dark eyes bright with a mischievous glow.

"Marie's taking a course in psychology—trying to figure me out I guess," Ted said.

"I know you, Teddy. Now Eric—that would be a real challenge," Marie said. "Come on Teddy, time to dance." She was the only one he knew who called him Teddy.

Eric led Liza on the dance floor. She whispered in his ear, "I like your friends."

"They're special. The ideal couple every boy and girl should meet in their lives," Eric said.

"That's sweet," Liza said. She melted in his arms. "If I were just Alice . . . ."

Eric held her close, and whispered in her ear, "You're a very perceptive young lady, but don't under-estimate yourself."

"I have no intention of doing so," she said with laughter in her voice.

Later, Eric danced with Marie. It seemed like old times. "Penny for your thoughts," Marie said.

"I was thinking how nice this evening is," Eric said. "Being with you, Ted, and Liza has given me a lift."

"I'm glad. We've been looking forward to seeing you again. Ted talks about you often."

"You both mean a lot to me," Eric said.

"We feel the same," she said softly. Her eyes grew misty. "Now—tell me about Liza."

"I've only dated her a few times. She's my brother-in-law's sister," Eric said. "I think she has a certain curiosity about me."

"You have that effect on people when they meet you," Marie said. "Liza is somehow different, I'm not sure how." Marie giggled. The wine had obviously taken effect—that hadn't changed either.

Later after several drinks, Ted's face took on that boyish look Eric remembered so well. "Do you ever think about Jason?"

"Yes. Sometime when I least expect it," Eric said.

"Me too," Ted muttered. "You know how emotional I get." He finished off his drink. "I try not to, but I get so sentimental."

"So do I Ted, so do I."

It was getting late. Ted dropped off Liza at her house. Eric walked her to her door. "I had a very nice evening. Marie and Ted are tops." She put her hand along the side of his face. "Good night Eric, I think I scare you a little."

Eric kissed her. "Maybe just enough." When he pulled her close, she pushed him away.

"Let's close this evening while it's still special," Liza whispered.

Ted then dropped off Eric. "We had a wonderful time," Marie said.

"We'll give you a call later," Ted added.

Saturday, Eric's father came into the shop about eleven. He took a puff of his rare cigar and said, "Let's talk. You gonna tell me what's on your mind the last week or so?"

"It was nice seeing Marie and Ted again. They're links to a special time in the past."

"It's nice to see old friends, but to dwell on the past can be defeating, especially in your case," his father said.

"I keep thinking of what might have been," Eric said.

"Might is the key word. You can't live in what might have been. You can only live for the future. If you do, it can tear you up, and there's not a damn thing you can do about it," his father said. "Memories can be self-defeating . . . . I've been watching you. This girl Liza—she's a pretty thing, but I don't know her well." He waited for comment, but Eric didn't answer, so his father continued. "What about Tyler?"

"It's over. It's just that simple. We broke up."

"I don't mean to be hard hearted, but maybe Tyler was there when you needed someone," Eric's father said.

"Maybe," Eric said. "I can live with that."

"I wasn't sure," he said flatly.

Eric was relieved when a customer came in. He had to get out of the shop before the walls closed in on him. "Do you mind if I take off?"

"Go ahead, I can handle it the rest of the day," his father said. "I hope I've helped."

"You have. It's going to work out—one way, or the other."

His father shook his head.

It was the first time he had been in the Twilight tavern since coming after Cindy after Jason's funeral. The place was only a couple blocks from the shop. Bryan was right. This place was a dump. On a sudden impulse, Eric decided a beer would snap him out of his mood. There were very few people for Saturday, but it was still early.

"Beer," Eric said. The same bartender looked at him. If he recognized him, he didn't show it. The sound of laughter coming from the other end of the bar broke his concentration. Idlers and Dexter were standing around the pool table. They looked his way. He thought of leaving, but the idea of running didn't appeal to him. Especially today.

"Hello there." The voice over his shoulder had to be Idlers. Dexter stood beside him with a stupid looking grin. "Silkwin—haven't seen you in here before."

Eric tried smiling, but his mood wouldn't let it happen. "I needed a beer after work—it's been one of those days."

"We all have 'em. I figured you were so wrapped up in religion and stuff, you wouldn't be caught in a place like this."

"Like I said, it's one of those days." Eric turned back to the front.

The bartender leaned forward. His eyes lit up as if someone had turned a light on in his head. "I thought I recognized you. You're Silkwin, some kind of healer or something." His excuse for a smile didn't hide the contempt in his eyes. "Another one?"

Eric thought about leaving, but knew he couldn't walk away. "One more," he said slowly.

"Old Dexter here is looking for Bryan," Idlers smirked. "He needs some lovin'."

Eric was stunned. He wasn't sure he heard right. He stared at Idlers. The bartender tried again to smile. "Why don't you just take off?" Eric said.

"I don't think he likes us. Maybe he's got something going with Bryan himself," Dexter said. He gripped the pool cue.

Eric knew he couldn't walk away. It was too late. "Maybe you'd like to tell me what you're talking about." Bryan's face flashed before him.

"Maybe he really doesn't know. How about that?" Idlers said. "Who'd want to admit his cousin is a queer?"

"You're crazy!" Eric shouted. The guys beside Eric quickly finished their beers and left.

Idlers' face turned red. His eyes seemed to bulge out of his head. "You're gonna apologize one way or another," Idlers said. "You don't have us trapped in a booth this time."

Eric tried again. "Why don't you walk away? You're the one shooting off your mouth!" A rare silence filled their end of the bar.

The bartender leaned over the bar, "I don't want any trouble in here." The look in his eyes said he was lying.

Idlers knew people were watching them. He'd gone too far to back down. He started to throw his right hand. In that brief second, instinct took over as Eric threw a left hook that caught Idlers flush and he hit the floor.

Eric felt the crack of the pool cue, then a trace of blood running into his eye. He heard the beer bottle hit the floor just before someone grabbed him. The police seemed to come from nowhere.

Eric tried to focus. The ringing in his ear slowly subsided. He heard the bartender trying to explain to the officer, "Silkwin threw the first punch—he started it."

The sergeant stared at Eric. "I'm pressing charges," the bartender was saying. "I won't have this kind of thing in my place—I got all the witnesses I need."

"All right," the sergeant said. He turned to face the bartender. "I'll bet you have. Come on, Eric. We'd better go."

Eric's head throbbed. It was the first time he'd ever been in jail. He called Johnny.

An hour later, the sergeant's voice startled him. "Johnny Bowers has put up your bail," Sergeant Hullman said. Eric snapped out of his daydream. "I've known you and your family for years. The drugstore was bad enough, but this . . . What were you doing in that place?"

"You won't catch me in there again," Eric said. Johnny and Ellen were waiting with Liza. Eric tried to control the foolish grin on his face.

"Eric, are you all right?" Liza asked.

"You ready to get out of here?" Johnny asked. Ellen just stared at him.

"What are you going to tell the folks? You'd better come up with something."

He didn't know what to say. *How could he explain about the fight without involving Bryan? How could he not know if it were true?* He had to think of something.

"Why, Eric?" Ellen asked flatly with the sound of disgust. "Just tell me why!"

"It just happened," he said. Eric heard the word queer over and over in his mind.

When they arrived at Eric's house, Eric asked, "Aren't you coming in?"

Ellen didn't answer for a few anxious moments, and then said, "For Colleen's sake, she needs me. Liza, weren't you going to the movies?"

"I'll take her to the second show," Eric said. "It's Saturday night."

"Why would she want to go with you?" Ellen snapped. She got out of the car. "You'd better take a look at yourself!"

"Ellen," Liza added quickly. "There has to be a reason."

Eric excused himself after experiencing the initial shock from his parents, and went to the bathroom. The eye was turning bluish black. He knew the bandage made it look worse. What really hurt was the third degree he knew he was about to face.

They were waiting on him. "You gonna tell us about this?" his father asked with an unfamiliar edge in his voice.

"Couldn't be helped," Eric said. "It was those guys I had trouble with in Grover's."

"Why now? That was a year ago!"

"I was in the right place at the wrong time." He knew his answer sounded all wrong.

"You never start these things, but they always happen to you. I know you've had your share of problems, but that's no excuse," his father said.

"I couldn't walk away."

"Why were you the only one arrested?" his father pressed. "Who swung first?"

Eric knew he wasn't going to win this one. "I did."

His mother stared at him without a word.

"There has to be a good reason," Johnny said.

His father leaned close to Eric and said, "Then what is it? *Make me understand*! Was it about Tyler? There's rumors going around that Tyler has a five-year-old son."

Eric felt anger and hopelessness. "No, it didn't have anything to do with Tyler," Eric said. He could feel his head starting to throb. He lit a cigarette, drawing the smoke deep in his lungs that seemed to steady him.

"Are you defending somebody?" Ellen asked suddenly.

Eric wondered how she could see through him.

Colleen's cry sent his mother hurrying off to the bedroom. In a moment, she reappeared with her; wide-awake, looking around with big, blue eyes. When she saw Eric, she cried, "Dada, Dada."

"Let me hold her a moment, then we must get going," Ellen said.

"I'm going to bed," Howard said, disappointment was in his eyes. Eric knew he'd let him down.

42

Martha said, "I didn't know Tyler had a son. Is that the reason you broke up?"

"No. Tyler's former boyfriend returned. Tyler said I was on a collision course."

"No comment," Ellen said.

"Liza, how about a trip to Cookie's Drive-in for a malt and hamburger—I wouldn't have to get outta the car?" Eric said.

"You seemed inclined to do what you want," Ellen said firmly. "We have to get back, the landlady's watching Elizabeth."

"I need someone to talk to and Liza is a good listener."

Johnny smiled at Eric, "You going to church tomorrow?"

"Yes, to quote an idol of mine, 'You can run but you can't hide.' Trust me," Eric said.

Ellen smiled in spite of herself, "Looks like we have to. Good night all."

Cookies' curb service was crowded until it started raining. Eric sighed, and then added, "Wouldn't you know it?"

Liza laughed and he felt better. "Did it have anything to do with me—Bryan, I mean?"

"I don't quite know how to answer that."

"Bryan and I just never really clicked." Liza watched carefully for the slightest hint of something she should know. "I have never felt with him . . . what I usually feel . . . with a guy."

He stared at her. At times, she was so blunt and outspoken.

"I haven't been able to get you off my mind," Eric said.

"I'll bet," she said. "Specially the part about jumping me in the back seat."

"Liza, what can I say . . . it just happened."

"Bryan once grabbed my breasts, then he apologized. I guess it was just curiosity more than anything. The feeling wasn't there, if you'll forgive the pun. I began to wonder if I had anything to offer."

"You're quite a woman. I've thought of you often."

The rain was letting up. She took a bite of hamburger, and then said. "I'm trying to cheer you up. Am I getting the job done?"

"Just being with you helps," Eric said.

43

"Bryan actually asked me if I had a good time with you—can you believe it?" Liza asked.

"Bryan loves you in his own way."

"Would you care to explain that?"

Eric didn't answer. He honked and the girl came to pick up the tray.

"I'm waiting for your explanation," Liza responded. A little later, he pulled in front of her house.

"I'm not going to comment on what's going through my mind—I can't," she whispered.

What could he tell her? Eric walked her to the door, pulled her close, and didn't want to let her go.

"Good night Eric. My attraction for you confuses me."

Eric didn't know what to say. He kissed her and left.

Next morning, Eric feigned illness and didn't go to church. He decided Bryan must come to him. He was thinking about the dream he had, and wondered if it had anything to do with what was going on with Bryan. When everyone returned from church, they saw Eric was still in his robe and had fallen asleep.

"Eric! Don't you think you should get dressed?" his mother yelled.

Liza laughed and Eric hurried off to his bedroom. When Eric returned to the living room, his father asked, "Was Bryan mixed up in that fight yesterday afternoon?"

"No. He wasn't with me. Why do you ask?"

"He wasn't in church. He was beat up last night," his father said.

"I can't believe it," Eric replied. "Is he all right?"

"A few cuts and bruises—somebody did a number on him." Eric resisted the temptation to laugh. The expression from his father sounded so strange. "It's strange both of you ran into trouble the same day," Howard said. "Very strange."

Eric stared at Liza. Her expression indicated the questions she asked Eric; she probably already knew the answers, too.

"I've asked Grace and David to dinner. They're gonna try and get Bryan to come," His mother added.

Eric felt things were closing in on Bryan and there wasn't a thing anyone could do. He suddenly felt sorry for him.

"You're not going to tell us any more, are you?" Ellen asked. There were times her perception was annoying.

"Trust me," Eric said.

The phone rang. He heard his mother's voice, "Yes, we understand. Thank you for calling." She returned to the dining room, "They're not coming. Bryan doesn't feel up to it and Grace won't leave him."

They all stared at Eric.

CHAPTER FIVE

Sunday's conversation did not include anything concerning Eric or Bryan. Colleen, as usual, helped ease the tension, but the family's glances searched for answers that Eric could not give.

Eric watched the expression on Ellen's face. "Dada, my dada," Colleen yelled.

Eric took her in his arms and hugged her. "How are you little one?" He turned to face Liza. "You wanta hold her?"

"Yes, you do like to tease me, don't you?" Liza said.

"Maybe just a little," Eric said. There was a knock at the door. "I'll get it," Eric said. "Oh Bryan—come in." Bryan looked a little bruised, but nothing looked serious. "How are you doing?"

"I'm all right, the folks are making something out of nothing," Bryan said. "I guess it's natural enough—especially in Mother's case. Liza—I've missed you."

"I've been thinking about you, too," Liza said.

"Bryan, you don't look too bad," Howard said. His grin vanished after seeing his wife's glare.

"It was just one of those things," Bryan said. Eric detected the sound of fear in Bryan's voice.

"I'm just glad you're both all right," Eric mother said. "Although with Bryan, I can't understand him being involved in such a thing." She looked toward Eric, but it was obvious words were not necessary.

Eric pulled Liza aside. "Will you go with me to the Club Commodore in Cutler City on Friday night?"

"I wouldn't want to be anywhere else," she said, with a look of mischief.

Two days later, Eric stopped in Grover's for a quick lunch, and saw Liza. He walked over to her table. "Mind if I join you?" She smiled and pointed to a chair. Eric placed his order and then looked Liza over carefully.

"Do you like my new dress?"

"Very much," Eric said. The dress was red with vertical white stripes and a white collar. She seemed to make the dress come alive. Eric looked up just in time to see Bryan walk in and head for their table.

"Mind if I join you?" he asked.

"Please do," Liza said.

The momentary silence was awkward. Finally, Eric said, "Marie and Ted are home on furlough. Liza and I, along with Stuart and Cindy are joining them at the Club Commodore in Cutler City. They're going back soon . . . You're welcome to join us."

"If you're sure you don't mind," Bryan said. "I'd like that very much."

Liza and Eric could only stare at each other.

Eric picked up Liza, and Bryan. He was well aware of the warmth of Liza's body next to his. Her perfume filled him with desires he had not thought of lately. She glanced his way and smiled. He was right about the dress.

The next stop was Wyler, where they would pick up Cindy and Stuart. After introductions, Cindy said, "Bryan, I haven't seen you for so long. You fighting—I'm not surprised at Eric, but you?"

"I was a little surprised myself," Bryan acknowledged

After arriving at the club, Cindy introduced Stuart to everyone.

"We're going to do it up right tonight," Ted said." It's on my dad and that doesn't happen often."

47

After dinner, Eric led Marie to the dance floor. "Ted mentions you often. He says you really brought us together," Marie said as she laughed softly, and then put her head on his shoulder, humming along with the music.

"You two were meant for each other," Eric said.

"I know, but we have had our moments," Marie whispered.

Eric could look at Ted and tell that he was about to fall into his familiar, melancholy mood, which was so much a part of him.

"I have been wondering what I want to do when I get discharged." Ted said, and added a smile.

Eric smiled back at him and said, "You mean you're not a career man?"

"No. With Marie and the baby coming—I have to look to the future more than I usually would."

"Seems like guys looking forward to their discharges usually get these kinds of thoughts," Eric said. "At least that's what I have heard."

"I'll figure it out," Ted added, watching Marie across the table.

Eric danced with Liza. Her mood seems to reach a new high. "I just love your friends."

"How do you feel about me?" He smiled and whispered in her ear. "You know, in a general range—nothing specific."

She threw her head back and laughed. "I refuse to answer on the grounds it may incriminate me." Her low, deep laugh became a giggle. "I can feel the wine," she said.

Later, Ted said to Eric, "I didn't want to mention it before, but this is our last chance to get together. I got a telegram to report as soon as possible. Naturally, Marie and I are disappointed, but you know the bottom line is duty!"

"I'm sorry," Eric said. "I just hope it isn't Korea—there seems to be some problems developing over there. I remember reading about the UN, warning us about the danger of civil war over there."

"Yeah. The fact that Russia tested its first atomic bomb doesn't help either," Ted sighed,

"It's getting to be a crazy world,—you don't know what's going to happen next."

"Things are changing so fast these days," Eric said.

"Marie's being brave through it all. With the baby and all, it makes it a little rougher. At least my folks and I have worked it out," Ted said with a big smile. "They really love Marie—I should have told them about her long ago. Dad and I—I think have come to an understanding, at least for a while."

"That's great," Eric said. There were times when Ted cursed the deep, sensitive feeling inside him. He sipped his highball, watching Liza and Marie whispering to each other. "You girls— would you care to enlighten us?"

"Girl talk!" Marie yelled over the music. Her bright, dark eyes expressing mischief.

Eric asked Cindy to dance. Things still okay with you and Stuart?" Eric asked.

"I'm so happy, but there will always be a place in my heart for Jason. Is there something I should know about you?"

"What can I say?" Eric replied, "She's also my brother-in-law's sister."

"What's wrong with that?" Cindy responded.

"Nothing, until you try to say it."

"Maybe," Cindy said. "You'd better get her out here again before we leave."

A few moments later, Eric led Liza on the dance floor. A song about being involved with a wonderful guy was playing. "I love that song," Liza said. "That pretty well says it all," she said with a teasing smile.

"You're very pretty, and a little loaded, too," Eric said.

"You're teasing me, but I'm gonna pretend you mean it."

"I do, lady," he said, on their way back to the table.

"Excuse me!" Bryan said suddenly and took off for the men's room. Eric waited a moment, and then entered the men's room with Ted and Stuart. Bryan straddled one of the toilet stools, vomiting.

"Is he going to make it?" Ted asked, a little pale himself.

"Hey Bryan, we've been there!" Stuart added.

"I'm so sorry," Bryan moaned. "I'm not use to drinking this much. This evening has been so nice and I have to spoil it."

"Hey," Ted yelled. "It's all right—don't worry about it. You get Eric to tell you about the time he had to get me out of the toilet on the train and believe me, there were other times!" A few minutes later, all four returned to their table.

"Sorry," a pale Bryan muttered, "I do feel better."

An hour later, they ate an early breakfast at a diner on the outskirts of Cutler City. "We really have to go, old buddy," Ted said slowly. Both Marie's and Ted's eyes were misty. "I'm not going to say goodbye, just so long for a while."

Eric could feel his stomach tighten. "Yeah—until later . . . You two take care of yourselves!"

"Cindy, it was good seeing you again," Ted said. "Stuart, it was nice meeting you."

Cindy hugged Ted and Marie.

"It was nice meeting you guys, too," Stuart said.

A little later Eric pulled in front of Cindy's house. "I hope you and Stuart enjoyed the evening," Eric said.

"We really did," Stuart said.

Cindy hugged Eric. "Eric, thank you for so many things. You know—just for being there for me, at the most trying times in my life," Cindy said.

"Seeing you look so happy makes it all worthwhile, we both fought our way back from hell and won," Eric said.

Eric pulled out into the early morning traffic and headed for Benford. The feeling of depression closed in on him. On the way home, Liza said, "I really sensed the bond between you and your friends. I've never felt anything like that before."

"Will you drop me off first?" Bryan said. "I still don't feel good—I gotta make church tomorrow." His attempt at a smile failed. "Sometime later, I've got to talk to both of you. It's important."

"When you're ready," Eric said. They watched Bryan until he went in the house.

"If it wasn't so late," Eric whispered.

"Not tonight, or should I say morning. I know you want me," Liza said, moving a little closer to him. "When I mean something more than a quick roll in the hay—don't laugh at me, Eric Silkwin!"

"You know you mean much more to me than that," Eric countered.

"I've seen you with Alice! When I can sense—at least part of the feeling you had for her—then we will talk about it," Liza said. "Kiss me good night and we'll take it from there."

Eric walked her to the door and gave her a quick kiss.

The Christmas of 1949 consisted of the usual activities, but with Colleen adding a special feeling. The following winter months finally faded into the early month of May. Eric had received several letters over the winter months from Marie and Ted. They were in England. They were looking forward to the baby and coming home.

Eric hoped Marie and Ted would remain in England until they returned to the states.

Eric had dated Liza a few times. Their relationship was progressing slowly. He hadn't heard anything from Tyler.

On a bright Sunday morning after church services, Reverend Langtree approached Eric. "Nice seeing you again, it's been awhile. My, how Colleen has grown."

"Yeah, she's almost two now," Eric said.

Eric joined his mother and father, who were standing near Ellen, Liza, Bryan, and Johnny. "Johnny has agreed to cook hamburgers on the grill if he has some help," Ellen said. "It's a beautiful Sunday."

"I'd volunteer if this guy would help," Liza said. She poked Eric.

"I could use some help," Eric said to Bryan. He felt time was running out. Bryan's eyes revealed a look of panic and fear, almost like a cry for help.

Later that afternoon, they were all in the back yard enjoying the first warm day. It was unceasingly warm. Colleen was in a plastic tub, splashing, and squealing with delight. "My dada, Dada," she yelled. Eric tried taking her out of the tub, and she threw a fit. It was the first time he saw her little temper.

"She's going to look like a prune," Eric's mother said, laughing as Colleen tried gripping the sides of the tub with her hands. Finally, she gave up.

Eric lifted her out of the tub and dried her off before handing her to his mother. Eric took over frying hamburgers while Johnny left for a while. The radio was playing in the background. Eric couldn't seem to take his eyes off Liza. She was wearing a blue polka blouse and dark blue shorts. "Hey Liza, can you come here? I could use some help."

"What kind of help are you looking for," she teased.

Move closer so I can feel you near me," Eric said.

"You'd better be careful about saying that you want to feel me," she said, with a deep soft laugh. "Someone might get the wrong idea."

He swatted her and she laughed. "You're just lucky there are people over there," Eric said. "I have this overwhelming desire to . . . ."

Bryan suddenly appeared. His eyes avoided theirs and his voice trembled. "Maybe we could talk later. You'll probably hate my guts," he said, with panic in his voice.

Ellen suddenly appeared before them. "A couple more burgers, Eric. You three are doing a good job—actually it's probably the woman's touch that's making the difference," she said and laughed at Eric and Bryan. She took the burgers and slipped away. Liza stepped away for a minute, and Bryan followed her.

"Liza, there's something I need to talk to you about," Bryan said. "I'm not sure how to say this." After a few awkward moments of silence, he said to Liza, "I can't be a real man to you. How can I explain this without sounding disgusting? You do not know . . . ."

"What are you trying to say?" Liza asked.

Before Bryan could respond, Ellen's voice startled them. "What are you two doing over here by yourselves? We want to take some pictures—it's getting late."

"We'll talk later," Bryan, said with a sigh of relief, and quickly disappeared.

Ellen finally got everyone together, but she could not find Bryan. "Liza, do you know where Bryan went?"

"I'm looking for him, too," Liza said.

Ellen couldn't help but notice the tone in Liza's voice. "Is everything okay, Liza?"

"I'm not really sure." Liza just walked away.

Ellen's expression demonstrated concern and confusion. After pictures were taken, everyone was getting ready to leave. It had been a long day.

Eric put Colleen in her crib. Right away, she fell asleep. "Thank God, I have you," he whispered. That evening he went to bed feeling tense, with a sense of panic he could not understand.

"Eric wake up—something terrible has happened," his mother shouted. He slowly opened his eyes. His mother and father stood beside his bed. She was crying.

"What's the matter?" Eric asked. "What is it?"

"They found Bryan in the basement," Eric's father said, his voice barely audible, "He's *dead.*"

Eric stared with disbelief. All he heard was his mother crying in the early morning silence.

Eric glanced at the clock; it was almost four o'clock. He got up, lit a cigarette, and sipped a cold cup of coffee. "So that's what the dream meant."

"Why would he do such a terrible thing?" his mother asked between sobs.

"David called a few minutes ago," his father said slowly, "All I know is they heard a shot and found Bryan in the basement." His father paused for a moment and then continued. "It just doesn't make sense, even for Bryan. He is not the type. They didn't even know he was home."

Eric winced. *If I had just pressed him—done something!*

"We're going over there . . . Eric, you hear me? Colleen's bottle is on the stove. We'll be back as soon as we can. Why does a terrible thing like this have to happen?" His mother added, "One of us will call you later."

He looked in on Colleen, pulled a light blanket over her. She stirred, and then curled into a ball. Eric sat in the kitchen, looking out the window at the early morning darkness turning to dawn. It was still unbelievable. He prayed for his cousin Bryan, who could not face the part of his life that had literally destroyed him.

The light of dawn began creeping over the rooftops, slowly filling the room with the light of a new day. He walked back into the kitchen, and reheated the coffee. The sunlight slowly moved across the floor. Another Monday morning and his life, and that of his family had changed once again forever.

The phone ringing startled him back to reality. He jumped up, fighting off numbness in his leg. "Everything is under control," his father said. "What took you so long to answer the phone?"

"My leg fell asleep. How are things, or should I ask?"

"Your aunt is under heavy sedation. The coroner and ambulance were here. They have taken his body away. We'll be home soon. I never felt so helpless. Your uncle is in shock, naturally, but seems to be handling things. He is calling Karen and Frank."

He heard Colleen stirring, "I've gotta go, Colleen is awake." She was standing up in her bed rubbing her eyes. The minute she saw him, she started jumping up and down. "Good morning sunshine," Eric said. He picked her up, changed her, and gave her the bottle. He jumped when he heard the front door open.

"It's just awful," his mother said. "They knocked out Grace, and gave David some pills. Karen and Frank should be here a little after noon. I'll fix something. Naturally, Karen's in shock and asking a lot of questions nobody has the answers to. You know how she is."

Bryan Silkwin, age 24 was found dead early this morning in his parents' basement . . . details will follow on a later broadcast . . . ."

Eric's father turned off the radio. His mother shook her head. "I still can't believe it—why on earth would he do such a terrible thing?"

"You got any ideas, son?" his father asked.

"No. I still can't believe it," Eric said. It was the first time Eric had lied to his father since he was small.

"He was all right yesterday," his mother added. "Bryan was a little moody—but that's not uncommon for him."

Eric said, "I've gotta get outta here for a while." He walked through the dining room with the phone ringing, but he did not stop to answer the many calls he knew would be coming. He got in his car and drove. The last few days flashed through his mind like a nightmare.

It was after two by the time he got home. He saw Frank's station wagon parked in front of the house. Eric felt the tension in his stomach. When he opened the door, he was shocked at Frank's appearance.

"I dropped Karen off at her folk's house. I know I look a little haggard, but it goes with the territory." He shrugged his shoulders. "Nobody seems to know why." He directed the statement at Eric. "There has to be a reason!" Frank said. "Karen and I have been going out of our minds since early this morning . . . It doesn't make any sense. You would think Bryan would be the last one to pull such a thing."

"I don't know," Eric said. "Bryan and I haven't been that close lately—I tried to talk to him several times, but he kept putting me off."

Frank stared at Eric. "I know Karen's going to want to talk to you."

A few minutes later, his mother said, "It's Karen. She just got through; the lines have been so busy." She looked at Eric and handed him the phone. "She wants to talk to you."

He took a deep breath; her voice shook, "Why in heaven's name?"

Eric took another deep breath, trying to shake off last night's lack of sleep. "I'm not sure—it seems so unreal!"

"That's not good enough," Karen said. "Mother is sleeping, I can't go near the basement, and even the thought of it gives me the chills."

"I know. What can I say, but you have to be strong."

"I am. You know me," she said. "I refuse to be any other way. I'm going with Dad to make funeral arrangements—let me talk to Frank a minute."

Frank mumbled something, and then he hung up. "I'm ready for a walk; I'm getting stiff from the long drive." Neither Eric nor Frank said much as they walked to the small park. After being seated, Frank said, "I think I have given you enough time."

CHAPTER SIX

Eric and Frank arrived at the little park in the town square. There were two women watching them with obvious curiosity. Eric stared and they looked away.

He lit a cigarette and took a deep breath. "I believe Bryan was a homosexual. I think he tried to tell me yesterday afternoon at the cookout, but couldn't," Eric said. "The only thing he did say was he couldn't be a man to Liza."

Frank did not say anything. He just stared ahead so Eric continued, "Several months ago, I was in one of those moods. I got in a fight with Idlers and Dexter in the Twilight tavern. They razed me about Bryan being queer."

"Yeah, I was in jail a couple hours before Ellen and Johnny bailed me out."

"You in jail? Anything else?"

"Tyler has a little boy. She was raped by a bum a few years ago, and she gave her son up for adoption. The boy's parents were killed in a car accident, so she adopted him." Frank looked stunned. He shook his head and stared at the water fountain. Eric continued, "One day Liza saw me go into Daily's and followed me. She'd split with Bryan and wanted someone to talk to and I needed a date."

"And Tyler?"

"She's back with her former boyfriend. She thinks he's more stable than I am. She says I can't let Alice go . . . and thinks I'm headed for trouble."

Frank grinned, "Wonder where she could get an idea like that?"

They both watched the police car pull up in front of the park. The two women, along with another couple, watched carefully. They gathered their children and moved to the park entrance, watching Sergeant Hullman walked straight toward them. "Eric, I gotta talk to you," the sergeant said. He looked over the area, and then stared at Frank.

"It's all right. Frank is Bryan's brother-in-law."

"Bryan was caught in the act at the train depot Sunday night," Hullman said. He paused for effect. "The guys you fought caught Bryan and the other guy before we spotted them. If Bryan hadn't tangled with them, we'd have missed 'em."

"I appreciate you telling us," Eric said.

"The other guy took off before I got to Bryan—I don't know who he was. Anyway, Bryan was scared and embarrassed." The sergeant continued, "I ran Idlers and Dexter off and asked Bryan if he was all right. He was shaken, but insisted he just wanted to get home."

"Idlers and Dexter, huh?" Eric felt anger building inside. "Thanks Sergeant, I appreciate it."

"You'll have enough to put up with when this comes out, and it will . . . What I'm telling you is, I don't want any more trouble!"

Neither Eric nor Frank answered.

The sergeant shook his head and walked back to his car, waving off the group of people.

"How in the world are we going to handle this? I wonder how long it's been going on and who else knows?" Frank asked.

"I don't have any idea," Eric said. "Liza did tell me Bryan never tried to make a pass at her."

"Damn!" Frank said softly.

When Eric and Frank arrived at Eric's house, Karen was waiting for them. She had been crying, but seemed under control. "It just doesn't make sense," Karen said.

Eric's father turned on the radio. The leading news story focused on the tragic death of Bryan Silkwin. A very detailed report came over the air. The facts were clear from the carefully worded newscast.

Everyone was stunned.

A few moments later, Karen said, "So that's what it's all about. I had no idea. Poor Bryan, what he must have gone through."

Eric's mother slowly responded as if in shock, "I'm going over to Grace. She needs me."

The funeral was Wednesday. It was a very warm humid day. Very few people came, even from the church. The people that came expressed their sympathy in polite, awkward gestures. Their references to Bryan as quiet, considerate, and religious failed to cover the obvious embarrassment in their faces.

Liza stood pale and silent. The procession started its trip to the cemetery. Bryan's mother sat silently through it all. She expressed no emotion. Frank held Karen's arm while she stared at the casket. A light rain began to fall, but the mourners stood their ground.

Reverend Langtree worded his eulogy with care. His sincerity and faith attempted to help support the loved ones left behind.

The lunch was at Eric's house. A few people came, and then quickly left. The table of food told the story. Karen, Frank, Eric, and Liza stood silently around the dining room table, aware of the awkward silence that filled the room. Karen's father came over to join them. "Karen, I'm taking your mother away for a couple of weeks. I've arranged to have the basement taken care of. I know you and Frank have to leave early tomorrow morning, so we'll say goodbye now. Take good care of those boys."

Karen hugged her father. "You and Mother take care of yourselves. We will keep in touch," Karen said.

Eric's heart went out to Bryan's family. "Karen, I would like to take you and Frank out to dinner tonight," Eric said.

"That would be nice, Eric," Karen said

"Liza, will you join us?"

"I would like to very much," she said softly.

Later that evening, they arrived at Morgan's. After they had ordered, they all waited for someone else to start the conversation. Finally, Karen said, "I feel Bryan is at peace now. I do not understand it all and probably never will, but I want to go on record saying it is over. Bryan will be in my thoughts. I will remember him in my own way."

Eric knew there would be times when she would have moments that only belonged to her and Bryan.

"I'm trying to get my old job back," Frank said. "Neither of us is happy. We're homesick and that job has literally put me through hell. Our home is here.

"That's my sentiment exactly," Karen added. "It seems all that glitters is not always gold. Now tell me about you two."

Eric and Liza stared at each other. "Eric sees me as Johnny's little sister." A frown formed at the corners of her mouth. "I'm twenty-four, five foot six, and every inch a woman!"

Even Frank smiled, and then looked to Eric for his comment.

"I don't doubt that for a moment," Eric said.

Later in the bar, Eric and Frank had whiskey highballs and the girls each had a glass of wine.

"I think we needed this," Karen said, "but we must be going. We have to get an early start. The boys are with our landlady. She's terrific with them and she knew this trip was going to be very stressful, but we don't want to take advantage of her."

Everyone was getting ready to leave when they noticed how people were staring at them, and whispering. "I'd love to tell some of these people where to go," Karen said, not lowering her voice. "How could they possibly understand?"

"We'll handle it," Eric said. Heads turned and guarded conversations became quiet as they left the restaurant.

"Bryan should've stood his ground," Karen said. "He was my brother and I loved him . . . It's such a tragedy to take your own life." She stared at Eric. "The family will have to put up with this kind of behaviour for some time. People are so judgemental."

Liza and Eric drove Karen and Frank back to Karen's parents' house. "Hang in there," Frank said solemnly. "We'll be seeing you soon, hopefully."

Eric watched them go in the house, wondering what thoughts must be going through their minds, especially Karen's.

Eric drove to his house. When he and Liza walked in, Ellen was helping Eric's mother clear off the table. Liza joined them while Eric talked to Johnny and his father. "I don't know what to do with all this food. It was barely touched," Martha said wearily, "I wished more people had come for Grace and David's sake."

Eric's father handed Eric a letter. "Johnny and I checked the house. There were two letters on Bryan's desk, one for you and the other to his parents."

Eric hesitated a moment, then opened Bryan's letter.

> *Dear Eric,*
>
> *If you are reading this, you know that somehow, I found the courage to do what I feel I must do. We both know I don't have the guts to face this terrible nightmare. I've been sitting here for close to an hour. I know in a split second it will all be over. I could not bear to face a life of ridicule and frustration.*
>
> *I'm only sorry for what the family will go through. I want to thank you for many things. I have carefully thought it out, and it's the only way that I can find peace. I do not understand these feelings; they seem to be beyond my control, and I can't live with that.*
>
> *May God forgive me!*
>
> *Bryan*

Eric folded the letter and stared off into space. He could visualize Bryan sitting in that basement all alone, waiting for a moment of courage. He felt chills down his back. What a senseless tragedy! So many people's lives affected. Eric prayed for Bryan in the only way he knew.

Saturday, Eric insisted that his father rest, and went to the shop. He dove into his work with a passion. Later in the afternoon, Mr. Quinlin stopped in.

"Hi Eric, I am so sorry about Bryan. Sometimes, it's hard for a man to understand," he said awkwardly. It was one of the few times that Eric saw him without a smile. "We were shocked . . . At first, we only heard the name Silkwin. Again, I'm so sorry; the whole family is."

Eric looked at this big man, searching for a way to express himself. It wasn't easy for him. "Join me for a cup of coffee, Mr. Quinlin?" Eric asked.

"Sure, I have a little time," Mr. Quinlin said.

Eric stared off into space, "So many people from our church never even bothered with the funeral," Eric said. "Bryan was such a faithful follower. Sometimes, I wonder if people actually practice what they're taught. They can be so judgemental."

"You're a bitter young man," Mr. Quinlin said. He sipped his coffee, and added, "Be careful, Eric. Bitterness can eat you alive. The family and I want to invite you to a cookout Sunday." Mr. Quinlin's face brightened, "Darryl's home, and he was asking about you. He looks great. He lost a little weight, but on him, it looks good. Maybe getting out would help you."

"Sunday sounds great," Eric said. "There's this girl . . . ."

"She's welcome too," Quinlin interrupted. "See yah Sunday."

Eric watched him walk past the front window in his easygoing manner. Eric called Liza right away. Her aunt answered. "May I speak to Liza, please? This is Eric Silkwin."

"Just a moment," she answered softly.

"Liza, it's Eric. How are you doing?"

"Hello Eric," Liza said, "I haven't been feeling too well."

"Sorry to hear that, maybe I can cheer you up a little."

She didn't answer for a moment, then, said slowly, "If you really want to. I'll be in the back yard. I'm really down and I may not be very good company."

"I'll take my chances," Eric said.

He stopped at Cookie's Drive-in and picked up a couple of malts. He tried to think of the right thing to say. A little later, he walked around to the back yard. She sat curled up in a lawn chair. Liza heard him and turned; it was obvious she had been crying.

"For you," Eric grinned and handed her a malt.

"You remembered—strawberry, my favourite," Liza said. Eric eyes moved slowly down her body and lingered on her long, slender legs. "I can almost read your mind, Eric Silkwin." She tried to smile.

"You have a nice smile; you should use it more often," Eric said.

"I'll try," Liza said. "I know I look a mess. I haven't slept well the last couple nights."

"You look good to me," Eric said. "We've been invited to a cook-out at Tyler's."

She grinned. "Tyler's, huh? You sure you want me with you?"

"I'm gonna tell you how much later." He bent over and kissed her, catching her off guard. "I just had to do that." He laughed and her smile came to life. "I'll pick you up tomorrow about one. You're right about every inch being a woman."

"Don't push it. Tomorrow, Eric," Liza said.

The following morning, Eric played with Colleen. She pulled Eric's ear, squealed, and took off running as fast as her little legs would move. Eric chased her until her laughter filled the Silkwin house. A few minutes later, he kissed her softly and carried her to bed. "It's time for your nap, little one," Eric said.

When Eric arrived at Liza's, she was waiting on the front porch. She wore a red blouse and dark blue slacks. "You look . . . ready," he said.

"You think I have the right outfit?"

"Perfect!" Eric said, and then added, "Smell good, too."

Red lipstick highlighted her smile, creating perfection.

The moment they drove up to the Quinlin house, Patsy and Evan ran to meet them, "Hi Eric, who's the girl? A girlfriend, I betcha."

"You're right Patsy. How are you, Evan?"

"Fine, thank you."

It wasn't long before Darryl and a cute, bright-eyed blonde joined them. Daryl looked good, the Navy must have agreed with him. "Eric, it's good to see' ya," Daryl said when they shook hands. "I'd like you to meet Lucy Owens."

"Nice to meet you Lucy, this is Liza."

Eric could see why Daryl was attracted to Lucy. She had a face full of freckles, and one of the nicest smiles he had ever seen. Everyone joined Jerry Yount, Tyler, and Reverend Webber. After introductions, a little later, Jerry yelled, "Hey Eric, how about a softball game later? You and Darryl can choose sides."

"Sounds great," Eric said. "Looks like it's going to be a good day for it. Tyler, you want to be on my side?"

"We've been on the same side before, Eric. I'm not sure that is a good idea," she laughed

Liza and Eric sat across from Tyler and Jerry. Eric noticed that Patsy was focused on a blond-haired boy named Jimmy Wooden, which probably was normal for a ten-year-old girl. Eric winked at her. Her face reddened, but she winked back and smiled. The afternoon moved along slowly. Eric felt an awkwardness and wondered if Tyler felt the same way. After eating, and some small talk, they played a double header. The afternoon faded into evening, which led to late night hamburgers and potato salad. Liza and Lucy helped Tyler clean up, while Darryl, Jerry, and Eric sat in a huddle.

"How do you like the Navy, Daryl?" Jerry asked.

"I was homesick!" Darryl said. "But when I saw the others in the same boat, I figured I'd make it. I really like the Navy. I'm thinking about making a career out of it."

"I had mixed feelings about my brief encounter with the military," Eric added. "I couldn't see myself as a career man."

"I haven't had any experience with the service, but I can tell you, college isn't a piece of cake," Jerry said. A little while later, the girls joined the guys. "You guys come up with any profound wisdom that will help us in the future," Liza asked and laughed.

"We didn't come up with any profound wisdom, but I do have an announcement to make," Jerry said. "Tyler and I are officially engaged." Jerry watched Eric carefully.

"Congratulations," Eric said. "I hope you're both very happy." Eric looked at Tyler to see her reaction. She didn't comment, but only smiled briefly.

"I'm happy for both of you, too," Daryl said. "Maybe that's something that might be in our future as well." He glanced over at Lucy.

The mild form of tension vanished. Jerry razed Liza about missing the fly ball that cost them the last game. They broke out in laughter. "I guess I'm just going to have to live with it," Liza said.

Later, on the drive back to town, Liza asked, "You loved her, didn't you? Tyler, I mean."

"Yes," Eric said. "She was there when I needed someone."

She waited for further comment, but Eric didn't say anything else until they arrived at Liza's house. "You can kiss me for a nice day." Liza said, and leaned close to him, "I had a ball."

Eric kissed her and said, "Me too."

When Eric arrived home, there was a strange car parked across the street. He started for the door.

"Hey Silkwin!" It was Dexter. Eric recognized his voice and walked over to his car. "I gotta talk to you a minute." Eric saw his folks looking out the window. Dexter's hand shook. He took a deep drag off his cigarette. "I hope you'll hear me out."

"I'm waiting," Eric said flatly.

"I admit Idlers and I teased Bryan. We didn't know he'd do something so . . . ." He saw the look in Eric's eyes and didn't finish. He quickly looked away.

Eric turned on him and shouted, "You worked him over the same night we tangled, didn't you?"

"Only after he hit me with a club," Dexter said, "Look at my arm!" His wrist was still bluish and bandaged. "I had to defend myself!"

"You ganged up on him," Eric yelled.

"Idlers hit him after Bryan charged after him," Dexter said. "I know it's hard to believe, but he was like a madman."

"What set him off?" Eric asked. He took another deep drag and flipped the cigarette out the window.

"We told him about what we said to you earlier. We were mad! How in the hell did we know he would . . . ."

"So Bryan knew that I knew about him on Sunday at the cookout!" Eric said.

"Idlers and I don't want any trouble. We're sorry. I swear I'm telling you the truth."

Eric looked in Dexter's eyes. Whatever these guys were, they never intended for something like this to happen. Eric saw his parents still looking out the window. "It's tragic, but over." Eric walked into the house.

"I can't stand any more trouble," Eric's mother said. "It won't bring Bryan back!"

"There won't be any," Eric said, "Dexter was apologizing." Eric picked up Colleen and kissed her. "That's from Liza, little one, and this one's from me."

Later that evening, Ellen, Elizabeth, and Johnny came over. Johnny had that look Eric was getting to know so well. "We talked to Liza; she said she's feeling much better. We've been worrying about her the last couple days," Johnny said. Ellen watched Eric with a smile on her face.

"We had a good time at the cookout this afternoon," Eric said. "I like Liza very much. One thing's for sure, she doesn't like to be referred to as Johnny's little sister. She said the other day that she was five-foot-six and every inch a woman."

"What did you say?" Ellen asked.

"I agreed with her," Eric said.

"I think her interest in you goes beyond that. I know her," Johnny said.

"Does that bother you, Johnny?" Eric asked.

"No, Eric. I just don't want her hurt."

"Believe me; I have no intention of hurting her."

Tuesday morning Tyler came in the shop, "I'm picking up my dad's shoes . . . I mean . . . ." He could tell that Tyler felt very self-conscious.

"I'm happy to see you, Tyler . . . I enjoyed the cookout Sunday," Eric said. "So when's the big day?"

"We haven't set a date yet," Tyler said quietly.

"We came close didn't we, Tyler?" Eric asked.

"Yes. I . . . You don't resent me, do you Eric?"

"No. You're special Maxine Tyler Quinlin. You helped me during a very rough time."

"I was filling in for Alice. I think we both knew that," Tyler replied.

"I loved you, Tyler," Eric said.

"Please Eric, I . . . I must be going. You're making me nervous." She took the package. For an instant, her hand touched his, and she pulled it back. He came around the counter. She watched him carefully with uneasy anticipation, as he quickly kissed her.

"I just had to do that," Eric said.

"Bye, Eric Silkwin," she said, after regaining her composure. She quickly turned and walked out of the shop.

"You are special, Tyler," he said aloud after she'd left, "More than you will ever know."

After work, Eric stopped to see Liza. It was five-thirty and still very warm. He walked around to the back yard. "Eric, what are you doing here?"

"I just wanted to see you—be near you," Eric said.

"You'd better watch talk like that, I take it seriously." Her smile was pure mischief. "Eric," she said softly her tone changing, "I have been doing a lot of thinking."

"That doesn't surprise me," he said. "You're really quite a girl."

"Woman, Eric!"

He laughed aloud, "Definitely a woman."

"I think you're a very sensitive guy under that rugged exterior. A guy who really cares. Alice knew that . . . If we're getting involved, I can't live in Alice's shadow. I've got to be the only one. I'm here if you're interested."

"I'm definitely interested," Eric said.

"You'd better take off Eric. I've got to do some soul searching." He kissed her and walked away. "Eric," she called before he left the back yard, "I can't or won't compete with a dead girl. I mean what I say. You'd better do some soul searching yourself."

"I plan to. It's time," Eric said.

When Eric arrived home, he was surprised to see Linda Hausler at his house. Her loveliness was replaced with a look of discontent. "Hello Eric," she said softly. She held Colleen, who obviously loved the attention.

"What a pleasant surprise," Eric said. He couldn't help noticing some of her perfection had slipped away.

"Colleen and I've been playing. She's terrific Eric, you must be very proud of her."

"I am," he said. "I'm just taking one day at a time."

"I'm here for a week visiting and I thought I would stop by to see everyone," Linda said. She glanced at her watch. "However I must be going. I'm joining Mother and Walter for supper."

"Think the lovely Mrs. Hausler would mind if I drove her home?"

"If you don't mind, I'd prefer walking. It's such a pleasant evening." They walked along the same familiar streets, but it wasn't the same, and they both knew it.

The attempt at conversation was awkward. Things had changed more than Eric realized.

"I was sorry to hear about Bryan, such a tragedy. Our lives are changing so much."

"So how have you been?" Eric asked.

She shrugged, and then continued, "Bill and I are having troubles. I am going back to him, but I do not know how long it will last. He's become quite a success—not only in business—but with another woman."

"I'm sorry," Eric said.

"Bill's afraid of a divorce," Linda said. "He needs me as a show piece. He's a selfish bastard." Her brief outrage didn't hide the tears in her eyes, nor the pleading in her voice. "Forgive me . . . I just had to get that out," Linda said. "We could always talk about almost anything. Are you seeing anyone now?" she quickly asked, changing the subject. "I get this feeling maybe there's someone special."

"I've been dating Liza Bowers, Johnny's sister."

"Is it serious?"

"I think it might be," Eric replied. "Linda, if there's anything I can do . . . ."

"Bring back the good old days, Eric," she responded.

"If only I could," Eric said.

"Get that look off your face, Eric. I'm not after you. We're friends. If there's regret between us, I don't know what it would be."

"Maybe not making love to you," Eric said. "I've always wondered what it would be like."

Just for an instant, there was the flicker of the old Linda in her eyes. "I should have guessed. Your bluntness hasn't changed."

"You asked me," Eric said.

She kissed him lightly just before going into the house. The unfamiliar look of hurt in her eyes was back. "Eric, as far as making love to you, I'm afraid you would be disappointed, and I couldn't take that."

CHAPTER SEVEN

A few weeks later, on a Friday morning Eric called Liza. "How would you like to go to Luckner's place tonight?" Eric asked. "Rita's having her grand opening."

"Sounds good to me," Liza said. "I heard Linda's back in town. I thought she had left . . ."

Eric responded, "She was at the house for a few minutes—I told you we're only friends. She's only going to be here for a week. She's having a rough time, and we could always talk. I'll pick you up about seven, okay?" Eric said.

"I'll be ready—bye," Liza said.

That evening Liza met Eric at the door. Her dark eyes revealed a hint of defiance and excitement all rolled into one. She had her black wavy hair in a slightly different style. Her dress was a bright red.

When they arrived at the restaurant, Rita greeted them. "I wondered if you'd make it," she said over the noise of the crowd. Eric introduced Liza. Rita smiled with a well-earned look of pride as she led them to a table. The indirect lighting and the red-checked tablecloths gave just the right atmosphere.

The candlelight cast faint shadows that danced across Liza's face, revealing that the woman in her was well under control. Sometimes, Eric had a hard time controlling his feelings. Could he be in love with this girl—who happened to be Johnny's sister?

"You're staring at me," Liza said.

"You're easy to look at and I like being with you," Eric replied.

"This is not the time to tease me, Eric."

He put his hand over hers, "I'm very serious."

"You sure it's not the candlelight?" Liza asked, with a smile.

"Now who's teasing who?" Eric said.

After dinner, Liza turned to Eric and said, "I'm ready to leave. Let's see how your sincerity holds up when there's no candlelight."

He drove to the park. It was a beautiful evening; they could hear music coming from the pool area. Several parents, taking advantage of the mild evening, pushed their kids in swings. The kids' laughter filled the park area.

"I hope what you got in mind is a kiss or two," Liza said. "Anything else is out of the question—it's the wrong time of the month. Let's walk. That expression on your face tells me you got something on your mind, Eric."

They strolled over to the pool. There were people swimming; kids yelling, taking advantage of the few minutes left before the final closing call.

"My life is very confusing," Eric said. I don't know where it will lead."

"You mean concerning healing," Liza said. She watched kids playing tag around the pool. "You're not the type to let your ego get in the way."

Her directness threw him off balance. She persisted, still not looking at him. "Tell me in your own way what you mean, Eric."

"When I feel the power flow through me, knowing it can help others. I can't let go for fear it will leave," Eric said. "I never felt this way about anything in my life."

Liza finally turned to face him, and said very seriously, "I honestly don't know whether you're blessed or cursed."

"Only time will tell," Eric said. "I admit my direction seems to lead to trouble—one kind or another."

"Eric, what direction are you talking about?" Liza asked.

"I know this sounds strange and it wouldn't be easy, but I have thought about having my own church someday, especially since there's so much controversy in our church. I never really told anyone about the church idea. I don't think my family would understand and I really don't want them to know."

"I won't say anything, Eric. Knowing you as I do, it doesn't surprise me about the church," Liza said. It was getting late. People were being asked to get out of the pool, over the protests of the kids. It had been a long day.

Monday morning at the shop, Eric caught up on orders. Business had slacked off the last few days. His father took the day off because he was not feeling well. When Eric got home, he saw Johnny's car in front of the house. Ellen and Liza were playing outside with Colleen. Johnny was inside, talking to Eric's mother and father while Elizabeth was taking a nap. Colleen saw Eric and ran toward him. He scooped her up and swung her in the air. "Hi honey, how's my favorite girl?"

"Daddy. Daddy home."

Eric looked at Liza. "At first, I didn't know who you were talking to," Liza said. Her eyes were full of mischief.

"What'd you mean?" Eric asked.

"Your greeting—I didn't know if you meant me or Colleen."

"Both of you really," Eric said. He bent over and kissed Liza. She calmly took Colleen out of Eric's arms and confessed, "I don't quite know what to say."

He stared at Liza. "I do," Eric said. "I'm ready to get my life together."

After regaining her composure, she asked, "Does what you say have anything to do with me? You'd better be careful, I have a witness."

"I'll say one thing, Eric," Ellen said, breaking their stare. "It's never boring when you're around. What does all that double talk really mean?"

"I'm about to find out," Eric said.

Eric took Liza's hand in his and strolled down the street. She looked at him. "What's going on?" Liza asked.

"I want you," Eric said.

"Nothing new about that . . . You wanted me in the back seat of your car, too."

Eric put his hand on her shoulder, "I love you, Liza." She stared at him, her expression refusing to reveal what was behind those dark eyes.

"I'm never sure when you're serious, Eric," Liza said.

Eric kissed her, and then said, "Will you marry me, Liza? We can get our license tomorrow morning and get married Friday evening."

"I think you really mean it, Eric?" She expressed laughter but her eyes were serious. "What would the family say? They'd think I was pregnant." She shook her head and grinned at him. "What if I took you up on it?"

"That's what I'm counting on," Eric said.

"Let's get back to the house before Ellen and Johnny leave. You can think about it in the next three blocks."

"Before I give you my answer, you should know I was in love with a guy named Mark Cannon. And I thought, a career in commercial art," Liza said. "Mark married someone else. He's out east somewhere, working for a tool company."

"You still in love with him?" Eric asked.

"I can't say for sure. I haven't seen him in over three years. As for my career, after much reflection, and an obvious lack of talent, I decided to give it up, at least for a while," Liza said.

"Maybe you didn't want it bad enough. You could still . . . ."

"I don't have the dedication or probably the talent to succeed, at least for now. Besides, I have my job at the paper. Maybe I'll get back to my commercial art someday, but I wouldn't bet on it." Liza worked for the Benford Daily News as a proofreader, with occasional artwork, and minor assignments as a reporter. They were both silent until they reached the front porch.

Liza smiled and said, "The answer to your question . . . I'm yours!"

Eric hugged and kissed her. They walked in the house when Ellen and Johnny were just about ready to leave. Eric asked them to take a seat for a few minutes. They looked at Liza and Eric with amused curiosity.

"We're getting married Friday night," Eric blurted out. "We want your blessing."

Eric's mother dropped her glass of milk and his father shook his head. Eric felt the grin on his face.

Liza only smiled at Johnny, and added. "I love him." Johnny hugged his sister.

"That's the way Eric usually does things," Ellen commented. The next couple of days Liza and Eric got their rings, license, and made arrangements with Reverend Langtree. Eric decided to call Karen and Frank.

"Hello Karen, Eric."

"Eric, this is a surprise. What's going on?"

"I'm getting married Friday."

"Eric, wait a minute, I gotta get Frank. He's gotta hear this." Eric could hear Karen laughing in the background. "Who are you going to marry?" Karen asked.

"I'm going to marry Liza. You know, my brother-in-law's sister."

Frank picked up the phone. "Eric, getting married. Have you been drinking?"

"No," Eric said. "I'm very serious. Liza and I have been going together for a while and our attraction to each other just grew stronger."

"Eric, are you sure this is what is really want?" Karen asked.

"Yes, we both love each other and we need each other." I realize you and Frank can't come back for the wedding, but I just thought it was important that you guys know."

"Eric, you never fail to surprise us. Congratulations, we'll be looking forward to seeing you and Liza when we get back in town. We appreciate you calling us to let us know."

The wedding took place Friday. It was small, only family and a few close friends were there. Liza knew that even though her mom and dad weren't there, they were there in spirit. The reception was held at Luckner's Place. Several tables were placed together in one section of the restaurant to form a temporary banquet room. Rita and her husband Paul congratulated Eric and Liza.

"I owe you, lady," Eric said.

"I wanted this for you two," Rita said. She took Liza's hands in hers. "I know this guy, honey. You'll have your hands full, but hang in there; I think he's worth it."

Eric's parents left early with Colleen.

Ellen kissed Eric and sighed, "The best, little brother."

Eric took Liza's hand in his, and faced Johnny. "I wanted you to know that I love her."

"I have suspected that for some time," Johnny said, and then he kissed Liza. "Be happy, little sister."

"I will, Johnny . . . Love you." It was time for Liza and Eric to start their new life together. They drove to Liza's aunt's house, where they would spend their honeymoon. It was a calm, chilly evening when Eric carried Liza over the threshold.

"You pour some champagne, and I'll join you in a few minutes," Liza said. The look in her eyes told him that the woman was about to rule supreme. When she returned, he took her in his arms and slowly removed the robe from her shoulders, taking in her slim beauty. Her low laugh filled the room, just before they became engulfed in passion.

A little later, he stroked her body. In a moment, her tongue searched his. Later, their exhaustion led to deep restful sleep.

"Eric, wake up," Liza said softly, then she laughed. "We fell asleep in the living room. Don't you think we should go to bed?"

The next morning, Eric woke up early. The light of a new day streamed through their bedroom windows. Liza was still sleeping. Eric showered and shaved, then peeked into the bedroom to see her sitting up in bed. The sleep was still in her eyes. She flashed a big smile, "Good morning, my husband. Why didn't you wake me?"

"I didn't want to disturb you. Besides, it's our honeymoon."

She reached for her robe, and wiped the sleep out of her eyes. "How long have you been watching me?"

Eric grinned. "Just a few minutes."

"You're a good husband," Liza said, "but right now, I need my cup of coffee."

She sipped her coffee and opened the door to inhale the fresh morning air. Eric smelled her cologne and took her in his arms.

She pushed him away and said, "You sit over there while I fix your breakfast." She looked over her shoulder with that little girl look he liked so much. Suddenly they stared at each other with a self-conscious awareness. "I wondered what it would be like the morning after," Liza said. "Do you think I'm silly?"

"No, I think you're terrific," Eric said. He lit a cigarette and watched her finish cooking breakfast. Eric could see the mischief in her eyes. "Am I as good on the living room floor as I am in the back seat?" she asked.

"That's a loaded question, lady," Eric said.

"I guess I'll have to settle for that. What're we gonna do today?" Liza asked.

Eric looked at her. "We might just have to find something to do inside, but how about we take a walk and get some fresh air first," Eric said. "I guess you know I have to be back at the shop Monday."

"I know. I'm gonna be good for you and Colleen," Liza said. Her dark eyes turned serious, "Maybe later, we can have a baby. In the mean time, I can work for a while. I'm flexible." They strolled hand-in-hand. She was like a little girl; she'd pull away and dare him to chase her.

After eating a late snack, they danced and finished off the champagne. Her eyes were bright and teasing, then she whispered, "Maybe we should make love."

Sunday afternoon, they drove to Eric's parents' for dinner. Ellen and Johnny were all smiles when Liza and Eric walked in the house. Colleen ran to them as fast as her little legs would carry her. "Leez and Daddy, I lube you!" He scooped her up in his arms.

"And we love you, little one." They all laughed.

"We have to work on a word or two," Ellen said. "You both look happy."

Liza looked at Eric, and then said "Very much."

"You going back to the house tonight?" his mother asked. "You could stay here."

"I don't think so," Eric said. "We're on our honeymoon until Monday morning."

Late at night, Liza and Eric sat before the fireplace eating hamburgers from the drive-in, laughing. "I could've fixed something. Why are we eating take-out?"

Eric grinned. "So we can spend the rest of this night holding each other."

"Sounds great," Liza said, and then flashed her smile. "My Aunt sent a letter. She felt bad that she couldn't be at the wedding. How would you like to be a house renter or homeowner? I didn't want t say anything until I felt the time was right ."

"I understand that," Eric said. "I admit I've been thinking about where we should live. You know we can't live at the cabin. They're going to put a state highway through that area. I can tell you have something on your mind."

"My aunt likes being by her sister . . . in fact, she likes it better there than here and would like to stay for a while, maybe even permanently. She wanted to know if we would be interested in renting the house."

"I like the idea," Eric said. "Who knows, maybe in the near future, we would have an opportunity to buy the place . . . I like it.

Liza laughed, "She mentioned something similar to that."

"Sounds like another women after my own heart," Eric said.

"Another . . . ." Liza said. "Who would be the first?"

"I can't say at this time—someone's ego might become too inflated,"

Monday morning, Eric dropped Liza off at work and went to the shop. His father was working his crossword puzzle and puffing on his cigar. "You look good, Eric. I think married life agrees with you," his father said, and grinned. "At least, the first few days."

"I feel great . . . We'll pick up Colleen tonight after work."

"I guess we'll miss her a little bit," Howard said slowly.

"What's the latest?" Eric asked, quickly changing the subject. His father always liked commenting on the news.

"You know, I wasn't too sure about that Truman, but I think he might be all right. One thing, you don't have to wonder what he means. I like that about him."

"But . . . ." Eric said with a grin.

"I hope he doesn't listen to that Senator McCarthy! You know, the guy who's looking everywhere for communists, and anything else he doesn't like," his father said. "He'd do anything to be one of the boys."

"I think Truman's his own man," Eric said. "I can't see him taking too seriously a guy that could ruin the lives of many innocent people."

"I guess we'll find out soon enough. Your mother and I think that Liza's a wonderful girl and we're happy to see you settled down. I admit you had us going there for a while . . . ."

It was the last words Eric's father ever said. He grabbed his chest and collapsed. Eric called an ambulance and then his mother. A few hours later Howard died peacefully in the hospital, surrounded by his family. He never regained consciousness. Eric knew nothing else could be done. He went back to the shop. As he walked in the door, smoke from his dad's cigar was still rising from the ashtray. Eric shook his head and quickly put the cigar out. He looked around, locked the door, and started the long walk back home with all kinds of thoughts going through his mind.

The funeral was crowded with his many friends. Eric phoned Karen and Frank and told them it wasn't necessary that they make the trip.

The graveside was too familiar.

Eric held Colleen, with Liza, his mother, Ellen, and Johnny by his side. A group of church members, as well as the Quinlins offered their condolences.

Too soon, it was over. A lifetime finished in a few minutes. It seemed, somehow, like there should be something more. Linda and her mother stood beside Walter, his dad's best friend, who sobbed openly. The years they had were suddenly ended.

The ride back from the cemetery seemed like a bad dream— the reality all too familiar. Liza and Eric offered to stay with his mother, but she would have no part of it.

She held up very well in the next few days. In her own words, it was a matter of accepting God's will. "I was grateful for all the years we had together," Eric's mother said. "I'd like to be alone with my Bible and memories. It's the way things are and we must accept them with faith."

Eric was restless the next few nights. He took comfort in holding Liza in his arms.

"Things happen so suddenly," Eric said. "It's strange how you expect something more . . . You'd think I could accept that by now."

Liza's only answer was the tears in her eyes.

Monday morning, Eric dropped Colleen off at his mother's house. She waited for them with open arms. "You get to work," she said. "Colleen and I will be just fine." Eric entered the shop. He sat in his father's swivel chair and stared at the pile of orders on the desk. For the first time, he realized that the total responsibility for the shop was his.

Almost five months had passed. Thanksgiving was just a few days away. It had turned cold and they had their first snowfall of the season. Colleen watched the snow with wide-eyed wonder. She was talking constantly, and each new word brought a scream of joy.

Eric talked to Karen and Frank. They were returning to Benford in December to stay. Two days before Thanksgiving, he closed early. The orders had slacked off with the approaching holidays. He picked up Colleen, who filled him in on her day.

Liza was at home with a cold, but she still managed a sense of humor. Eric walked to the stove and kissed her. "Soup and sandwiches tonight," she said, and she smiled, despite a red nose. "I did manage to bake a pumpkin pie."

"Pie," Colleen shouted, tugging at Liza's dress, and then she raced into the living room. She looked into the corner, and said to herself, "No, Colleen," and then she would run off in another direction. Liza and Colleen had this game, where Liza would hide her teddy bear and Colleen had to find it.

Eric put his arm around Liza and kissed her. "You look much better."

"Yes, and I think you're building up to something," she said.

"Look, me found!" Colleen shouted at them, her eyes bright with joy.

"Why don't you give your teddy bear a name?" Eric asked. Her smile faded quickly, looking from Eric to Liza. There was the same look of wonder in her face that Alice had. "Me teddy bear's name is Doodles." They both laughed.

After supper, they sat staring into the fireplace. Colleen snuggled between them. She crawled on Eric's lap; it was her way of being ready for bed. Her eyes were almost closed. "Doodles sandy-eyed," Colleen yawned, "Me put him to bed."

Eric carried her to her room, with Liza following, as they did every night. She held Doodles close. They kissed her goodnight. They returned to their favorite spot before the fireplace. "You sure you feel up to . . . ." Eric asked.

She put her finger over his mouth, smiled, and then stretched out on the couch. "Maybe, just maybe, this could be a cure for my cold."

"It's worth checking out," Eric said. Later she molded into his arms as only she could do. He kissed her softly as the night overtook them.

Thanksgiving came and went with a depressed feeling of missing his father. The family tried to keep the holiday spirit, but they realized it was the beginning of their dad's favorite season. Liza helped Colleen make out her Christmas list. Eric and Liza received a letter from Marie and Ted. They were doing fine and overjoyed with their daughter, six-month-old Tina. Karen and Frank were due home the first weekend in December. They were moving back into the house that Frank's father had left him.

Early Monday morning, Eric snapped out of his daydream when he saw Linda enter the shop. "Hello Linda," Eric said. "Home for the holidays I would imagine."

"I know this is a little late, but congratulations on your marriage, Eric. Mother told me about you getting married to Liza Bowers."

"Thank you, Linda"

Eric poured her a cup of coffee. "I still think of your father now and then," she said. "I really liked him." Linda grasped the cup and stared at Eric. "Bill and I are awful close to a divorce. Some *Christmas*, huh?" She started to cry, and then suddenly, just like always, she took control of her emotions. "He thinks he's in love with someone else."

Eric stared at her for a moment, then said quickly, "How about I buy you lunch at the Grover's, like the old times?"

"I'd like that. I have to run some errands. I'll be back before twelve." She dried her eyes and instinctively took out her pocket mirror, touching up her face. Some things never changed.

"You're still lovely, lady."

"You're always saying that, and if you ever stop, I don't know what I'd do."

At Grover's, Linda and Eric sat across from each other in a booth they had used many times. She still had that look that made him feel lucky just to be with her. "I'm staying with Mother and Walter. I'm trying to get my old job back at Mullaird's," Linda said. "I . . . I know Bill and I have had troubles . . . . She's probably a lot better in bed than I am!"

Eric didn't know what to say. It wasn't like the old times. Their lives had changed so much. He didn't answer so she continued.

"That would be very important to him, and all you men— being good in bed, I mean!"

"I don't know, but in my limited experience, it's a matter of giving yourself to each other," Eric said.

"I've never felt that," Linda said softly. "I guess it just isn't there." When their orders arrived, Eric was relieved. "Well anyway, I'm going to try to get my life back together."

"I know what you mean. You'll make it," Eric said.

She glanced at her watch, "I better get going; I've got an appointment at Mullaird's this afternoon. Thank you for the lunch and the conversation. I'll be all right; I have my whole life ahead of me, isn't that true?"

"Yes, it is," Eric said. "Don't let what has happened keep you from the good life you have coming."

For the first time she smiled. "You still have the strangest way of expressing yourself that I've ever heard, Eric Silkwin. Say hello to Liza and Colleen for me."

That evening, Liza was in a very odd mood. "I heard Linda's back in town." She waited a moment, watching Eric. "I heard she's getting a divorce and staying in Benford."

"Yes, I talked to her this morning," Eric said. "As a matter of fact, I took her to lunch. She's hurting and we could always talk." Eric felt that familiar grin on his face. "She said to say hello."

Liza tried to be serious, but her grin broke through. She stood defiantly with both hands on her hips. "The thoughts that go through my mind . . . I guess I should be ashamed of myself, but she's so pretty."

Eric put his hands on her shoulders, and laughed when he saw a smudge of flour on her nose. "You're right. She is pretty, but she doesn't have that look about her—that combination of the little girl and the woman."

"I guess I have to hear things like that once in awhile," Liza said.

"You will. Now what's for supper?" Eric asked.

She grinned. "Stew and me."

"Sounds like a winning combination," Eric said.

She suddenly turned around and threw her arms around him.

"I don't know what brought this on, but I kinda like it," Eric said.

She pulled away and looked him in the eye. "I just felt like it, right at this moment."

"Sometimes you're a strange lady," Eric said, kissing her nose. "But I wouldn't want it any other way."

CHAPTER EIGHT

Saturday evening Karen and Frank came over. "Welcome home," Eric said.

"It's good to be home," Karen said.

"That goes double for me," Frank added. They both showed the strain of the last week, getting moved into their house.

"I'm sorry we couldn't make your wedding," Karen said. "Everything was so hectic. Frank's job has been tearing us apart."

"That's an understatement," Frank added. He looked even worse than when he was here for Bryan's funeral. Eric guessed he'd lost about fifteen pounds. He'd changed even more than Eric realized. Karen was the same, plus a few pounds.

"This is a nice place," Karen said. "This is your aunt's house, Liza?

"Yes, she is spending time with her sister, so we are renting the house for the time being."

"We were really sorry to hear about your dad, Eric," Karen said.

"I really miss him," Eric said. "I sense his presence in the shop once in a while."

Karen looked at Frank. "I guess you're still involved in healing?" Frank said.

"I help with healing at Mayville once in a while."

"What about you, Liza?" Karen asked.

"Not that much really. I sat in on some of the Bible study classes," Liza said. "I help with an occasional dinner and mostly support Eric."

"Bible study classes?" Karen pressed. "I had the impression there was more to it."

Neither Liza nor Eric commented.

"I've heard things at the plant since I've been back," Frank said.

"People have to have something to talk about," Eric said, with an edge in his voice. He could not understand Karen and Frank's resentment after all this time.

"Any word about the cabin? We saw the construction." Frank added.

"I'm still waiting to hear something," Eric said.

"How do you feel about selling the cabin?" Frank asked.

"Not too bad. It was a special place at a special time," Eric said. "Besides, I don't have much choice with the highway coming here. How are the boys?"

"They're fine; in fact, we have a sitter watching them, so we can't stay to long. Time goes so fast. Just think—Christmas is only about a week and a half away. I'll give you a call and see when we can get together for Christmas," Karen said.

After Karen and Frank left, Colleen fell asleep. Eric helped Liza clear off the table, but she insisted on doing the dishes. After she had finished, she joined Eric. "You've been staring into that fire for almost an hour. Have a cup of coffee and hold me."

He put his arm around her and suddenly felt better. She often had that effect on him.

"Maybe Karen and Frank do have a point," Eric said.

"Yes, but is it the point that clears things up, or only confuses you and creates more doubts?" Liza asked.

"I don't have the answers," Eric said, "and I'm beginning to wonder about some of the questions."

"I thought healing meant so much to you," Liza said. "It seems every time you get around Karen and Frank, you begin to doubt yourself! How can they possibly know or understand how you feel?"

"I don't know," Eric replied.

"Even your mother has said to pray about it. I remember you telling me that you knew what you wanted to do, and it wouldn't be easy."

"I remember, but sometimes doubt and frustration just closes in on me," Eric said.

86

"Remember when you were trying to get to me? Did doubt and frustration stop you then?" Liza asked.

Eric smiled. Liza's timing, as usual, was perfect.

"What would you rather do?" Liza asked. "Get in one of your moods, or close in on me?"

After loving her to the point of exhaustion, he whispered, "Why can't all my decisions be like this?"

She laughed and said, "If you'd put half the energy into your decisions that you used a few minutes ago, you'd know what path to take without question."

"Have I told you today how much I love you?" Eric asked.

"No, but your demonstration pretty well nailed it down."

Monday morning came quickly. Liza looked at Eric and smiled, "How do you want your eggs?"

"Over easy."

"I somehow figured that," she said.

"Mornin', Daddy," Colleen yelled.

"Good morning, cutie. You know, I just might run into Santa Claus today. I'll have to tell Santa something if he asks about you. You got your Christmas list made out?"

Colleen looked to Liza then back to Eric, "I think. Me good," she said between spoonfuls of cereal. "I'm *over* two years."

"I know little one." He dug into his eggs and winked at Liza, "How about Momma?"

"Good too," Colleen said with big eyes. "Doodles too."

Dr. Emery was waiting in front of the shop, huddled against the doorway. The light snow was tapering off, but it was getting colder. "Good morning doctor," Eric said. "It's been a while. Join me for a cup of coffee?"

The doctor accepted the cup and said, "This coffee helps on a cold morning like today. Eric, I have a patient. Are you interested?"

"Yes." Eric said. "If I can help, and it's okay with Dr. Hedwick?"

Dr. Emmery smiled. "Patient's request. I'll handle Dr. Hedwick. You want any details?"

"Only where and when," Eric said.

"How about after you close up, Eric? We can meet at the office."

"I'll be there," Eric said.

After Dr. Emmery left, Eric's thoughts turned to Alice. This time of year was when he thought of her the most. He buried himself in his work until it was time to meet Dr. Emmery.

"Hello Eric, how are you? How's married life?" Sherry asked.

"Great," Eric answered.

"Come in, Eric," Dr. Emmery said. Dr. Hedwick was examining a boy about ten or eleven. "I'd like you to meet Billy Hagger and his mother."

The mother gripped her purse. "How do you do?" she said softly. "I'm so sorry. I'm very nervous . . . ." She looked at Eric and said, "I want you to know, it's not that I lack faith in you, it's just that I've never done this kind of thing before. It's just with Christmas and all . . . ."

"We understand," Dr. Emmery said. "It's quite all right."

"Billy has a stubborn case of pneumonia," Dr. Hedwick said.

Eric shook the boy's hand, "My pleasure Billy, you about ready for Christmas?"

"Yes . . . you gonna make it a good one for me?" The boy's eyes stared straight into his.

"I'm gonna try very hard—with the help of these doctors, of course."

"I like your order of billing," Dr. Hedwick added. He was his old self.

"I don't have much money," the mother said, "but I'm not a charity case!"

The boy suddenly went into a series of spasms. Eric quickly placed his hand on the boy's chest, and prayed. *In the name of Jesus—thy will be done.* He felt the power rushing through him. The boy's face turned bright red, and then slowly took on a natural color. Gradually, he began to breathe easily. In a few moments, perspiration broke out on his forehead.

Eric heard a voice in his head. *"The boy will have his kind of Christmas."* Then he felt the power fading away.

The mother thanked them, helped the boy with his coat, and started to leave.

Just before they left, Eric said. "Don't mention my name; only the doctors."

"A sudden touch of modesty?" Dr. Hedwick asked.

"The important thing is the boy," Eric said. "Besides it's Christmas."

It was just a little before seven when Eric walked into the house. Colleen ran to him, "Hungry Daddy?"

"Starved," he said, scooping her up and over his head. Her laughter filled the room.

He explained to Liza about the healing he had given Billy Hager.

"How'd you feel about that?" she asked.

"Great. After hearing that voice I realized—whatever happens, I should never doubt or question this source of healing again."

"Sounds like you got your answer," Liza said. Later after supper, Eric read Colleen a story until she fell asleep. Liza joined him on the couch. "I'm happy for him—the boy, I mean," Liza said. "I don't understand how something that could help a little boy can be considered bad."

Next morning, Eric stopped in to see his mother. She insisted on fixing him breakfast. She listened carefully while he explained the little boy, and his reaction.

"Thank God," she said, looking into his eyes. "My prayers for you have been answered. Not exactly as I wanted, but you're blessed with a gift beyond our understanding. We should be very thankful."

"I hope this blessing doesn't have too many thorns," Eric said softly.

"What?" his mother asked.

"Nothing Mother, I was just thinking out loud. Hey, I've gotta get to work."

As Eric was walking toward the shop, he saw Linda. "Happy Holidays," Linda said. "How's the family?"

"Great," Eric said. "How about joining me for a cup of coffee and tell me what's behind that light in your eyes."

"Bill's here. He got in yesterday. We talked last night and agreed to try to work things out. Maybe there is a Santa."

"I wouldn't be a bit surprised," Eric said.

"I didn't tell you the other day, but . . . I'm pregnant. Bill didn't know, and Mother insisted I should tell him."

"It could make a world of difference," Eric said.

"It's the reason Bill and I are trying to work it out. I'll be honest with you; I'm a little afraid." She looked down at the floor and said, "At the time I conceived, if I remember right, it wasn't exactly a loving time." Her face reddened. "This is very awkward for me, but do you think it will make any difference?"

Eric grinned. "I think it works under any circumstances."

She joined him in laughter, but her face was beet red. "Silly. That's not what I mean . . . You think it could affect the health of the baby?" Her smile vanished.

Eric realized how important it was for him to say the right thing. "You and Bill just love each other and the baby's development will be fine."

"I'm just glad nobody else is hearing this conversation," Linda said. She then turned on one of her loveliest smiles. "They'd never understand."

"But we do and that's the real difference," Eric said.

"Bill's taking me out for dinner at Morgan's. Maybe becoming a father is what he needed." The tone of her voice suggested confirmation.

"It wouldn't surprise me at all," Eric said.

Eric finished his Christmas shopping and headed home. Liza and Colleen met him at the door. "Karen called," Liza said. "We're supposed to have Christmas Eve supper at their house." Colleen tugged at Eric's pant leg, trying to get his attention.

"You see Santa?" Her eyes glowed with the look of wonder. Eric kissed her, and picked her up.

"Yes. I gave him your list."

"Tell him me good?"

"Yes, but I think he already knew."

Eric put her down.

She yelled, "Happy me," and took off into the living room.

"What'd he say about me?" Liza asked. She was stirring a pot of homemade soup. He looked over her shoulder.

"He never mentioned your behavior," Eric said with a big grin. "But he did say he loved you very much."

"Good enough," she said.

Everyone met at Karen's house. Eric hadn't seen his aunt and uncle since Bryan's funeral. His mother, Johnny, Elizabeth, and Ellen came later. The usual feeling of family unity wasn't there. The tension was like an invisible barrier. Nobody mentioned religion, but it was still awkward. Christmas Day seemed the same as any other day with the exception of the kids, whose joy saved the Christmas season.

The holidays passed quickly into April. The countryside took on the appearance of early spring. The leaves were gradually replacing the naked branches of the trees. Karen and Frank visited occasionally, but it wasn't the same. Each family seemed wrapped up in their own problems.

Eric hadn't worked with healing since the Hagger boy before Christmas. For some reason or another, they hadn't made it to the Mayville church in months.

Eric received a letter from Marie and Ted. They were back in the states and his parents were coming to Texas for a visit.

That evening, Eric sat before the fireplace. He was deep in thought, holding Colleen, watching the flames dancing about the logs. "Read me story, Daddy."

He picked up the book and began to read, but his gaze wandered beyond the pages. *"Once upon a time, a little boy had two paths to choose from. One was easy. The other, he felt was right, but could also lead to dragons that waited for him . . . ."*

Early Sunday morning, Eric walked out into the yard and worked out on the heavy bag with a vengeance. "How about a break?" Liza yelled. He wiped his brow and watched them walk toward him. Liza always seemed to manage a smile.

"Your timing is perfect. I'm ready to knock off." Eric took Colleen in his arms and they walked hand-in-hand back to the house.

"Tyler and Jerry Yount's marriage is to be in October," Liza said casually. "It was in last night's paper."

""I'm happy for them," Eric said, seemingly trying to convince himself in his mind.

"I'm hungry," Colleen said.

"What's unusual about that?" Eric asked, "What have you been doing this morning?"

"Looking at my book," she said with pride. Liza and Colleen worked together almost every day. Colleen's interest and Liza's patience made each new thing Colleen learned a joy.

Liza and Eric both insisted Colleen refer to her mother—Alice—as Mommy One, and Liza as Mommy. Some of the family didn't seem to agree, but couldn't come up with a better idea.

The next week consisted of visits from the family and his father's old friend, Walter. It was the first time Eric had seen him since his father's funeral. Linda's mother had received word that Linda had a miscarriage.

Eric received a letter from Marie and Ted. They had extended his tour because of Korea.

The shop orders picked up so much that Eric was working overtime. He had heard Linda and Bill Hausler were going through with their divorce. It was almost ten when Tyler came into the shop. She slowly made her way to the counter. "What a pleasant surprise, Tyler. We haven't talked in a long time," Eric said.

"I guess it's been a while," she said. "I came to invite you and the family to my wedding. It's going to be a small affair. By the way, Patsy asks about you."

Eric grinned. "I think about her every now and then—and you, of course . . . ."

"Now Eric," Tyler said.

"Hey lady, we're friends, aren't we?"

"I'm being silly," she said as she turned away trying to avoid looking at him directly.

That night, Eric told Liza that Tyler came into the shop to invite them to her wedding.

"I wonder if you're still in love with Tyler," Liza said. It was one of the few times that she was wide-eyed and serious. "I wonder if sometimes a person can be in love with two people at the same time . . . Eric, get that grin off your face. That was a legitimate question, and I'm trying to be serious."

He pulled her on his lap and kissed her. "Lady, you sure come up with some good ones," Eric said. "You have quite an imagination."

She got off his lap and stared at him with her woman's stare. "It happens."

He held her that night like always, but his mind couldn't release her words.

A couple of weeks later, Eric received a phone call. "Hi Eric, this is Patsy."

"Hi Patsy, How are you?"

"I'm doing okay. I just wanted to let you know that Tyler's and Jerry's wedding has been call off. I knew they wouldn't get married."

"Sometimes, things happen for a reason," Eric said. "Thanks for letting me know." Eric knew Tyler could never marry someone she didn't love.

CHAPTER NINE

The dog days of August were here, when Eric received a letter from Ted. He'd finally gotten his discharge after four years. They were due back in the states with one-year-old daughter, Tina. Liza stared at Eric as she handed him a couple more letters. Eric knew these were more letters from anonymous people, who questioned his right to heal.

"Why do we still get these things?" Eric asked. "I haven't given a healing for months." The letters were all much the same and never signed. Tension between Eric and Liza increased. After Colleen was in bed, Liza cornered Eric.

"Talk to me!" she said. "The last few days, I've felt your unrest. Is it because you haven't been more involved with healing, or just because of these letters?"

"It isn't the people as much as it is my concern about Colleen's future," Eric said.

"Why in the hell don't people mind their own business?" Liza asked, with an edge in her voice. She stood with her hands on her hips, her dark eyes blazing, "Who are these people to question your right to live your own life?"

Karen and Frank came over the next evening. Liza and Eric hadn't seen them in a couple of weeks. Frank was moody and Karen was outright defiant. She read the letters and handed them to Frank. "Although it's none of their business, I basically agree with what they say—I think the family has been through enough. This is a small town. You know how people are."

Eric didn't answer.

"I agree with Karen," Frank said. "We have to think of the kids, especially when they start school. What're you trying to prove Eric?"

"Believe me," Eric said. "I've been thinking about the kids . . . but I believe in what I'm doing! You've never understood."

"You sure?" Karen asked. "You know the doctors only use you occasionally for their own benefit . . . and that church in Mayville!" Karen shook her head and looked at Liza "What do you think? Don't look at Eric. Just forget that you're defending him for a moment. You want the children ridiculed?"

"Of course not," Liza said.

"Just tell us in your own words, Eric," Frank said. "Surely you can't believe you're really chosen." Eric didn't say anything, so Frank continued. "Even the doctors explained that there wasn't any evidence you helped Mr. Winslow. As for that boy with pneumonia, he was under the doctors' care."

"It isn't just the healing; it's the little girl and the people in the dreams reaching out to me. There's much more at stake than you realize," Eric said.

"If you really have this power . . . how come it didn't help Alice?" Karen asked.

"I wish I could answer that," Eric said. "I've asked myself the same thing many times."

"You haven't been right since Alice died," Karen continued. "We don't want to hurt you—even Tyler couldn't take it. You want to put Liza through the same thing?"

"I think somehow you've blown this all out of proportion," Frank added.

In a way, Eric realized Frank's position. He had advanced in Nathan Lock Company. He was a good foreman; he worked hard, and was considered one of the company's best assets. Recently Frank had become an officer in the family church.

"Whether you like it or not, other people are involved!" Karen snapped. "That's the part you refuse to understand . . . there's no way to avoid it. You have to realize you're taking all of us with you—especially the children. We have to go," Karen said calmly. "Just think about it."

After Karen and Frank left, Eric was very quiet. Liza wasn't quite sure what to say.

"Eric, since we're going to your mothers for dinner, what do you think about going to the Mayville Church this evening?" she asked. "Maybe it will help you find the answer you're looking for."

After the church service, Elaine Caulfield and Steven Loulder greeted them. "We were wondering what happened to you two," Elaine said. "There've been several people asking about you."

Eric felt at home in the little healing sanctuary—a place where all the doubts and fears vanished. Later Eric, Liza, Elaine, and Steven sat down to talk.

"Your doubts are obvious," Steven Loulder said to Eric. "We know what you're going through . . . . Believe me; all of us have experienced it one time or another."

"In fairness, neither Steven nor I have had a marriage partner or children to contend with," Elaine said. She explained how both she and Steven had family problems. "People look on the morbid side. They condemn the church and everything related to it. When you go against traditional churches, you're an outcast."

"I guess we have a lot to think about," Eric said.

Liza and Eric drove back to Benford in silence.

The phone rang. "Eric, this is Ted. We're home at last! I'm discharged."

"It's great to hear your voice, Ted. How about meeting me at the shop tomorrow and coming over for dinner tomorrow night?" Eric asked.

"Sounds good to me," Ted said. "We've missed you people."

"We feel the same. It's great to have you home." Eric hung up and joined Liza. "That was Ted, they're home for good. I invited them over for dinner tomorrow night"

"Great," Liza said. "It'll be nice to see 'em again. Tina must be over a year old."

"Colleen, we're going to have company tomorrow night," Eric said.

"Super, Daddy," Colleen yelled. Super seemed to be her favorite word these days.

Liza and Eric reminisced about the last time they'd seen Marie and Ted. "Don't you think it's time for you to get some sleep, little one?" Eric asked.

Colleen looked in Eric's eyes, "I'm bigger now."

"Whata you mean?" Erik asked.

"How long am I a little one?" she asked, staring at him.

Eric took her in his arms. "You're bigger, but to me, at least for a while, you're my little one. You think that'd be all right?"

"Okay, but I am bigger!"

"Good night, honey. Dream nice." After her prayers, he tucked her in bed. "Good night, bigger one." Her big blue eyes smiled with approval.

Liza stood in the doorway smiling. "You got any of that sweet talk for me?"

"I have more than talk for you, pretty one."

"I'll bet," Liza countered.

At noon the next day, Eric fought off the August sun as he walked to the drugstore.

It was very hot, with perspiration soaking through his shirt. He felt a sudden chill passing the floor fan, just inside the drugstore entrance.

He saw Linda sitting at one of the tables. She motioned for him to join her. "I haven't seen you for quite a while, Eric," she said. She looked cool and fabulous in a pale blue dress. Linda always knew what made her look special. "How are you?"

"Hot. This is some day," Eric said. "I didn't realize you were back home."

"I've been back for a while. How about joining me for lunch, and we can talk? My treat," Linda said.

"How can I refuse? It's a deal." He didn't want to lead the conversation, but she seemed to be waiting on him to say something.

Eric glanced at the several people staring at them. Evidently, some things hadn't changed at all.

Eric looked into Linda's eyes and said, "I was so sorry to hear about you losing the baby." Linda didn't respond, but her expression said it all. Eric changed the subject. "Ted Faulkland, his wife Marie, and daughter Tina are joining us for dinner. We haven't seen them for almost two years. I'm guess I'm a little excited."

"I can imagine," she said, then added, "Bill's working for Mullaird's in Engineering. I wouldn't have mentioned it, but he's headed this way."

"Well now," Hausler said, "The lovely Mrs. Hausler, and her old friend, Eric." He pulled up a chair and joined them. It was obvious he'd had a few. He had gained weight and looked flushed and bloated. Eric noticed a receding hairline that he guessed would cause undue alarm in Bill Hausler. "So how's everybody?"

"Martinis lunch?" Linda asked.

"Strictly business, lady! I'm trying to put across a new design." Hausler waved off lunch and ordered coffee.

Linda glanced at her watch, "Have to rush. Some of us have to work regular hours."

"Honey," Bill said, with a smile, "Ease up on me, I've changed. How's the family, Eric?" Hausler asked. He couldn't seem to take his eyes off Linda.

"Liza and Colleen are fine," Eric answered.

"Linda and I almost had a child. The miscarriage . . . was one of those things," Hausler added. "A tragedy, but I think we should try again." His grin returned, "If you'd just give me another chance."

"What would your women think?" Linda asked.

"That would stop. We love each other and you know it."

Linda picked up the check, ignoring his comment. "Nice seeing you, Eric. Give my best to your family," Linda said, as she hurried off.

"How about another cup of coffee, Eric?" Bill asked.

"I guess I got a few minutes. I've got a business to run," Eric said. If Hausler detected any sarcasm in Eric's voice, he ignored it.

"I'm serious about wanting Linda back," Hausler said. "I didn't realize how much I needed her until the last year or so." The waitress refilled their coffee cups.

"From what I've heard, you can't blame her," Eric said, expecting an outburst. "I'm sure she has a hard time believing you from past performance."

"That's true," Hausler said. "It's always been too easy for me—other women, I mean." It was true. Ever since Eric had known of Bill Hausler, he always had the girls after him. What some guys would treasure evidently had turned out to be a curse for him. "I like to think I've matured, and have more self control," he said seriously,

"I've gotta know Eric . . . have you and her ever been more than just friends?" Hausler asked.

"That's hard to say," Eric admitted.

Hausler watched him carefully. "Tell her I love her if you get the chance. I can't change things— but I can do something about 'em. I've seen her out with a couple guys, but what I can't get out of my mind is you and her."

Eric got up to leave. "I'll tell Linda, but the rest is up to you."

It was late afternoon when Marie, Ted, and a cute little girl named Tina, entered the shop. "Eric!" Ted yelled. He flashed that boyish grin. Eric looked them over carefully; they had both put on weight and looked very happy.

"Tina's beautiful," Eric said. "Like her mother."

"Oh Eric," Marie said. "I knew you'd say something like that."

After Eric closed the shop, Marie and Ted followed him to his house. Ted and Eric sat at the dining room table watching Liza and Marie fix supper. "It's good to have you home," Eric said

"It's hard to believe I'm really out of the service," Ted said. "It seems so long since we went in." He winked at Colleen. "Come here honey, and let me look at you. My, how you have grown."

Colleen looked at Eric, smiled, and then walked slowly to Ted. "I'm over three-years-old," she said.

"Such a big girl and so pretty, too." He leaned close to Eric, whispering, "I need a drink. Maybe if you suggested it a little later—Marie's kinda—you know . . . ."

Eric took a close look at the guy who couldn't handle whiskey a few years ago. He smiled to hide his concern. "Sure old buddy—for the old times. You're not really hooked, are you?"

"Maybe a little," he grinned. "I'm working my way out of it. It takes time, you know. What a terrific meal. Eric, you're a lucky man," Ted said.

"We both are," Eric countered. "How about a drink to celebrate your homecoming?" Eric watched Marie's smile fade for an instant. After a highball, Ted seemed more at ease. He and Eric went for a walk in the backyard.

"As great as this homecoming is," Ted said, "I'm a little scared. I've got Marie and Tina to worry about now."

"How about your father's insurance company?" Eric asked.

"They've cut back."

"Don't worry, you'll find something," Eric added.

Ted finished his second highball, and tried to smile. "You still hooked on religion . . . healing wasn't it?"

"Yes, but not too active. Liza and I go to a church in Mayville once in a while; they practice healing," Eric said. He watched Ted's reaction. "The family's not too happy about it."

Ted surprised him by saying, "Marie and I attended one in England. It's more common than you would imagine."

"Marie's Catholic," Eric said.

"So am I—for Marie's sake—but we both found the church fascinating, even more than I suspected. You know me," Ted said, fiddling with his cup of coffee. "I don't fit in orthodox religion."

"I've been getting the heat because of my involvement with healing from Karen, and Frank," Eric said.

"Interesting, to say the least," Ted said. "What are you going to do?"

"Haven't really decided. Karen and Frank have changed. Things like this didn't used to bother them a few years ago—especially Karen."

"We've all changed," Ted said seriously. "Time has a way of doing that. You know, I enjoyed that church. Strange as it sounds, it's the only time I felt like I really belonged." They walked back into the kitchen. The girls had dress patterns scattered all over the kitchen table. Ted laughed. "Look, I think the girls are creating."

"Now Teddy, you behave yourself," Marie said. Their conversations went on into the evening, until it was hard to know what to say.

All of a sudden, Eric asked, "How about a picnic Sunday, at the park?"

"Sounds like a winner," Ted said, Eric knew enough about Ted's expression to know something else was on his mind. He was right.

"I'd like to go with you to Mayville sometime," Ted said.

"Mayville? What are you talking about Teddy?" Marie asked.

Ted explained Eric's involvement.

Marie listened carefully. If she was surprised, it never showed. She looked to Liza, "What do you think?"

"Mixed feelings," Liza said. "I'm not involved in healing like Eric. I attend a class once in awhile . . . It's just that there's so much controversy."

Marie faced Eric, "I guess Ted has told you about our experience in England . . . . Why do I have this feeling you're thinking of becoming a minister?" Marie asked.

It was the first time anyone had mentioned it since his mother, years ago. "I don't know," Eric said slowly. "Strange you should mention it, because that's something that's been on my mind, but I don't know if I'm ready for that kind of responsibility."

"That doesn't surprise me that much Eric," Ted said.

"I think this is something that deserves a lot of thought," Marie said. "But right now, we really need to be going. It was good being together again."

"We feel the same way," Liza added.

Later in bed, Eric listened to Liza's deep, easy breathing. She cuddled next to him as usual. He glanced at the clock. It was after one. Suddenly a ball of white light appeared in front of him, and he heard the words, *Believe in yourself.* Then the light disappeared. Eric stared at Liza and whispered to himself, "If only I could."

The next day Eric had trouble keeping up with his work. Just before noon, he picked up the phone. "Hello Karen, this is Eric. Marie and Ted are home, how'd you like to have a picnic at the park tomorrow?"

"I'm all for it," Karen said. After a few moments, Frank was on the line. "Eric, a picnic's great . . . . You mind if I invite Sally and Bert Simmon? Bert's my boss."

"No problem," Eric said, although he wasn't sure. The Simmons belonged to the family church. They hadn't said more than a few words to him in years. Mr. Simmon was an officer in the church and a supervisor at the Nathan Lock Company where Frank worked.

It was a beautiful August Sunday, and as expected, the park was crowded. Kids played ball, waiting for the taste of hamburgers and hot dogs, whose aroma filled the air.

Frank introduced the Simmons to Liza, Eric, and the Faulklands. The Simmons, who insisted on being called Sally and Bert, seemed friendlier than he remembered.

After eating, the women cleared off the table while the men took a walk.

They finally settled on a recently vacated bench near the ball diamond. A group of screaming kids were in the midst of a close game.

"What are your plans, Ted?" Frank asked. "Now that you're a civilian."

Ted grinned and replied slowly, watching the ball game, "Not sure. The only experience I have is insurance, and that's limited. They're cutting back where my father works."

"I've heard there's an opening for an insurance clerk at Griffin's in Benford," Bert said.

"Griffin Insurance?" Frank said, "Where Tyler works?"

Bert Simmon cleared his throat and spoke, "I know some people over there; maybe I could put in a word or two?"

"I'd appreciate it," Ted said. "I'm not too excited about going back in the service, but sometimes you don't have a choice. If push comes to shove, I'll check into the GI Bill. Maybe something can be worked out there." Ted finished his can of beer and tossed the empty into the barrel nearby.

Eric watched the kids. He didn't know whether he envied them or not. The late afternoon sun slowly cast shadows across the ball diamond.

Ted called Eric a couple of days later. "Can you believe it? I got the job at Griffin Insurance! I start next Monday."

"You see, things are working out," Eric said.

"Now if we could just find an apartment," Ted said.

Ted and Marie had been staying in a small upstairs apartment. The house was recently sold and they had thirty days to find a new place.

The following week, Marie and Liza went apartment hunting. They found a lower two-bedroom apartment just off Main Street. Liza called Ted and asked him to meet them. It wasn't long before Ted and Eric came.

"It's an adorable apartment," Liza said, "Marie and I took measurements for curtains, after seeing it."

Ted put his arm around Marie, in the middle of their empty living room. "Well honey," he grinned, "We're starting over with nothing but each other and Tina . . . How can we miss?"

"We can't Teddy, long as we realize the deposit, and the furniture will put a big hole in our discharge pay. But like you said, we got each other."

Liza and Eric watched a couple of friends who were obviously crazy about each other.

Saturday evening, Liza and Eric helped Marie and Ted move into their new apartment. On a radio parked in the corner of the living room, Hank Williams was belting out Marie's favourite song about a cheating heart.

"Marie," Ted said wearily, "Eric and I have moved this couch three times." He stopped a moment and wiped his brow. "Don't you think you could decide where you really want this damn thing?"

"Now Teddy, this is very important to us girls. Right, Liza?"

"Very true." Liza laughed. The girls, in many ways looked like sisters, except Marie was putting on a little weight.

"We want a beer, don't we, Eric?" Ted moaned.

"It would hit the spot," he said. The late August evening was warm. Eric walked to the door. The sounds of children playing under the street light cut through the stillness of the evening.

"Here." Ted handed him a beer, "We earned it, and we're not through yet. Women are something else!"

"What would you do without us, Teddy? I might be good to you later tonight!"

He grinned. "Sounds like blackmail to me, but you got it, honey . . . if I'm able. Come on Eric, let's take a break on the front steps."

The kids across the street protested when called in the house. "It never changes, does it?" Ted asked. "The kids, I mean. I remember going through the same thing."

Eric sighed. "Me too." He heard the girls laughing inside. It was a good feeling. "At times, I still cling to memories of you, me, and Jason—you know, the old days."

"Yeah," Eric said. "Every once in a while."

"I guess we'd better get back in there," Ted said. "I've got a promise for tonight—and I don't want to screw it up—know what I mean?"

Eric laughed. "Sure do."

"What's so funny?" Marie asked.

"I told Eric I didn't want to screw up my promise."

"Teddy—the way you talk." Marie quickly changed the subject

The year was 1952. It was the first day of September. It was like any ordinary day, except Liza seemed unusually quiet. "Is there something bothering you, Liza?" Eric asked.

"Yes," she said. "I saw this ad in the Benford Daily News Paper and I'm not sure if I should tell you about it."

"What do you mean?" Eric asked.

"When I was proofreading, I saw an ad that had a Baptist Church and a house for sale. The only other information was to contact a Wallace Woodstock, and it gave a phone number."

"Talk about a sign," Eric said.

"Talk about goin' out on a limb," Liza countered.

Eric pulled her close. "Scare you?"

"Maybe. Wait until Karen and Frank hear about this." Liza said. Eric put his hand on her leg and her concern turned into a smile. Her voice became a whisper. "You think that's gonna take you off the hook."

"I'm not sure—but right now . . .making love to you makes my life worthwhile," Eric said. "I have no idea what's going to happen with this church business, but tonight I'm gonna make love to you like it would solve all our problems."

Later, when he held her, she snuggled close. "On a scale of one to ten, what do you think?" Eric asked. She didn't answer but he heard her low, soft laugh that led to a night of contentment.

It was the middle of September, when the bank finally notified Eric that the cabin was sold. The cabin, which meant so much to him and Alice, was to be replaced by a new interstate highway. Eric's mind now shifted to the little white empty Baptist church in town. He had been negotiating with part-time real estate tycoon/gentleman farmer Wallace Woodstock for the last couple of weeks. He had an early lunch and went to Woodstock's office for his appointment. "I'm ready to close the deal on my previous offer, or forget the whole thing," Eric said. "I plan to start my own church."

Woodstock leaned back on his chair and puffed on his cigar. He grinned and slid the papers across his desk. "I have the application for your permit and license, along with the final papers. I just wanted to make sure you didn't change your mind. Your own church, huh?" he asked.

"Yes, I have been planning this for some time."

"I know the people around here for miles. You don't fit in," Woodstock said. "You strike me as a man who wouldn't stay where he wasn't wanted." He groaned and shifted his over two hundred pounds in his office chair. "I know your healing reputation, which frankly don't matter to me one way or the other. What does your family think about this?"

"The only one who knows about this is my wife, Liza," Eric said. "That's the way I want to keep it."

It was almost noon the following Friday when Wallace Woodstock walked into Eric's shop. He flipped a set of keys on the counter. "You can check the house and church in the next couple of days. Right now, we need to go to the bank and court house."

A few minutes later, Eric was facing a clerk in the City Council's office. The clerk's pale eyes stared at him through thick glasses. He glanced at the papers on the counter and smiled. "Mr. Silkwin, you want to open a church at Chestnut and Elm . . . nondenominational?" For an instant, a gleam appeared in Woodstock's eyes.

"That's correct," Eric said.

"I cannot understand how you can possibly think Benford could, or would support another church, especially the kind you're talking about."

"That's beside the point. It doesn't matter. It's irrelevant," Eric said quickly.

"I did not mean . . . ." The clerk glanced at Mr. Woodstock for an instant then back to Eric. "Of course. It's one of our basic rights. When would you want this permit?"

"I'll contact you," Eric said. Mr. Woodstock said nothing, but the grin on his face showed his approval.

The next day, Eric decided it was time to tell his family about his new home. He called Ellen and Johnny first and later Karen and Frank. He wanted to tell his mother in person a little later. Everyone was to meet that evening at Eric and Liza's new home, located at the corner of Chestnut and Elm. Eric and Liza arrived first. It wasn't long before Karen and Frank pulled in the driveway. Eric heard a knock at the door. "Welcome to our new home," Eric said.

"Hey, this is great," Karen said.

"Nice," Frank added. "When did all this happen?"

"We've been negotiating for the last couple weeks or so, I guess," Eric said. "We didn't find out we got it until yesterday. We wanted to surprise everyone."

Karen looked out the window. "Whose church is that?"

"Mine," Eric said. He grinned; he couldn't help himself. Karen's expression was priceless.

"Whose?" she asked. "Wait a minute—let me see if I understand this—you have bought a house with a church—right here—in Benford?" Karen shook her head and turned to face Frank who finally snapped out of his trance.

"I can't believe it," he said. "What are you going to do with it?"

"I'm not sure," Eric said. "I haven't worked out all the details yet." A few moments later, Karen and Frank settled down.

"How could you, Eric?" Karen asked.

"It's something I have to do. There are some things I have to work out, it won't be right away."

"I can't believe it . . . You're going to start a church in Benford?" Karen asked. "Mayville was bad enough—but *this*!" She threw her hands up.

"You're a Methodist, Eric," Frank added, glancing at Karen. "We're talking about the family church! How can you . . . ."

"One of the reasons I'm considering this is because Reverend Langtree is catching too much pressure from too many people," Eric said. "Besides, this church is going to be nondenominational."

"As if that makes a difference!" Karen said. "I hope for all our sakes you know what you're doing. You have thought this out—right?" Before he could answer, the sudden knock jolted them. It was Ellen, Johnny, and Elizabeth. They barely got in the door when Karen turned to them.

"Come in. You are just in time for a meaningful conversation . . . You heard about Eric's latest?"

"No," Ellen said, "But very few things surprise me anymore."

"Ha!" Karen yelled. "It beats all—even for him." She stopped to catch her breath. Her eyes got bigger. "Look out the window. He's starting a nondenominational church here in Benford," Karen said. "Can you *believe* it?"

Ellen looked out the window. "No, I can't." She stared at Eric. "You going to tell me this is some kind of misunderstanding. You're upsetting people and I got a feeling it's just the beginning," Ellen said, with an edge in her voice. "What would the folks think?"

"What can I say?" Eric countered, "I made Wallace Woodstock an offer, and he accepted it."

Karen turned to face Ellen. "He's *your* brother."

Ellen shrugged, and then said to Liza, "You're Catholic. It has to affect your life. What does all this mean to you?"

"I'll remain a Catholic. What I do not understand is you people knew of Eric's involvement with healing for some time. Why are you suddenly surprised? Didn't it ever occur to anyone that Eric might end up having his own church someday?"

Nobody answered for a minute, and then Karen spoke up, "We didn't take him that serious. If it were only him, but this will affect the whole family. What about when the children start school?" What do you think it's going to do to them?

Eric said, "I can't answer that."

"What does your mother think about this?" Karen asked.

"I guess we'll find out soon enough," Eric said.

Karen and Frank left. Ellen looked at Johnny, "You haven't said much. It's your sister and my brother."

"We can't decide for them," Johnny said. "Karen and Frank seem more concerned about their image than anything else."

"I'll admit to that," Ellen said, putting her hand on Eric's shoulder. "I'm against it—but it's your life and I know you well enough to know you're going to do what you want."

The following day, Eric stopped at his mother's house. When he entered the room, he saw his mother sitting in her favorite chair reading the newspaper.

She looked up, startled. "Eric, what a nice surprise."

"Hi Mom, thought I'd stop by, I've got something to tell you."

"What is it?" she curiously asked"

"Liza and I just bought a house with a church."

His mother looked confused. "What are you talking about?"

"The house we just bought has a church on the property," Eric said.

"Eric, that's wonderful. I wasn't going to mention anything, but I've been praying that you would be led and now it seems my prayers have been answered. I'm so happy for both of you," she said.

"Thanks Mom, maybe both our prayers have been answered."

Eric stopped in at Grover's. He saw Claude Stratman motion to him. Eric ordered coffee and joined him. "I've heard rumors; something about a church?" Stratman said. "Seeing you with Wallace Woodstock gives me reason to believe there may be something to it. Talk about the odd couple!"

Eric grinned.

"When I wrote about Nathan Winslow's death, I covered it the only way I could," Stratman said. "The only reference I was allowed to make, concerning his unorthodox treatment, was limited. My editor, Louis Cowler and Winslow were close friends. For the family's sake—I believe was the way he phrased it . . . I felt I owed you an explanation."

Eric took a sip of coffee, "It's okay, I understand," he said.

Stratman glanced at his watch. "As usual, I'm on a deadline . . . . I was sorry to hear about your dad."

"Thank you. I never know how to reply to something like that," Eric said.

"You fascinate me. I still have this hunch that there's going to be a big story about you. I'm pretty good on my hunches." Stratman flashed his rare grin and got up to leave. "Keep me posted. I have no idea what this story will be . . . However, it will be special! I meant it when I said I would do it right. I promised you a fair shake."

"I believe you. Otherwise, I would have never agreed to give you the exclusive."

"Take care," he said, again flashing that rare grin.

Eric paid his check. He had a feeling Stratman was right.

On the last Sunday in September, Eric and Ted moved furniture into the Silkwin's new home. That night, after getting Colleen to bed, Liza said slowly, "Eric, are we ready for something like this? It's kind of strange."

"Time will tell. We must go forward among the wolves."

"That's the part that scares me," Liza said.

The following Sunday evening, at about eight o'clock, the church door opened. Eric looked up from the trim he was paint-ing, to see Cindy and Stuart in the doorway. "Welcome," Eric said. "It's great to see you again."

"You never cease to amaze me, Eric," Cindy said. "I'm gonna run over to the house and see Liza and Colleen."

"Looks like you've got your hands full," Stuart said, after Cindy left. They sat on the front pew. Stuart ran his hand over the smooth wood. "This place reminds me of when I was a kid, years ago. I have some time on my hands. I'd be glad to help you get this show on the road."

"Sounds good to me," Eric said. A few minutes later, they went to the house. "My company moved to California," Stuart said, "but, amazingly, I got another job driving a truck for a construction company. I never felt like I belonged to any church. You might have a couple members from Wyler."

"We had only been back in Wyler a couple weeks when we heard the rumors," Cindy said. It wasn't long before Marie and Ted pulled into the driveway.

"Ted, Marie," Cindy said, "It's good to see you."

"It's good to see you guys, too," Ted said. "How are you, Stuart?"

"I'm doing alright. Cindy thought we should check up on Eric. We've heard some pretty amazing things and we had to see for ourselves that everything was going okay."

Later in the afternoon, everyone relaxed in the backyard. Marie glared at Ted after his fourth beer. "We put this rubber mouse in Tyler's desk," Ted said, with laughter. "You should have seen her jump off her chair and scream. I never saw her move so fast."

CHAPTER TEN

Colleen had just celebrated her fifth birthday. It seemed impossible time had passed so quickly. During the month of June, Liza and Eric went to Mayville every Sunday. He felt a power in the little white church that was special and hard to explain.

Karen and Frank had drifted into their own routine. Liza and Eric seldom saw them. Ted had a few problems with his work—to use Marie's words. He had managed to curb his drinking problem. That summer evening, Eric and Liza had just returned from Mayville to find Ellen and Johnny at their mother's house. Ellen rushed to him, tears in her eyes. "Oh Eric! Mother had a stroke about an hour ago. The ambulance rushed her to the hospital."

"Is she all right? I mean . . . ."

"We don't know," Ellen said. "It happened so suddenly. We were in the living room talking when she turned pale, grabbed her chest, and collapsed."

They left Elizabeth and Colleen at Marie and Ted's, and hurried to the hospital. It was an hour before Dr. Emmery joined them.

"She's holding her own," Dr. Emmery said. "That's all I can say at this time. I'm sorry Eric—this isn't exactly the way I hoped we'd meet again."

Karen and Frank showed up a little later.

"You people will want to stay here. We'll help take care of the girls," Frank said.

Time moved slowly into the night. "I should do something," Ellen said to no one in particular. "We were just sitting there like always and then . . . ."

Their silence was only interrupted by nurses and the sound of the support system.

"There's no reason we should all be here," Eric said. "We don't know how long before she regains consciousness. I'll stay tonight. I'll call if there's any change. The rest of you can work out a schedule." Ellen didn't respond.

It was after ten-thirty before they left. Eric settled down for the night in the lobby. The activity changed into an occasional page for a nurse or doctor. A feeling of fatigue closed in on him. He called on his guide Tawnya, for healing.

Eric heard the early morning activity at about the same time Johnny tapped him on the shoulder. He stretched, and felt the discomfort of cramps in his shoulders and legs. The early morning light was just beginning to stream through the windows. "How's Ellen?"

"Restless," Johnny said. "She finally fell asleep early this morning. You look terrible. A shave and shower would help." A few minutes later, Dr. Emmery joined them in the lobby.

"She's the same. I feel that I must tell you this could go on for some time, then again . . . ."

Back at the house, Liza was fixing breakfast. Eric inhaled the aroma of bacon and eggs. "I'll relieve Ellen, if you want, or maybe I should be with her," Liza said.

"I'd prefer you two together. Johnny and I can handle it the rest of the time," Eric said. "How's Colleen doin'?"

"Asking a lot of questions I can't answer. For a child her age, she seems well in control."

"I'm hungry," Colleen said. She had her blanket in one hand, and Doodles, her teddy bear in the other. "Hi Daddy, is Grandma at the hospital?"

"Yes. She's resting. She'll be home when she feels better."

"Can't she rest at home?" Colleen asked. Liza smiled at Eric, placing his breakfast before him. He sipped his coffee, while Colleen waited for an answer. She never took her eyes off Eric.

"Grandma can get better sooner in the hospital because there're doctors and nurses there to take care of her," Eric said.

"She's not goin' to heaven like Grandpa?"

"No," Eric said. "I don't think so."

The answer seemed to satisfy her. She dug into her cereal with a passion.

On the third day, Eric's mother regained consciousness. She was paralyzed on the right side of her face. It left her with only partial speech. Dr. Emmery explained that she could have occasional memory lapses.

"How should we react?" Ellen asked.

"As if nothing happened, unless she questions you," Dr. Emmery said. "We don't know how the mind will react at any given time."

"Thanks doctor," Eric said. "We'll be as normal as possible—for us, I mean." It was the first time in three days that Ellen cracked a smile.

"My family's around me," Eric's mother said, early the next day. The partial paralysis slightly affected her speech.

The next several days, she talked about Jesus and her husband. "He's doing so well, no aches, pains, and he looks wonderful, like he did years ago."

"Who, Mother?" Ellen asked.

"Your father, of course. I talk to him. He has a beautiful home, but he wouldn't take me there."

Liza's face took on an expression that Eric had never seen before. Ellen looked to Eric, who shrugged.

"You were dreaming, Mother," Ellen said. "You were unconscious the last two days."

"It wasn't a dream," Martha insisted.

"Whatever you say, Mother," Ellen said.

"The crib. He was talking about the crib for Colleen," Martha said. "He couldn't wait to see Alice's face."

116

Ellen started to speak, but words failed her.

"I'm sorry," the nurse said, "Your mother must rest."

"I must get home." Ellen added slowly, "Johnny will be home for supper before long. It's strange; she spoke as if Alice were . . . ."

"I'll see you later," Eric said.

The following day, Eric's mother came home. Early in the day, she seemed in excellent spirits and knew everybody. Later that afternoon she changed. "I want to see my granddaughters," she said firmly. "You people have got to quit watching over me like I'm on my last legs."

"If you insist, Mother," Ellen said.

"I certainly do!" Elizabeth talked to her grandmother for a while. Ellen watched closely, despite her mother's protests. "You have beautiful hair, like your mother's," Martha said calmly touching Elizabeth's soft curls. "Maybe I'll rest awhile."

The three of them filed out of her room. Ellen said to Eric and Johnny, "She's acting strange. Why is it I'm afraid of what she's going to say next?"

"We have to expect anything," Eric said. The next few days and nights seemed to run together. Eric was grateful that Walter Blanchard was watching over the shop. An hour later, Ellen shook Eric who had fallen asleep in the chair. "Mother's awake. I'll fix her something to eat."

"I'm better, Eric," his mother said. "Don't forget to wake your father; you know how he feels about being late for church." Eric didn't answer. He took Colleen's hand and left.

As soon as Eric got home, Liza asked how his mother was. Eric explained the best he could. After supper, Colleen went in the living room; soon the sound of the radio filled the awkward silence.

"I'll try to help, but I'm not sure I can take it," Liza said. "You mean she just slips out of time, in a matter of minutes?"

"Yes. It's strange. She looks great. The only paralysis is slight, but her eyes are not the same, they actually change."

"How do you mean?"

"Clear one minute, glazed and distant the next."

"I'm sorry Eric," she said slowly. "What about your plans for the church in town?"

"I'm not sure. Maybe I'll have to put it on hold." He shaved, showered, and crawled into bed. He couldn't sleep, his whole body felt weak and tense. Colleen walked into the bedroom and lay beside him. She clutched her toy dog.

"What's the matter, honey?" Eric asked.

"I'm thinking about Grandma," she whispered. She snuggled closer and said, "Grandma told me she saw—you know— Mommy One?"

"Colleen, she gets mixed up and forgets things sometimes. You understand, don't you?"

"I think so . . . You not going to be sick are you, Daddy?"

"No, I'm just tired." It was the first time Eric realized just how sensitive she was. Evidently, she felt his depression. "Tomorrow, I'll be rearing to go," he tickled her and she laughed.

"See ya." She got off the bed and looked at him. "Sleep good tonight, Daddy."

Sometime during the night, Eric felt Liza cuddle next to him or thought he did.

"Eric it's almost eleven o'clock," Liza yelled. He gazed out the window at the bright sunshine.

He called out to Liza, who suddenly appeared. "I guess I was really out," Eric said. "I don't ever remember being so tired— right now I'm starving."

"I'll fix some bacon and eggs," Liza said, "It's too early for dinner. Colleen had to look in on you twice before she'd go out and play.

"All this has been a little rough on her," Eric said. "My mother asked Colleen about Alice."

"Oh no," Liza gasped. A little later, they sat looking at each other over the table. What happened to us? Eric thought. They had to reach out to each other. "What about a movie tonight?"

"I don't feel up to it . . . I appreciate your asking," Liza said.

"It was just an idea." The following three weeks, most of Eric's mother's friends, relatives, and members of the church stopped in to see her.

Liza and Eric got together with Marie and Ted on Saturday night. They went bowling and to the movies. They stopped in Smokey's after the movie. Liza was in a rare, good mood. "That was one of the most dramatic military movies I've seen in a long time," Liza said.

"I agree," Frank added. "Sinatra won an Academy Award for that movie; it brought his career back on track."

"Yeah. I just love Frank Sinatra," Marie sighed.

"He's all right I guess," Ted added. They all laughed.

Liza and Marie excused themselves and went to the ladies room.

"How is your mother doing Eric?" Ted asked.

"She is doing better; she is walking with a cane now," Eric said. "She seems content, but she slips back and forth in time."

"I want to ask you some questions about your mother—if I'm out of line just let me know . . . . This thing with her talking to your father, do you think she really she sees him?"

"Yes, I do," Eric said. "I can't be sure. I think she sees Bryan, too. I've heard her mention him a couple times. Her sub-conscious mind somehow confuses her with the present reality."

Ted shook his head. "Wouldn't it be something if it were true, to know our loved ones are really close?"

"I've always believed that," Eric said. "It's what helps keep me going. People consider it morbid. It's something they can't see, so they refuse to believe it. In a way, I guess it scares them. I've never been able to figure that out."

"When are you going back to Mayville?" Ted asked. "I would like to go with you, if it's okay."

"This coming Sunday, I hope," Eric said. "Liza has been acting very strange lately."

"I got that impression," Ted said. "Tyler's been acting very moody and withdrawn lately at work, too. I don't know what comes over these women."

Marie and Liza returned to the table. Ted glanced at Marie after ordering his third drink. From her expression, it would be his last for the evening.

"Eric, Liza was telling me that your mother seems to be doing a little better. Have you thought about giving her a healing?" Marie asked.

Liza watched his reaction. "I don't know. I laid my hands on her once, but we both felt awkward. She never asked for a healing, at least not from me."

"You tried—what more can a guy do, right honey?" Ted asked.

"Right, Teddy. I'm just glad we all agree this is our last drink for the evening." They all laughed. It was good to see Liza enjoying herself. Eric put his hand on hers and for a while sensed a closeness between them.

Later that evening, when Eric and Liza were alone, Liza said, "I had a very good time tonight. Being with Marie and Ted was special."

When they were getting ready for bed, Liza asked. "What were you and Ted talking about in your huddle?"

"He was curious about my mother and her conversations with my father.

The next day, Karen and Frank were at his mother's. It was close to one o'clock. Evidently, her conversation was fairly normal from the expression on their faces. Bruce and Barry sat on chairs like a couple little gentlemen.

"That Mrs. Dunly shouldn't have made such a fuss about you and Alice, when you tried to give Alice a healing on her knee," Martha said calmly. Karen and Frank stared at her. "Your father agrees with me," Martha continued.

"How's work?" Eric asked Frank, who seemed to be unable to take his eyes off Eric's mother.

"All right I guess, about the same as always."

"The weather is beginning to change," Karen said. "I'm afraid we're in for a long summer."

"The flowers at the cabin must be beautiful," Martha said. "You and Alice are so lucky to have such a nice place. I'm going to church next Sunday," she said. "I miss it so. I haven't seen Liza and Bryan, but then young people in love are always so busy." Colleen watched the conversation go back and forth with wide-eyed fascination.

"It's getting late, honey," Frank said.

Karen and Frank left. "Eric, I think I'll lie down for a while until Ellen and Johnny get here," his mother said. "You don't mind, do you?"

"Of course not." He helped her into her room. In a few minutes, his mother was asleep.

"Daddy, was the cabin Mommy One's and yours?" Colleen asked.

"Yes honey," Eric said.

"So now the cabin is Mommy's instead of Mommy One's?"

"Yes Colleen. I'm afraid my little girl is growing up," Eric said.

"I told you. I am bigger now!"

"So you did. Remember when I showed you where the cabin was when they were building the new highway?" Eric asked.

"I think so," Colleen said.

Liza, Ellen, Elizabeth, and Johnny came a little later. Ellen peeked into their mother's bedroom, and then came back to the dining room. "Let her sleep," she said. "We should talk, although I'm not sure what I should say to her."

"You should've seen Karen and Frank's face awhile ago," Eric said. "Evidently, they had no idea about the extent of her condition. It's strange how quickly she slipped into the past."

121

"I guess that's what bothers me the most," Ellen said. "But it's like you say; what choice do we have?"

Ted walked in the shop the following day. "How about a couple games of pool?" Ted asked. "I told Marie I'd lay off the drinks for a while."

"I think we need something a little different," Eric said. "Wait until I finish closing."

Layn's pool hall is usually busy, especially after six. They beat the crowd and got a table near the front counter. The pool hall was a long narrow building between the dime store and a furniture store.

"Your break," Ted said. He looked over the pool cues. He won two games of eight ball and one of rotation before they wrapped it up. "You're not with it," Ted said. "Come on, let's get a cup of coffee at Rita's then I gotta get home."

"Hello gents," Rita said. She smiled and faced Eric. "I actually saw you in our church last Sunday."

"Rare occasion," Eric said. "I'm gonna try and make it more often. How's it going with you?"

She sighed. "Busy constantly. The price of success is demanding, but that's what we wanted. Ted, you're unusually quiet. I can almost tell the mood you guys are in when you walk in the front door. I haven't seen Frank for a while."

"He's busy. He's a foreman now," Eric said. "I wish I had his ambition."

"You do look out of it, Eric," Rita said. "Where's that fire you used to have?"

Eric shrugged, "I'm not sure."

She stared straight into his eyes. Rita—like his sister Ellen—had an uncanny ability almost to see through him. "You have that discontented look . . . Oops, I'm talking out of turn."

"Don't worry about it. It's all right," Eric said.

"I got a hunch I should get home," Ted said with a grin. "See you later, Rita."

"Me too," Eric added. "Don't work too hard and stay off those fire escapes."

Rita's face turned red for a moment. She finally smiled, "Why would you mention that after all this time?"

"I thought to myself—how could I shake Rita up a little? Then I pictured . . . ."

"I get the message," she said, and broke into laughter.

"It was a good time," Eric said. "See you." It was one of the rare times when Rita's mouth was wide open and she had nothing to say.

"You're late," Liza said. "I'll reheat this stuff."

"Sorry. Ted and I played pool and I lost track of time."

"Hi Daddy." Colleen ran to him. "You going to Grandma's?"

"Tomorrow night, honey. Did you have a good day?"

"Yes. Mommy and I played all kinds of games. Will you read me a story after supper?"

"Just one, then off to bed," Eric said.

Later that night, Liza brought them a cup of coffee and they sat together in front of the fireplace. Eric was surprised to see the mischief in Liza's eyes. She put her hand on his shoulder. He took her in his arms and held her close. They watched the flames dancing in and around the logs. The only sound was the crackling of the fire.

Eric kissed her and she kissed him back. She put his hand on her leg. He gently moved it higher and pushed her back on the couch. Her low, sexy laugh was like music to his ears. Later, she lay in his arms exhausted. The last thing he remembered before falling asleep was her sigh.

The phone rang. Eric jumped and glanced at the clock. It was after 1:00 a.m. "Mother's been taken back to the hospital!" Ellen said. "We're with her."

"I'll be there in a few minutes," Eric said.

"What is it?" Liza asked.

"Mother's back in the hospital. I've gotta go—I'll phone you later."

"She's resting," Ellen said. "She regained consciousness. I talked to her for a few minutes."

"Hello Eric," his mother whispered. Ellen and Eric moved closer to her bed. "You know I'm sorry about that dog you wanted."

Eric hadn't thought about that in years. He couldn't have been more than five or six. It was a stray hound that he wanted to keep and his mother refused. It wasn't until the following Christmas, when he got his new bike that he got over it.

"It's all right, Mother," Eric said.

"That bothers me," she said, then smiled. "Now I feel better and more at peace than I've ever felt. No back pain . . . Alice talked so nice to me last night; she's such a lovely girl."

Ellen had tears in their eyes.

"Look how nice your father looks." Eric's mother motioned to the front of the bed. "He's so handsome. He's reaching out to me . . . ."

They were the last words their mother ever said. She suddenly hemorrhaged. Ellen turned quickly. Eric took her in his arms. The nurses came quickly with the doctor. He examined her and turned to them, "I'm sorry. She's gone."

Eric led Ellen out of the room. "Listen to me. Our mother has joined our father. Be happy for her. For both of them!" She stared at him. "Ellen! I know what I'm talking about."

She tried to smile. "I am, Eric, because it's so important to me at this moment."

The funeral was one of the most crowded the little white church ever held. People stood in the aisle, huddled in the doorway. The family stood grouped together. Colleen and Elizabeth stared in silent, wide-eyed wonder.

The people gathered at his mother's house much the same way as they had for his father. She would have been so proud. The Quinlins were there, along with Linda, her mother, and Walter Blanchard.

That night after they all had left, Liza, Ellen, Marie, and Karen all pitched in to help clean up. As usual, Karen's parents were going out of their way to do what they could. They all left but Ellen, Liza, Eric, and Johnny, who sat around the familiar dining room as they had for years. "First Dad, then Mother. I just can't accept . . . ." Suddenly, Ellen burst into tears.

"You have too, Ellen!" Eric said. "Mourning is normal, but remember—if you don't let them go, you're going to hurt their progression . . . They'll be held close because of your depression."

"I never thought of it that way," Ellen said. She looked into Eric's eyes and whispered "Eric, you're not yourself! Even your voice is different . . . it's like I'm talking to someone else!" She turned to face Johnny, who seemed stunned.

"*Thank you, Tawnya—how could I not know that you were with me and the family at a time like this?*" Eric was thankful for the comforting words from his guide. That night, Liza and Eric tucked Colleen in bed after her prayers. She hadn't said anything. It wasn't like her.

"Honey," Eric said, "You better get rid of that long face." He hugged and kissed her.

"Grandma's in heaven?"

"Yes, with Grandpa and Mommy One. Yes, they're happy."

"I'm so glad," she said, and then she rolled over and fell into a deep peaceful sleep.

CHAPTER ELEVEN

Eric called Ted the following Saturday. "I just wanted to let you know we're going to Mayville tomorrow evening, if you and Marie would like to go."

"We'll look forward to it," Ted said.

They stopped for dinner on the outskirts of Mayville. A few minutes later, Eric introduced them to Elaine and Steven Loulder. The Loulders were married in June, and still had the glow of the newlyweds. "We decided suddenly," Elaine said. "We've been in love for some time, but this guy was too bashful to pop the question."

She playfully poked him. Eric joined Steven and another man in the healing room. Ted observed and later received a message that he had healing power.

After services, Eric explained buying a church in Benford.

"There'll probably be controversy. It's a big step," Reverend Larry Watts said.

"What I have in mind is to find four visiting speakers at least for a while."

"I have four people who might be able to help you," Reverend Watts said. "But, maybe someday you should consider serving in the ministry, besides just being involved with healing."

"I think you're right," Eric said.

Eric went to join Ted. They overheard the girls talking.

"Eric's moody," Liza added. "He's up one minute and down the next. You never know what he's going to say or do next."

Marie laughed. "Teddy being a healer doesn't surprise me. He is so sensitive. I know he joined my church for me. I just hope he can stand the flack I know is coming his way . . . That's the part that bothers me."

"I've heard enough of this conversation," Ted said as he grinned. "Have faith in me. As I've said before, together we can do almost anything."

"Sounds good to me," Eric said.

It was six when they arrived back in Benford. They dropped off Marie and Ted after picking up Tina and Colleen at Ellen and Johnny's.

The Loulders made a couple of trips to Benford. They helped with suggestions and voiced their approval for Eric's church. In late October, the weather had turned cold, and resulted in a light snow. The heating bill stood out on the kitchen table. Liza stared at it, and then at Eric. "When're we going to get this show on the road?"

"I like the way you put that," Eric said.

"Loosen up. I'm in your corner," she said.

"Sorry, but I've been asked that same question by several people, and I don't know whether they're with me or waiting to see me to fall on my face."

"Both," Liza said. "But that's beside the point."

"Tomorrow, Mayville," Eric said. "I gotta get somebody for the first Sunday in November. I think we should celebrate. I've got a bottle of wine . . . We could dance to the music on the radio and you know . . . ." Eric stared at Liza. She was in one of those rare moods.

"First the dishes," Liza said. "You can whisper in my ear and touch me now and then."

After Liza returned from her shower, Eric handed her a glass of wine and then lit a cigarette. She stared at him, finished her wine, and cuddled in his arms. The damp aroma and freshness of the shower clung to her. He kissed her, carefully removing her robe from her shoulders.

"*Now,* take me *now!*" she whispered. He carried her into the bedroom. Their movements began a fierce tempo that exploded in a climax. They lay caressing each other in complete silence until they fell asleep.

Next morning at breakfast, she glanced at him with a faint blush. Her smile slowly spread across her face. "What can I say?"

"Don't say anything," Eric said, just let me know last night was not a dream."

Her eyes gleamed. "It was real. Believe me! We have this chemistry," Liza said. You know for a few moments, it was as if we were the only two people in the world . . . I know it sounds silly but. . . . ."

"I felt the same way, almost unbelievable," Eric said.

She laughed. "The way we talk, I'm glad nobody else is hearing this conversation."

Colleen wandered in the kitchen rubbing her eyes, with Doodles in one hand and her blanket in the other. "I sleep a long time, I think." She yawned and stared at Liza and Eric.

"You hungry, honey?" Liza asked.

"Yes," she replied. "You sleep good, Daddy?"

"It was one of the best nights I've ever had," Eric replied.

Colleen saw the snow, and ran to the window. "Lots of snow, it's super!" she yelled.

"I guess so—in some ways," Eric sighed. It was the heaviest snow this early he could remember. A blanket of white quickly covered the ground. In two weeks, Eric's church would have its first service. A feeling of strange anxiety engulfed him.

"You're staring at me," Liza said, tugging at her robe, which to Eric's delight, exposed part of her firm, small breast. She pulled the robe together. "I don't know about you . . . ."

"I keep picturing you last night," Eric said.

Colleen was trying to handle a mouthful of cereal. Eric leaned forward looking at her bowl. "It's getting soggy, honey."

"I like it that way. You work today, Daddy?"

"No. You're going to your Aunt Ellen's. Your mother and I are going to Mayville."

"I get to see Liz?" Colleen asked. "*Super!*"

Eric winced, silently hoping Colleen would pick up a different word to express herself. She looked at him out of the corner of her eye, like Alice used to do. "Daddy, dig in your cereal."

"I'm going to handle that right now," he said, winking at her.

"Super!" Eric winced and Liza laughed.

Eric and Liza took Colleen over to Ellen and Johnny's. "I don't approve of this church business," Ellen said firmly. "I haven't from the first. I am telling you straight out. When is the grand opening?"

"The first church service is two weeks from today. You make it sound like a supermarket opening—are you coming?" Eric asked.

"I'm not sure," Ellen said. Eric and Johnny just grinned, and looked at each other.

After pulling into the Mayville driveway, Eric said, "You look terrific, Liza." She wore a light red blouse with a white collar, and a dark blue skirt.

"Thank you," she said. "Now let's get inside before you try talking me into the back seat."

Reverend Elaine Loulder agreed to be the first guest speaker at Eric's church.

Steven Loulder had lined up other speakers for the remaining months. Eric worked in the healing room with a couple people that the Loulders had brought with them. He felt his strength increase throughout the healing service.

It was after six when they picked up Colleen. Eric did not volunteer any information and Ellen never asked.

The following two weeks passed quickly. The pressure of the first service closed in on him with more tension then he expected. Ted and Eric watched Marie and Liza checking details at the church. "Look at the girls," Ted said. "You'd think they were getting ready for a party. Can you believe Jason entered my mind earlier, as if he were here?"

"Maybe he is," Eric said seriously. "If I were a gambling man, I would bet on it. I didn't mention it, but I sensed his presence, too."

"All right, guys," Marie said, in the best form of a direct order as she could manage. "Let's get everything in order. Teddy, get your chin off the table."

"I don't have my chin on the table. Aw, Marie!"

That night, Eric could not sleep. He slipped out of bed, went to the kitchen, and reheated the coffee. It was after two when he finally fell asleep. The last thing he remembered was a prayer for guidance.

"Wake up, Eric. It's after ten." Liza shook him. "You were really out."

He sat up in bed, "The time is here," he said to Liza.

A moment later, Colleen raced in the room and jumped on the bed. "Daddy, you sleep a long time." She crawled into his arms and hugged him.

"Come on Colleen, your daddy has to get up. Breakfast is waiting for us."

"Come here, Mommy," Eric said. He opened his arms, and grinned. "One kiss and we'll start the day."

"Kiss her, Daddy. I wanna see," Colleen said.

"Maybe one kiss," Liza said. He grabbed her and pulled her beside him. "Eric, control yourself!" Sometimes I don't know about you. I mean—don't you think you should get dressed?"

"I got something to take care of first," Eric grabbed her, looked at Colleen, and then kissed her.

Colleen clapped her hands and laughed, "Mommy kissed Daddy, and I saw it."

"Settle down, young lady and let your father get dressed. This is a big day for him and we're running late."

Karen had arranged an early dinner because of the church opening. Eric and Liza felt as ill at ease as Karen and Frank. "Relax Karen. I don't expect you to be at church," Eric said. "I'm serious. I understand your view, and you should understand mine. I don't want you pressured any more than I want to be."

"I get it," Karen said.

A few minutes after Eric opened the church, Elaine and Steven Loulder arrived. They joined Liza and Eric over coffee. Steven watched Eric closely, and then said. "It's only natural to be a little up tight. Let's just throw our faith out and see what happens."

Eric greeted the people who slowly filed into the little white church. He tried to ignore a few people across the street with picket signs. Most of them were against him, as well as the church. The demonstrations seemed peaceful enough—at least at this time. Eric sent out a silent prayer that they would continue to remain that way.

Linda, her mother, and Walter Blanchard arrived a little later. The church was almost full, to Eric's amazement. He looked back over the crowd to see many strange faces among the few he recognized. Colleen sat close to him, wide-eyed, captivated by the crowd of people.

CHAPTER TWELVE

The bright sunshine fought the cloudy, overcast day. Eric, feeling uneasy, looked out over the group of friends and strangers. Suddenly a sense of peace overtook him. He addressed the congregation, "Ladies and gentlemen, welcome to *The Chapel of the Healing Light*."

After Reverend Elaine Loulder's sermon, a message service took place. Reverend Loulder gave messages to an overwhelmed curious crowd. Afterward, Reverend Steven Loulder added a brief message of faith and unity. Eric announced that next week, a healing service would begin at one and regular service at two.

"May Christ's presence be with you," Eric said. "Coffee and cake will be served in the basement. Everyone is welcome."

Most of the people left after the service. Some of the faces showed open scorn and ridicule, yet seemed reluctant to leave. Later, after a few congratulations, Marie, Cindy, Stuart, and Ted helped Liza and Eric clean up, while Ellen and Johnny watched the kids.

Eric faced Ellen. "What'd you think of it?"

"I'm reserving judgment," she said.

It was almost seven o'clock before they finished cleaning and getting Colleen to bed. Eric and Liza collapsed on the couch. "I couldn't relax at first," she confessed. "I was afraid of what might happen. I'm sure that everyone was surprised by the beautiful service."

"I'm very tired," Eric sighed. "A happy tired. The name of the church came from somewhere outside of myself."

"I think it's a wonderful name," Liza said.

The following month faded into Christmas. The church had leveled off to about twenty people. Some were still curious, but the novelty was wearing off. Karen and Frank invited Liza, Eric, Colleen, Ted, Marie, and Tina for Christmas Eve dinner at Karen's parents' house. Nobody mentioned Eric's church until late in the evening, when Karen's curiosity took over. "I hear your church is doing fairly well. The healing service is one thing," Karen said, "but the message services . . . Come-on, Eric!"

"Let's put this discussion aside for a while," Uncle David interrupted.

"One last point, and then I'll drop it," Karen said. "How about those messages taped to your shop window—I heard about them."

"It's true," Eric said. "I received a few negative messages since the church opening. I tore 'em up."

"You didn't tell me," Liza said in a surprised voice.

"They're harmless. I didn't want to worry you," Eric said. "At least they didn't paint the windows."

"Hey!" Frank said, "It's Christmas Eve, how about the feeling of good will toward each other?" Frank had gained weight, plus the addition of a mustache, which seemed out of place. If its purpose was to add distinction, it failed miserably.

Frank and Ted sipped highballs. Ted didn't say much. He was in one of his moods.

"You gotta be what you gotta be!" Ted said suddenly after an evening of silence. "God, I wish I knew what I gotta be!"

"Teddy," Marie said. "What in the world are you talking about? You're not yourself tonight."

The boyish grin was a little slow coming to the surface. "Sorry folks, a little self-pity."

It was a strange Christmas Eve. The evening ended with several family members putting their feelings out for someone else's approval and usually failing. Eric realized it was the first Christmas without his mother or father.

They all gathered at Liza and Eric's for their New Years Eve party. The tension vanished early in the holiday spirit. It was obvious that Ted had a few earlier at the office party. "I'm telling you," he said, cornering Frank and Eric, "Tyler really had a couple of drinks."

Marie was bright-eyed, trying to balance a glass of wine. "Whatever happened to her marriage?" she asked.

"Don't really know," Ted said. "She and Jerry—what's his name—evidently just drifted apart. She never talked about it. Tyler is dating a guy at the office, but she keeps her distance, if you know what I mean."

Frank seemed more mellow than usual. He turned to Eric, "Karen and I have decided not to monitor what you do, concerning your church."

Karen put her hand on Eric's shoulder, "Forgive us?" she asked, clutching her highball. "It took us awhile to figure out what was important."

"Nothing to forgive. If you didn't voice your opinion, you wouldn't be the Karen I know."

"Hey! A toast to President Eisenhower," Frank yelled.

"If you insist," Ted said. "I guess it is New Years . . . How about The Yankees winning their fifth consecutive world series over Brooklyn?" He then raised his glass to Eric. "And last but not least, a toast to our new heavyweight champion, Rocky Marciano!"

"You would mention those kinda things. Although I guess, that's better than talking about Russia's hydrogen bomb," Karen said, slurring her words. "However, there is something so tragic about the Rosenberg's execution! A real human tragedy."

"That's for damn sure," Frank said. "What about the kids driving us crazy with that song about a doggie that's in the window."

"Amen to that!" Karen added, and they all laughed. The music drifted through the living room. Soon they were dancing between the sounds of laughter and sentimental memories of the past. The feeling of togetherness brought on the New Year with toasts for the future. Everyone began to relax, some removed their shoes; it was that time of the evening.

The early months of 1954 brought little change in Benford. Eric was surprised when Linda's mother came in the shop. "What a surprise—how are you, Mrs. Blanchard?"

"Call me Mary."

"All right, Mary. Would you like to join me for a cup of coffee?" He offered his father's chair. "I need a break. It helps me make it through the afternoon."

"One of those days, huh?" she asked.

"I'm afraid so," Eric said. He couldn't help staring at her. She was still a very attractive woman. It was easy to see where Linda got her looks. "Sorry, I didn't mean to stare."

She laughed. "Relax Eric. You've always been uptight around me. I wanted you to know that I encourage Walter's interest in your religious activity. The controversy doesn't bother me."

"Somehow that doesn't surprise me," Eric said. "I know Walter's a very sensitive man."

"Yes he is. I've known that for years; that's why I married him. Thanks for the coffee. I have to get going, I have an appointment," she said.

"It's been my pleasure," Eric said. "Say hello to Linda for me."

"I will," Mrs. Blanchard said. As she left the shop, she said, "I wish the best to your family."

The summer of 1954 passed into August. Colleen blossomed into a tomboy of six.

Cindy and Stuart took off out west to another construction job. Stuart never stayed in one place for long. Marie and Ted became like family. Karen and Frank were still close, but there was still an invisible barrier between them and Eric and Liza.

Eric saw Tyler occasionally. Her life was obviously wrapped up in Evan, who was about to start the fourth grade. She never mentioned Jerry Yount.

"I still don't know why I have to go to school," Colleen said seriously, her big blue eyes staring at Liza and Eric. "I can't read or write."

Liza and Eric tried to keep from laughing.

"Honey, that's why you're going to school," Liza said. "You'll meet new friends."

"Boys?" Colleen's eyes widened. "Like Bruce and Barry? Sometimes they're mean, but I'll handle 'em," she said with a look of defiance. Eric noticed her baby fat had vanished. Earlier that spring, she had bloodied Barry's nose.

The big day arrived in early September. Liza walked her to school, four blocks from their home. Her eyes were big with the anticipation of a new adventure. Eric felt a lump in his throat. He hugged and kissed her. "I'll be good, Daddy. It might take some getting used to."

Eric's business had grown beyond his expectations. After a hectic and busy day, he hurried home to hear about Colleen's first day.

She talked for several minutes before stopping for a breath. Her eyes shone with excitement. "I like my teacher, Mrs. Morris," she said between bites of supper.

"Any special boys?" Eric asked.

"None I can't handle," she said flatly. "Connie and I eat lunch together. We're friends."

Friday morning, Colleen sighed at the breakfast table, "I'm ready for a Saturday," she said. Liza and Eric just looked at each other and tried to keep from laughing. Later that morning, Karen stopped in the shop and told Eric that Frank would be gone for a couple of weeks. He left for Glenville, Ohio, on a special job assignment for Nathan Lock Company.

Later that night, after Colleen was in bed, Eric read the paper and listened to the radio. He glanced over to see Liza working on some type of project. Eric tried to get her attention. "Why don't you come over here and sit on my lap?" he asked.

She looked up from her sewing, a little self-conscious about her newly acquired glasses. "Promise not to get fresh?"

"No. I can't do that," Eric said.

"All right." She put her sewing aside and walked over to him. "Wait," she whispered removing her glasses. "Just in case."

"Mommy, Mommy," Colleen called.

"Damn!" Eric sighed.

"Maybe you're not ready to be a minister. You still have some rough edges, Eric Silkwin." Liza rushed to Colleen's room. Eric lit a cigarette, leaned back, and relaxed.

"I had to lay with her for a while. You want to lay with me?" Liza asked

"I was afraid you'd never ask," Eric countered.

He scooped her off her feet. "You don't have to carry me," she yelled.

"It gives me a feeling of conquest," Eric said.

"Take me, you brute! Wait, I have my dress on and . . . ."

Afterwards, she laughed softly, "I guess I should get up and get undressed. When I said take me, you didn't waste much time."

The following evening, Colleen put her head on Eric's shoulder and whispered, "Tell me about Mommy One." Liza motioned for him to take her in the living room. He picked her up and she put her arms around his neck tighter than usual.

They settled into the big, easy chair. *How could he tell her about that special way Alice looked at him? Her joy at Christmas over a book of poems, and the way her eyes expressed her feelings.* "What do you want to know, honey?"

"Like a story, Daddy."

"Okay," Eric began. "Do you remember the cabin? I took you out there a couple of times. Anyway, Mommy One and I loved it. We had a picnic, ran in the snow, and threw snowballs at each other. Before we left, we made a big snowman."

"A snowman with eyes, mouth, and a nose?" Colleen asked.

"Yes. Your mother put a scarf around his neck and funny hat on his head."

"What was his name?" The visions flowed through Eric's mind like a movie. Alice's eyes big and bright, with a look of mischief and love simultaneously. He glanced up to see Liza standing in the doorway with tears in her eyes. She turned and went back in the kitchen.

"Daddy, what was the snowman's name?"

"We didn't name him, honey. There just wasn't enough time. We just . . . ."

"Is Mommy One the lady in my bedroom?"

It startled Eric for a minute, but after looking at Colleen, he could see she didn't show any fear at all, just curiosity. "I don't know for sure," Eric said, "But I think so . . . Are you frightened?"

"I was the first time, a little," Colleen said.

"She loved you so much, Colleen."

"I know, she told me, Daddy. Nice story, but my eyes can't stay open." Eric carried her into her bedroom holding her a little tighter than usual. She knelt beside her bed, with her hands folded, and said her prayers.

He tucked her in and kissed her softly. Before he went out the door, he heard her say,

"She doesn't have to open the door like you do, Daddy." Colleen expressed a sense of calmness that surprised Eric and made him feel relieved. She closed her eyes with a look of complete peace.

"I didn't mean to eavesdrop," Liza said softly. "She really sees Alice, doesn't she?"

"Yes, she does," Eric said. "She accepts it as a natural thing."

"Oh Eric!" Liza suddenly started to cry. "I wish it could've been different . . . That Alice had some time with her."

"I have a feeling that Alice is spending more time with her than we know."

Liza sighed. "I'm so glad." She snuggled in his arms. "Sometimes, I think I don't belong here . . . Don't interrupt me. I don't know what it is, but it's so real sometimes, it scares me."

A week later, Tyler came into the shop. "Hello Eric. I was just in the neighbourhood and I thought I would stop by."

"It's nice to see you, Tyler. How is everyone? How's Patsy doing? It's been so long since I've seen everyone."

Tyler didn't answer right away. "Maybe I'm being silly," she said, avoiding the look in Eric's eyes, "But Patsy's been going to dances, even dating. She's only fifteen, Eric."

"So that's the reason you came to see me?" Eric asked.

"Oh Eric, you make me feel so guilty." She looked into his eyes, and then quickly looked away.

"You're really worried about her, aren't you? Eric asked.

"Worried enough to ask you if you could talk to her. She always listened to you before. She's . . . she's growing up too fast," Tyler said. "I've tried to talk to her, but I don't think she's taking me as seriously as she should."

"I'll see what I can do, Tyler," Eric said.

"Thank you, Eric. I'm sure the family would appreciate it. How would you, Liza, and Colleen like to come over for supper? It's been such a long time since you've seen everyone."

"I think I would like that," Eric said.

"I'll call you tonight and we can set something up. I don't want Patsy to know that I put you up to this."

"Patsy's always been special to me, but then, so have you," Eric said.

The expression on her face was strictly Tyler. After a brief smile, she quickly left.

At home, later that evening, Eric told Liza that Tyler had stopped in the shop earlier in the day. He explained, "Tyler was upset about Patsy and asked me to talk to her. She is going to call later to invite us over for dinner."

Monday night, Eric and his family arrived at the Quinlins about six. They were welcomed by their usual easygoing manner.

"Eric, I'm glad that you and Tyler ran into each other. It's been so long since we've seen you," Mrs. Quinlin said.

Eric was surprised at how much Patsy had changed; then he realized it had really had a long time since he'd seen her.

After supper, Liza, Colleen, and Tyler went in the other room to look at a dress that Tyler was making. Patsy grinned at Eric. She had obviously developed quite a bit in the last few months; the pigtails and awkwardness were gone. The quick, friendly smile he remembered seemed to be missing.

"How about a walk?" Eric asked. "We haven't talked in a long time, I think about you now and then."

"I wonder how I knew this was coming," Patsy said. They walked in the backyard, with the voice of Johnny Ray belting out the haunting lyrics of *'Don't Cry.'*

"Don't be so hard on me," Eric said. "I've been busy and from what I hear, so have you."

Patsy grinned. "I know Tyler put you up to this."

"She's concerned about you. Naturally, I am too," Eric said. "Maybe I'm taking advantage of our friendship."

"This has nothing to do with our friendship," Patsy said. "I know one of the reasons you didn't come to the house was Tyler. I'm not blind."

"It's your imagination."

She only smiled. They were in the side yard, by the old swing that Patsy had loved. Her face softened. "Colleen is great, Eric, and Liza is pretty . . . but you and Tyler . . . ."

"Let's talk about you."

"I'm going with Jimmy Wooden. You met him at our cook-out. Mom, Dad, and Tyler are worrying over nothing. Sure Jimmy and I are close, but . . . ." Her voice trailed off. The freckles she was so concerned about had become one of her most attractive features, and so much a part of her. "I imagine this is going to be about sex," Patsy said. "Tyler couldn't handle it." Patsy looked disappointed. Her attempt to shock him didn't work. The young girl had matured in many ways.

"No lecture. Just use your head. Sex is special with the right individual at the right time."

"How original! You're just not my idea of a knight on a white horse . . . Oh! Eric, I didn't mean that—I'm so sorry," She said with a hint of tears.

He put his arms around her, "It's all right. Fifteen is a rough age, if I remember right." The smile he remembered was back. "I'm a friend who will always remember this little girl who understood my feelings at the lowest point in my life . . . Friends?" Eric asked.

"Always," Patsy said.

Eric and Patsy walked back to the house. Everyone was in the living room.

"Did you two have a nice walk?" Mr. Quinlin asked.

"Yes," Eric said. Patsy just smiled. "Well, I think we better be going," Eric said. "It's getting late."

"Thanks a lot for supper," Liza said. "I enjoyed visiting with you."

"I enjoyed it too," Mrs. Quinlin said. We'll have to get together again soon and not wait so long."

On the way home, Liza seemed quiet. Colleen seemed wound up. "I had fun, Daddy," she said. "Even if Evan is a boy, he's not too bad.

It was a sunny day, although a little chilly. It was their last picnic of the season and the park was crowded. Ted and Eric came early to reserve picnic tables. Liza, Marie, and the kids came later. Everyone helped set up the picnic area. It wasn't long before it was time to eat.

"It was tragic—yet kinda funny," Ted said, with a beer in one hand and a hamburger in the other. "This guy I work with is a real character. A little like Jason, anyway he was a little loaded Friday morning . . . Yeah, in the *morning*," Ted said again for emphasis.

"What's so funny about a man being drunk?" Marie asked, wide-eyed.

"You've got to hear the whole story," Ted said. "First, the guy's a clerk like me. You can smell the stuff on him every day, especially when he comes back from Smokey's at lunchtime. Anyway, we have this employees' sign-out board; you know what I mean. He's signed out about ten-thirty—after his name, he had put the time, and reason for leaving as *gone to get drunk*!"

"He wrote that on the board, in those words?" Liza asked.

"Those very words," Ted said. "We knew he wasn't happy with his job, but that's the first time he signed out like that. I heard later that he got fired that afternoon. I talked to him a little later and he didn't seem upset at all; in fact, he seemed to be in a good mood."

"That's terrible, Teddy," Marie murmured, then stared into Ted's eyes. "Did you go with him for lunch at Smokey's?" Her eyes never left his.

"Maybe a couple of times," Ted said softly.

Smokey's was a small bar recently opened to cater to mainly office people for lunches and the after-five business crowds. The small, dimly lit bar was in the middle of the business district and its specialty was convenience.

The girls started to clear off the picnic tables. Frank looked tense, and withdrawn. He'd returned from his two-week trip to Ohio the day before. Eric had the feeling that there was something going on besides work. Eric watched Ted play ball with the kids for a while, and then suggested a walk. "I hate to see this fall come," Frank said as they walked toward the swimming pool.

"Me too," Eric said. He knew he had to wait for Frank to get around to what was on his mind. That much about him hadn't changed. The kids were enjoying the pool as the sun lowered behind the trees. Suddenly Eric couldn't resist, "Was she worth it?"

Frank's first reaction was surprise, and then anger that vanished quickly, replaced by a sick, painful expression. "How did you know?"

"It is just an impression I get—plus, the look on your face," Eric said. He looked Frank in the eye. "You never answered my question."

"It was a one night thing. This young woman sat next to me in a couple meetings, and we got together for a couple of breaks," Frank said slowly. "She was friendly and outgoing. One thing led to another. I took her to lunch a couple times, and the first thing I know . . . I swear—I don't even know how it happened."

"Does Karen suspect anything?" Eric asked.

"She thinks my preoccupation is my work. I feel like hell. It only happened once and . . . ."

Eric tried not to smile. "It's a little like getting pregnant. It only takes once."

"Don't mention that word," Frank sighed. "It's happened, and no matter what I do, I can't change it . . . Do you think I should tell Karen?"

Eric waited a moment. "Knowing Karen, it's hard to tell."

"It's making me sick. Sometimes I think I should tell her, but then I chicken out. I'm not . . ."

"Come on Dad, play ball with us?" Six-year-old Barry tugged at Frank's pant leg.

He sighed. "All right. We're ready to walk back anyway." He held Barry's hand as they walked back across the park to their table.

"What've you two been up to?" Karen asked. She looked at Eric, and then she stared at Frank, whose face reddened. "You take confessions, Eric?" For a minute, time stood still. Karen's face suddenly broke into a smile.

"Confessions!" Eric mumbled. "What are you talking about?

"You two always reveal what's on your mind. Two overgrown boys who never really managed to grow up."

"What's going on?" Marie asked. Nobody answered. It was the last call for hot dogs on the grill. "Ted, I think you've had enough beer," Marie said without her usual humor.

"This is it, honey," Ted replied opening another. "It's a picnic, and tomorrow the week starts all over again."

The quiet, warm sunny day was passing into the late evening. The kids, who had their own little picnic area seemed to be slowing down after a full day of activity. A sudden cry interrupted the silence. Bruce ran toward them holding his nose. "Mommy, Colleen hit me," he yelled, with Barry tagging along behind him as fast as his little legs would carry him.

"What happened now?" Karen yelled.

"I'm bleeding," Bruce cried. Frank held his handkerchief to Bruce's nose.

"It's not bad," Frank said. "Blow your nose. You're all right."

Eric looked down at Colleen, "What'd you hit him for, honey?"

"He put his hand on my leg and he wouldn't stop!"

"What!" Karen gasped, and then tried hiding her grin. "Bruce, why did you put your hand on Colleen's leg?"

"I dunno," he said, and then he quickly lowered his head. "I felt like it."

Colleen's big eyes showed anger with her chin stuck out. It was the first time Eric ever saw that expression.

Ted turned away, trying to keep from laughing. Colleen spoke up, "I popped him in the nose, Daddy . . . He's no doctor man!"

"We'll talk about this later," Karen said, obviously trying to control herself. "Like father, like son." Suddenly they were all laughing, with the kids staring at them.

A little later, everyone pitched in to clean up the area. Karen walked over to Eric. "I want to talk to you while the others are loading the cars. I know about Frank. I could always read you two; besides, it shows all over him."

"He's really sick about it, Karen," Eric said.

"He should be! He needs to stew awhile," she said. "I'm a realist. I think we can work it out if it doesn't happen again. I know he loves me, and the boys. That's the difference."

"I don't know what to say," Eric replied.

"If I know him, and I do, he got involved, not realizing it until it was too late."

"You're quite a woman," Eric said.

"I've been telling you that for years," Karen said. "I'm hurt, but I'll survive. They are coming back. Let's knock it off.

It was Sunday morning. The whole congregation watched Liza, Colleen, and Eric walk down the center aisle of the church. Reverend Langtree's smile helped offset the stares of the congregation.

"I'm pleased to see you and the family again," Reverend Langtree said after church.

Mrs. Winslow joined them, and said, "I want to thank you, Mr. Silkwin, for working with the doctors on my husband. Just before he died, he told me how much your healing helped relieve so much of his pain and helped his breathing. My son and I will always be grateful."

"I wish it could've been more—much more," Eric said.

"We all do what we can. Never underestimate the power of your gift. I'm sorry you and your family have such controversy."

He didn't know what to say. Liza and Colleen stood silently beside Eric with a look of pride.

Gradually groups of people broke up and shook Eric's hand. Their smiles were faint but they existed. "These are not bad people. They just don't understand what you're doing," Rev Langtree said. "It isn't as if they are against you. They're afraid of the unknown, and yet, they've heard of the good you've done . . . It's a classic case of human nature."

Eric had lunch at Rita's the following day. "Hello stranger," she said. "Give me a few minutes and I'll be right with you." The jukebox was blaring away. Eric glanced around the room, noticing how her business had grown. Many of Bedford's businessmen had lunch at Rita's through the week. Her food was great, and reasonably priced. Although it had stepped up in popularity, to Eric it had lost that special feeling it used to have.

"So what's new?" Rita asked. "We haven't talked in quite awhile. This business keeps me busy most of the time. The trouble with success is you have to pay the price. But that's the way it goes. Enough of this stuff. You appear to have mellowed, Eric."

"I'm getting older," he said.

"You—older? You gotta be kidding me. Come on, you gotta do better than that. Try again."

"I'm not sure," Eric said. "Maybe it's the business and the church—especially the church. Sometimes I wonder what I was thinking of . . . ."

"It'll take time," Rita said, "You have conflict that pulls you both ways—you knew it wouldn't be easy. You're missing that drive you use to have. You've gotta stand up for what you believe."

"You're very perceptive," Eric said. "But where did it really get me?

"Maybe you're not sure where you want to go! Things happen that we have no control over. I have no idea why, they just do," Rita said. "Maybe it's just one of those days—believe me—we all have 'em!"

"Maybe you're right," Eric said. "You still wrapped up in that poetry, and what was it? The classics?"

"Yes and no." She laughed. "I guess what I'm trying to say is I'm reading and expanding my interest more toward the classics."

"I have just been reading about this senator and his so-called communist infiltration into the US Army," Eric said.

"I know exactly who you're talking about," Rita interrupted.

"Do you think there's anything to his witch-hunting and whatever else this clown is up to?" Eric asked.

Rita's usual smile faded. "To put it in my own perspective—
I think he's a big windbag, seeking far more publicity than he
deserves. This so-called list of communists that he fails to pro-
duce . . . ." She stopped for a moment to serve a customer coffee,
and then she picked up right where she left off. "I don't even
want to think about how he's ruined the lives of many innocent
people in this process. His self-appointed judge and jury role
really bugs me."

"I'm getting that impression," Eric added. "I don't know
how somebody like him gets so much power."

"It happens sometimes," Rita said. "I also read what happened last year when the USSR exploded a hydrogen bomb. I
guess that's what some people would call progress—but it scares
the hell outta me!"

CHAPTER THIRTEEN

Eric decided to close the shop for a week so a new furnace could be installed. It seemed unusually dry for the month of May. It was a good time to help George Quinlin with his hay for a few days. Putting up hay wasn't as easy as Eric remembered. "You look like you could use a break, Eric," Mr. Quinlin said. "How about let's stop for lunch?"

"Sounds good to me," Eric said. He noticed that Mr. Quinlin seemed quieter than usual. "What's on your mind, Mr. Quinlin?"

"Just call me George, Eric. Patsy took my truck and scraped the fender. She cut too close to a piece of machinery. I know she didn't mean to do it, but it really upsets me."

"I can understand you being upset George, but sometimes things just happen. Patsy's young. I'm sure we've all done things; I know I have."

"I guess you're right, Eric."

The next day, Mr. Quinlin went into town for parts. Patsy and Evan were allowed to skip school so they could help get the hay in before it rained.

"He was really mad," Pasty told Eric on the ride back to the barn. "I just cut a little too close," she said, flashing that freckle-faced grin. Suddenly her face got pale. She hopped off the wagon and vomited.

Eric yelled at Evan and he stopped the tractor. "Hey Patsy, you all right?"

"Upset stomach," she said after regaining her composure "Dad really chewed me out about that truck." After she skipped lunch, her mother made her go upstairs and lie down.

Just before one o'clock, Tyler drove into the yard. "What are you doing here, Eric?"

"I closed the shop for repairs, so I thought I'd help your dad." Evan grinned and watched Tyler blush.

"I'll drive the tractor," Tyler said. "You two load the hay. With any luck we'll make it before dark." Tyler looked at the clouds moving in, "Barring rain, and Eric's age and condition," she added with laughter.

Eric soon realized just how out of shape he really was. He was puffing and panting in less than two hours. "Eric, why don't you throw those cigarettes away?" Evan asked.

"It's sure worth thinking about," Eric responded. They rushed back out into the field right after unloading the wagon.

"Sure you can make it?" Tyler asked.

"Yeah. Remember I was a little younger when I did this before. I know—it shows." Eric added, "You gonna split a beer with me?"

"I'll think about it," Tyler said. "How are Liza and Colleen?"

"They're great."

"Colleen's sure pretty," Evan said, and then looked at both Tyler and Eric before turning red. "Why Evan," Eric feigned shock. "I believe you're after my daughter."

"She's only starting school. Come on you two; I happen to like Colleen—we're friends."

"I know and I think it's great," Eric said. He glanced up at the approaching rain clouds gathering in the distance.

"You ready to hit it, old man?" Tyler asked, after crawling on the tractor.

"You just drive and we'll take care of the rest," Eric said. "Right Evan?"

"Right you are. Hit it, Mom!"

"Is that anyway to talk to your mother?" Tyler yelled, but could not resist a smile.

Eric's mind went back a few years. He could almost see her with that scarf, old shirt, and blue jeans. What scared him was the way he still thought of her. She looked at him then quickly away when she saw him staring at her.

Her father returned to help before they finished the next load. They got in the final load before the rain started. "I

151

appreciate your help, Eric. What'd you say we all have a beer?" George Quinlin asked.

"You still upset about the truck?" Tyler asked her father.

"A little," he said. "I was really hot and heavy when I first saw it . . . but I realize how things like that can happen."

A few minutes later, Patsy came outside and joined everyone. She sat next to her father, looked at him, and grinned. "Dad, why don't you tell us about when you and your brother sneaked your father's old Model T pick-up truck?"

He smiled. "You think that will get you off the hook, huh?" He hesitated a moment then grinned, watching the light rain bring a freshness to the air. "My brother Jack, who was a couple years younger than me, and myself couldn't resist taking my dad's truck for a spin."

"Was it new?" Patsy asked.

"About a year old, I guess," he said. "We thought we had it figured out, and we did, except one thing—we didn't know how to stop it. So we just kept driving around in the field until it ran out of gas. It seemed like it took all afternoon and we began to panic because our dad was due back anytime."

Tyler grinned. "You didn't make it did you?"

"Almost," he said. "They pulled into the yard just before we ran out of gas."

Patsy laughed. "Where was this wood shed?"

He pointed at an old rotting shed. "Over there—it wasn't our first trip, or our last." He sipped his beer, and his smile faded. "My brother died of pneumonia that winter. Long time ago," he said. "Jack and I fought each other, but when it came down to it, we stuck together. I guess that's the way life is," George Quinlin said.

"So maybe I'm not so bad?" Patsy asked.

"I'm really not sure yet. Let's get to the house. Your mother should have supper ready. Eric, how about joining us?"

"Thanks, but I can't stay. A couple girls are expecting me and I promised to read Colleen a story. I enjoyed your story, George," Eric said. "Patsy, don't worry, you're not the only one who gets into trouble. Asking Tyler to split a beer with me speaks for itself."

"Now Eric," she shook her head, but could not resist a smile. Mr. Quinlin shook Eric's hand. "Thanks for helping Eric."

"My pleasure," Eric countered.

It was late Saturday evening in early July when a freckle-faced girl walked in the church with a tall blond-haired boy, who seemed vaguely familiar. "Hello Patsy," Eric said. He had not seen her for a couple months.

The expression on Patsy's face showed panic. "Hello Eric," she said softly. She looked into his eyes. "You got time to talk to an old friend. You remember Jimmy Wooden?"

They shook hands. "Yes." The boy was six feet tall, husky, with serious brown eyes. Eric faced Patsy and said, "I've got as much time as you need."

"We need to talk," Jimmy said in a quiet, nervous voice. "We have a problem and . . . ."

"If I can, I'll try to help," Eric said, feeling the tension. "Patsy's a special friend. How about a cup of coffee? I have some in the basement."

"Sounds great; I like your church," Patsy said. "Jimmy and I have been here a couple times but we didn't hang around." Suddenly she broke into tears. "I'm pregnant." The words rang through the stillness. "I'm at least three months, naturally time is running out. I thought maybe you could come to supper some evening so we could . . . ."

"I'll be glad to," Eric interrupted. .His mind drifted back over the last few years. He looked at the tall, gangly girl, whose sensitivity touched him when he needed it the most, "You call me, and I'll be there. You know, your father loves you very much, Patsy."

She didn't respond.

"I love her," Jimmy said. He put his arm around her. "We made a mistake. We'd be grateful if you could be there for us."

"I'll call you tomorrow," Patsy said.

Eric put his arm around her. "It's gonna be all right. Worrying won't help."

After Patsy and Jimmy left, Eric thought to himself, George Quinlin was one of the nicest easygoing people he knew, but he would not understand this. As Eric walked back to the house, he heard Liza's voice. "Eric, it's late and Colleen is waiting to be tucked in. What are you doing?"

"Patsy and her boyfriend Jimmy were just here. Patsy's pregnant!" he said, and then regretted saying it.

"It happens sometimes," Liza said.

"I know," Eric said, "but Patsy's a special friend."

"And you're supposed to make it right because she is?" Liza said.

Eric didn't say anything else; he knew he had already said too much. Liza's reaction didn't really surprise Eric. Lately she seemed to be drifting away from him.

The following day, Patsy called to invite Eric and Liza for supper that evening. When they arrived at the Quinlins, Eric noticed Jimmy Wooden's Ford coupe. "Welcome you two," Mrs. Quinlin said. "My, how Colleen's growing. She's such a pretty little girl; look at those big blue eyes."

"Hello," Tyler said to Liza and Eric. Colleen starred at Evan. He surprised everyone by taking hold of Colleen's hand, and going outside.

"I've never seen him do that," Mr. Quinlin smiled. "You never know what kids are going to do next. Come here Eric." Mr. Quinlin put his hand on Eric's shoulder. "Jimmy and Patsy are trying to explain television to me." Mrs. Quinlin, Liza, and Tyler went off to see the dress that Tyler was making.

"Have a seat," Mr. Quinlin motioned to Eric. "Doesn't your brother-in-law have these televisions in his shop?"

"Yes. He just got some new ones last week. The last few months, he has been studying them. He says they're expensive—but the coming thing."

"Expensive is right, from what I hear," Mr. Quinlin added. "I guess that's what they call progress, but I'm not so sure."

"Evan is getting so big," Eric said. "But, Patsy is the real surprise. She's grown into quite an attractive young lady."

"Careful Eric." Mr. Quinlin's hearty laugh filled the room. "Remember she had quite a crush on you."

"I think it was mutual—now, I'm an old married man."

"Old! You don't know what old is. Wait until you get in your seventies."

"I would have never guessed you were that old; you sure don't look it," Eric said.

"That's because I married a women almost twenty years younger than me," Mr. Quinlin countered.

After a wonderful meal, they lingered around the dining room table. Eric could not keep his eyes off Tyler, but a quick glance from Liza convinced him to look elsewhere.

"George, how about a walk to settle this terrific meal?" Eric asked.

"Sounds good to me," Mr. Quinlin said. Eric wondered how to break the news. The look on Patsy and Jimmy face revealed how urgent it was. Eric knew that this was his only chance.

"What's really on your mind, Eric? I know you, remember," Mr. Quinlin said.

"Patsy and Jimmy came to see me last night."

"Why is it I'm afraid of what you're about to tell me?" The friendliness left his voice.

"Patsy's pregnant."

George Quinlin stopped walking. The big man's face turned red. Suddenly, he started back to the house. Eric put his hand on his shoulder and he shook it off. "I knew they were too close," he said with an unfamiliar edge in his voice.

Eric grabbed his arm. "Wait. Talk to me!"

"A little late, isn't it!" Mr. Quinlin said.

"No. Those two kids love each other—these things happen," Eric said.

"Guess you'd know about that!" Mr. Quinlin said.

Eric ignored his remark. "Stop and think. It's happened. What you say or do can affect a lot of lives."

He stared at Eric with a look that sent chills down his back, "I'm going to wait until you and your family leave. Later, we're going to have a little talk," Patsy's father said. "I should've kicked his ass out of here a long time ago."

"Try and understand," Eric said.

"Understand what! That Patsy's a tramp?"

"You know better than that!" Eric yelled. He felt like hitting him for the first time in his life, but after looking in his eyes, he knew better. "My God! How can you say such a thing?"

"I didn't mean that," he said slowly.

"We both love her, and she needs our help and understanding," Eric said.

"You're right." He cracked a smile. "You were going to swing at me, weren't you?"

"Close," Eric said. "Just for a split second."

"I think it would have been a big mistake on your part," Mr. Quinlin said. "We'd better get back to the house."

Eric silently agreed with him.

It was as if the conversation never took place. George Quinlin was his charming self again. Patsy and Jimmy avoided his eyes the rest of the evening. Liza never spoke on the ride back to town; she just stared out the window.

A few days later, Eric and Liza received an invitation to the marriage of Patsy Quinlin and Jimmy Wooden on July 23rd, 1955.

The following day, Eric ran into Linda Hausler at Grover's. Eric couldn't help but notice the light in Linda's eyes was missing.

"Hi Linda. How are you?" Eric asked.

"I don't know if you heard Eric, but Bill and I are getting back together—evidently we deserve each other; it's like a tragic comedy," she said.

"The lovely Mrs. Hausler is actually becoming bitter," Eric said. She ignored his statement "You're too hard on yourself Linda. We all change, maybe that is the tragedy of growing up. Somewhere our dreams seem to get lost in time."

The last three or four years left more wrinkles on Linda than Eric would have ever imagined. For some reason, he thought she would be the last person that would happen to.

She tried to smile. "I must be going. Eric, you don't have that confident look anymore either. Where'd we go wrong?"

"I don't know. I wish I knew . . . You still look lovely, lady."

"Not any more, Eric Silkwin—not anymore."

Later that night, Eric noticed Liza staring at him. "What's on your mind, Liza?"

"You can't expect the people at Mayville to keep carrying the church. It hasn't been able to support itself. I think you should close it," Liza said with a bitter tone in her voice. You could tell the closeness between the two of them was quickly fading away. Neither of them knew why, but both were aware of it.

"I've been thinking about it," Eric said.

"I think you should," she said before falling asleep.

The phone rang, startling Eric. He jumped out of bed and ran to answer it. Tyler's voice cried out, "There's been an accident! It's Patsy and Jimmy . . . It happened on the curve, just west of town."

He glanced at the clock. It was after one. "I'm on my way." He hung up and got dressed.

"Eric, what is it?" Liza asked.

"Accident. Patsy and Jimmy—I've gotta go."

157

He saw the flares, police car, and ambulance in the distance. He parked on the side of the road and rushed to Tyler's parents who were talking to the police. One of the ambulances was leaving with their sirens shrieking in the night.

"It's my fault!" George Quinlin cried. His body shook. "Why'd I have to get so angry?"

"Patsy . . . ." was all Eric could say.

"The other ambulance took her to the hospital. We're going there now," Mrs. Quinlin said. "Tyler must be worried sick."

"Don't worry, I'll go check on her," Eric said. He rushed to the Quinlin's house with a feeling of panic. Tyler was looking out the window when he drove up. She rushed to him. Her slim body shook with her sobs. "Patsy?" she whispered.

"They've rushed her and Jimmy to the hospital. Your folks are with them. They'll call as soon as they can."

"Did you hear anything yet, Mom?" Evan asked.

"No," Tyler said. She became aware of being in Eric's arms. "I must control myself." She spilled the coffee and sobbed, "I'm so afraid, Eric!"

"Here let me help you." He finally got her settled down. The small talk failed to take her eyes off the phone. When it rang a few minutes later, she jumped but did not move. "I'll get it," Eric said, trying to keep the edge out of his voice.

"Eric," Mr. Quinlin's sobbing voice said, "Patsy died in the ambulance on the way to the hospital. Stay with Tyler until we get home. Just say we're with her."

"All right," he said, trying to control his voice. "Your folks are with Patsy and . . . ."

"She's not . . . ."

"No," Eric lied. This was a Friday that Eric would never forget. *Less than two weeks ago, we were having dinner together*, Eric thought. The only thing he could think of was the eight-year-old girl with pigtails, digging her bare feet in the grass at the cemetery, years ago. He tried talking to Evan; anything to get that blank stare out of Tyler's eyes. It wasn't long before the Quinlin's drove up and Eric, Tyler, and Evan ran to meet them.

It was the first time Eric saw George Quinlin look so completely defeated. Tyler knew the minute she saw their faces. "Thank you for staying with Tyler and Evan," Mrs. Quinlin said.

Eric felt helpless. "If there is anything at all I can do."

"*You knew!*" Tyler screamed at Eric, beating her hands on his chest, "You knew and didn't tell me!" Her eyes were wild with rage.

Her father held her, "Cry it out, honey—I told him not to tell you." When Eric got home, he told Liza all the details. It seemed like hours, but it was only a little after two. Eric lay in the darkness, praying for the Quinlin family and fighting off the vision of Patsy's smile.

Sunday morning Eric sat in the living room, staring out the window. He heard the newspaper hit the front door. He opened the paper and on the front page was the accident. The picture of Jimmy's car wrapped around the tree left no doubt that anyone could have survived. Jimmy Wooden was thrown clear, with minor cuts and bruised ribs. He was held for observation and released. The passenger in the car, Patsy Quinlin, did not survive.

The funeral was two days later. Eric, with Liza by his side, sat behind the Quinlins. He stared at Patsy's closed casket. The graveside service was the hardest. Evan cried openly as did Jimmy Wooden, standing off to one side.

They attended the dinner later at the Quinlins. Tyler stared at him only once and quickly looked away. "Thank you for coming," Mrs. Quinlin said. "George is upstairs under sedation. He blames himself. It was one of those things," she said. "Who could have known?"

The months passed quickly. Eric hadn't really seen or heard from the Quinlins the last few weeks He did see Ted, who told him that Tyler had become a loner and that she seldom spoke or smiled. As Eric thought about the events that happed several months ago, he heard the shop door open and looked up to see Jimmy Wooden. Eric didn't know what to say. Jimmy looked bad. It was the first time he had seen him since Patsy's funeral. Eric looked in Jimmy Wooden's eyes.

"I dropped in to say goodbye and thank you for being there for Patsy and me," Jimmy said, his voice breaking for a second. "I didn't know whether you've heard, but I enlisted in the Army. I have to get away."

"Just before Christmas?" Eric asked.

"Yes. My bus leaves tomorrow. I don't want to be around here without Patsy, especially at Christmas. She talked about you often, Eric. I haven't talked to the Quinlins—I can't face them—if I just hadn't been going so fast!"

"Don't torture yourself over the details. It doesn't change a thing. Believe me, I know," Eric said.

The last thing Jimmy said before going out the door was, "I've heard it takes time. I'm going to do the best I can. It isn't as if I have much of a choice"

"Good luck." Eric knew that he was right about time.

Christmas Eve, Liza and Eric tried very hard to put their differences aside for Colleen's sake, but even Colleen sensed the lack of harmony. For the first time in years, the Silkwins were not together for Christmas. Karen and Frank were at her parents, and Marie and Ted were in Cutler City with Ted's parents.

Christmas afternoon, Colleen played with her presents. Eric helped Liza with the dishes. Their conversation barely existed. Their movements were mechanical. After finishing the dishes, Eric suggested a drive to the cemetery. "It's snowing Eric," Liza said. "I'll stay with Colleen. You go ahead. Alice will be expecting you."

The snow was tapering off; the sun looked like it might come out any minute. Eric stood before Alice's grave. He lowered his head, staring at the snow covering her headstone. "This Christmas," he said after several minutes, "It's been one of my most difficult ones. Guess you know that Liza and I are drifting apart. I needed to be near you." And then with a heavy heart, he walked slowly to Patsy's grave.

"People don't understand me being out here talking to you, but you would, Patsy. I'll pray for you, your family, and Jimmy. You'll always be special to me."

Later the following evening, Liza said with a tone of disgust, "Eric, you have to snap out of it." They had just finished supper and Colleen was getting tired after a long day. "We feel your depression. You, more than any of us, should be able to deal with these things. I know Patsy meant a lot to you, but . . ."

"Oh grave, where is its victory, oh death, where is its sting?" Eric said softly.

"What in the world are you talking about?" Liza asked.

"The real sting of death is in the survivors—the ache that tears you apart!"

"It's a part of life," Liza said flatly. "You're too sensitive. Far more than I realized, and at times it frightens me. You are selfish! You more than anyone should realize that there is a reason for all things, no matter how tragic. Why don't you take some of your own advice?"

"If I only could," Eric said.

That night they made love with a driving physical desire that left—for the first time—emptiness. Eric thought of Liza's words a couple weeks ago. *If we could turn our physical desire for each other into real love, we would have it all!*

In early 1956, the marriage between Liza and Eric fell apart. The last of March, she asked for a divorce. "We made a mistake, Eric . . . We're neither the first nor the last." She stared at him. "The only thing we got in common is sack time. I am going to level with you; we both tried and it didn't work. Mark is free— he's divorced. I've received a few letters from him under a post office box number," she said. "It wasn't as if I cheated."

Mark Cannon, Liza's first and evidently only love, had worked with Liza in Benford until becoming sales manager for a tool company and moving out east a couple of years ago. "I don't know if things will work out between Mark and me, but I want to try. I've also decided I have to pursue commercial art . . . It's my last chance."

"I won't stand in your way," Eric said.

"You're going to make me the heavy, aren't you?" Liza said.

"No. I sincerely believe everyone should be with the one they truly love."

"Is that your religious or personal view?" Liza asked calmly.

"Both," Eric said. "I think it's a tragedy for two people to remain together who are in love with someone else."

"Like you and Tyler. Everybody knows that is why she did not marry Jerry Yount. A girl like Tyler would never marry a guy she didn't love."

"I know," Eric said.

"I'm sorry I can't be her or Alice for you. You must despise me," she said with pain in her voice.

"You will always be special to Colleen and me. I was hoping that we could still remain friends," Eric said.

She did not fight the tears in her eyes. "I sincerely hope so." She finished her packing, and closed her suitcases. She tried to avoid his eyes but could not.

"What are your plans?" Eric asked.

"I had planned to stay with Ellen and Johnny tonight," she said. "There's a train leaving tomorrow morning that I hope to be on," Liza said.

"You want me to drive you?" Eric asked.

"No, I'll call a cab . . . Throw something!" she screamed. "Hit me—*do something!*"

"Is that any way for friends to act?" Eric asked.

Her slender body was suddenly wracked with sobs. "Oh God, Eric . . . I'm so sorry."

"I'm sorry, too," Eric said. "I'm going for a walk. Lock the door when you leave."

CHAPTER FOURTEEN

A couple days after Liza left, Eric told Ellen and Johnny that he and Liza were getting a divorce. "It just didn't work out," Eric said.

Ellen looked into Eric's eyes. "I think you and Liza are both irresponsible," she said.

"What can I say? We tried hard—very hard," Eric said, "But we couldn't ignore the fact that we both loved someone else. It's like Liz said, '*You can't substitute love; either it's there or it isn't.*' I know it sounds like a cop out, but it is what it is. Everything will be all right. Colleen and I are not exactly helpless; we just have to adjust. Liza is special to me; she and I will still continue to be friends."

"Doesn't that bother you?" Ellen asked.

"No. Liza is happy. It's the way it should be."

Ellen just shook her head.

The following week, Eric closed the shop a few minutes early. The chilly late afternoon was bringing on a light shower. He walked into the insurance office where Ted worked. Ted looked up from his desk, and his boyish smile broke through. "Why Eric, what a surprise. How about I buy you a drink in about five minutes?" Ted asked, glancing at the clock, and then added, "Look who's coming."

"Hello Eric, how are you?" Tyler asked softly, with a smile that brought on those irresistible dimples. "I want to thank you for comforting me after Patsy's . . . ."

"I wish it could've been more," Eric quickly interrupted. "I felt so helpless."

"We all did," Tyler said.

Eric looked into Tyler's eyes. "I came to invite Ted for a drink at Smokey's. Would you like to join us?"

"No thank you, Eric. I've got something else I need to take care of."

Ted grabbed his coat. "I'm ready if you are, Eric."

Smokey's was even more crowded than usual. Ted grabbed a booth. His timing was uncanny. Maggie the server turned on her professional smile, "What'll it be, men?"

"Jim Beam and water, and don't crowd it with a lot of ice," Ted said quickly. "I'm still surprised about you and Liza. It is just such a damn shame. You're both such nice people."

"We tried, but it just didn't work out," Eric said

"Why do things have to be complicated? God knows the time I spend trying to figure things out." Ted said, signalling the waitress.

A couple of drinks later, Eric glanced at the big clock over the front door. "Ted, it's six already. This is it. I don't want Marie mad at me."

"You're probably right," Ted said. He quickly finished his drink and rushed through the crowded bar. "I'll see you later, Eric."

Eric finished his drink, and started to leave when he heard a familiar voice over his shoulder.

"Hello Eric." He turned to see Linda standing beside him. She waved to a girl who was leaving. "She's a friend I work with—buy a girl a drink?"

"My pleasure," Eric said, "What'll you have?"

"The same as you're having. I need to lift my mood," Linda said. He stared at her. It was almost like old times. She still drew attention from the guys at the bar.

165

"Things really never change. I guess . . . some things," Eric said.

Linda glanced at the people at the bar and smiled. "Seems like we've been in this situation before . . . next thing I know, you'll be asking me to take the long way home through the park."

He matched her smile and felt the warm glow of the whiskey. "That was so long ago."

"Yes, many tears ago," Linda said. "Get that look off your face. I am not going to bury you with my problems. It's Friday night."

They stared at each other, the music drifted through the crowded bar from the brightly colored jukebox. *"You'll never know how much I love you. You'll never know . . . ."* The lyrics reached down inside Eric—touching feelings he didn't want to surface—not tonight.

"I heard you're a free man," Linda said. "There's a lot of that going around." It was obvious that she had had a few drinks before joining him. "So, Eric, what are you up to?"

"I don't know. I was just asking myself the same question."

"Since you're not sure, want to walk me home?"

"Yes. I think we should get outta here," Eric said. "Something tells me getting loaded is not going to do either one of us any good."

"I'm ready," Linda countered. "This is just like the old days."

"Yeah," Eric muttered. "The old days." They finished their drinks and left.

The warmer than normal evenings brought on the signs of an early spring. The light snow melted as soon as it hit the walk. They walked down familiar streets, holding hands, desperately trying to recapture the past. They arrived at her house like many times before. "How about a cup of coffee and a dance or two?" Linda asked with unfamiliar desperation in her voice.

Eric held her close, blending their moves with the sound of the music. He knew it was time to leave and kissed her lightly. She was in his arms kissing him back, with a passion that was unfamiliar. "Linda, I think you've had a little too much to drink."

She pressed herself against him. He took her in his arms, kissed her and she responded. "Stay with me Eric," she whispered.

"You don't know what you're saying, Linda."

"All the talk about making love to me was just . . . ."

"It wasn't just talk, believe me. I am human," Eric said. "I don't want you hating me later. We've been friends to long."

She kissed him again, with a passion that he could not resist. He felt the fullness of her body, his hand shook when he began to unbutton her blouse, as he whispered, "Are you sure about this?"

Later, she lay in his arms as the rain beat against the window. "Was I . . . ." Linda's voice was so soft he barely heard her.

"You're special . . . like I always figured," he said softly. "I can't bring back the things you're looking for. I wish I could."

"I had to try," she said. "Have you lost what little respect you had for me?" she asked with tears in her eyes.

"No. It was a pleasant surprise on my part. You and I will always be special friends."

"I hope so," Linda said. "Would you mind if I asked you to leave? It was pleasant and I think we surprised each other, but the neighbors . . . ." The real Linda was back in control.

He dressed and then turned to her, "This will probably never happen again, will it?"

"Probably not," Linda said, softly "It had to happen once."

"You're still a lovely lady," Eric said. "Believe me. I'm in a much better position to know . . . Beyond a doubt."

"Good-bye, Eric Silkwin."

"Good-bye, Linda Maynard." The sound of her gentle laughter was like music to his ears. He kissed her cheek, and added. "Maybe we can't go home again—but we can capture some of those precious memories." Her answer was a smile mixed with tears.

The following week, Eric spent his evenings reading stories to Colleen. He would get her breakfast, see her off to school and together they would have their evening meal. They were closer than ever before. Marie and Ted were at his house often. Marie insisted on fixing meals.

The nights were the loneliest. Eric received his divorce papers. Liza wanted to remain friends and keep in contact.

Friday night Eric stopped at the insurance office to see if Ted wanted to go for a drink. Smokey's was crowded as usual. Ted ordered and a big grin spread over his face. It wasn't long before Eric was feeling his drinks. "I've got to see her!" Eric said suddenly over the blare of the jukebox and the endless surrounding conversation.

"Who?" Ted asked.

"Tyler. I have to let her know I love her. God, how I need her—I just can't sit here!"

Ted grinned. "You're loaded, Eric."

"That's beside the point. If I don't get through to her," Eric said. "It will be too late. I'm serious Ted . . . Will you drive me out there?"

"If you insist," Ted said. "I'll call Marie and explain things." He started to leave the booth, and then said, "What in the world will Tyler's folks think?"

"I've got to take a chance," Eric said. "Tyler is too important to me."

"Alright," Ted said. "I'll be back in a minute . . . Love can sure screw a guy up." He looked at Eric again for verification.

"Well, look who is here," Bill Hausler said. He slapped Eric on the back. He was with another couple and a blonde hanging on his arm like he would suddenly vanish. "Hey Charlie," Hausler yelled at the other guy, "Get us a booth and I'll be right with you . . . Eric, what's a spiritual leader like you doing in a place like this?"

"A time for reflection," Eric said, feeling the warmth of the whiskey. He stared at Hausler, who had had a few himself.

"Reflection, in your case is a dangerous thing, Silkwin. It's usually a sign of failure. By the way, this is Annie."

"Silkwin, I've heard that name." Her smile looked painted on.

Ted returned. "Let's go." He downed his drink and stared at Hausler.

After they left, and found their way to the car, Ted said, "One thing I'm sure of—I'm doing the driving. Marie said we're both crazy and you're asking for trouble."

Eric sighed. "What else can a guy do?"

"Tell me about it," Ted said

When they pulled in front of Tyler's house, Ted shut off the lights and added, "You sure about this? Maybe tomorrow would be better."

"If I don't do it now, I'm afraid I won't get it out—my love for her, I mean."

"You want me to wait here?" Ted asked.

"I'm not sure," Eric said. "What if I just get out and see how it goes?"

"You better do something—somebody's looking out the window," Ted said, and then laughed. "I'm sorry buddy. I hope it doesn't turn out to be as funny as it seems right now"

Eric walked slowly to the house, stopped and started back to the car when the porch light came on. "Eric is that you?" Mr. Quinlin's voice called from the porch.

"Yes." Eric said, trying to think of what to say. "Thought maybe I . . . we came to visit."

"Well, don't you think you should come in the house?"

"Come on, Ted," Eric yelled back at the car, "I think we're at the critical moment."

"Watch it!" Ted yelled about the same time Eric fell over a block planter.

"You all right?" Ted pulled Eric up. "I guess you know this is kinda embarrassing."

"How do you think I feel?" Eric moaned.

George Quinlin walked out to them. "Eric, you hurt? You've been drinking?"

"Some," Eric said, feeling foolish. "I suddenly got the feeling this isn't such a good idea."

"Well, you're here now. You'd better come in before you hurt yourself. How about some coffee?" Mr. Quinlin asked. "From what I see, you need it." Eric and Ted slowly entered the house.

"Hi Eric, you all right?" Evan asked. The only thing missing was Patsy.

"I kinda fell over the planter." For a moment, Eric thought he was going to be sick.

"Hey Mom, we got company. Eric and a friend came to visit us."

"I see," Tyler said, fighting a smile. "Or should I say, I heard. What in the world are you doing this time of night? Eric, you never cease to surprise me."

"I'll put something on your forehead," Mrs. Quinlin said. "The coffee's almost ready."

"The weather is nasty out," Ted said, trying to make conversation. "It's drizzling . . . I don't know what is gonna happen next." An awkward silence fell over the kitchen.

"You've been drinking," Tyler said, no longer trying to hide the smile.

"Here's your coffee," Mrs. Quinlin said. "I think the rest of us should go in the living room."

"What I have to say," Eric said, taking a deep breath. "I love you Tyler, and deep down I know you love me. I know it every time we look at each other."

The smile left her face. "Liza and I—we're divorced. We tried to make it work, but our love only involved the bedroom."

"Eric!" Tyler yelled.

"Sorry," he said quickly. "You don't know how hard this is for me. Everyone knows I love you—Liza knew. Don't you understand? I have to say these things . . . You can't make yourself love someone."

"Eric please!" Tyler said, she got up and poured Eric and Ted another cup of coffee.

"You had to know tonight," Eric said, with desperation in his voice. "Don't you see that we've wasted years?"

"I think we should leave," Ted said, "You're pressing your luck . . . I think you got your message across. In any event, I think we screwed up."

"Maybe you're right," Eric said. "I never did have much tact . . . It's just . . . ." Eric got up slowly, the pain of a headache beginning to take over. Tyler left the room. He heard her slam her door.

"What's a guy supposed to do?" Eric said. Ted steered him to the door. He turned to the Quinlins, who had rejoined them. "Let me talk to her through the door." Eric pleaded.

"Only if she agrees," George Quinlin said.

Eric knocked on her door, "Tyler, listen to me. If you tell me now you don't love me . . . I'll never bother you again."

"I'll talk to you later," her voice had the sound of tears. "Not now Eric."

"Well okay, but I want you to know that I'll love you forever!"

Later in the car, Eric felt himself begin to sober up, "I really screwed up, huh?"

"I'm not so sure. What else could you do? I'll admit it should've been handled differently—but that's not your style."

"What time is it?"

"It's only a little after nine. Can you believe all this has happened in just a little over two hours?" Ted asked. "I remember how it was with Marie. You were there for me."

"Wanta couple drinks?" Eric asked. "Colleen is staying with Ellen and Johnny."

"Yeah—maybe we can figure it out. I'm not sure, but I think she loves you. Who understands women?"

Smokey's had thinned out; it was that time of evening. Ted steered him toward the back, away from Hausler and his party.

"Back again?" the waitress smiled, "Jim Beam and water?"

"I can't believe what I did a few minutes ago," Eric yelled over the jukebox. "What was I thinking of?"

"It was probably a stupid impulse," Ted yelled back. "I've had a few of them myself. Let's face it! Love can shake a guy up. Wait right here, and I'll call Marie. I'll be right back."

"Hey Silkwin!" Hausler's voice bellowed over the noise. Eric glanced at them. Hausler walked back to their booth, the blonde right behind him and the other couple not far off.

"Cheer up Silkwin, you can't tell me Liza wasn't keeping you happy . . . Hey—maybe that's the problem." He leaned closer, yelling, "Maybe it's the other way around!" The couple stood beside him. "Hey Charlie, did I ever tell you about a girl named Liza?"

"Knock it off, Hausler—I'm not in the mood," Eric said. Ted returned to their booth, his grin quickly faded away. "Maybe we'd better go."

"I wanta hear about Liza," the blonde said.

"Let's go," the guy named Charlie said. He did not look like the kind of guy who wanted trouble. The faded blonde-haired woman on his arm looked disappointed. "She's a hot number, especially in the back seat," Hausler said. "You don't believe me—ask her!" The people near them suddenly focused their attention on what was going on.

"Why don't you just leave us alone?" Ted asked.

Hausler ignored him and put his hand on Eric's shoulder. "Trouble with Eric here is he could never get it on with Linda."

Eric grinned. "Wrong! That is no longer true."

Hausler's smile faded. "What'ya trying to say? You couldn't get next to Linda and you know it." His eyes watched Eric closely. "You're a lying bastard." Hausler's face flushed. His eyes took on a wild look.

"Come on, Bill!" Charlie tugged at his arm and he shook it off.

"Gentlemen, please." The waitress said. She looked over to the bartender.

"What I really regret," Hausler yelled, "Is not getting some of that Alice."

Eric jumped up. Ted tried grabbing him but was too late. Hausler's right crashed into Eric's face, knocking him back in the booth. Eric tore loose from Ted and drove his right deep into Hausler's gut, doubling him over. He threw a left hook, which Hausler blocked, but Eric's right uppercut caught him flush. He fell over the table and hit the floor with a sickening thud. Hausler did not move. People suddenly closed in around them. Ted bent over to look at him, and then his face took on a pale expression, as he yelled into the crowd, "Get an ambulance . . . My God—I think he's dead!"

Eric was arrested and held until his trial. Karen and Frank were due back in Benford the following weekend. The Nathan Lock Company had sold out and Frank was trying to get into Mullaird's. Eric received a letter from Tyler. She mentioned visiting him but Eric didn't want that, he didn't want Tyler to see him like this.

Eric's trial was May 20th, 1956. He was found guilty of manslaughter; sentencing was scheduled for the following week. Ellen and Johnny were taking care of Colleen. Walter Blanchard, who had worked with Eric's father, agreed to run the shoe shop. He insisted he needed to keep busy.

The most pitiful sight Eric had seen during the trial, other than Colleen, was Linda. The lovely woman had faded badly.

"Silkwin!" The guard called, "You have a visitor . . . Miss Maxine Quinlin."

"Thank you," he said. The guard released his cell door and Eric followed him into a holding area. There, Tyler was sitting, wide-eyed, looking carefully around the room. "Eric, I'm so sorry. In a way, I feel it is my fault. If I had talked to you, instead of rushing in my bedroom . . . I'm a little nervous," she said.

His need to hold her was so strong he gripped the edge of the table. "Tyler—don't ever think that! You had nothing to do with it. I know coming here isn't easy for you."

"Why wouldn't you see me earlier?" Tyler asked.

"I couldn't face you, as much as I wanted to."

"I'm not here out of pity, Eric. The night you were out at the house, you said many things I have thought over carefully . . . I have always loved you—that is why I never married Jerry. I knew for sure after you married Liza, but it was too late!"

Eric hoped time would stand still for the next few minutes. "My lawyer has worked out second degree manslaughter. I could get a year—but with good behavior I can be out in six to eight months."

"I don't know what to say!" Tyler said.

Eric felt the pressure of time. Suddenly he said, "I want you to wait for me—I know it's a lot to ask." Tyler didn't say anything.

The guard signalled him to wrap it up. He could feel his gut tighten.

"Write me Tyler, I love you."

Tyler managed a smile through her tears. "I love you too, and I'll be praying for you."

Karen and Frank came to see Eric a few days before he was to leave for prison. Frank looked serious, but tried, in his own way, to cheer Eric up. As usual, Karen spoke first. "You look good, Eric."

"So do you, Karen. How is it going with you, Frank? Hey— get that look off your face—I'm the guy in here."

"Eric, what can we do for you?" Frank asked.

"Colleen—I have to make her understand. I'd appreciate it if you could help hold things together. Tyler knows that I'm still in love with her. She was here."

"You shouldn't be in here," Frank said, "I mean . . ."

"I know," Eric replied. "I tried to tell these guards the same thing, but they just don't understand."

"Still a sense of humor, I see." Karen countered.

"It's one of the things that keeps me from losing my mind," Eric said. He tried to smile, and then added. "It's kind of ironic that I'm leaving for prison the same day as Colleen's birthday party. Having it at the park was a great idea. I really appreciate everything you're doing for her. I don't know if this will happen, but I've requested permission to stop at the park on the way to the penitentiary to see her. I've explained to the sergeant that she was having her birthday party there; she's going to be eight years old."

"I hope you can make it," Frank said.

The guard walked slowly toward them, "I'm sorry—it's time."

"Oh Eric," Karen started to cry.

"No crying in here—it's not allowed," Eric said. "Frank, I hope you get in Mullaird's. I can do the six or eight months, because I have so much waiting for me."

Later that afternoon, Marie and Ted came. "We'll watch over Colleen," Marie said.

"I know," Eric said. "I appreciate it. Ted, get your chin off the floor. I need you to be strong for me."

"I will. Eric, if you just hadn't . . . ."

"We'll pray for you," Marie added.

The next day, Claude Stratman came to the police station. "My name is Claude Stratman. I believe my editor; Louis Cowler got permission for me to do interview with Eric Silkwin."

"Yes, I remember," Sergeant Hullman said. "Wait here."

"Eric, there's a Claude Stratman here; wanting to interview you. Of course, it's up to the officer in charge and you."

Eric looked to the man who was taking him to prison. "It's alright with me," Eric said. "He gave me fair coverage through my trial."

The officer in charge who was taking Eric to prison looked at his watch. "We have several miles to go. It's okay with me, if you make it quick."

Sergeant Hullman returned to the main office, "Follow me, Mr. Stratman."

Claude Stratman had his pad and pencil posed for action. "Eric, do you have any general statement concerning the results of your defense?"

"No. I thought Mr. Gardener represented me as well as possible under the circumstances. I wasn't too crazy about how things turned out."

Claude Stratman's laughter was short lived. "What about your sentence? Do you think it was fair?"

"I honestly don't know—it could have been worse. Then again, maybe it could have been better. I'm not a lawyer," Eric said.

"What about your church?" Stratman asked.

"I'd rather not comment at this time."

"If you don't close it, then who would run it?" Stratman persisted. Eric knew he was asking the questions set forth from his editor. It was his job.

"Like I said—no comment."

"Is there anything you wish to add?" Stratman asked.

"Yes." Eric saw the officer checking his watch. "It was an unfortunate accident . . . Yes, an accident. I am truly sorry," Eric said. "I sincerely apologize to the Hausler family and don't know of any other way to express my deep regret.

It was the day that Eric was to be transported to the penitentiary. The officer who was assigned to transfer Eric looked at him carefully. "The sergeant here has given his word that you would conduct yourself within reason if we allowed you a few minutes with your daughter."

Eric nodded. "I'm going to ask if you could remove the cuffs while I say good-bye to her."

"It's against every regulation in the book," the officer said, "But I think there are times when a little adjustment should be made."

Eric sent out a silent prayer of thanks.

"I'll vouch for him," Sergeant Hullman said. "I've known him and his family for years and it's his daughter's birthday party."

When Eric and the officer arrived at the park, Eric saw several people watching the police car drive around the curve and then stop.

"All right," the officer said. He unlocked the cuffs. "Don't make me regret this. I'm trusting you. Do not greet the others. Your daughter must come forward to meet you."

"I appreciate this more than you'll ever know." Eric felt a lump in his throat as he watched his eight-year-old, dark-haired daughter run to meet him.

"No sudden moves among the crowd—straight back here," the officer in charge said.

"Yes sir. I understand," Eric said. He scooped Colleen up in his arms. He saw the officers motioning for the others to stay back. "You look so pretty, little one . . . Happy Birthday."

They sat at an empty table a few feet away. "Listen honey. I want you to be a brave little girl. Ellen and Johnny will watch over you."

"I will Daddy—I'm a trooper like my mommy," she said. Her eyes moved to the police car in the distance, "Did you really kill a man dead?"

"Yes honey. It was an accident, and I'd do anything to undo it. I know I'm asking an awful lot of you, but I don't have a choice. Do you understand?"

"Yes Daddy, like when I had to stand in the corner at school—Oops!" He held her tight, "I'll pray for you every night."

Eric held back his tears. "I'll be home soon."

"I know, Daddy. I'm not gonna cry!" Her little chin started to quiver. He hugged and kissed her, and took a long look at those big blue eyes."

"I have to leave now, remember I love you, Colleen," Eric said.

"Me too, Daddy. I love you."

He turned and slowly walked back to the awaiting officer. Just before getting into the police car, he waved at Colleen, who frantically waved back.

"Thank you," Eric said. He placed his hands in front for the cuffs. Eric watched until the group of people passed out of view . . . especially one little girl.

CHAPTER FIFTEEN

They arrived at Raulington Prison late in the afternoon on June 2nd. Eric was processed, fingerprinted, and photographed.

The first night in the cell was the roughest. The clang of the cell door behind him brought a feeling of mild panic, then depression. He fought off the vision of Colleen's face, praying that sleep would overtake him . . . His prayer was soon answered.

During most of the first week, Eric was getting adjusted to prison life. A couple of days later, he was assigned to the prison library. The mail arrived in about ten days. His first letter was from Ellen. He noticed his hand tremble as he read it.

> *Dear Eric,*
>
> *Colleen is really something. She and Elizabeth are getting along fine. She says she is being brave for her daddy. Tyler and her folks were here this week. She gets along great with Colleen; I think she really cares about her.*
>
> *Everything here is the same. Walter Blanchard is doing well with the shop. Johnny says hang in there. I must close; you know how I am. I have to start supper soon. We all pray for you.*
>
> *Love, Ellen.*

Eric laid the letter aside and opened Tyler's.

> *Dear Eric,*
>
> *What can I say? We will make up for wasted time. I can only pray that time will pass quickly and we will be together. I see Colleen now and then. Do not worry about her. She is fine. She says you will be home soon, and we will go on a picnic.*
>
> *She mentions seeing her mother sometimes at night. It does not scare me anymore. I don't know quite what to*

*say. Your faith is mine now; do not lose the special gift
you have. There is a reason behind all of this.*
　Love & Prayers, Tyler

Eric lay back on his bunk until the vision of Colleen and
Tyler flooded his mind.

"Does it really help? Thinking about it, I mean," Louis Halpren asked. The voice from the overhead bunk brought him back
to reality. Louis was a good-natured guy, with curly blond hair and
green eyes. He had an uncanny ability to accept almost anything.

"It helps me," Eric said softly. "My daughter and girl are just
a dream away."

"There you go," Louis said, with his usual laughter. "Lucy is
with me too, at least mentally. Still, speaking from experience,
what she's up to lately? I can't be sure."

Semi darkness came with silence, except men in distant
cells clearing their throats, and settling down for another night
of confinement. On some nights, Eric could hear the lonesome,
haunting sound of an inmate, singing softly into the darkness.

The light from outside the cell cast the shadows of bars
across the bunk, crawling up the wall.

"How do you feel about that, Louis? Your girl, I mean?" Eric
asked.

"Hey, whatever will be will be," he said with an abrupt
laugh. "I haven't met the girl who's going to ruin my life, a least
not yet. Everything is temporary—three squares a day, and I get
to work in mechanics. I admit I miss touching a girl now and
then, but you can't have everything."

The sound of a hymn filtered through the cell. Others soon
joined the voice. It had the feeling of bringing peace to end
another day. They were the loneliest sounds Eric ever heard.

Louis Halpren was twenty-four; in and out of reformatories
since he was a kid. "It's my love of cars that gets me in trouble,"
Louis laughed, "Almost anybody's car!"

The one thing Louis very seldom mentioned was family.
Eric thought he detected pain in his eyes when he did mention
them. "I'm my own family," was all he ever said.

The work at the library was easy. For the first time in his life, Eric began reading something besides the Bible, even classics that he had never read. The books about far Eastern religion caught his attention. He concentrated on healing and practiced Yoga, which led to new understanding.

"I don't see what you get out of those meditations," Louis said. "I mean—what has all that stuff got to do with cars? I do remember going to a little white church when I was a kid. I don't remember it affecting me either way."

"It's hard to explain," Eric said. "I guess we're all looking for something. You know Louis, you have a way of keeping a sense of humor," Eric said. I envy that."

"One thing I learned the hard way is that bitterness, temper, and hate will eat you alive if you let it," Louis said thoughtfully. "It can get you in a lot of trouble. I speak from experience. I know somewhere down the line that things are going to work for me. I don't know about calling it faith . . . I just feel it."

The next day, Eric met Henry Iceland, Louis' friend. Henry Iceland was twenty-two years old, but looked seventeen. He was medium height, with short, dark wavy hair, and a baby face. "Henry doesn't have many friends," Louis explained. "I'm one of the few. There are too many creeps in here; you have to be on guard. Henry was raped; that's why he has a cell by himself," Louis added seriously.

"I got mixed up with the wrong crowd and held up a grocery store," Henry said. "Nobody was hurt, but it got me three years. I was the lookout," he continued. "I panicked when I saw the police, and messed my pants. It was one of my most embarrassing moments of my life."

The three sat together in the mess hall. Louis slapped Eric on the back, "Eric here is a librarian. In other words, he has a gravy job. He has this fascination for Far East religion."

"Does it really work?" Henry asked. "I need something, that's for sure. I'm getting out of here, and I don't want to come back."

Eric smiled. "My temper got me in here," he said. "Maybe if I'd learned a little control before, I wouldn't be here, and a guy would be alive."

"Hey, if I hadn't stolen that beautiful convertible, I wouldn't be in here either," Louis said. Then he laughed. "That car was beautiful—I mean it was something else."

"I remember praying for a blue bike when I was a kid," Henry said seriously, "But I never got it. I did get a bike the following year, but it was red."

"You're a character," Louis said.

"Yeah I know," Henry replied. "Red wasn't all that bad."

Eric worked out a system of reading and meditation that helped eliminate most of his loneliness. The first three months became routine. It eased the tension but increased the boredom. Walter Blanchard wrote a letter and said the shoe shop was running smoothly and it helped him feel useful since his retirement from Mullaird's.

The third of September Eric received a letter from Frank.

Dear Eric,

I know you are surprised to hear from me. This is probably the second or third letter I have written in my life. Karen and I are okay. I got a foreman's job at Mullaird's.

I want you to write to Ted. He's gone off the deep-end, drinking too much. Karen and I are closer to them since you went away. You know Ted; he is the most sentimental, sensitive person I ever met.

All he talks about is Jason, Cindy, Alice, and you. He seems locked in the past. Tyler is well under control. This self-reliant girl's shyness—if it ever existed—is gone.

One other thing—I admire you for standing up for what you believe. Something I am not sure I could do. How would you like for Karen and I to bring Colleen

*and Tyler for a visit? I am going to close now. This is the
longest letter I ever wrote in my life.
   As always your friend, Frank*

Eric wanted to see Colleen and Tyler more than anything
but the idea of them coming here bothered him. He managed
to write to Frank and Ted before lights out. The familiar sound
of cell doors closing and the restless feeling of another night
of confinement became part of a routine he was very familiar
with.

The next day at evening chow, Lou said, "Isn't this one of the
best meals you've ever had?" He held up a drumstick. "What
else could a guy want?" They heard a couple snickers mixed
with laughter.

"What do you mean, Lou? This is a terrific meal," Henry
added in a serious tone, "We need more like it."

"Maybe your new friend can pray for that," the voice of a
stocky man with the crew cut from across the table said.

Lou laughed with a controlled determination to play the
remark down, and said, "Hey Stark, maybe you're right. What've
we gotta lose?"

Stark's dark, beady eyes showed that he did not appreciate
Lou's attempt at humor. The guy next to Stark whispered in his
ear. Stark's stare turned into a grin, "You're telling me that guy,"
he said, pointing his spoon in Eric's direction, " . . . killed a man
with his fists?"

"Ignore him, Eric," Lou said in a low voice, "Stark probably
got up on the wrong side of the bed. Don't let him con you. He
had a shot at the pros; I think his brains are in his fists."

"I heard that," Stark bellowed. "Personality Lou, and lover-
boy Henry have filled their three of a kind with a religious
freak!"

Henry blushed, and lowered his head.

Lou stared at Stark, holding onto his grin, "You crowd me or my two friends, and I'll have you in solitary. You know I can handle it, and you can't!"

"You want to crawl into the ring?" Stark countered.

"No. You'd probably kill me, and I couldn't give you that satisfaction."

"You're a real comic, Halpren . . . ."

"Trouble here?" The guard interrupted. He stood by their table, beating a nightstick with a deadly rhythm in his left hand.

"Naw," Lou said. "Just shootin' the bull."

The guard glared from one to the other. "Hold it down. I don't wanta have to come over here again."

Eric began to have second thoughts about Colleen and Tyler coming here.

"You going to church services tomorrow morning, Eric?" Lou asked.

"Yes. It's what keeps me going."

"Henry's going; think I'll go, too." Lou added softly, "Who knows—maybe I can probably pick up a few pointers."

Louis, Henry, and Eric sat together in the chapel. Lou stared awkwardly at the other inmates. He whispered to Eric, "Do you realize that this is the second time I've been here in over three years?"

Henry laughed, "Yeah, the first time you had to be here."

After services in the mess hall, Henry spoke up, "I liked it. It's like I have someone on my side. I've never been aware of a feeling like that before. Oh, I don't mean you guys," he added. "But someone who really cares about me . . . I never had that before."

Eric leaned close to him. "There is someone, and they're closer than you think."

Henry's only answer was a big grin.

Eric paced the cell, visiting hours were only a few minutes away, and his nerves were getting the best of him. "They'll make it," Lou said thoughtfully. "From what I've heard the last three months, nothing will keep them away. Hey, you're the man with the faith, remember?"

"It's not lack of faith. I guess it's seeing me in here, especially my daughter." It wasn't long before the guard came.

"Silkwin, you have visitors, follow me. I want you to know you were given a special privilege because of your daughter's age. You will meet in a special visitors' room. Remember, no physical contact."

"Thank you, sir. I really appreciate this," Eric said, holding back his tears.

When Eric walked into the visitors' room, Colleen ran toward him and he scooped her up in his arms. "Daddy!" she yelled. She put her arms around him and held him tight.

Eric saw the guard motion to avoid physical contact. "My little one," he said. "Let me look at you. You're getting so big."

"Bigger every day, Daddy . . . look over there," Colleen said. She pointed to Tyler, Karen, and Frank. They sat at a table across the room.

Tyler smiled, bringing those incredible dimples to life. "It's good to see you, Eric." The sound of her voice was like music to his ears.

"It's great seeing all of you," Eric said softly. "It means so much to me."

"Where's the bars, Daddy?" Colleen asked with wide-eyed wonder. She looked around the room with curiosity.

"They're not in this area, honey."

"Is this the visit room?" she asked.

"Yes Colleen." He noticed her freckles, just like Alice.

She tugged at his sleeve, and said, "Where's the shooters, Daddy?" she asked.

"Shooters?" Eric asked with a grin.

"I'm afraid it's the effect of television," Karen said.

"They're in another area, honey."

The laughter was subdued. "Connie and I talk all the time," Colleen said seriously. "Glen pulled my hair in school and I popped him one—right in the nose . . . Oops."

"Did you have to stand in the corner?"

"Yes. Sometimes I have to for talking in school."

"Really, I'd never have guessed that." Eric's expression changed, "Do kids in school tease you about me, Colleen?"

She looked Eric in the eye. "Sometimes I stand tall—like you told me."

"I'm proud of you, honey, but I don't want to see you hurt."

"I don't cry . . . much. I'm strong," she said with a look of defiance. "Uncle George says he's always here for me, no matter what."

Eric looked at Tyler. "He's a good man and his daughter is someone special to me."

"You mean Evan's mom?" Colleen whispered. She said pointing to Tyler. "She's really super, Daddy." Eric was amazed at how much he missed those words. "Bruce walks me to school and watches over me. He is brave. He pops kids if they're mean to me."

Eric looked to Karen then Frank. "It's not serious," Frank said. "The boys get a charge outta watching over her. Most of the time she takes care of herself."

"That's true, Daddy," Colleen said seriously.

"I know you're concerned about Linda," Karen said. "We've had lunch several times. She does not blame you. She knows the circumstances. Besides . . ." Karen's face brightened, "She's going with a guy who works at Mullaird's. She told me to tell you to hang in there."

"How are Marie and Ted doin'?"

Karen lowered her head and said. "You take this one, Frank."

"He hit a car and got picked up for drunk driving. He's not seriously hurt, but he was in the hospital for three days with a fractured leg," Frank said. "I talked to him yesterday. He'll be laid up for a while—that's the reason he and Marie are not with us."

Karen took over. "Marie's torn between anger and pity. She is worried about Ted's state of mind more than anything . . . She is also pregnant."

"Just before I left, Ted's parents showed up and they really got on him. Naturally, his father's lawyer put up the bail," Frank said. "He's gonna have to pay a fine, and go for counselling—Ted looked so pathetic. He reminded me of an older little boy, if there is such a thing."

"Poor Ted," Eric said slowly. "He's always manages to get in trouble one way or the other . . . Where in the world is Colleen?"

"Over there," Tyler said. "She is talking to the guard. She's not afraid of anyone."

A few minutes later, Colleen returned looking temporarily defeated. She poked Eric on the arm. "You can't go back with us, Daddy," she said seriously.

"What're you talking about?"

"I asked that man . . ." she said, and pointed to the guard she had been talking to, " . . . if you could go home with us, and he said he didn't think so. I said please!"

"Thanks for trying, honey," Eric said. He looked at the guard who smiled.

"I'm working on the farm at the Quinlins," Colleen said. Eric thought she looked tanned, healthy, and happy. "Uncle George calls me a windjammer."

"I wonder why?" Eric said, enjoying the laughter.

"How do you like working in the library?" Tyler asked, "What're you reading?"

"It's great. I've read several novels. The books on meditations help. They've opened up a new outlook. I understand more about what I've been involved with."

"Glen walks with me. He doesn't pull my hair anymore!" Colleen chimed in.

Eric grinned.

Colleen stopped for a second to reach for another thought, "I have a dog at the Quinlins. His name is Custer, a puppy who licks my face. We run and play together . . . Uncle George says he's a hound, and I say he's a good hound, and I love him."

"You take good care of him, Colleen and pet him for me," Eric said.

"I will, Daddy," Colleen said. "Just before they left, we put roses on Mommy's grave. She loves you too, she told me. I pray with her sometime. She don't stay long, but she said she's always with me. Daddy, I can't remember all the things I wanted to tell you."

"Listen to me honey. I'm with you, too," Eric said, "Close your eyes. I'll bet you can feel my arms around you—try hard now."

Colleen closed her eyes. "I'm trying hard as I can!" For a moment, her little lip quivered. "When are you coming home?"

"Soon honey. Before Christmas," Eric said. "Always remember—I'm with you in thought." Eric picked her up and hugged her. "Write me Tyler, and remember I love you."

Eric looked at Karen and Frank. "It means so much to see you again; you take care of yourselves, thank you for watching over Colleen." The guards led everyone out. Eric could see Colleen was close to tears. She waved and Eric waved back. He knew she would cry later, but then, he probably would too.

Henry's parole was next week and Lou had a month to go. The month passed quickly. The night before his release, he and Eric talked into the night. "Lucy and I are getting married, and we're both going to work for a garage . . . Hey, I'm good. I can fix anything mechanical. With any kind of luck Eric, you'll be home for Christmas," Lou said. "Just hang in there. Remember the best is yet to come." It was the last time they talked.

The following day Eric met another young man who was assigned to his cell. "My name is Garnet Leonard. I'm black!" The tall, gangly, young man said, with a look of fear and defiance all rolled into one.

"So you are," Eric said. He extended his hand, "Silkwin, Eric. I'm white!"

"This is all new to me," Garnet said, " . . . and I'll admit I'm confused, lonely, and a little scared."

"I know the feeling," Eric replied. "Have you been assigned a job yet?"

"Laundry for now," he said pitifully. He lowered his head. "They said if I behaved myself, and followed the rules, maybe I'd later have a chance at something else . . . It wasn't very encouraging." Leonard Garnet never said much the first week, and then he gradually opened up. "What're you in for?"

"Killed a man in a bar accident," Eric said. "I lost my temper for a few seconds, a man is dead, and I'm spending my time with guilt."

"I and a buddy held up a liquor store," Leonard countered. "My first job . . . I'm the lucky one. They killed my friend. I just froze and here I am."

Eric later found out that Garnet Leonard was an artist and a good one. "Someday," Garnet said, "I hope to paint."

"You'll make it," Eric said. "In the words of Lou Halpren . . . Think positive."

"You make it sound easy," Garnet said.

"It's not supposed to be easy. We screwed up or we wouldn't be here. All I'm saying is to make it positive as you can. Take it a day at a time."

"I'm gonna try—believe me, I got your message," Garnet said slowly.

Two days later, Eric received a letter from Bill Hausler's parents. It was the first time he had heard from them.

Eric Silkwin

I imagine you are surprised to receive this letter. The hate we have held the last few months has come close to destroying us. Hate does not change things and it is virtually eating our high-spirited nineteen-year-old daughter alive.

Kay is now a bitter young woman, instead of the happy-go-lucky girl we loved. She saw Bill as her big

brother, who could do no wrong. I think I know the lone-
liness you are feeling, being separated from your loved
ones.

I want you to write to our daughter and explain your
feelings. We are trying to keep her from destroying her
life, and our sanity. I am sitting here wondering how to
close this letter. The only way I can think of this moment
is, "Peace be with us all."
Mr. & Mrs. Elliott Hausler.

Eric felt the sincerity of a mother and father. Bill's father, Elliott Hausler was one of Benford's prominent citizens, and Vice President of The Merchants Bank. Eric rarely saw him. He was tall, with wavy, gray hair and handsome stoic features.

"Looks serious, from the expression," Garnet said. He looked up from his sketchpad.

"How's a guy supposed to save a nineteen-year-old girl from destroying her life . . . Especially after killing her brother?"

"That's gotta be rough!" Garnet sighed. "I don't envy you— but I can see why you've gotta try."

Eric told him the whole story.

"You and this religion thing you talk about should give you an edge," Garnet said. "Use what you think will do the job. Does it haunt you? I mean like nightmares?"

"Sometimes I wake up in a cold sweat," Eric said. "I go over it in my mind. All I can think of is the stupidity of it all. One guy's dead and the other's in prison. I think of the families who'll never be the same."

"Dig deep," Garnet said. "You can't change what's already been done, but you gotta give it all you got."

Eric knew he had to respond to the Hauslers' letter. He started the letter, calling on Tawnya, his spiritual guide. *I need you to help me heal a troubled girl—so many lives depend on it.* After several crumpled sheets, Eric said, "I can't get a handle on this, no matter what I write."

"It'll come," Garnet said. "Stick with it."

"I can't bring him back!" Eric screamed. "I can't change things or I wouldn't be here.

"Every guy in here fells like that," Garnet said.

"You're right. I'm just going to write what I feel."

A few minutes later, Eric finished his letter.

> *Miss Hausler,*
>
> *Please read this letter through before destroying it. In a few seconds, I took your brother's life and put myself in prison. It was an accident, a sudden, tragic accident. There's no way I can bring your brother back and I'm truly sorry. I will have to live with what I've done for the rest of my life*
>
> *I exist here day and night, missing my loved ones, in one of the loneliest places in the world. I worry about the effect it will have on my eight-year-old daughter, who tries so hard to understand. Your family is worried about you, too.*
>
> *Hate can destroy you and your family's life. Forgive me. Not so much for myself, but for you and your parents. Your brother would never want you living your life with such bitterness.*
>
> *I know this letter is crude; I hope in some way it can help you.*
>
> *Sincerely, Eric Silkwin.*

Eric reread it and handed it to Garnet.

"I know it doesn't do exactly what I want it to, but maybe it'll get my point across."

Garnet read it. "It sounds sincere. Remember there's only so much you can say. Mail it and put it out of your mind."

CHAPTER SIXTEEN

The next day, Eric received letters from Ellen and Cindy.
Dear Eric,

We all miss you so much. Everyone is fine. Johnny has mentioned picking you up when you get out; hopefully very soon. He is working all kinds of hours, learning about televisions. Naturally, the church is closed since you left. Walter Blanchard keeps it clean, and checks on everything. He is always around to help others, no matter what happens.

We pray for you. I know your strength will see you through. I better close now, I have to do the dishes now, you know me. Take care of yourself.

Love, Ellen, Johnny & Liz.

Eric put thoughts of Ellen aside, and opened Cindy's letter.

Eric was surprised to receive a letter from Cindy. It had been a while since he heard from her.

Dear Eric,

It's been a long time since we talked. Stu and I found out about you when we came back for a short visit. I am sorry for everything you've been going through. Please let me know if there's anything I can do. Stu told me to bake a cake and put a file in it. You know him.

He is working construction and we live from day to day, but doesn't everybody?

Colleen is really something. I guess Stu and I are not meant to have children, but we keep working at it. Our thoughts are with you. We are looking forward to a reunion with you at Christmas. I am going to hold that thought, and give that cake a little more thought.

With Love and Prayers.

Cindy & Stu.

A few days later, Garnet told Eric he got transferred to the sheet-metal shop. It'll give me a chance to learn a trade—something I can build on. You heard anything from the Parole Board? I heard rumors about the review board or whatever they call it."

"Nothing yet," Eric replied.

"Man Eric, I feel your depression."

"Yeah, if it wasn't for the workouts and meditations, I don't know what I'd do."

The next day, Eric received a letter without a name or return address. He was almost sure he knew who it was from, and he was right.

> *Eric Silkwin,*
>
> *You will probably be coming home soon and, of course, Bill never will. I have to give you credit for your nerve. You make it sound like you're the victim, not us. I do not intend to relieve your conscience. Because of you, my brother no longer exists.*
>
> *I will do what I can for my family. I do feel sorry for your daughter. Nevertheless, I remind you of who is putting her through this nightmare. You are right about one thing; hate can destroy a person.*

He handed the unsigned letter to Garnet and sighed, "She didn't get the message. My best wasn't good enough. I failed."

He did not say anything until he read it and handed it back. "You tried. There's only so much you can do."

The gym was crowded. It was one of the few releases from tension for men with too much time and nowhere else to go. Eric watched a couple guys work out for a few minutes then moved to the heavy bag, slowly banging away, and then increasing the tempo.

Eric heard a voice. "Not bad—I gotta admit," Stark said. "But then, that bag don't punch back."

Eric grinned; he thought of Sergeant Hanley, who would have said the same thing.

"What's so funny?" Stark asked, with a sneer.

"Just remembering someone else who told me the same thing, a few years ago."

Eric wondered if laying a few punches on Stark would release that extra tension, but then decided against it.

"Hey Maddox," Stark yelled to the big black man in the ring, shouting instructions to a couple welterweights. He called time, climbed out of the ring, and walked up to Stark. Eric ignored them and pounded away at the heavy bag.

"Those two are not going to do anything," Stark said glancing at the welterweights.

"What's on your mind?" Maddox asked. He stared right into Stark's eyes. Eric had heard Maddox was a good prospect until a late night party ended with him drunk, standing over a girl whose neck had been broken. He had been here over eight years, serving a life sentence.

"Silkwin and I need a little action in the ring. I outweigh him by a few pounds but not that much."

Maddox stared at Stark, then Eric. A group gathered around them. Stark had evidently been through this before. "What'd you say, Silkwin? Stark takes his frustration out on about everybody around here—but *me*." Maddox's smile caused Stark to look away.

"Why not?" Eric said.

In the next few minutes, he found himself in the ring with headgear and eight ounce gloves. Maddox called them to the center of the ring. "You sure about this?" Maddox asked Eric. Stark refused headgear. Eric told his second to remove his.

"You should wear it," his corner man said. "Stark was a semi-pro!"

"Maybe you're right," Eric said.

The crowd had surrounded the ring, only a couple guys on speed bags worked their rhythm in the distance. "No low blows," Maddox said, looking at Stark. "In case of a knockdown, the man scoring the knock down will go to a neutral corner and stay there until I wave him in. If necessary, I'll stop the fight for an eight count—understood?"

Both men nodded. The bell rang and Eric moved to the center of the ring on his toes, wishing he had worked out more. Stark moved toward him—bobbing, and weaving. Eric faked a jab and Stark sneered, banging both gloves together. He charged and threw a left hook, which landed high on Eric's head.

Eric grabbed and held on to Stark for a moment, trying to clear his head. Stark pulled away. Eric faked a jab, and then jabbed again, which landed. Eric threw a right uppercut, which caught Stark coming in. Stark staggered, but quickly recovered. Rage filled his eyes.

Eric started to block a left hook, which never came. He felt Stark's right dig into his midsection and he gasped for breath. He never saw the left hook that dropped him. "Three-four-five." Eric was on one knee watching Maddox yelling in his ear. He got up slowly. "You want to continue?"

Eric nodded and Maddox waved Stark in. Stark dug both hands to the body. Eric felt his legs turn to jelly. He grabbed, but Stark pushed him back, dropping both hands, motioning for Eric to come in. Eric feinted a jab then threw a right, which landed high on Stark head. The crowd was going wild, which increased Stark's rage.

Suddenly, weakness filled Eric's arms. His legs felt like lead. He tried to dance away but his legs would not respond. He raised his left to block the right he had seen coming, but it was too late, it landed, and Eric felt himself flat on the deck, shaking his head. "Six-seven . . ."

He got up on one knee at the count of nine, but his legs would not support him. Maddox moved in and shouted, "You've had it. You all right?"

"I think so," Eric said. He sat on the stool. "I guess I was really out."

"You sit still for a few minutes!" Maddox said.

That evening after chow, Garnet asked, "You a fighter, Eric?"

"No," he said, with a slight grin. "If there was any doubt, it was cleared up earlier."

"I'm surprised at you letting Stark con you," Garnet said. "I saw him in the chow hall. He didn't seem as cocky as usual. You losing your cool is what surprises me."

"A moment of sudden impulse," Eric said. "You'd think I would know better by now!" Garnet shook his head and handed Eric a couple of letters.

Dear Eric,

Happy Birthday, it is a little late, but I am with you in thought. Ted and I got a raise. He seems better. I am planning for the day you will be released. Colleen is doing well. She tells me about seeing Alice as if it were the most natural thing in the world.

She is a very unusual little girl. I thank God every day that she trusts me. She's so good for my parents. In some ways, she takes Patsy's place. I am sitting under the tree where we split a beer. It seems so long ago. I am closing with prayers for you. Write when you can. What do you think of this?

Love you, Tyler

Eric stared at the picture of Colleen, Tyler and a white and tan hound named Custer sitting on a hay wagon with Evan between them. He couldn't help but smile.

The second letter he opened was from Walter Blanchard.

Dear Eric,

I know you are surprised to hear from me. I felt it necessary to keep you informed. The shop is doing fine. I have all I can handle, but it is good to feel useful. Linda got married to a nice guy; she seems happy. Wallace Woodstock has asked me what your plans are, concerning the church and I told him I did not know. I can only imagine the depressing atmosphere you are in, but you will come out with new strength.

Hold fast to your faith. It is still your destiny. I must close now. My prayers are with you.

Sincerely, Walter Blanchard

"Eric," Garnet said, "I got it straight. Rumor has it that the Parole Board is meeting tomorrow."

"It's about time," Eric said. "Do you ever get the feeling these walls are closing in on us?"

"I try not to think about it" Garnet said seriously. "You shouldn't be either."

Eric received notice to appear before the Parole Board the next day. The reality of it finally happening drove him to a nervous anxiety.

"You'll make it. You gotta believe."

"It's so important," Eric said quickly. "They sure know how to put the pressure on a guy. I hope I say the right things."

"It'll come," Garnet said. "Let's play chess. It'll help you relax." Garnet had constantly beaten Eric, although he was getting better—much better. It was Garnet's move, and he shook his head. "You're getting rough, Silkwin—either that, or I'm a good teacher." It was Eric's first win. "It's a good sign," Garnet said. "You're on a roll."

The Parole Board consisted of six people, two of which were women. At least two of them clearly revealed the power they held.

Eric sat directly in front of them, with a guard behind him. He looked around the room, and then straight at the Parole Board, trying to read their expressions.

"Mr. Silkwin," the man in the center of the table spoke with the sound of authority. "We have your record which has been reviewed with care. Do you have a statement to make before our questioning?"

Suddenly, all the things he carefully thought about vanished. He sent out a silent prayer. "To kill a man is a terrible thing," Eric said. "In just a moment, I took a man's life. I go over and over what happened and realize there's nothing I can do to change it."

"Then you're sorry?" The woman at the end asked.

Eric looked at her. What compassion there might be, he felt rested with her. "Yes ma'am. I've been sorry since the moment it happened." He realized how he must look, with a faint trace of a black eye.

The man in the center said, "This man—Hausler—you knew him personally?" He looked over the papers in front of him. "Didn't he marry the girl you were going with?" The man's eyes showed the love of power he held.

"Yes," Eric said slowly. "The girl and I were friends."

"Didn't he accuse you of having an affair with her?"

"Yes," Eric said. "Until just before the . . . er . . . accident."

"I understand your wife died in child birth?" The woman with compassion asked.

"Yes. I was in the service at the time." A second woman glared at him, and kept adjusting her glasses. She was well-groomed. A few short years ago, she had to have been a very attractive lady.

"Weren't you arrested in a bar before this incident?" she asked.

"Yes. Two guys who held a grudge against me had tried to provoke me into a fight by insulting my family. To set the record straight, one of those guys threw the first punch, I only defended myself," Eric said. Her dark eyes concentrated on him. Eric realized she was the main one he somehow had to make understand what really happened.

"I see," she said flatly. Her cold, tight smile, revealed nothing but contempt. "How does a man—with such religious interests . . ." she paused to check her notes, " . . . apparently from early in your life, manage to get in so much trouble in bars?"

"I honestly don't know . . . . Actually, I've spent very little time in bars. Both incidents have been because of insults directed at my family—not me—but my family." He watched the expressions on the faces of the Parole Board and knew he had just scored a point.

"You have the resemblance of a black eye," the lady countered. "Fighting, Mr. Silkwin?"

"Boxing," Eric said. "It was nothing but a gym workout to relieve tension and frustration."

The rest of the questions were about his plans if parole was granted, and his attitude overall. He thought the questions were over when the dragon woman went for a knockout. "I understand you have received mail from the family of the deceased?"

"Yes. The family wrote to tell me that hate was destroying their lives."

"That's not what I meant, Mr. Silkwin. There's a young impressionable daughter . . . Why don't you tell us about her?"

So that was it, Eric thought. The woman was going for the kill. He had to wonder what made this woman so bitter. "They asked me to write to their daughter," Eric began slowly. "They were afraid this hate was also destroying her life, and by me writing to her, maybe she could let go of that hate. She answered my letter and told me that she doesn't forgive me and infers that she has no intent of doing so in the immediate future."

"What a shame, a young lady's life torn apart by her brother's death—all over a bar room brawl."

"Believe me; I realize how tragic it is. I have been living with this ever since it happened. I'm sorry I can't go back and change it. I must live with it for the rest of my life."

"It could have been avoided," she pressed.

"All accidents, in some ways could have been avoided," Eric countered. "Yet for some reason they still happen."

"Do you feel you can resume a productive life in society?" another member of the panel asked.

"Yes. I have a daughter and a girl I love, who are the most important things in my life."

"Let's talk about your daughter. How do you think your being here has affected her?" the compassionate woman asked.

"It's been rough on her—naturally—she's only eight. I'll spend the rest of my life making it up to her. She understands what happened and knows how much I love her. I pray, and ask for forgiveness every day. It's the only thing I can do." The woman's face took on a smile. Eric knew she understood.

The dragon lady couldn't resist a final word. "You killed a man with your fists; do you realize what that really means?"

"Yes," Eric said. "As I said—I live with it night and day . . . but there's one thing that helps me live with it."

"What could that possibly be?" she challenged.

"We were both throwing punches. It could've gone either way." The woman stared at him and lowered her head.

That night, Eric told Garnet, "I keep wondering what I should have said."

"Don't let it bug you. They surely understand the pressure a man's under, or at least they should—it's their job."

"That's the part that bothers me," he said, thinking of the dragon lady.

"I have a feeling you made it," Garnet said. "Now let's see if that win of yours was just a fluke." It was. Eric lost two chess games in a row, but his thoughts were on his future. A few days later, Eric's hand shook when he received the Parole Board's letter. Their decision had been on his mind constantly. Now it was in his hand.

"It won't change," Garnet said. "Open it. You made it."

Eric's eyes skipped over the details, he would be released November 15. He felt relieved and a sudden feeling of joy overwhelmed him. "I made it!" Eric shouted.

"You can handle the next week and a half standing on your head," Garnet said.

The following days were the slowest Eric could remember, but they finally passed.

Eric went to the gym for the last time. Stark walked over to him and extended his hand. "I'm glad you made it." He looked down at the floor then into Eric's eyes, "You done good against me."

"Not good enough," Eric said, rubbing his jaw. "But I can live with that."

"Hey Silkwin," Maddox yelled from the squared circle. "Keep your nose clean." He gave him a victory sign and a big smile. For the first time in a long time, Eric felt the joy of just being alive. The pain, frustration, and loneliness were fading away like clouds on a gloomy day.

The day arrived. In an hour, Eric was going to walk out of Raulington prison. He received papers, lectures from the warden, and a few dollars.

"This is it," Garnet said. He extended his hand. "You know, those talks we had about your beliefs were strange, but they helped . . . I'm grateful. If you get the chance—say a few prayers for me. I know I can get it together if I get another chance."

"I will," Eric said. "You have my word."

The guard led him through the cellblocks, among shouts of congratulations from men he never knew, but understood.

Eric walked into the lobby, greeted Tyler, and put his arms around her. It was a feeling of nearness he had missed . . . He kissed her. "Just let me hold you for a minute and look at you."

"My turn," Karen said with outstretched arms. "It's good to know you're with us again—welcome home. Colleen is fine. She is in bed with a cold. You don't know what we had to go through to keep her there."

"I can imagine," Eric said. "What do you say we get outta here? I want to see this place from the outside."

Frank grinned. "Sure you don't want to hang around and say goodbye to the boys?"

"It's taken care of," Eric said. He put his arm around Tyler's waist. They walked several feet, and then Eric stopped. He had to see the gloomy gray stone walls for a last time.

The day held a hint of cold weather. They were on the road for over an hour, Eric gazed out the window at the farmhouses, and the fields with the look and smell of early winter. Frank pulled into the parking lot of a roadside diner. "It doesn't look that special."

"It does to me," Eric said. He felt awkward. The waitress and people at surrounding tables stared at him with knowing glances.

"We can leave," Frank said.

"No, it's all right," Eric said. "They can't get to me. I'm free—and I'm going home."

They drove for another hour. The music from the car radio put Eric in a relaxed, mellow mood. The next few miles, the familiar sights came into view. Tyler put her hand in his.

"Look out the window, Eric Silkwin," she said.

They were entering the city limits. "My cup runneth over," Eric said. "I never knew Benford could look so good or mean so much."

CHAPTER SEVENTEEN

Colleen sat up in bed, surrounded with books, blankets and a cloth pinned around her neck. Eric walked in with Tyler, and Colleen reached for him. "Daddy," she whispered.

Eric put his arms around her and held her tight. "You've got a fever, honey."

"I gotta cold bug too, Daddy," she sniffled, and rubbed her red nose. "I'm gonna chase these cold bugs away with happy thoughts like you always told me to."

"That's my girl. You'll be up and at 'em in no time."

Colleen looked at Tyler, "You going to be my mom now?"

Tyler looked to Eric then smiled. "That's up to your Daddy."

"Super!" Colleen yelled, and Eric smiled.

Karen and Frank peeked into Colleen's bedroom. "We're going," Karen said. "We've got to pick up the kids. It's good to have you back, Eric."

"Goes double for me," Frank added.

"It's good to be home," Eric said.

After they left, Ellen said, "Tyler, how about helping me with my dress. Eric needs a nap and a certain young lady promised to take one after she saw her daddy."

"Me huh?" Colleen sniffled. Eric kissed Colleen again. He suddenly felt weakness in his legs and almost fell.

"You're worse than I thought," Ellen said.

"Just give me a couple hours. All this is catching up with me," Eric said. "I haven't slept too much the last couple nights."

Eric woke up and glanced at the clock on the dresser. It was after six. He heard voices in the kitchen, which were music to his ears. There was a slight knock on the bedroom door. "You awake?" Tyler's soft voice said through a half-closed door.

"No, come in," Eric said. Tyler entered the room. "Hold it," he said. "Let me look at you . . . I've dreamed of this." She walked toward him. He grabbed her and pulled her on the bed.

"Eric, you . . . ." His mouth was on hers. "Let me up—what's Ellen going to think?" She pulled out of his reach and smiled.

"I had to know I wasn't dreaming," Eric said. "You're really here."

"I'm real," she said keeping her distance. "You better get cleaned up, and for goodness sake shave." Tyler said rubbing her cheek.

After a shave and a hot shower, Eric felt better. "I'm really *home*," he said. The face in the mirror smiled back at him. Outside the bathroom door, Colleen yelled, "Daddy, I got to use the bathroom, quick too."

Eric opened the bathroom door and walked into the kitchen, where the smell of pot roast filled the room. "You look better," Ellen said. "How do you feel?"

"Like a free man." He put his arms around Tyler. "This girl here has given me new life."

"From the sounds in the bedroom, I can understand why . . . Tyler, I'm only kidding," Ellen laughed. "Johnny should be here soon; he's working all kinds of hours."

Colleen ran into the kitchen and into Eric's arms. "Daddy, hug me a little more."

"My pleasure," he grunted. "You're getting so big and pretty."

"Like Mother One?"

"I see," Eric said. "It's mother instead of mommy now, huh?"

"I'll be in the third grade, Daddy."

Eric smiled. "So you will. I'm proud of you." Colleen crawled in his lap and looked up into his eyes. "Did you know any shooters, Daddy?"

"No, I never met any."

"Oh," she said, looking disappointed.

"Welcome home, Eric," Johnny said as he walked into the kitchen. He took Elizabeth in his arms. "How does it feel, Eric? To be surrounded by all these people?"

"It's something I've missed," Eric said.

After dinner, they all sat around the table in awkward silence. Eric felt the tension, "I'm open for questions; don't be afraid to ask anything," he said.

"All right," Ellen said. "What about you and Tyler?"

Eric looked at Tyler and grinned, "We're getting married as soon as we can. I don't intend on losing her again." Tyler just smiled. "We could get our license next week," Eric said. "Thanksgiving is only a week and a half away."

"That isn't that long," Ellen said. "You two should have some time alone; it's something you both need. Colleen, how about staying here with us until your daddy gets settled in?" Ellen asked. "I'll take you to school. You can help me with Elizabeth."

"What do you think, Colleen," Eric asked.

It's okay, Daddy," Colleen said. "But only 'til vacation time." A short time later, Colleen was fast asleep. Eric kissed her on the cheek. *She's getting to be quite a lady*, Eric thought to himself.

"Well, I guess I better get Tyler home," Eric said. "It just hit me—my car?"

"It's at your house." Johnny added, "Frank took good care of it for you. I can take you home."

"Let's walk," Tyler said quickly. "We need it, after spending most of the day in the car."

"It's about twelve blocks you know," Eric said.

"I can handle it," Tyler said in a flirting way. "How about you?"

Eric just smiled. "I'll see you tomorrow sometime," Eric said, facing Ellen and Johnny. "All of a sudden, I don't really know what to do first."

Eric and Tyler walked the familiar streets, hand-in-hand. They passed Alice's house. Eric glanced through the picture window, and the vision of Mr. Dawsher sitting there crying after the night Alice died. "Memories are painful aren't they?" Tyler asked softly. Eric knew she was thinking of Patsy.

"Tell you what," he said, "We'll make our own memories—good ones for the rest of our lives." He pulled Tyler closer and kissed her. "I'm trying to control myself."

She laughed. "I think we should keep walking." A few blocks later, they arrived at his house. He unlocked the door, and looked around. Someone had spent a lot of time keeping the house in order.

"You have anything to do with this? It's as if I never left."

"Marie, Karen, and I cleaned, and Frank took care of the car," Tyler said.

"I'm grateful for that," Eric said. "I haven't even asked you about Evan."

"He's great, and looking forward to seeing you. Wait until you see how he's grown."

"I'm anxious to see him," Eric countered.

Eric noticed Tyler's expression change, something he was well familiar with. "You and I have—in your own words—screwed up our lives somehow," Tyler said seriously. "We have to be sure beyond a doubt about our relationship. There's not going to be another time for us."

"You mean—the controversy and all the . . . ."

"Yes," Tyler said seriously. "All of that."

Eric was silent for a moment. "All I know is, and I think you feel the same way, we were meant to be together. I want us to be together 'til death do us part. I think we have to look toward the future and not focus so much on the past."

"I really think you're right, Eric."

"It's getting late, Tyler. I'd better get you home."

"Yes. It's been a special day for us; I'm really glad we talked," she countered.

Eric drove to the same spot they had been to before they split up. He stopped and parked. "For sentimental reasons," he said. Suddenly feeling a little foolish, he finally had Tyler beside him and he wanted her. He lit a Camel, and said, "How can I make this seem right?"

"It's all right. I'm here for you." Eric put his arm around her, and kissed her and she kissed him back. He kissed her again harder. The closeness of her increased his desire. Suddenly the feeling was gone.

"It's all right," she whispered.

"I'm embarrassed. This never happened to me before," Eric said. "I guess it's because it's been so long. I . . . ." He cracked the car window, drawing the cool night air into his lungs, "And wouldn't you know it, it's starting to rain." He flipped the Camel out of the window. She was in his arms, and in a moment of understanding, they laughed together.

"We'll have our time together," she said softly. The rain beat against the roof of the car with a steady rhythm. When they arrived at her house, the rain had slowed down. "Welcome home Eric," Tyler whispered. I've been waiting, too." She walked toward the house.

"Wait, Tyler!" He ran to her, taking her by the shoulders. "All the times I've dreamed of this, and now—I'm scared."

She put her arms around him and touched his face. "So am I, but we're going to make it. Now get going it's raining harder . . . Call me tomorrow."

On the way home, Eric kept going over everything that had happened in his mind.

Eric opened the front door. The silence seemed unreal. He put coffee on and collapsed in the easy chair. Street noise took over the sounds of the night. The sound of cars, and flashing lights through the window had changed his world again.

He woke up in the middle of the night, went to the bathroom, and absorbed the reality of being home. *It is not a dream this time.* The next couple of days, Eric adjusted to the life he had missed so much. Colleen was feeling better, and he and Tyler were rediscovering their relationship.

Tyler went to pick up Colleen at Ellen's house. When they arrived at Eric's, Colleen ran into the house. "Daddy, I'm all better and we're out of school until after Thanksgiving," she said. Her face was red and flushed from the cold air. "Look. It's starting to snow."

Tyler stood in the doorway watching her, "Well, Mr. Silkwin, you going to get out of bed?"

She wore a red flannel shirt and blue jeans, which made her about the cutest thing he ever saw. She stood with her hands on her hips. Colleen sat on the bed, watching them.

"I'd better," Eric said sheepishly. "Any chance breakfast might be an option?"

"You talk to your daughter, and I'll see what I can do."

"Super fine," Eric said. "Right, little one?"

Colleen stared at him, and said, "I'm not little anymore."

"I forgot for a moment," Eric said. "Somewhere along the line you have become a big girl."

"Yes. I brought my bag . . . I am staying with you, right?"

"Of course, honey."

"I just wasn't sure."

Eric took her in his arms. "I wouldn't have it any other way. We're together. It's what I've dreamed of for a long time. Tyler and I are going to get married."

"We gonna be a family? Evan too?" Colleen shouted.

"Yes, we'll all be together."

The week of Thanksgiving, Mr. and Mrs. Quinlin arranged the wedding. Ellen was Tyler's matron of honor, and after winning odd man out by flipping coins, Ted Faulkland was Eric's best man. It was going to be a small wedding, but there was still much work to be done.

Eric took Tyler to the movies for the first time in over two years. Afterwards, they went to Grover's drugstore. The only difference was the young man behind the soda fountain.

"I remember when you got kicked out of here," Tyler said. She sipped her soda, and stared at him. "It seems so long ago." The music from the jukebox drifted through the busy store. *"Fairy tales do come true, it might happen to you, if you're young at heart . . .."*

Eric tried to ignore the whispering and occasional glances from people. "Just listen to the song—never mind these people. It's just me and you!" Tyler whispered. He saw Linda coming in the front door. She saw them and came to their table.

"Eric," she said, with an unfamiliar ring of joy in her voice. "I'd like you to meet my husband, Jim Callan."

"My pleasure," Eric said. They shook hands. He was not the kind of guy Eric would expect Linda to marry. He was plain looking, with short blond, curly hair and a warm smile.

Eric looked at Tyler and smiled. "I would like to introduce my fiancée, Tyler," Eric said.

"I can see by Eric's expression that congratulations are in order," Linda said.

Tyler responded with her matching smile.

"Eric, I've heard some pleasant things about you," Jim Callan said.

"What can I say?" Eric responded, "Linda and I go way back." Eric turned to Linda. "This is awkward for me," Eric continued. "I knew I'd have to face you eventually, but . . . ."

"I feel much the same way, Eric, but I have no ill feelings toward you."

"I work in accounting at Mullaird's," Jim Callan added. "I know Walter Blanchard quite well. He is an exceptional man. I talked him into introducing us and we seemed to click. I only hope she's as happy as I am."

"I'm very happy," Linda said. "Colleen is getting to be quite a young lady. You must be very proud of her, Eric."

"I only hope," Eric said slowly, "I can make up for some things I've . . . ."

"*There* he is! *Eric Silkwin!*" The young woman's voice called from the front of the store. People stared at her as she rushed toward their table. "I'm Kay Hausler, and you're the man who killed my brother. Linda how could you?" she screamed. Her eyes were bright with hatred. She spit out the words, "*Killer!*"

The young man with her tried unsuccessfully to take hold of her arm. "Come on, Kay . . . This is not the time or place," her escort said.

"We have to be going," Linda said.

"That's right, Linda. Run. You've always been good at that!" Kay Hausler screamed after her.

Eric saw the Callan's almost run into Karen and Frank as they were coming in.

"Kay, please," her escort said, looking self-conscious.

"I could hear you people from the front of the store," Karen said. She and Frank took a seat as if nothing was happening. "So, how's it going?" Karen asked.

Kay Hausler's eyes blazed with anger, her voice bitter. "*Killer!*" she repeated. She grabbed his coffee and threw it in Eric's face. He calmly wiped his face with a napkin.

"He's served his time!" Tyler said, with a sharp tone in her voice Eric had not heard before. "What do you want from us?"

"He killed my brother," Kay screamed out.

"It was a tragic thing. I feel sorry for you and your family," Karen said. "However, your brother shot off his mouth, causing his death and Eric's six months in prison." Karen raised her voice. "*Look around you!* There is not a person in here who does not know it—including yourself. *What do you expect him to do?*"

For the first time, Kay Hausler looked stunned. She started to say something, but her words seem to fail her. "Either we go right now, or I'm leaving you," the escort said. She turned and stormed out, with him following her.

"Karen, you and Tyler are something else." Eric said.

"You and I know she had it coming," Tyler said slowly. "We can't run and hide. Besides you're on parole."

"Tyler's right," Karen added. "You can't start married life by running and hiding."

"You and Tyler are both very special," Frank said. "Don't let other people try to change you."

Thanksgiving came and went, leading to the morning of November 28th, Tyler and Eric's wedding day. Frank, Ted, and Johnny watched him dress. All three grinned. "You'd think . . ." Eric said, " . . . the third time I could handle this occasion a little better."

"Just because you're a little pale," Ted said, and broke into laughter. "With different shades of socks."

Eric looked at his feet and shook his head. "I remember when I had to keep you from falling apart, Ted."

"Yeah. Now it's my turn," Ted said.

Maxine "Tyler" Quinlin and Eric Silkwin were married in Tyler's church. Eric felt nervous until the ceremony began. The wedding march started, when suddenly, Eric felt a strange sensation, and his attention was drawn toward Mrs. Quinlin. Stunned, he saw a beautiful vision of Patsy, smiling back at him, as if to say, everything was going to be alright now. The vision disappeared as quickly as it appeared. Later, he would share this with Tyler. George Quinlin escorted Tyler down the aisle. Her beauty cast an aura of loveliness. She could sense Patsy's presence. Later after the ceremony, Eric and Tyler greeted everyone. After all the congratulations, laughter, tears, and final good wishes, they took off for Mayville in Eric's car. The cans tied to the back of Eric's car only increased the laughter from everyone. Eric couldn't wait to tell Tyler about the vision he saw of Patsy smiling at him.

"Eric, I'm glad you told me. Now I know she was there, and that means so much to me."

Mayville's finest hotel was theirs for forty-eight hours. They had dinner, and retired to their room, where a bottle of champagne waited on the table. "You can pour; I'm going to change," Tyler said. "I'm going to make you realize just how lucky you really are . . . I hope!"

Eric sipped the champagne.

"What do you think?" Tyler's soft voice cut through the silence; the incredible dimples were never more evident, with a nightgown of blue satin and lace. Her eyes held the promise of a love he had dreamed of for years.

He started toward her, but the sight of her nightgown being slowly removed froze him in his tracks. She never said a word. All the promise was in her eyes. She came to him slowly.

The promises were fulfilled in an act of love that he always knew existed. He held her in his arms, watching her drift off to sleep.

Later, Eric carefully removed his arm, got up, and stared out the window, watching the lights of the city. The sky was bright with stars that emanated a feeling of contentment.

"Eric," Tyler called out from the darkness, "Where are you?"

"Here at the window, honey." Her perfume still clung to her. He put his arm around her in the semi-darkness.

"You can't sleep?"

"Counting my blessings. Here I am, lucky enough to experience a love that some guys never find and for a second time. I'll never be far away from you again," he whispered.

Eric and Tyler arrived at Johnny and Ellen's. Colleen yelled when they opened the door.

"Welcome home," Ellen said. "The look on your faces answers any questions we may have had."

"Are we a family?" Colleen asked.

"Yes," Eric said. "I think we should pick up your brother, don't you?"

"Yes, I need a brother." Colleen talked constantly on the way to Tyler's parents. Tyler tried to answer the many questions. He just looked at her and winked.

"Come in," Tyler's mother said. "You look wonderful."

"They surely do," her father added. "Yet, that's the way it's supposed to be." He shook Eric's hand and hugged Tyler. "There's a young man waiting, probably wondering just how he's going to fit into all this."

Evan looked to his mother, then to Eric. "We're a family," Eric said, and embraced him.

"I'm your sister, Evan," Colleen said. "Aren't you going to hug me?"

Eric could sense the loneliness the Quinlins already felt. "If you think you're getting rid of these two . . . you're wrong. You will also find yourself with a little girl here, who asks endless questions."

George Quinlin smiled. "We can handle 'em. We welcome the opportunity."

Colleen and Evan carried on an endless conversation in the back seat, amid laughter. You could hear the sound of happiness. "Thank you for understanding how Mom and Dad felt," Tyler said. She kissed Eric on the cheek and the kids laughed.

"You see that?" Colleen asked Evan.

"Yeah . . . isn't it great?"

"Super duper!" Colleen yelled and both Tyler and Eric smiled.

Christmas was a time of joy and happiness. Karen, Tyler, Ellen, and Marie were busy preparing dinner. Ted, Johnny, Frank, and Eric kept the kids under control while carrying on a conversation. Barry and Bruce were arguing about how to put a puzzle together, while Colleen, Elizabeth, and Evan watched in amazement.

"Oh, the joys of Christmas," Frank sighed. "There's what you call a classic example of brotherly love for each other."

Ted held Tina, who slept through it all.

Although hectic, everybody was in a holiday mood.

Later after the kids finally got to bed, Tyler and Eric sat looking at the opened Christmas presents, boxes, and wrapping paper, scattered all over the floor near the Christmas tree. The lights on the tree cast flickering shadows about the room.

Eric held Tyler in his lap. "It's a very special Christmas night," Eric said. She laid her head on his shoulder with a sigh. A gentle snow was falling outside, which made the evening even more relaxing. Tyler sighed. "I should get up and do something."

"Tomorrow. This is our night," he said softly. "It's just you and I." She snuggled and a few minutes later, fell asleep.

"Eric, I'm sorry," she said about half an hour later. "I must have dozed off . . . Don't you think we should go to bed?"

"I'm wide awake, maybe we could . . . ." After making love, they held each other with a closeness that made words unnecessary.

The next morning, Colleen ran into the living room with Evan not far behind her. She had her new dress on.

"Do you think my dress is pretty?" Colleen asked.

"Yes," Eric replied. "What do you think, Evan?"

"Not too bad for a sister," he said, displaying a rare sense of humor. Through all the teasing, it was obvious he was proud of his new sister.

"You two start putting away your things."

After seeing the look in Tyler's eyes, Eric said, "This is normal after Christmas day."

"What's normal around here?" Evan asked.

The doorbell saved his mother's comment. "Come in Walter, it's good to see you again," Eric said.

"You'll have to excuse the mess," Tyler said quickly. "Eric and the other two kids," she laughed, " . . . are supposed to be cleaning."

He joined her in laughter. "It's great. It looks like it should be the day after Christmas."

"Walter, would you like a cup of coffee?"

"Sounds good to me," he said and then smiled.

"I . . . spent yesterday with Linda and her husband. It's good to see her happy again . . . She told me about the drugstore incident."

"One of those things," Eric said. "It'll take time—more for some people than others."

"I was wondering about the church," Walter said. "You going to reopen it?"

Eric looked to Tyler. "I don't know," Eric said. "At times it seemed right, but now I'm not so sure. It's a big gamble—more now than ever."

Tyler stared at Eric, "I decided before we got married to cast out my fear. If this church is meant to be—we can handle it. If it isn't, we can handle that, too," Tyler said.

Eric put his arm around her. Walter only smiled. "I have to be going. Stay in touch, if you need any help call me." After Walter left, they went to the church. The stillness seemed almost haunting.

Later that afternoon, Eric and his family drove to Tyler's parent's house. All felt the absence of Patsy, but eventually because of the kids, the joy of the season touched them all.

Evan took Patsy's picture off the bureau and stared at it. He did not say a word. He just kept looking at it. "We all miss her, Evan. Especially at this time of year," Mrs. Quinlin said. "I know she's with us in spirit and would want us to enjoy Christmas and not mourn." Eric and Tyler just looked at each other; they knew Tyler's mother was right.'

"We received a letter from Jimmy Wooden, asking for our forgiveness. That poor boy is still feeling guilty. George and

I both wrote him that our forgiveness wasn't needed, but if it helped his peace of mind, he had it."

"I think things are back to normal," Tyler said, "Patsy's spirit is always with us. That's what Eric has been trying to tell me all this time."

CHAPTER EIGHTEEN

The warm, unseasonable weather melted most of the snow. The sun reflected off the trees in blinding beauty. Tyler and Eric stood before the loved ones' graves with their heads bowed in silent prayer. "I think Patsy thought we would end up together," Eric said. Tyler had tears in her eyes.

"She sensed things, I knew that the first day I met her," Eric continued.

Alice's was the last grave. "It's been so long since we stood here together," Tyler said. "I never told you, but the last time we visited their graves together, I saw a vision of Alice and Jason, just for an instant. They were smiling as if to show their approval. I really feel they know we're here," she said.

"I have no doubt. Sometimes, their presence is so strong I almost feel I can touch them," Eric said.

They walked back to the car. They stopped at Tyler' parent's house to pick up the kids and ended up staying for supper. "I think it's good that you went to the cemetery," Tyler's mother said. "So many people forget after a time, and it seems wrong to me."

"We're reopening the church," Tyler said. She watched her parent's faces. "Eric needs to work with healing."

Eric leaned over and kissed her cheek.

"They do that a lot," Evan said.

"Even at night sometimes," Colleen added. A familiar redness appeared on Tyler's face. Mr. Quinlin laughed and Tyler's face got redder.

Mrs. Quinlin thought to herself, *it was good to see George laughing again.*

217

The ride back to town centered on the kids arguing over who was the funniest clown on television. Tyler only looked at Eric and shrugged.

Karen and Frank had the New Year's party at their house. They finally got the kids settled down to play Monopoly. Frank had gotten rid of his moustache, and put on fifteen pounds. "Eric, I thought you dropped the idea of your own church since . . .."

"We're going ahead," Tyler said quickly. "In fact, we're planning to go to the church in Mayville soon.

"I know you've heard this before," Frank said. "Do you think there are enough people in Benford to support it? There is a lot opposition."

Ted waved his highball to get attention. "There are always some people against what you want to do." Marie shook her finger at him, "Honest honey, I'm under control."

"You'd better be or I'll shut you off," she said, surprising everybody, including Ted.

He feigned shock, "How can you say that? Sex is a valuable part of life—Oops!"

The kids suddenly stopped the game.

"Daddy, what does Ted mean?" asked eight-year-old Barry.

Frank grinned. "I'll explain it when you get a little older, but I'll tell you this much, it's something you'll look forward too."

"Everything good is always when I get older," Bruce muttered.

"I've noticed that," Evan added.

"I'm confused too, Daddy?" Colleen blurted out.

"Someday, your mother will explain all this to you later," Eric said.

"You're right," Colleen said. "All the good stuff is always later, when you get older. Let's get back to the game; I've got Park Place."

"You see what you started, Teddy?" Marie punched him playfully on the arm just as the doorbell rang. Frank answered the door. Ellen, Elizabeth, and Johnny walked in, followed by Liza and her husband Mark Cannon. "This charming couple dropped in and we thought you wouldn't mind seeing them," Johnny said.

Eric and Mark shook hands. Liza kissed Eric on the cheek. "Hope you don't mind. We're only here for a couple days."

"Of course not. It's good to see you looking so happy," Eric said.

Liza stared at Eric a moment, and then glanced at Tyler. "I could say the same," she countered.

Marie watched Ted, determined to control his drinking. It was Karen and Frank who were having too many. "Well, old Buddy . . ." Frank drawled in his loaded voice, " . . . have you noticed how we keep getting older every New Year's, with a few more kids?"

"Yes, and I feel it," Eric said.

The kids' goal of staying up until twelve faded. It was a little before the New Year and everyone had their arm around someone. It was that time of evening. "See that look in Eric's eyes?" Liza said. She was obviously a little loaded. "I only saw that twice, once when he was with Alice, and now . . . I'm happy for both of us."

Eric raised his glass to support Liza's observation.

"I feel guilty about not supporting your church," Frank said, suddenly on a talking spree, weaving back and forth with Karen holding onto his arm.

"You understand don't you?" Karen asked her eyes bright from drinking wine. "Frank's been worrying, and he's finally getting it off his chest."

"Frank," Eric said, "I don't expect you to leave the family church—I never have—it wouldn't be right."

"Then we're still close friends?"

"Forever," Eric said. "Now let's bring in the New Year on a positive note."

"I'm glad that's over," Karen sighed and they all laughed.

"Happy New Year," they all shouted at the stroke of midnight.

"I love you, baby," Ted kissed Marie waving a highball. "Thought I'd better tell you tonight."

"I love you, Teddy," she said. Her dark eyes brighter than the wine she held. "I'm glad that's your last highball!"

"Women!" he said seriously, "What can a guy do?"

It was a little after one when Ellen, Liza, and Tyler finished helping Karen to clean up. Marie had talked Ted into leaving earlier.

Frank, Johnny, Mark, and Eric stood huddled together, discussing the events of the last few months and the coming a new year. "Television is the future," Johnny said. "It's going to revolutionize communication. It's going to be the entertainment off the future."

"Cheaper, I hope," Frank said.

"Yes. In a few years there'll be at least one in every home."

"I agree," Frank said. "The things we use to read in comic books will . . . ." He suddenly turned white and slumped forward. Johnny and Eric grabbed him and eased him to the floor.

"Call an ambulance!" Johnny yelled. Tyler and Karen ran from the kitchen. Ellen stood frozen in the doorway as Eric rushed to the phone. Johnny gave Frank artificial respiration, while Tyler held a pale Karen in her arms. Mark put his arm around Liza to comfort her.

Frank Karland had a mild heart attack. Ten days later, he was out of intensive care, resting in his own room. Tyler and Eric stood by his hospital bed along with Karen. "They tell me to lose at least fifteen to eighteen pounds," Frank said. "Which is understandable." He seemed in good spirits and looked well. "I'm going home in another few days, but I've got to stay in bed for a while."

"I'm going to put the clamps on him," Karen said, looking worse than he did. "And he's going to lose weight, one way, or another."

"We're just glad you're doing better, Frank. We do have some news we want to tell you. Tyler is pregnant."

"That's great," Karen said.

"Yeah, great," Frank muttered.

Karen tugged the light blanket around him. "Momma, you're going to spoil me silly."

"I think we need to be going; you need your rest, Frank."

"Thanks for coming," Frank said in a weak voice.

"He's going to be all right," Eric said as they walked toward the car. After leaving the hospital, Eric and Tyler decided to visit the church in Mayville.

The little white church was as he had remembered. Some people were vaguely familiar. He took Tyler's hand. "I know it's your first time here, but don't worry, I'll be with you."

"I'm not worried. Just show me around and I'll be fine," she said. "I wonder if you're the one with second thoughts."

"I am a little uneasy," Eric admitted.

"Welcome back, we haven't seen you in so long," Mr. and Mrs. Loulder said. "We thought maybe you'd forgotten us."

The service had not changed. He watched the healers work in the back room and suddenly felt more at ease. "We can use you, Eric," Steven said. "You ought to be in here, like always—and there are many people who need our help."

Eric felt the power he had not used for so long. After services, Eric told Elaine and Steven Loulder about being in prison. He explained in detail the time he spent searching and praying for guidance.

"Sometimes it seems our faith and confidence can be shaken," Steven said. " . . . but when needed, it will come back even stronger."

"I'm thinking about reopening the church," Eric said.

"We're with you," Elaine said. "You know, there will be moments you'll regret it, but if you feel deep inside it's right, you'll make it."

On the way back home, Eric and Tyler decided to stop at Tyler's parents' house. After hearing the news about the baby,

Mrs. Quinlin hugged Tyler and Eric. Mr. Quinlin smiled and congratulated them. Although his good-natured mood was back, his eyes expressed concern—especially after hearing, he was going to be a grandfather.

"We're behind you in your church, but it's going to get rough at times," George Quinlin said. "People's gonna be against the church," he said. "More so now—your license will be a problem."

"I don't want you worrying," Eric said. "If it gets too bad for Tyler and the kids, I'll close it again. As far a getting my license back, something will work out."

"We have to be going," Tyler said. "The kids will be wondering where we are."

"They still fight a little?" Mr. Quinlin asked.

Tyler and Eric laughed. "Only now and then."

Eric sat in the courthouse waiting for his appointment. He knew Wallace Woodstock was in control in the background. "They're ready for you, Mr. Silkwin," the clerk said.

"Thank you." Eric walked in the room, nodded to Woodstock and went to the counter.

"Mr. Silkwin," the clerk said slowly. He shuffled some papers, and then faced Eric. "Your license has been taken under advisement and denied."

"Would that have anything to do with Mr. Woodstock?" Eric asked, as he looked Woodstock in the eye.

"See here now," the clerk said, with an expression of being insulted. He could not tell if the man was frowning or smiling except the tone of his voice, "You're a convicted felon."

Eric handed the clerk a group of papers they had prepared. "Maybe you should check your papers again. You'll notice the application is in my wife's name."

He looked at Eric, then Woodstock, and back to the papers, reading them carefully. "That's true," he mumbled.

Woodstock walked to the counter. "Let me see those." He looked them over quickly and dropped them on the counter. "Why do you insist on this church?" He stared at Eric, and then added, "You just can't resist looking for trouble can you? You are going to push this, aren't you? Seems to me you'd have learned better in prison."

"You wouldn't want to tangle with the right of religious freedom, would you?" Eric asked.

"Can't do that," he admitted, but not with the tone of defeat. "I've heard about that healing nonsense."

The clerk did not know for sure whether to smile or not.

"Why can't we be civilized about this?" Eric asked.

"Civilized!" he shouted. "It'd be interesting to hear your definition of the word. I don't have the time or patience. Give his wife the permit. He'll have to learn the hard way. It may be the only way he understands."

"Yes sir," the clerk said. Woodstock stormed out of the office. The clerk stamped the document and Eric paid the fee with a smile.

The next morning after Tyler's recovery from her brief morning sickness, he showed her the papers. "I really own a church?" she said, and then the dimples came to life because of the big smile that spread across her face. "I never owned a church before." Eric kissed her and went to work.

It was one of those days where nothing seemed to go right. Eric was reworking a job that should have been done hours ago. "What is the matter with me today?" he said aloud.

Walter Blanchard smiled at him. "You know what they say about people who talk to themselves?"

"That's normal for me," Eric said. "I got the permit, thanks to your suggestion about putting it in Tyler's name."

Walter hid his modesty, as usual, behind a shy smile. He quickly changed the subject. "You going to be a minister? I've always thought someday you would."

"I'm not sure," Eric said. "What else is on your mind?"

"You know me pretty well, don't you? I want to be a part of it," Walter said.

"Your timing's perfect," Eric said. "I want you looking over my shoulder, giving advice. Someone I can trust to keep me in line, and that someone is you, Walter."

"I've got to be going, Eric," Walter said. "Feel free to call on me anytime."

Eric went back to work and everything seemed to fall into place—even better than usual.

Tyler was happy, even clowning around that evening with the kids. With the baby coming, she seem to be on her own high. "You kids get your homework done. The holidays are over," Tyler said firmly.

"Daddy, you going to be a preacher?" Colleen asked.

"I'm not sure, honey. Evan, what do you think about all this?"

"I don't know, Dad. Sometimes, kids just stare at me once in awhile," Evan said. "I don't think they understand about the church and what it's all about."

Eric frowned. "Keep me posted. It's only the beginning. You too, little one."

"Daddy, don't call me that!"

"Sorry honey, I forgot. I'm gonna work in the church awhile," Eric said. Tyler turned her cheek to him. He ignored it and kissed her on the mouth. "Now, isn't that better?"

"Now that you mention it . . . ."

Eric added coal to the furnace, and walked back upstairs when he heard the front door open. At first, he did not recognize the young woman. He looked at the approaching figure in the semi-darkness. "I saw a light," the voice said and he knew it was Kay Hausler. "I'm not going to say I was just passing by," she said.

"I've been standing outside for half an hour." She sat on a chair a few feet from him, pulling her coat around her.

"It'll warm up in a few minutes," Eric said, wondering what he should say. He sat next to her. Her expression revealed nothing.

"Do you pity me or despise me?" she asked. Her voice echoed through the church.

"Neither," Eric said. "It wouldn't change anything."

"I can't eat, sleep, or function," she said, with irritation in her voice. "My mother and father are worried about me. I've talked to my parents, a doctor, a minister, but in my heart, I knew I had to meet with you face-to-face."

"I think we had to meet," Eric said. He gave her a hot, steaming cup of coffee. She held it between both hands, sipping it slowly.

Her eyes stared into his. "I know you didn't start the trouble, but in my mind, I had to blame you!"

"That's understandable," Eric said.

"Out of curiosity," she said, a little more relaxed, but still looking hurt and defiant. "I hear you're going to be a minister— out of guilt for my brother?"

"No. I think it has been in the making for years. Frankly, I wasn't ready before."

"I remember hearing about you years ago." Her face flushed for an instant. "You were involved with healing, I believe." Eric did not reply, so she continued. "I have to justify my belief about my brother. I'm confused, and I don't like feeling ashamed of myself."

"You have no reason to be . . . I can understand your feelings."

"It's getting late. I am apologizing, but only for my actions in the drugstore. I'd had a couple drinks, and . . . I can't forgive—I don't know if I'll ever be able to."

Eric finally spoke. "I hope you can, it would be important to me."

I'm a B-plus student. I can't have this preying on my mind," Kay Hausler said. "I don't know for sure whether I'm going to be a doctor or a lawyer. There's something about the law that intrigues me."

The back door opened, and Tyler brought in a tray of dough-nuts. "If I'm intruding, I'll leave. I thought maybe you'd like something to eat."

"I would like that," Kay Hausler said. "I wanted to apologize for the drugstore incident."

"Eric and I can understand your feelings. We just hope and pray that it doesn't destroy you or your family."

"I'm leaving tomorrow—I've put this off until . . . "

"It took courage to come here," Eric said quickly.

"For some reason, I like the word guts better." She finished her doughnut and coffee. "I appreciate you hearing me out . . . I'll work this out somehow. I do not suppose you would you pray for me. I'm very serious."

"I already have. I feel, in part, those prayers have already been answered," Eric said. "In the near future, would you please drop me a line and let me know how you're doing?"

"I'll do that," she said as she walked down the aisle.

Tyler called after her, "Good luck in college."

"Thank you," she said and then walked out the door.

Tyler sipped her coffee, glancing at Eric. "You suddenly look much better than you have for a long time."

"I can't be sure, but I have a feeling a terrible weight has just been lifted."

The winter months passed quickly into late summer. Marie had another girl—Lindsay. The church was to reopen the first day of October.

Eric received a letter from Kay Hausler. She would try to forgive him; she thanked him for releasing her from her torment.

Paul Silkwin was born the 7th day of September, 1957. He was seven pounds, eight ounces of boy, with dark hair and dark eyes. "Let me hold him, Mom," Colleen asked after

Tyler returned home. "He's so little, with wrinkled hands and feet."

Evan stood by the bed with a big grin and much pride. "At least he's a boy," Evan said.

"Big deal," Colleen countered.

The church opening was three weeks off. Eric ignored the usual letters of protest, except one that, for some reason, bothered him more than usual.

The only physical damage was a broken window, which was replaced, and a slanted editorial in the Benford Daily News, which both Tyler and Eric accepted as publicity.

Eric stood, as he had for the last ten years, before Alice's grave. "Here I am again. A little older, but I still think of you. Tyler and I have a son, Paul . . . . Colleen is great. I'm not sure about becoming a minister. I don't know what else to say." Eric absorbed the peacefulness of the cemetery. He turned to go and suddenly saw Alice looking at him for just a second. The vision came so fast he almost missed it. "Thanks for coming, Alice. Wish you could hang around longer." He waited a few minutes, and then left for home.

Later that evening, Tyler and the kids did the dishes while Eric held a squirming Paul. "I get the feeling that there was something special that happened today," Tyler said, watching Eric closely.

"I went to the cemetery today. I saw Alice for a split second . . . ."

Colleen looked at Eric. "I saw her. I think I saw Uncle Bryan too last night." Her expression suddenly changed. Colleen looked like she was going to cry. "He didn't scare me, but I still felt scared. It was like he was . . . It was like a . . . a warning. I don't understand, Daddy."

Eric took her in his arms. "It's all right, honey. He's been on my mind too lately."

"But what does it mean?"

"I'm not sure, honey," Eric said carefully. "Maybe in the next few days, we can figure it out together."

"I hope so," she said. "I didn't know if I should tell you or not."

"Honey, listen to me," Eric said slowly. "It's nothing you should worry about. It didn't matter if you told me or not."

He watched the expression of fear on Tyler's face.

CHAPTER NINETEEN

The Chapel of the Healing Light reopened the morning of October 1st. Reverend Elaine Loulder and her husband Steven were to be the guest speakers. The few hecklers outside did not dampen their enthusiasm. The guest's consisted of about twenty people, mostly friends and relatives. It turned out to be a beautiful service. Many people stayed after the service to congratulate Eric and Tyler on the Church's reopening.

The next day, Eric came home from work late.

"Where have you been?" Tyler asked. "We're invited to Marie and Ted's for a night out. Maybe a movie or bowling."

"I was talking to Rita." He put his arm around Tyler. "What are you making?"

"Homemade soup for tomorrow."

"Sounds good," Eric said. He went into the bedroom. Paul was sleeping with his thumb in his mouth, lying on his stomach with his butt up in the air. Soon, Tyler came in the room.

"Look, he's sleeping like a baby."

Both laughed. "How original!" Tyler said. "It won't be long before Colleen will be home from school. Have you noticed she seems a little down lately? You don't think it has anything to do with your cousin Bryan, do you?"

"I don't think so. She seemed to have forgotten it the last few days. I'll find out."

"That's a heavy burden for a nine-year-old girl," Tyler said. "I know you're worried Eric. You can't fool me."

He read the paper until he heard the back door open. "Hi honey, how was school today?"

"Good Daddy. Connie and I had a nice lunch. We talked about boys." She looked at him out of the corner of her eye. "I saw Evan holding a girl's hand."

"How about you—anyone special?"

"I might like Glenn better if he didn't try to hold my hand. He hangs around us a lot. I'm just glad it's Friday."

"How'd you like to stay at your Aunt Ellen's tonight?" Eric asked.

"Great. Liz and I can talk about boys and things."

Evan came in the house with a sheepish grin. "Dad, I gotta talk to you after supper."

"What happened to your pants?" Tyler asked.

"I fell off my bike and skinned my knee," he mumbled.

"The way you handle that thing," Eric said. "Were you the only one on the bike?"

His face reddened. He looked at his mother. "Not exactly."

"Time to eat," she said. "You two get washed up. Colleen, you want to help me set the table?"

"Yes, but I got a lot on my mind too—girl things."

After supper, Tyler fed Paul, while Evan and Eric slipped off into the living room. "I'm waiting," Eric said.

"First off, I was wondering if I could have a couple bucks. I am taking Shelley to the movies tonight. I know I've been a little late cleaning up the shop after school." He looked down at the floor.

"Shelley being the reason?" Eric asked.

"Yes. I really like her."

"I understand. I've been there a couple times myself." Eric gave him three dollars. "You sure that's enough? It could get embarrassing."

Evan grinned. "Maybe a couple dollars more for back-up. I'll work it out, I promise."

Tyler stood in the hallway, hands on her hips. "I want to hear how you skinned your knee. I'll try to fix your pants."

He blushed. "Where's Colleen? I don't want her hearing this."

"She's in her room, changing clothes."

"You want all the details? I know you'll laugh at me . . . Oh, all right. I talked Shelley into riding on my bike." He hesitated a moment, then looked at his mother. "She got on the bar and we . . . Mom, you sure you want to hear this?"

"Go on."

"I pulled away from the curb; everything was fine until . . . ." His face reddened, " . . . I looked at her legs and ran into the bumper of a parked car."

Eric's grin vanished when he saw the look on Tyler's face. "Why? Couldn't you have turned the other way?"

"I couldn't without hitting the lady on duty at the school crossing."

Eric laughed. "I'm sorry."

"You know what shocked me the most? Shelley calmly got back on the bike, and said 'let's give it another try.' It was embarrassing. Several kids laughed at us, and some guys really gave us the business, but she never lost control," Evan said.

"Sounds like quite a girl," Tyler said. "Things like that happen to all of us sometime in our lives—being embarrassed I mean."

Colleen came into the room, "What did I miss?"

"Nothing. I was just telling Mom and Dad about my accident."

"You're laughing," Colleen replied. "How can falling off your bike be funny?"

Marie and Ted came over with their daughters, later that evening. Everyone decided to stay in and play cards. Lindsay was fussy, but Tina seemed contented to play with her dolls.

Eric told Marie and Ted all about Evan's experience. "I can almost understand how Evan felt," Ted said. "I think all guys have embarrassing experiences, usually with a girl."

"I just hope he's not getting serious," Tyler added.

"Puppy love!" Ted said. "Eric—you're really quiet tonight."

"I was wondering about the pressure the kids must feel in school because of the church. They don't say much, but I know it's there."

"They'll survive," Tyler said. "How are things at the office, Ted?"

"About the same, nothing too exciting. Eric, I heard about the group of young people in your Wednesday night Bible class," Ted said. "That could be where the pressure will really come from.

"I was thinking about that," Eric said. "What can I say? They just started coming. I still get some calls from different people. They are all the same—the work of the devil, and that kind of thing."

"Some of mine are a little different," Tyler said. "Some are filthy. I usually hang up on them. Lately I blow this whistle into the phone. Since doing that, I've had fewer calls."

"Those . . . er . . . people. They're cowards," Marie said. "They hide behind phone calls and letters."

"When do you reach the point of no return?" Ted asked Eric.

"I wish I knew," Eric said.

It was getting late, when Ted and Marie left. Everyone turned in for the night.

"Eric, what's the matter with you," Tyler laughed softly. The kids are still awake. I don't know about you."

"It's your fault—I have this attraction for you, which at times seems uncontrollable."

"This is not the time," she whispered. "Good night, my man.:

A few weeks later, Stuart Praust came into the shop. "Hi Eric. How'ya doing?"

"Stuart, what brings you into town?"

"Cindy's at the house in Wyler. Our renters moved out, leaving the place in a mess. We're back for a while. I don't know for how long. How's the family?"

Eric handed him a cup of coffee, "Great. Colleen and Paul are growing so fast. Evan should be by in a few minutes. He's almost fourteen and has a girl."

"Sounds normal. I remember when my definition of a dangerous girl was one you wanted to hang around after you got out of bed."

Both laughed.

Evan came in a few minutes later. Eric stared at him after he noticed the bruise under his left eye. "Don't worry, Dad. It didn't have anything to do with you or the church," he said. He grabbed a broom. "This guy I know shot off his mouth once too often. We had to tangle. It's been in the making for a long time. It was in the parking lot across the street. This guy started to bug Shelley. She told him she didn't want anything to do with him, but he wouldn't leave her alone," Evan continued. "I . . . we had enough. There was no other way."

"I understand," Eric said. "I'm wondering if your mother will. Women sometimes have a hard time understanding these things."

Stu laughed. "Been there a few times myself. Sometimes a guy has to do what he's gotta do, especially when a pretty girl's involved."

Evan grinned at him. "I won, Dad. I know you're just dying to ask me. It was short. I got him with a left hook, followed by a right . . . After he caught me with a lead right."

"He caught you with a lead right?" Eric asked.

"Well," he grinned, "I made the mistake of looking at Shelley at the wrong time."

"What did Shelley say?" Eric asked.

"Nothing. She kinda babied me." He finished sweeping the floor and emptied the barrels.

"That's what counts," Stu said.

"My first fight in school was over a girl. I was a little younger than Evan," Stu said. "Her name was Betty. A cute little blonde who did her best to ignore me . . . The funny thing about it was this kid and I staged the fight." Stuart stopped for a moment; a smile spread across his face. "He hit me and I got mad, so we really tangled. I won the fight but lost the girl. It was just one of the many dumb things I did."

Eric laughed.

"Gotta run along—Cindy will be wondering about me. I'm supposed to be getting a fixture for the bathroom. We'll see you later."

When Eric and Evan got home, Tyler was in the kitchen. "What happened?" she asked as soon as they stepped in the door. "Did you have a fight?"

"It's kind of a long story," Evan said.

"Couldn't you have just walked away?"

"Not and kept his self-respect," Eric said.

"You men," she said, glaring at both of them. "You never change, young or old."

Eric grinned. "Old?"

She finally smiled, "I didn't mean—oh, I don't know what I mean." Tyler set the table in silence until Colleen came in.

"I saw you fight. I was in the crowd. Your eye's turning black," Colleen said.

"I know," Evan muttered.

They ate supper with very little conversation. Finally, Colleen said. "Evan really popped him! It was . . . ."

"Colleen, please!" Tyler said. After supper, Colleen and Evan did the dishes while Tyler gave Paul his bath. It was getting late, and the kids went to bed. Tyler cuddled next to Eric. He kissed her, and ran his hand along her leg until reality hit him. "Sorry honey," she said softly, "We'll make up for it."

The last think Eric heard before falling asleep was her gentle laughter when he said "I feel like keeping a score card."

It was just before noon when a tall, slender man that Eric did not recognize walked in the shop. He extended his hand. "My name's Jim Cleary," he said. "Shelley's father."

"My pleasure meeting you," Eric said. "Shelley's a delightful girl. We all think a lot of her."

"Would you like to have lunch with me at Rita's?" Mr. Cleary asked. "It would give us a chance to talk."

"I'd like that, give me a couple of minutes to close," Eric said. Cleary nodded and looked around the shop.

When they got to Rita's Place, it was filling fast.

Jenny, Rita's new waitress, took their order and hurried away, only to return a moment later with coffee. "Mind if I smoke?" Eric asked.

"No. Never got hooked on them myself."

Eric grinned. "One of my few vices." He never responded.

Rita looked at them with her usual curiosity.

"Good meal," Mr. Cleary announced, "You're probably wondering why I had to talk to you. I think Evan is a good boy. I . . . I don't quite know how to say this . . . ."

Eric felt it coming. The feeling in his gut was never more evident. "Why don't you just say what's on your mind?"

"Shelley's mother feels . . . Evan should stay away from Shelley—at least for a while."

"Why? Those two kids like each other. You can see that every time you look at them," Eric said.

Mr. Cleary wiped his mouth with a napkin. "I personally believe in the freedom of religion, but my wife feels different." He watched Eric closely, and then continued. "She doesn't want Shelley mixed up in any kind of controversy." It was obvious he felt relieved.

"Have you mentioned this to Shelley?" Eric asked.

"My wife is going to deal with her tonight. This is my part."

Eric looked him in the eye and he lowered his head. "Dessert, gentlemen?" Jenny asked.

"Not for me thanks," Mr. Cleary said, glancing at his watch. "I must get back to work. You know, the usual routine."

"Separate checks?" Jenny asked.

"I invited you to lunch," Cleary said. He took out his wallet, but his gesture lacked confidence.

"Let's go Dutch; I insist," Eric said. Jenny made out separate checks.

He took his with a brief smile, "I've enjoyed our little talk."

"I wish I could say it's mutual," Eric said. Mr. Cleary's face reddened. He left with a brief stop at the cashier and hurried out without looking back.

A moment later, Rita moved in the booth and sat across from Eric. "Bring me a cup of coffee, Jenny. I gotta rest these feet of mine, and bring us a piece of peach pie. It's on me . . . You gonna tell me why you suddenly look like you've been hit in the gut?"

Eric told her all of it.

"I'm sorry. I have seen those two in here a few times. Both are great kids."

"They are," he said. "That's why it doesn't make sense. Why do people—respectable people—have to be that way?"

"I'd say ego, image, or fear. Sometimes a combination of all three."

"I gotta get this afternoon in," Eric said. "Sometimes I . . . ."

"I know," Rita replied. "I've had a few myself."

Eric tried to work, but Evan and Shelley's face kept getting in the way. "Damn it," he said. He left the shop and went home.

"Where's Evan?" Eric asked.

"He's late," Tyler said. "It'll be a little while before we're ready to eat—enough time to tell me what's bugging you." He told her the story.

236

"It's unfair!" she cried. "Why take it out on the kids? What's wrong with those people?"

"Hi everybody," Evan said. "What's the matter?"

She ignored his question. "Evan—would you please get your sister in here to eat?" He looked at his mother, shrugged and went into the living room.

The laughter from the television seemed out of place. During dinner, everyone was waiting for someone else to speak. "Shelley cancelled our date," Evan said. "I called her just before coming home. Something about a family discussion."

"I got a B in Arithmetic," Colleen said.

"That's good, honey," Tyler said. She looked to Eric. "What do you think about our daughter?"

"I'm proud of her, like I'm proud of our son."

"Huh," Evan said. "Hey a B is great, but why do I get the feeling we're not talking about grades at all? Hey Dad, this is the first night at the shop I've missed this week."

"We gotta talk after supper," Eric said. "It has nothing to do with grades or the shop."

Eric told him about lunch with Shelley's father. He did not say anything. "Talk to me," Eric said. "I know it's my fault."

"No, it isn't. It is those narrow-minded parents of hers. Don't you think I felt their resentment toward me? Oh, smiles were on their faces, but I could tell. I talked to Shelley—it may be a little rough, but we're going to see each other."

Eric wondered if there was not more to it, but knew the time for questioning should come later.

Later that evening, Colleen asked, "Why are we having our own church? Connie asked me in front of some kids . . . I didn't know what to say."

"Tell them it's what we want," Evan said with an edge in his voice. "Why should we have to explain our life? I'm tired of people crowding me in a corner." He stopped long enough to smile. "Except the family, of course."

"Where does Shelley go to church?" Eric asked.

"The Baptist Church," Evan answered. "You know that big brick church just west of town."

Eric hesitated a moment then asked, "You ever think of attending there?"

"Do you really think it would make any difference to her parents?" Evan asked. "Not really! Shelley and I will work it out!"

Eric sighed. "Maybe you're right."

The next morning, Tyler rushed Colleen and Evan off to school, and grabbed a cup of coffee. "Seems like we're all running behind this morning," Tyler said.

"I know," Eric said, and kissed her the same time the phone rang. Tyler answered it and motioned for Eric just before he went out the door. He grabbed the phone with impatience. "Hello. Oh, how are you, Dr. Emmery? Yes. It's been awhile. Okay, I'll see you then." He hung up the phone and shook his head. "He wants to see me after work. You know he wrote to me a couple times when I was in prison."

"You can bet it's important," Tyler said.

Eric worked steady to catch up. The day went fast. It got dark much earlier. He could feel the chill in the air; winter was not far away. He closed the shop at five and walked the few blocks to Dr. Emmery's office. "Come in, Eric," Sherry smiled. "How are you? How's the new baby?"

"Fine; active, very active," Eric said.

Dr. Emmery motioned for him to come in his office. Eric entered the office, and noticed how much Dr. Hedwick had aged. "Hello Eric," he said, with a mildness that seemed unnatural for him. "I imagine you are surprised to hear from us?"

"Yes," Eric said. "I want to thank you for the letters while I was in prison."

"I'll come right to the point. I want you to give my mother a healing," Dr. Hedwick said slowly. "It won't be easy. She has contempt for doctors—including me—and about everything connected with them."

Agnes Hedwick was one of Benford's most respected citizens. She was a direct descendent of the founding family. She wore her prestige proudly, along with her independence. From all the stories Eric had heard, she was the woman behind the man who built and managed the Benford Daily News and the Century bank. Agnes Hedwick was the major influence on the Board of Directors of Benford's leading bank.

When her husband died over twenty years ago, she took over and built the newspaper and bank into very successful institutions. She had to be in her eighties.

"She knows about me?" Eric asked.

"Yes. She doesn't miss much until recently," Dr. Hedwick said. Eric knew the doctor's life was dedicated to his mother and his love of medicine. He had never married. "She's going to give you a rough time," he continued. "She has been known to swear at doctors—including myself."

"You want *me* . . . an unorthodox healer, to meet her head on?" Eric asked. He shook his head.

"That's it!" Hedwick said as a rare smile appeared on his face for the first time. "If you can handle her. She is so unpredictable. You should be prepared for some abuse and contempt."

"Where and when?" Eric asked

"Tomorrow evening after your work; about six." Hedwick added, "Naturally, I'll be there."

"Naturally," Eric said. "I'll do what I can. I'll be looking forward to it . . . I think."

When Eric got home, he told his family all about the challenge that lay ahead. "I've heard about her," Evan said. "I don't envy you. She is an institution in herself. I've heard she's about a hundred years old."

"Not quite," Eric said. "She's in her eighties. The last time I saw her, I was a senior in high school. She's a striking figure."

"Eighties are close to a hundred," Colleen said seriously.

CHAPTER TWENTY

The Hedwick Estate was one of two estates in Benford, the other being the Wyatt. Both were located in the northwest section of town. Most top executives lived in that area, on Country Club Drive. The Hedwick and Wyatt Estates held the traditional distinction of being the homes of Benford's founding fathers.

"Getting cold feet?" Dr. Emmery asked, as they walked up the flagstone steps leading to the hundred-year-old mansion.

"I'm not sure," Eric answered seriously. It was starting to snow harder. Dr. Hedwick met them at the door. The interior was about what Eric expected—right out of the movies.

"This way please," the butler said politely. His face showed years of control and loyalty. The massive waiting room had an odor of time. The room was massive. The furniture from another era looked expensive and uncomfortable.

"I'll see if she's ready," Dr. Hedwick said quietly. His voice had the effect of an echo in the large room. "Make yourselves as comfortable as possible."

Eric looked around the room. It was like stepping into another time.

"It's the third time I've been here myself," Dr. Emmery said. "The room has an almost hypnotic effect."

"Yes, it does," Eric said. "It's like you want to take in every detail, and yet you're afraid you'll miss something."

"That's the feeling I was talking about . . . An aura of power from yesterday."

"She's ready," Dr. Hedwick said. "This way, please." Then he whispered, "All I can say is, be ready for anything."

The butler led them into the library. Thousands of books filled one wall, from the floor to the ceiling. Eric could tell the wine colored drapes had recently been drawn open. The gigantic room needed fresh air and sunlight. Eric and Dr. Emmery sat on a large leather sofa.

Agnes Hedwick entered the room and sat directly in front of them on a large leather chair. Her son sat beside her at attention. The coffee table between them held a tray of glasses, and two large silver pitchers. She sat upright. A tall, heavyset woman with silver hair carefully swept back on each side of her head. Her left hand held a cane that looked like a tree branch. Eric watched her clouded, blue eyes, behind heavy, large thick glasses.

It was the first time he felt in awe in someone's presence. Her voice suddenly cut through the stillness. "Coffee or tea?"

It was loud and clear. Eric was surprised. "Coffee with cream, please," he said, with more control in his voice than he expected.

The maid started to move forward. Mrs. Hedwick held up her hand and the maid stopped at once, as if mechanically controlled. "You're excused. I do believe we can handle this . . . Do you smoke, Mr. Silkwin?"

"Yes I do, now and . . . ."

"Louisa, would you please get an ash tray?" she said.

"Yes, ma'am."

"I don't know, Mother—maybe it would be better if . . . ."

"Nonsense!" Mrs. Hedwick said. "My husband smoked cigars for years. I do believe I would like the smell of tobacco. It's been a long time."

Raymond only nodded.

Eric lit a cigarette and discovered that his hand was shaking.

She noticed it at once. "Relax, Mr. Silkwin," her voice echoed through the room. "I'm not as bad as they have led you to believe. I have reviewed your life since you worked with my son and Dr. Emmery. I had to pry it out of Raymond here, who was reluctant to tell me. At times he's a snob!"

Raymond Hedwick's only response was a mild smile.

"Your life seemed to have its complications," she said. "But we all do. Especially if we believe in something a little different from the ordinary."

"Yes ma'am," Eric said, drawing the smoke deep in his lungs. He felt self-conscious of the smoke, which hung in the air like a fog.

"You killed a man in a bar," Mrs. Hedwick said. "I read about it. You are remarried, divorced, and remarried again. You have a daughter from your first marriage and a son from your third," She stared at Eric then continued, "Raymond has told me about your healing. You have a church with, what—a couple dozen members?"

"Average of about twenty-eight or so," Eric said.

"The people in this town have given you opposition in several ways," she said. "I know Wallace Woodstock. He is like me in many ways. He's the only man I ever met who is at least as strong-willed as I am."

"I found that to be true," Eric said. He put out his cigarette. He thought for an instant that he saw a twinkle in her eyes.

"Opposition builds character," she emphasized. "If you do not know that by now, you never will. The important thing is how much you believe in what you're doing." She took a sip of tea and her eyes bore into his, waiting for him to comment.

"I believe in healing," Eric said. "My wife and children are behind me, but the abuse of my daughter and son troubles me. At times, I wonder if I'm doing the right thing."

"That's good," she said. I do not mean your children's abuse—they will survive if they are made of the right stuff. Doubt forces you to analyze things, and that can either destroy or strengthen your belief. It's not easy. It isn't supposed to be."

Eric did not know what to say. He did not expect this much conversation, but his respect for this woman increased. "Raymond and Dr. Emmery are good doctors. Dr. Emmery has more vision. My health is naturally deteriorating," she continued. "I don't expect miracles. The headaches I have recently have taken on more power, but I am going to tolerate them if I can. I'm a strong willed woman, but with a respect for a power beyond our comprehension."

"You have to respect medical science," Raymond said. It was only the second time he spoke. "It's come a long way and is a proven science. I don't mean to be critical, but this stuff Eric is doing is . . . unreliable."

"Let's just see what spiritual healing can do," Mrs. Hedwick said. "Don't misunderstand me, Mr. Silkwin. I did not mean that remark as a challenge. You dictate the conditions." The woman held a very large Bible in her hands.

Eric seated her on a straight chair. The doctors stood beside her. After she removed her glasses, Eric lowered his head in prayer and placed both hands on the woman's head. He felt the heat passing through his hands almost at once. She flinched a moment and then remained still. After a few minutes, he stepped back.

She noticed Eric's hands were swollen. Dr. Hedwick led him to a bathroom.

When Eric returned, she was on the couch and had a smile on her face. "My headache has almost completely disappeared, but I'm very tired—I must retire. Mr. Silkwin, I enjoyed our visit. What is your fee?"

"I never charge for healings."

"A very rare thing today. Rare indeed!" she said, and smiled just before leaving.

"I'll have you know this was her idea," Raymond Hedwick said quickly, after returning from escorting her to her room. "She usually gets what she wants."

"I got that impression," Eric said. When they left the house, Eric said. "I enjoyed meeting her; she's a remarkable woman. I believe she has given me strength in a way she doesn't know."

Dr. Emmery smiled. "Don't be so sure."

There was a larger than usual crowd at The Chapel of the Healing Light service, the following Sunday. Reverend Elaine Loulder smiled, as she got ready to begin her lecture. "I think it's wonderful," Reverend Loulder said. "To be used as a healing instrument is truly one of the most precious gifts of all."

A voice from the front row yelled, "You're a lady of the *devil!*" The familiar woman's face took on the appearance of someone deranged. She rushed to the front of the church. "It's not too late to *repent.* You can *still* save your *soul.*"

A young man Eric had seen before rushed to her side. *"Repent! Repent!"*

After the initial shock, Reverend Loulder raised her hand and tried to restore order.

The troubled woman suddenly quit talking and stood defiantly with her hands on her hips.

"I am a child of the living God," Reverend Loulder said calmly, "and so are you. We each have our own beliefs; why condemn me?"

"Your influence can lead our children astray," a woman in the back yelled. "We heard about you and your Wednesday night class, if you'll *excuse* the expression—*Bible class*! We are here to protect our children from negative influences they may never overcome. We have been trying to get that point across for some time. We must challenge you!"

"These children, as you call them, are young adults," Reverend Louder said, "Why don't you let them decide? They are going to search somewhere!"

"Nonsense! We have to protect our children!" another man yelled, and several people stood with him. "You're not wanted here, and neither is the Silkwin family."

"Why don't you get the hell out of here!" Ted yelled.

"Teddy!" Marie gasped. "You sit and watch your language."

"Now's not the time, honey. These people came to *us*, looking for trouble."

"It's not funny, Frank," Karen poked him. "I wouldn't have missed this for anything. I didn't know Ted had it in him."

Karen finally grinned. "Neither did I."

Stuart walked to the front door. "If you object to our services, please leave!" he said.

"We all have the right of choice," the deranged women yelled.

"That is exactly what we are trying to tell you!" Reverend Louder said. "This is our choice!"

A few people started filing out, but several people stood in open defiance. The two women and the man who spoke up controlled the movement. "It is my duty to defy you and this church, for the benefit of the righteous."

"I repeat—if you continue to disrupt this service, you must leave," Stuart said calmly.

"You can't talk to my wife that way," the man next to her said.

"I just did. It's my job to maintain order," Stuart said.

The man rose to his feet pointing his finger at Stuart, "You're out of line, mister. My wife has a right to express her opinion!"

"That may be, sir. But not here, she doesn't," Stuart said with an edge in his voice. The woman in charge signalled to the rear of the church and a man came up front with a camera. He took some pictures of Stuart towering over the woman's husband and another of Stuart pointing his finger at both of them.

Several people blocked the entrance until the man with the camera got away. The woman who started the commotion, with her youthful companion smiled. "You haven't heard the last of me!"

They filed out of the church without another word.

The following day, the Benford Daily News had pictures on the front page. One of the pictures was the husband of the women who created the disturbance at church pointing his finger at Stuart and the other of Stuart charging down the aisle. Under the first picture the caption read, *"This is a religious service*? The other picture: *Can this be a bouncer at church*?

Eric threw the paper on the floor. "We were set up all the way! No wonder our attendance increased so much the last two weeks." Tyler did not answer. "I'm gonna talk to the editor," Eric shouted.

"I think you should," Tyler added calmly.

Eric stood facing Louis Cowler, the editor of the Benford Daily News. His reputation was that he was a rough, but an honest newsman. He rose to shake hands. Mr. Cowler was a big, burly, dark haired man, with gray at the temples and strong glasses, which failed to cover his bushy eyebrows.

"I assume you've seen last night's paper?" Cowler said. His office door opened and Claude Stratman glanced at Eric, and then gave his editor some papers.

"Excuse me a minute," Cowler said. He quickly read them, crossed out a couple of lines, and handed them back.

"Why are you persecuting me and our church?" Eric asked.

Mr. Cowler closed his office door and re-lit his cigar. "I'm not. I am in the news business and right now . . . you're news."

"The editorial?" Eric questioned.

"Freedom of the press I think is what they call it. What I wrote is my opinion. I thought I handled it with extreme care."

"It's slanted," Eric said.

"Naturally." He looked at Eric carefully. "I have a view point. I'm going to be honest with you," he said. He looked through his door and the adjoining office. "I'm an editor who's doing a job! I have guidelines I have to follow! Frankly, you are in the hot seat. You've upset too many influential people who pull a lot of strings."

"You're told what to write?" Eric countered.

"No. Let's just say I'm led in a certain direction," Cowler said. "I have thirty-three years in this business. This job is the end of the line for me. Off the record—between you and me—crusades are for those who can afford them. If you repeat anything that I am telling you, I will deny it. You follow me?"

"Yes, I'm afraid I do," Eric said.

"I shouldn't tell you this, but you could print a counter editorial," Cowler added. "I'd have to print it. Anybody who can express their position in an intelligent and clear point of view has that right."

"Yes, they do," Eric said, thinking of Walter. "Then you'll print it?"

"Yes, in the interest of fair journalism, if it's handled right," Cowler said. "Now if you'll excuse me, I have a hell of a lot of work to do."

Eric left and figured Walter Blanchard might be just the person to help him with this.

When Eric got home, he walked into the kitchen. "You satisfied?" Tyler asked.

"Maybe," Eric said. He picked up the phone. "Depends on a certain individual." Eric dialed Walter Blanchard's number. He explained to Walter what happened when he went to the Bedford Daily News.

"After that scene yesterday, I welcome with open arms, the opportunity to tell our side of the story," Walter said.

"Hey Dad," Evan yelled. "You know a man named Idlers? He was killed earlier on a motorcycle west of town—about two hours ago."

"I know him," Eric said. Although Dexter and Idlers were a source of trouble, about all they had was each other. He was surprised that he felt sorry for Dexter.

Walter Blanchard's editorial appeared a few days later. It was a classic piece. Even the editor admitted that it was well written. He doubted that it would have little, if any, effect on the public.

He was right.

That evening, Eric was sweeping out the church and he heard the front door open. He looked up and saw Dexter, not saying anything, just standing awkwardly with his hat in his hand.

"You want a cup of coffee?" Eric asked.

Dexter nodded and walked forward. "I gotta ask you something," he said following him. "Idlers never had a church that I know of. We never talked about religion. What I'm tryin' to say is; I wondered if you'd have his funeral service, or whatever you call 'em."

"Doesn't he have a family?" Eric asked.

"No. He's an orphan—I'm all he's got," Dexter said.

"I've never had one. Still, there has to be a first," Eric said. "I guess I could get someone for the eulogy."

"You mean talkin' over him?"

"Yes," Eric said. He could see this was hard for Dexter.

"I figured you," he said slowly. "I know you'd have a hard time saying something kind about Idlers, but at least you knew him. I'm gonna need mourners. I don't want him planted with just me and a couple guys from the shop—if they'd come—which I doubt. Fact is, there just wasn't many people who cared for old Idlers . . . There were times I didn't like him much myself."

It was the first time Eric had ever experienced a tragedy with such a comic overtone.

The following morning at eleven, Eric gave his first eulogy. He tried to say the things he thought Dexter wanted to hear. Dexter sat in front, watching the casket and listening carefully. Ted, Frank, and Johnny, along with a few church members volunteered to be pallbearers.

Dexter had told Eric before the funeral that they had bought a plot together once when they'd been drinking. "We only had enough money for one—whoever needed it first got it and the other was on his own . . . Old Idlers won, I guess," Dexter said.

At the cemetery, when they lowered the casket, Dexter's poker face broke down. He cried openly, his body shook, and then suddenly he stopped. He looked down in the grave, raised his hand in a farewell salute, and motioned for the men to fill the grave.

"You done good, Silkwin," he said afterwards. Dexter looked at the group of men Eric had talked into coming. "I wanna thank you men for comin'. Old Idlers woulda been proud." He faced Eric, "I quit my job. I'm goin' back home . . . We never talked much about it, but I don't think Old Idlers ever knew any of his family. We just met at the rooming house and kinda got along. Thanks again—I'm obligated to'ya." He turned and walked away.

Eric called after him, "At least you cared!"

"Who else was there?" he yelled back.

Dexter was right. The guys from the shop never came.

"It felt so strange," he told Tyler and the kids that evening. "The casket in front of me with Johnny, Ted, Frank and Dexter's poker face staring back at me."

"You, preaching a eulogy," Tyler grinned. "I would've liked to been there."

"Me too," the kids said. He only returned their smiles.

"I think it's so sad," Tyler said. "Maybe some of us girls should have been there."

"He didn't want any girls there, and I was afraid to ask why."

The winter months came and went. Everyone wondered what the New Year would hold for them.

CHAPTER TWENTY-ONE

It was the spring of 1958. The picnic was in full swing. The kids played ball, while the men gathered, discussing the world of sports. The women were busy preparing hot dogs and hamburgers. A car stopped near the picnic area, and a boy with blond hair walked slowly toward them.

Eric watched Colleen meet him and lead him to their table. "Daddy, I'd like you to meet Glenn Sawyer." The boy shook hands after she nudged him. Eric introduced him to the others. His blue eyes brightened and a smile crossed his face. "I wanta thank you for inviting me," he said.

"Our pleasure, Glenn," Eric said. "Colleen talks about you often."

His face reddened. "I talk about her, too."

Colleen just smiled and said, "Glenn lets go watch them play ball."

As they walked away, Frank said, "Now I'm really feeling my age."

"Me too," Eric sighed. "My baby with a boyfriend."

Johnny laughed. "It comes with time."

"Time to eat!" Karen's unmistakable voice called. "I'm surprised you guys aren't ready." Everyone seemed to have a great time.

That evening Tyler, Evan, and Colleen reviewed the day. Eric read Paul a story, put him to bed, and then returned to the living room. "What's all the conversation about?" Eric asked.

"Colleen is asking questions that I can't answer," Tyler said.

"Tell your dad what's on your mind, honey."

She looked at him with that wide-eyed wonder her mother had. "You remember my friend Connie, at school? I told her sometimes, I see people's faces that are . . . you know. We tell each other secrets. She said I was . . . touched. I asked her what that meant, but she didn't know."

"You still friends?" Eric asked.

"I think so, only she acts a little different."

"Colleen, I believe that you have been given a special gift of seeing visions. Sometimes, when people cannot see these same things, they think there is something wrong with us. What they don't understand, they sometimes are afraid of, or think it is bad. If people are really true friends, they will like us for who we are, even if we are different." Eric had tried to explain as best as he could.

"I wanna go to Mother's grave for a few minutes, please."

"Take her," Tyler insisted, "You have an hour or so before dark. Maybe it'll help."

Eric and Colleen placed flowers on Alice's grave. Eric felt like he was intruding. He looked out over the cemetery, and saw a soldier standing at a familiar grave.

"Colleen, I'm gonna leave you for a few minutes. I think you should be alone with your mother for a while."

"You're right, Daddy," she said. She stared at the headstone.

"I'll be back in a few minutes." Eric walked within a few feet of where the soldier stood. He didn't want to intrude, but he felt he knew him. When he was closer, he was sure. It was Patsy's grave. Eric waited until the soldier turned to face him and extended his hand. "It's good to meet you again, Jimmy. Or should I say, Sergeant Wooden? It's been a long time."

The grin was as Eric remembered—so was the serious look in his eyes. "Eric Silkwin. It has been a while," Jimmy Wooden said. "I had to come to Patsy's grave. It's been over two years. I've been overseas for about a year—Japan." He took out a cigarette and offered Eric one. Both lit up.

"How are Patsy's parents doing?"

"They're fine," Eric said.

"How have you been, Eric?"

"Tyler and I got married. We're really happy together."

"I thought you were married to Liza?"

"Liza and I got divorced. She left me. It didn't work out, but we're still friends."

"You and Tyler sound right. What happened to Jerry Yount?"

"He took off out east somewhere. I haven't heard about him for a long time. You discharged?"

"No, I've got a few months to go. I'm trying to decide what to do with my life. My folks want me to stay here. My dad's getting too old to run the farm and . . . I just don't know yet." Eric noticed a wedding band on his finger. "Yes, I'm married. I have been for about a month. I met her at my home base in Texas. I've been back in the states for a few months. I knew her before I went overseas, but she was leaving for college and I was going overseas, so we went our separate ways."

"You gonna see the Quinlins?"

"I should. It's been on my mind," Jimmy said slowly. "My wife Peggy knows all about Patsy. She thinks I should see 'em. I've gotta be going. They'll be waiting for me for supper. I enjoyed seeing you again."

"I hope things work out for you," Eric said. He looked over at Colleen who was watching them. "Remember my daughter Colleen? That's her over there." Eric pointed at her, "She's ten years old now."

"That just doesn't seem possible," Jimmy said. "I'll see you around—may even stop at your shop."

"You do that," Eric said. He watched him slowly walk away.

"Dad, who was that man?" Eric told her about Patsy and Jimmy Wooden.

"I don't remember them," Colleen said. "But when you were talking, Mother and I had a talk. If you don't mind, I'd like to keep it to myself for a while."

"I understand, Colleen. You tell her I love her?"

"I always do, and she loves us, too. I'm not worried about my visions now. I think I understand."

"I'm glad. Always use the gift you've been given for good."

"I promise. I will," Colleen said. They left just before darkness began closing in around them.

It was late summer. Eric had just finished cleaning the church when he heard the front door open. He was shocked to see Dexter standing in the doorway, clutching a lightweight, tan jacket. He walked toward Eric.

"It hasn't changed much," Dexter said. "The church I mean. I wondered if you'd still be in business."

"It's only been a few months," Eric said. "By the way, Dexter—what is your first name?"

"Buck," he said slowly. "After my cowboy idol, Buck Jones. I'm not really much like 'em. I'm gonna go back to work at Mullaird's."

"What happened at home?"

"Things. People changed in the last few years," Dexter said. "I wasn't too popular before, come to think of it."

"How about your folks?" Eric continued.

"Both died years ago. If I remember right, they never seemed to cotton to me much, either. You need help cleanin' up this church?"

"I can always use help," Eric said. "Why would you . . ."

"I need to belong somewhere to something," he said flatly. There was no sound of bitterness, only defeat. "Never thought much about it until Idlers went and got his self killed. He had about as much use for a motorcycle as I have with a submarine—but it's past now. You hear anything from Bryan? You know—those visions, or whatever you call 'em?" Dexter asked.

"I've sensed his presence sometimes, but that's about all."

Dexter looked disappointed. "I'm here to belong. How'd I start?"

"Eric!" Tyler called. The sound of her on the basement steps took over Dexter's complete attention.

"Howdy, Mrs. Silkwin," he said, hat in hand. He stood awkwardly as she walked toward them with a surprised look.

"Hello Mr. . . ."

"I'm Dexter. Buck's the first name, ma'am."

"When's the last time you ate, Dexter?" Tyler asked.

"Had coffee and what somebody called a hamburger, at a dump this morning, before noon. I'm here to tell you, I promised myself I'd stay outta that place."

"You're welcome to join us for supper, Mr. Dexter. We're having leftover stew."

"Sounds good, ma'am. I'd be like grateful."

Tyler faced Eric. "The kids should be home from the movies any time, so we should eat soon . . . It's after five." Less than an hour later, they all sat around the kitchen table.

Colleen and Evan watched Dexter with an amused, curious look. "No family, Mr. Dexter?" Tyler asked.

"Buck, ma'am. Only distant relatives—and most often than not—the more distant the better. This is great," he said, digging in the stew. Both kids seemed content to listen to the conversation.

Buck rose from the table, "Gonna get goin' and get squared away at the roomin' house. I'll start cleaning the church after work tomorrow night, if you'll line it up."

"You sure?" Eric said, "I can't afford . . . ."

He held up his hand, "Don't want pay. It's my way of startin' to belong. Thanks for the meal. I'll be see'n ya." He left.

Tyler, Colleen, and Evan stared at Eric. "What can I say? I turned around and there he was."

The following evening, a little after five, Buck showed up. He cleaned off his feet in the narrow hall before entering the church. Eric handed him a broom.

He waved off supper with a shrug. "I came to be of help—not a burden."

Later that night, Marie, Ted and the kids came over. It'd been over two weeks. Eric told them about Buck.

"It's a strange situation," Ted said.

"I think it's kind of him," Marie added. They all watched television.

"I'm going to get me one of these things," Ted said, and then he looked at Marie. "Maybe a little later."

Buck attended the following Sunday church service. He came early and helped clean the entrance. "I appreciate your help," Eric said. He stopped for a moment to catch his breath, "At times, it's a little more than I can handle."

Reverend Elaine Loulder gave a beautiful sermon, followed by the message services. Eric became fascinated, watching Buck change his seat several times. He finally settled behind a woman and her daughter. It was plain where his interest was.

After services, when the people filed down to the basement, Buck led Eric to one side while watching the young woman and her mother. He said in a whisper, "I'm interested in that woman,—think you can get her downstairs?"

"I'll try," Eric said. He approached them before they left.

"I'm Lynn Goss," the young woman said, "and this is my mother Edna." The mother had short, straight, brown hair, much like her daughter. Both had a light shade of green eyes. Eric got the impression that neither of them smiled much.

"Won't you join us for coffee and cake in the basement?" Eric asked.

Lynn looked at her mother.

"We welcome you," Eric said, pushing more than usual. "I think you'll find the people friendly."

"Long as there aren't any of those scary people who caused that ruckus here last time," the mother said. "Damn crazy people—I dunno what's wrong with 'em."

"Mother! Watch your language!"

The mother broke into a slow grin, and said. "Sorry—those people disturb me."

"Me too!" Eric said, with a half smile. Later after introductions, Eric joined Tyler, Marie, and Ted at their table. They watched Buck manage to sit across from Lynn. Ted grinned. "I hope Buck makes it. The guy evidently has his sights on her."

"I think it's romantic," Marie added.

"What I wouldn't give to be in on that conversation," Ted said. "If he can get by that mother's stare, he might have it made. I wonder where in the world he got that tie."

When Lynn Goss and her mother left—Buck followed them. Ted laughed. "Love conquers all—I read that somewhere."

It was the last day in October. The Karlands, Faulklands, Prauts, and Silkwins gathered at the park for the last picnic and softball game of the year. Colleen and Paul had spent the entire summer on the farm with Tyler's parents. Shelley evidently had worked out something with her parents, because she and Evan were dating steady. They were both in junior high school.

"It's a beautiful day," Marie said. She watched Ted's quantity of beer carefully. He grinned at her, sitting in a huddle with Eric, Frank, Stuart, and Buck, who had just joined them. The men sat around a picnic table, watching the kids play ball. They played cards, and even talked the girls into a softball game.

"I think a young girl named Shelley has too much control over Evan," Eric said,

"Women always have an influence over us guys," Ted said.

"What other way could it be?" Stuart said, and they laughed.

It was the first time Buck took part in their social events. He watched the kids playing ball with intense interest. "Remind you of your younger days?" Eric asked him.

"No—nobody wanted me. I tried a couple times, but I was always the last one chosen."

"I was the same way." Ted added, "How much education you got?"

"Sixth grade, by the skin of my teeth. My brothers weren't too hot either."

"How many brothers?"

"Two. They're out and gone somewhere. I tried to find 'em when I was home, but they'd been gone for years."

"That's too bad," Ted said.

"Don't matter none. We never got along anyway," Buck added.

"I'm safe!" Colleen yelled after sliding in to second base.

"No, you're not!" Bruce yelled back. He threw his glove on the ground. The other kids gathered around them. Evan waved his hand and Colleen walked back to home plate with her head down. Just before dark, they lit campfires, roasting marshmallows and hot dogs. The starlit sky wrapped up a wonderful day.

"I wanna earn money like Evan—my allowance doesn't go far," Colleen said late one evening, three weeks before Christmas.

"What'd you have in mind?" Eric asked. He looked to Tyler and she just grinned at him and shook her head.

"Let me sweep and clean the shop; Evan's working with you."

"All right, young lady. You can start tomorrow after school."

"You sure, Colleen?" Tyler asked.

"Why not?" Evan joined in. "She's a tomboy. She plays ball, climbs trees, and everything else. Besides, I need some relief." Colleen came home the next day, changed clothes, and entered the shop. Evan handed her the broom and showed her the routine. Two hours later, although tired and dirty, she joined them for supper with a look of satisfaction on her face.

Eric and his family spent Christmas day at the Quinlin's. "Grandma, this is the first time we spent Christmas day at your house," Colleen said, after she finished eating a large turkey dinner.

"I know, honey. I hope you're having a good time. I heard about you working in the shop after school. I'm so proud of you."

"I need more allowance," Colleen said. "I'm bigger and older!" Tyler's father sat in his favorite chair, rocking Paul.

"It was a great dinner, Mrs. Quinlin," Shelley, Evan's girl said, "I'm so happy you invited me."

Tyler noticed Evan put his arm around Shelley. When Shelley left the room for a few minutes, she couldn't help but say something. "Evan, don't you think that you and Shelley are getting a little too serious?" Her dark eyes watched his reaction.

Evan turned to Eric. "What do you think, Dad?"

Eric couldn't avoid Tyler's dark eyes staring at him. "I hadn't thought about it. I hope you and Shelley use your heads." From Tyler's stare, Eric figured he broke about even.

Later that night, Tyler said, "I think you should've been clearer about . . . You know."

"Sex?" Eric asked. "He's only fifteen years old. Don't you think you're rushing things a little bit? Those are two pretty level-headed kids."

"You're right, but kids that age are more . . . active now days," she said. "They could start necking and . . . you know."

Eric grinned. "Not exactly." He put his arm around her, "Why don't you show me."

"The kids may not be asleep and this bed . . . ." she said, before he could kiss her. A half smile formed at the corners of her mouth. "Your son can hear us."

"He understands." Eric kissed her, and he pulled her down on the rug beside the bed. "Don't you think?"

Later they lay, holding each other. The stillness of the night engulfed them. "Who said it can't get any better?" Eric said.

"I don't know," she said softly. "But can you imagine us on a rug. It's—I dunno. What are you laughing about?" Tyler asked.

He laughed aloud. "I was thinking of something," Eric said. He rubbed his knees, recalling a certain fire escape years ago.

The following morning, things were hectic. Christmas vacation was over and everyone was trying to get back to their normal routine.

"Paul, eat your oatmeal," Tyler said. "Where is that girl?"

"Colleen's in the bathroom," Eric said,

"That's why I get up earlier," Evan chimed in. "Women stay in the bathroom longer." He looked at Tyler and smiled, "Right Mom?"

"It just takes us longer," Tyler said.

Colleen dug into her breakfast, glancing at the clock. Evan grinned at her as she wrinkled her nose. The day proceeded on with the normal happenings. Evan came home right after school. It wasn't long, and Eric followed. Although resented by a few of the students, Evan was still popular. Eric had heard he was one of the best basketball and football players in school.

"No practice?" Eric asked.

"Not tonight. You know Dad, I've been thinking about learning the business."

"What brought this on? Don't you have enough to do with your basketball and football? I want you to concentrate on your studies. You can always work in the shop."

Evan looked closely at his father. "Shelley and I . . . we . . . ."

"You kids are very young, you know that," Eric said with more conviction than usual. "You two have plenty of time. Whatever you do, don't mention this to your mother."

Several months passed. The warm May temperatures seem to put everyone in a better mood. That evening, Tyler and Eric went to see a new movie, *Marjorie Morningstar.* It was the first time they'd been out in over a month. Tyler had a special feeling for Gene Kelly. "I just love to see him dance—he's so romantic," she whispered, right after the movie started.

Eric put his arm around her. "Eric, what're you doin'? You're acting like a teenager," she whispered. "People are going to . . . ." She put her head on his shoulder and whispered, "I guess I should just relax and enjoy it. We don't get away that often." After the movie, Tyler and Eric went home.

"Evan's not here," Colleen said. "He had to talk to Shelley."

About half an hour later, Evan came home. "Sorry I'm late." Tyler glared at him.

While Eric and Tyler were getting ready for bed, Eric said, "It's only a little after eleven."

Tyler turned her stare on him. "Did you talk to Evan?"

"Yes. Everything's under control."

"I wonder. It better be," Tyler responded.

On a late fall morning, the phone rang. "It's for you, Eric," Tyler said. After a moment of silence, Eric hung up. With a look of shock on his face, he said, "A woman is coming to the church tonight; with a committee, which will, I quote, *Air out differences and come to a reasonable agreement.*" Eric smiled to himself. "From experience, I'm almost certain I know what those agreements will be."

"Watch yourself, Eric," Tyler said. "I knew something like this was coming."

The evening was unseasonably warm. It was only a few minutes before the committee would appear. The silence in the church helped free his mind of tension. *Don't these people realize that their children are searching? Was he overstepping his boundaries, and where should he draw the line?*

A few minutes later, the couples filed silently into the church. Eric recognized a couple of the men and their wives. The men began by introducing themselves.

"I've got lemonade and coffee in the basement, please follow me," Eric said.

Their quick, awkward, curious smiles revealed how much they wished they were somewhere else.

When the committee settled down, Eric said, "I want everyone to feel at ease and ready for open discussion."

"I guess I'm essentially the spokesman," a tall, thin man said. He tried smiling, until he looked at his wife. He wiped his brow. "I don't know exactly how to say this." Eric could see his wife glaring at him from his lack of aggression. "We don't want our children coming here . . . Period!" he finally managed to say. He quickly took a seat, looking relieved.

Eric didn't say anything at first. He looked over the group, and said, "I see. And how am I supposed to stop them?"

"Discourage them!" one other man said. The look on his face showed surprise at his own aggression. He glanced at the woman beside him, who smiled her approval.

"What about your own responsibilities?" Eric asked.

"See what I mean," the representative's wife said. "What could we expect?"

"We're seeking a solution," the representative said.

"These young people seem to have an attraction for this . . . er . . . church," Eric said calmly, "I don't intentionally try to appeal to them. They're searching, or they wouldn't be here."

"A fad," the wife said. "They could lose their traditional values of family and religion and undermine their whole lives."

"Don't you think that's a little extreme?" Eric said. "My doors are open to all."

"I told you he wouldn't help," one woman yelled. She then turned to the woman beside her. "He doesn't care."

"You're wrong," Eric said. "I care very much . . . Out of curiosity, why aren't your church leaders here? I would be willing to meet with them."

"Really!" the woman said. "Let's go. This is a waste of time."

"I'm sorry. What do you think I'm doing that's so wrong?" Eric took his Bible in his hands, "This is the book I use. I welcome discussions."

"You're running a cult!" The woman yelled, no longer trying to control herself. "Or is it the occult?"

Eric grinned, which infuriated her. "The occult simply means unknown and there's a lot in the Bible that's open for discussion."

"You're twisting things," the other man said.

"From what view point?"

The first and only man who appeared under control said slowly, "You would agree to meet with our church leaders or religious representatives?"

"Yes, I welcome an open discussion. I'm not so close-minded that I refuse to accept discussion and criticism from anybody."

"What in the world is an ex-con doing with a church?" the woman yelled from the back of the church.

"Helen, that's uncalled for." She got up and started toward the basement steps, "You people coming? The man's not going to help. I know enough of the Silkwins to know that."

They all left without another word.

When Eric got home, he told Tyler all the details. "From the look on your face I'd say you lost the discussion," she said. "Those narrow-minded people would love to dictate your religious freedom."

"They just don't understand, Eric said. They're afraid for their children, but what they don't understand is that the kids are going to search somewhere. They want answers and they're going to go where they can find them."

CHAPTER TWENTY-TWO

Eric sat sipping coffee, watching the late Friday afternoon shoppers walk by the shop window. The slow rain was slowly turning into large flakes, the first snowfall of the season. The street noise intruded on the stillness of the shop. He felt drowsy and began to relax when he saw Ted walk past the window and enter the shop.

"You look like you're sleeping," Ted said.

"I guess I almost was," Eric said. "Aren't you taking off a little early, Ted?"

"Maybe a little." He looked around. "Things a little slow, huh? It's the first time I remember the shop being this quiet."

Eric stared at him. "Ted, what's really on your mind? I know you—remember?"

"All right, there's this girl at work. A cute little thing. I've been kinda flirting with her," Ted said. "Nothing serious. You know . . . I like being . . . she's just . . ."

"What'd you mean? Kinda flirting?" Eric asked. "Why are you telling me this?"

"I really don't know," Ted said. "I guess you're still on parole, huh?"

"Yes. If you're suggesting a drink, I might go for a club soda," Eric said. "But what's all of this mean? Are you meeting this girl?"

Ted looked down at the floor. "She might be there."

"If I go with you, I want you leaving with me in about an hour!"

"I promise," Ted said.

Smokey's was living up to its name. With the stale smoke and the dim lights, Eric could barely see. The people in the crowded bar didn't seem to notice.

"What can I get you men?" the waitress asked.

"Bourbon and beer chaser," Ted said quickly

"Club soda would be fine," Eric said. The waitress looked at him, shook her head, and took off. It was the first time that Eric had been in here since the Hausler tragedy. He was glad it was a different waitress that waited on him. Ted looked around. It was crowded, with people table-hopping, among the laughter and conversation. Suddenly Ted's face brightened. Eric suspected the young woman was here. "She's here isn't she?" Eric asked.

"Over there," he yelled pointing. "She's with another girl. They both work in the office . . . After all, she did take Tyler's place."

"What's that got to do with it?" Eric said.

"Nothing really," Ted said. "Just something I thought I would mention." The waitress came with the drinks. "Ted, what are you trying to prove?" Eric said.

"You know me. I'm just foolin' around. I'll just invite them for a drink. I mean, after all, I do work with them." He caught their attention, and motioned for them to join him.

Her name was Peggy. She was short, cute, with close-cropped brown hair and big eyes. Her friend Doris was blonde, blue-eyed, with a tan that looked out of season. "Teddy!" Peggy said, "We haven't seen you since a few minutes ago." She slid in by him. Doris sat next to Eric.

"Imagine seeing you in here," Doris yelled over the jukebox. "Isn't it just great? It's Friday night, with a weekend coming up. Who's your silent friend?"

Ted introduced Eric. "Ladies, meet Eric Silkwin."

"The name sounds familiar," Doris said. "Wait a minute, don't you run a church or something?"

Peggy's smile vanished. "You're the one who killed a man in this very bar about two year ago. I remember!" She stared at him in disbelief. Eric didn't answer.

Ted quickly ordered drinks—both girls seemed speechless. "Just one and we have to go," Doris said quickly. "Can I ask you what you're doing in this bar? Aren't you a minister or something?"

"I just stopped in for a quick club soda with my friend," Eric said.

"For goodness sakes," Doris said. "I don't know why I asked such a thing. I'm sorry; I hope you're not offended."

"I try not to be," Eric said.

"So, what're you girls up to?" Ted asked quickly.

"We'd like to go to a dance somewhere. What we'd really like to do is go to Cutler City. There are all kinds of things going on there," Peggy said nudging Ted. "I mean, it is Friday night."

"Excuse me a minute girls," Ted said. "I've got to go to the little boy's room and make a phone call."

"Tell me, Mr. Silkwin—I mean Eric—what's it like to kill a man?" Doris asked. Her eyes watched him closely. "I've often wondered about something like that—I'm curious."

"It was the most terrible thing that ever happened to me," Eric said.

"Doris," Peggy asked, "Why'd you ask such a stupid question like that?"

"I meant no harm. I said I was curious."

"I'm back," Ted said. He glanced at Eric, and then the girls. "Just don't take me long."

Doris giggled. Her attempt at embarrassment failed. Eric glanced at the clock over the doorway. It was close to five-thirty. He couldn't believe they'd been here half an hour.

"Like I said, there are dances in Cutler City," Peggy said, with a big smile. "A couple girls shouldn't go unescorted though." She looked at Ted, leaning close to him.

"Refills?" the waitress asked.

"Yes." Ted looked at Eric. "It's still early."

"We got a half hour," Eric said flatly. The next few minutes fell into an awkward silence. Eric glanced at the clock, and then to Ted. He finished his drink, "Sorry girls, we have to be going," Eric said. Doris looked disappointed.

The fresh air felt good; there was a steady mixture of rain and light snow. Ted didn't say anything. "You sure you know what you're doing?" Eric asked.

Ted smiled as they walked toward their cars. "I just had this feeling to be near this girl for a few minutes. I know it sounds odd . . . Didn't you ever have a feeling just to be with somebody and really not get involved?"

"I know it's none of my business, but I'm afraid that you're heading for trouble."

"Maybe that's the only thing I got going for me," Ted said seriously.

"You're something else, Ted."

The next day, Dr. Hedwick came to Eric's shop.

"My mother asked for you. She's in the hospital," Dr. Hedwick said. It was the first time he'd been in Eric's shop. He looked around with mild curiosity.

"She's not well . . . ." He almost broke into tears, "I'm afraid she's failing."

"Naturally, I'll do what I can," Eric said. It was after four. "I'll meet you at the hospital in a couple hours." Dr. Hedwick nodded and quickly left. Eric closed the shop and went home.

"Imagine him coming to you," Tyler said over supper. "You can bet people will take notice of that. Maybe I shouldn't have said that."

"You're on the spot, Dad." Evan added, "The lady is probably on her death bed, and if she dies, People will say you failed."

"Nevertheless, she asked for your father," Tyler said.

"Yes," Evan persisted. "Still, the part that bothers me is that they will remember that she died after you were there."

Tyler and Eric stared at each other.

"Come in," Dr. Hedwick said softly. He looked withdrawn and pale. The hospital room took on a familiarity that Eric knew very well. Agnes Hedwick was propped up in bed. A faint smile crossed her face.

"It was kind of you to come, Mr. Silkwin," she said. Her voice was husky, but faint. He took her extended hand in his. Her son pulled another chair next to her bed. Her clouded eyes stared into his. "I have these terrible headaches that the good doctor here has failed to alleviate. You helped me before and I seek your healing effort again."

"I'll do what I can," Eric said. "Whenever you're ready."

"Maybe we could chat a few minutes," she said. "I heard that you met with some of Benford's citizens. I assume you consider it a temporary roadblock?"

"Sometimes doubt closes in on me," Eric said.

"As long as it doesn't defeat you," she said with conviction. "Get that hang-dog look off your face, Raymond. I'm not ready to die—I have my plans, and there are things I need to do. I've had Raymond read me the editorials. I have the feeling this Walter Blanchard is the right man to have on your side. He impressed me with his counter editorial." She stopped a moment, and then continued. "His sincerity rings throughout the article." She sighed and leaned back to catch her breath.

"He's quite a man," Eric said.

"He believes in what you're doing. The evidence is throughout the article. I want to meet him and . . ."

"Mother, you should rest awhile," Dr. Hedwick said quickly. He felt her pulse as an automatic reflex. Eric gave Mrs. Hedwick a healing.

"I'm going to write an open letter to Mr. Cowler. I think he's a fair man. The ridiculous separations of the churches defeats progress," Mrs. Hedwick said. "People should find a way to resolve differences. Benford demands it!" she gasped, leaned back and closed her eyes, and then said slowly, "I'm all right, just give a few moments."

Her son's eyes misted over. Eric saw his look of frustration and helplessness. This dedicated man of medicine reaching out to the mother he loved.

"You rest, Mrs. Hedwick," Eric said. "I have to make a couple telephone calls."

"Now?" Dr. Hedwick said, with a stunned look on his face.

"Trust me," Eric said. Eric walked down the hall to find a phone. He lifted the receiver called Ted. "Hello." Marie's unmistakable voice answered. "This is Eric, let me speak to Ted. Ted—can you come to the hospital right away, room 103? I need you for a healing."

"Give me ten minutes," he said. Then he dialled Johnny's number. "Johnny, this is Eric. I need you at the hospital to help with a healing; come to room 103."

"I'll be right there," Johnny said. They arrived simultaneously. Both entered the room with a look of curiosity. Eric introduced them and placed each of them according to the still small voice in his mind.

"Where do you want me?" Dr. Hedwick asked.

Dr. Hedwick took his position without a comment. His mother watched carefully. She had the look of faith and confidence in her eyes.

Eric placed both hands on her head, after a moment she flinched as if jolted by a shot of electricity. The perspiration flowed down her forehead as fast as her son could wipe it off. *The voice was right.* Eric had never felt so much power flowing through his body as he did then.

"The feeling of weight in my head is gone," Agnes Hedwick said. "I can't be sure, but I'm almost certain I heard a snap."

Eric stepped back when a nurse entered the room. Raymond quickly dismissed her with authority. After Ted and Johnny left, Eric and Dr. Hedwick sat over coffee in the hospital cafeteria. "I'm going to tell you what's really wrong with my mother," he said. His voice broke, but he continued, "She has an inoperable tumour on the brain . . . I've known for some time."

"I'm sorry," Eric said. "I only hope we could relieve some of her pain."

"Out of curiosity, why did you call in the other two? It's the first time I've seen you do that." Eric knew Dr. Hedwick. He would never understand the voice. Yet Eric felt he owed him an explanation. "To supply as much energy as possible—it was a sudden hunch."

The explanation seemed to satisfy him. He sipped his coffee and stared into Eric's eyes. "It hasn't been easy for me—at times I felt I should've told her, but decided against it."

"I understand. You have to do what you think is best. I gotta be going. Tyler and the kids will be wondering what happened to me."

"Thanks for coming. You're a lucky man to have a family." Eric felt the doctor wanted to say more, but he couldn't. Eric watched him slowly head for the elevator.

It was after eight by the time he got home. Tyler, Evan, and Colleen were waiting. Tyler looked up from the paper and adjusted her glasses. "What happened, Dad?" Evan asked. Eric explained.

"She's better, huh? I mean is the headache gone?" Evan asked.

"She said it was, just before she fell asleep. She had a peaceful look on her face."

"I got a good feeling tonight," Tyler said. "It was like there was something special with that healing."

The following afternoon, Eric received a phone call at the shop. "I've got to talk to you," Dr. Hedwick said, with more anxiety than normal. "Could you stop after work at my office?"

"I'll be there when I can," Eric said.

Just before five, Ted stopped in the shop. His boyish grin spread across his face. "Hey Eric, how about a drink on me? I think I'm getting a raise. How do you think we did yesterday with the old woman? I mean Mrs. Hedwick?"

"I gotta stop in and see Dr. Hedwick right after work."

"Tell you what. I'll wait in Smokey's for you. Calling you so soon must be something important . . . How about it?"

"I don't know how long I'll be," Eric said.

"I'll wait," Ted said. "At least for a while—I gotta know about this."

Dr. Hedwick glared at Eric from across his desk. Eric sipped coffee. The doctor's expression was not easy to read. "I don't know how to tell you this," he said slowly, "and I don't understand. Nevertheless, the tumor is gone. It has, and I repeat, literally disappeared."

"You sure?" Eric asked.

"Positive. We ran x-ray tests *twice*. The tumor is *gone!*"

"That's great!" Eric said. "How's your mother?"

Dr. Hedwick stared at him with a look of disbelief. "Do you *understand* what I'm saying? The tumor *disappeared!*"

"I heard, and I think it's great!" Eric said as he watched Dr. Hedwick's shocked expression with amusement.

"Do you really think this is a common occurrence?" Dr. Hedwick asked.

"No, of course not. You have to understand, I don't look at things like you. In other words, I don't consider healing beyond the realm of possibility," Eric said with conviction. "You can't place limits or underestimate the power of the spirit."

"The spirit?" Dr. Hedwick whispered.

"Yes. The greatest power in existence!" Eric said.

Dr. Hedwick shook his head. "I have to think about this! I do believe we should discontinue this conversation at this time."

"You're the one who called me," Eric said. "Where's Dr. Emmery?"

"He's taken some time off," Dr. Hedwick said. He stopped for a moment, obviously trying to collect his thoughts. "He met a lady doctor at a medical convention a couple weeks ago and hasn't been the same since. Actually, I'm quite happy for him. I've always felt he was a lonely man."

Eric only smiled.

"I'll let you go," Dr. Hedwick said. "I don't think we should let this out among the public."

"I agree," Eric said. "Good night, Dr. Hedwick. I'm happy about your mother. I like her. She's a remarkable woman." Eric started for the door when he heard a voice behind him.

"Thank you, Eric. I'm sincerely grateful." It was the first time he'd humbled himself in Eric's presence.

"My pleasure, doctor."

The snow was coming down hard when Eric stopped off at Smokey's.

Ted had obviously had a few. It was almost six o'clock. Smokey's was crowded and noisy, as usual. Eric felt out of place. He saw Ted with the girls with whom he worked. "I wondered where you were. You remember Doris and Peggy?"

"Yes," Eric said. The one named Doris made room for him. "How's it going, girls?"

"Another day's work down the tube. Time for play," Peggy laughed, and then nudged Ted.

"One more and I have to hit the road," Ted said. "We're having pre-holiday drinks. Will you girls excuse us for a few minutes? Why don't you powder your noses?"

"All right, Teddy—we'll give you about ten," Peggy giggled. They went off into the crowd.

"Aren't you ready to leave?" Eric asked. "You know you're overdoing this girl bit, don't you? Like I said before, you're headed for trouble."

"I can handle it," he said. "Tell me about Mrs. Hedwick."

"She's better," Eric said. He had to yell for Ted to hear him. "She had severe headaches."

"That's all. You holding out on me?" Ted asked.

"She had a brain tumor," Eric said. Then he immediately regretted it.

"And . . . ."

"They think it's gone."

"If I know Hedwick, he's sure; otherwise he'd never admit it. Isn't it fantastic? Do you really have any idea what this means? Eric—you're a celebrity!"

"We want to keep it quiet. I'm not the celebrity type."

"Oh, I'm sure the good doctors would love that. You can trust me—after all, I was a part of it. I still can't believe it!" The girls returned with smiling faces.

"I'll see you later," Eric said. "Remember tomorrow's a work day."

"Don't remind me," Doris moaned.

The cold, fresh air felt good. Suddenly the thought hit him; *Why did I tell Ted?*

When Eric returned home, he explained what happened to everyone while Tyler fixed supper. "You're a hero, Daddy," Colleen said.

"I'm not a hero. I'd be grateful if you kids would keep it this among yourselves."

"Karen and Marie were here earlier," Tyler said. "They were looking for Ted . . . I thought he was with you."

"He was." Eric looked at the clock, and then finished his cigarette and coffee. "I'll be back later; I think I know where he is."

"I'll wait up," Tyler said. "I mean . . ."

"Don't worry, Mom. Colleen and I will be in bed," Evan said. "Mom, I do believe you're blushing."

When Eric arrived back at Smokey's, Ted was still sitting in the same booth.

"What are you doing back here?" Ted yelled out.

Peggy and Doris were still with him, and another guy had joined them. Ted's voice was enough for Eric to realize he'd had several.

"Running a little late aren't you?" Eric said.

"Hey, it can't be that late." Ted glanced at the clock. "Damn—I gotta take off. You girls take it easy. Don't do anything I wouldn't do."

Peggy laughed. "That leaves a lot of territory."

"See you people later," he said, and headed toward the door.

"That didn't take long. Did you find Ted?"

"I found him," Eric said.

"The kids are in bed," Tyler said. She had fixed her makeup. The freshness of a shower clung to her. He grinned to himself. "What are you grinning about?" she asked.

"I feel you're in the mood."

"You do, huh? How can you tell?"

"Little ways. How about I grab a shower, hold you in my arms, and with a little wine . . . Who knows what can happen," he said.

"Wine?" She gave him her rare sexy grin. "You're on parole."

"Not with you. Besides, I feel a little reckless." He peeled her robe away, and then followed her back on the couch. "Occasionally a guy's gotta take a chance."

Her laughter was music to his ears.

Eric told the Quinlins about Mrs. Hedwick's tumor disappearing.

Tyler's father held Paul, and shook his head. "No telling what you'll go through, once the word gets out. At least you got to spend the night here with peace and quiet."

"Why does such a blessing have to cause so much trouble? Why can't people just accept it for what it is?" Tyler's mother asked. "It's such a shame."

"Teachers' conventions come in handy occasionally, don't they?" Tyler's father said to Colleen and Evan.

"They surely do," Colleen said. "We get Friday off."

"We have to get going, Mom," Tyler said. "Spending last night out here was delightful. It looks like we could be getting quite a bit of snow.

"You know you're welcome any time," her mother said.

"Maybe word won't get out until Monday," Eric said. "We'll see you later. We had to warn you. I'm not sure what you should expect."

"Just take care of yourselves. We'll handle our end . . . It's a shame that such a blessing has to receive such publicity. You kids behave yourselves," Tyler's father said with a big smile.

"Oh, grandpa!" Colleen yelled to him just before they pulled out of the yard.

Eric glanced at Tyler on the way back to town. He almost knew what she was thinking. Just before arriving at their house, both saw a crowd of people in the front yard.

"What are all those people doing in our yard?" Evan asked.

"Hey Silkwin! What do you think of Mrs. Hedwick's tumor disappearing?"

Another reporter shouted, "We need a statement. How do you account for it?" The photographer took pictures.

"Please—give me a chance!" Eric said. He tried to yell above the constant barrage of questions hurled at him. "I don't have a statement now!"

"Mrs. Silkwin, what's your reaction?" another yelled as they fought their way to the front door.

Eric took Tyler's hand, leading the way, as wide-eyed Colleen and Evan stayed close by him.

"Please!" Eric said. He opened the door and ushered Tyler and the kids inside. "Later!" he yelled and closed the door.

"How could they know? About Mrs. Hedwick, I mean?"

Tyler stared at Eric, and said. "I can't imagine Dr. Hedwick saying anything. It could've been anybody at the hospital."

Eric immediately thought of Ted. "I shouldn't have told Ted last night."

"I doubt it makes any difference. You can't keep anything like this from people. It was bound to get out . . . I was just hoping it would take longer," Tyler said.

The next morning, when Tyler looked out the window, there were even more people and reporters in the yard; she let out a scream. "Eric, what are we going to do?"

Evan and Colleen rushed in the room and looked out the window. They were both in their pajamas. "I can't believe what's going on?" Evan said. "Where do all these people come from?" You'd think they'd be freezing out there.

"You kids get dressed. The sooner I can get you to school, the better," Eric said. He looked at the windows.

"Dad, there's a teacher's convention, remember?" Evan said.

"I forgot for a minute," Eric said. "That could be a blessing in disguise."

CHAPTER TWENTY-THREE

"I'll get the phone," Tyler said. She picked up the receiver and looked at Eric, no one was there. He shook his head.

When the phone rang again, Eric grabbed it. "Hello? Oh Walter! I'm sure glad you called; we have reporters here and I can't handle it. All right, I understand." He hung up and turned to Tyler. "Walter suggests telling them that we will make a statement early tomorrow; otherwise they won't leave us alone."

When Eric opened the door, reporters fired questions at him from every angle.

"I'll make a statement tomorrow morning," Eric said.

One of the reporters shouted, "Where and when?"

Eric hesitated, looking over the anxious faces. "The Benford Daily News building at ten," Eric said.

"Are you agreeing to an open question and answer session?" Claude Stratman asked.

"Yes!" Eric replied. He shut the door.

"You're a celebrity, Dad," Evan said.

"It isn't funny," Tyler said, slamming the silverware on the table. "We must handle this with care.

The next morning, Tyler and Eric ate a late breakfast.

"Eric, what're you going to say to these reporters?" Tyler asked. "I saw you tossing and turning last night."

"Wouldn't you?" he said with an edge in his voice. "Sorry."

"I do have an idea," she said. "Let Dr. Hedwick field the questions. He's a professional."

"I'll call him," Eric grabbed the phone. He felt his hand shake. "Hello, Dr. Hedwick. I told reporters that I would make a statement this morning at the Daily News office. I had to say something. I need you to answer their questions."

"I'll be there," he said. "Meet me a half an hour before the meeting, in my office."

It was a cold crisp morning. The warmth of the sun made the day more tolerable. Everyone met at the Benford Daily News building in a conference room. Louis Cowler, the Managing Editor fielded questions from reporters to Dr. Hedwick.

"Calm down, Eric," Dr. Emmery said. "We'll handle things. I know you didn't ask for this, but we have to deal with it."

"I don't know, I . . . ." The crowd interrupted Eric's voice.

Suddenly, Mrs. Agnes Hedwick, accompanied by her chauffeur, walked in. The room became silent, except for the sound of her cane. She walked slowly toward the conference table. She faced her audience with pride. "I can and will speak for myself," she said.

The flash of photographers didn't phrase her. Louis Cowler recognized a woman reporter. "Mrs. Hedwick, I realize what a trying mental and physical strain this appearance must have on you. What is your reaction to Silkwin and your son?"

"Respect for both. I've always been proud of my son, although I'm sure, there have been times he doubted it. Mr. Silkwin, I believe, is an instrument of God."

"Then you do believe he's helped you?" the woman asked.

"Obviously."

Louis Cowler recognized another reporter. "Mrs. Hedwick, a woman of your stature . . . ."

"This has nothing to do with stature!" Mrs. Hedwick's strong, firm voice interrupted, "I don't want this turning into a side-show . . . Benford deserves better! I accept this incident—or to put it in more familiar terms—*God works in mysterious ways*."

Wallace Woodstock's voice roared through the room, "Do you support the Silkwin church?" All eyes were upon him for an instant, and then they shifted back to Mrs. Hedwick.

"Yes I do, Wallace. You more than anyone else in this room, should realize that Mr. Silkwin is doing what he believes in . . . despite the opposition. The same damn thing you'd do!"

Laughter exploded in the room. "That's beside the point! My concern is for the citizens of Benford!" Woodstock shouted.

"So do I, but obviously times have changed. Children are searching, as we all should be. If traditional values were doing what they should, children wouldn't be searching elsewhere! They're not fools! They'll find their own way, and that's the way it should be . . . If you'll excuse me, I'm getting very tired and I must leave." Mrs. Hedwick's companion and chauffeur helped her up and guided her out of the room. A form of respect held the silence, except the sound of her cane until she left the room.

"These questions can go on forever," Louis Cowler said. "I suggest we close this meeting. I have a paper to run."

"One last question for Eric Silkwin," Claude Stratman, Benford's own asked. "Would you care to enlighten us of your plans?"

"Believe me, I have no idea!" Eric said firmly. He noted the smiles on both doctors' faces.

Eric told Tyler all the details. "I've had at least four phone calls this morning," she said. "One was disgusting. Strangely enough, two for your support, and the other was just concerned."

"I'm afraid it's gonna be this way for a while," Eric said. "The church will probably be overflowing tomorrow. I'm glad Elaine is speaking."

She finally smiled. "Since the day I met you, I've had this feeling that something is going to happen, and I didn't know what. You're a strange one, Eric Silkwin."

"Who loves you, Tyler Silkwin"

"I love you, too. That's what's gonna bring us through this," she said.

"Daddy," Colleen said. "A girl and her friends said . . . you're working for the devil!"

"I'd never work for the devil. Colleen, you must believe that. You remember the talk we had not too long ago, about how people react to something they don't understand? They may think it is bad . . . ."

The phone rang, and Tyler answered it. "Hello . . . I guess we could—let me ask Eric. Marie and Ted want us to come over and play cards about seven. Evidently they've worked out their differences."

"Sounds good," Eric said. "I haven't seen Ted since last week."

"Don't worry, I'll stay in tonight and watch over the little ones," Evan said.

"Ha!" Colleen protested.

"Come in, you two," Ted said sheepishly. Tyler and Eric brushed the snow off their coats. "Hey, you look great. Marie's in the kitchen, she's fixing some snacks."

"Great," Tyler said. "Maybe I can help her."

After Tyler left the room, Ted managed to look at Eric. "I heard about your ordeal this morning. Me and my big mouth."

"It had to come out, don't worry about it."

"I think I'm still in the dog house," he whispered.

Eric grinned. "I suspected as much."

During their card game, Marie glared at Ted, "Can you believe this guy of mine . . . He was *kinda flirting*!"

Tyler never commented. Eric looked at Marie, Marie at Tyler, and then suddenly they all broke out laughing at the expression on Ted's face. "Aw Marie, it wasn't that bad."

"I believe you, Teddy. Otherwise, there'd really be trouble."

"Does that mean I'm forgiven?"

"I don't know—I'm still thinking about it."

The knock on the door interrupted them. "I'll get it," Ted said.

"Is Mr. Eric Silkwin here?" the voice said. "Name's Norris, reporter for the Cutler City Daily and I . . . ."

Eric stepped forward. "No more interviews, Mr. Daniels. I have nothing to add."

"An exclusive can do you a lot of good, Mr. Silkwin. You know the way I slant this story is up to you."

"Sorry," Eric said. "I've said all I'm gonna say at this time."

"I don't think you realize what you're saying. The Cutler City Daily is not exactly a small-time newspaper. You're news! People want details. They need to know about you, your family, and friends."

"Like I said, I've had it. Good night, Mr. Daniels." Eric shut the door in the middle of the man's muffled objection.

"I don't envy you," Ted said as they joined the girls. "The guy was here earlier and I refused to talk to him. He'll bug anybody. He's not the type of guy to take no for an answer."

The phone rang. Marie answered it, "Hello. Yes Karen, they're here, just a minute." She looked at Eric, "Karen wants to talk to you."

"Eric, one of those reporters was here again," Karen said. "Frank got fed up and took off. You know all this has to end somewhere. People can only take so much!"

"Don't' worry, I'll talk to him. He's probably at Smokey's."

"I gotta find Frank," Eric said. "He blew his top over some reporter."

"A lot of that is going around," Marie said. "Teddy, you can go with him if you behave yourself—you're walking a fine line, you know."

"Believe me—I know," Ted said.

Eric saw Frank at the bar. He looked up with a slight grin, the one where he'd had a few. "Well . . . The celebrity has joined the common folk. How 'ya doin' Ted?" The guy next to him looked at Frank and shrugged.

"How about a table in back," Eric said. "We need to talk."

"After you," Frank said flatly.

Ted ordered a shot and a beer. "Hey I'm here. I might as well . . . ."

"Karen called me," Eric said.

"That's funny, I thought she was getting as fed up as I was with those damn reporters."

Eric looked Frank in the eye. "She is, but she can't just take off and leave the kids."

"I get your point," Frank said. "As usual, you're right. You know, it's not just the reporters. It's where this thing is taking us!"

"One more," Ted said. "And I promise I'll . . . ."

"Let the guy have a damn drink!" Frank yelled. He got up from the table. "I know I've said this before, but . . . Eric, you are strange, and always have been. Your idea of religion is . . . What's the use? We've been through this before," and then added before leaving, "I'll see you later." He slowly walked away.

Ted glanced at Eric and said. "Hey, I'm ready."

Eric and Ted returned to Ted's house. Tyler told them that Karen had called and Frank got home all right. It was getting late. "I think we better call it an evening," Eric said.

When Tyler and Eric got home, the kids were already in bed. Tyler seemed more relaxed than usual. "I'll have you know, Marie and I had a little wine while you were gone," she said.

Eric grinned and explained his talk with Frank.

"In a way, you can't blame him," Tyler said. "Those reporters will drive you crazy. As for your conversation with Frank," Tyler giggled. "You are kinda strange, you know."

"You're just saying that because you had a glass of wine, and you're kinda cute."

"Kinda! You had better watch your hand. I heard the kids awhile ago and you do have church service tomorrow."

"What's one thing got to do with the other?"

"I'm not sure," she said. "Let's just say I owe you."

"One of these days, I'm gonna start collecting and you're going to be a very busy young lady." Eric fell asleep right after he heard her gentle laughter.

"It's unbelievable," Walter Blanchard said. "The Service won't start for fifteen minutes and people are standing in the aisles. There's even people lined up outside."

Marie added, "They completely ignored the pickets across the street. Ted wants to know what he's supposed to do?"

"Two services. It's the only way we can handle it," Eric said. "I talked to Elaine a few minutes ago, and she's agreed to speak at another service after Steven.

It had been a long day. It was close to seven o'clock before Tyler and Eric ate supper. Colleen and Evan had taken Paul to the movies earlier.

"What a day," Tyler said, digging into their scrambled eggs, "I'm going to shower and maybe we can go to bed early?"

"We should have about an hour before the kids get home," Eric said. "They'll probably stop at the drugstore." Tyler put the dishes in the sink and hurried off. Eric lit a cigarette, reflecting over the day. The disturbances were few, but so many strange faces.

"I'm through," she said, standing in the hallway.

"I'll join you in a couple of minutes," he said, hoping the shower would wash away her weariness. Dressed in a red nightgown, she sat up in bed staring at him. He took her in his arms, and she joined him with an aggressiveness that surprised him.

"How was the movie?" Tyler asked the next morning over breakfast.

"Great," Colleen said. "I'm glad to hear your church services went okay"

Evan said, "You know we're behind you!"

"I've never doubted that for a moment," Eric replied.

Reporters were waiting in front of the shoe shop that morning. Eric dreaded the questions he knew would be coming. "Mr. Silkwin, what is your reaction to the overwhelming attendance at your church?" Miss Wilson asked. The other reporter, Claude Stratman, from the Benford Daily News stood next to her, eager but letting her take the lead.

"I'm sorry; I've forgotten your name."

"That's quite all right," she said with a big smile. "Ada Wilson, from the Cutler City Times. You're becoming quite a celebrity, Mr. Silkwin."

"It's not intentional—believe me," Eric said. "I have a business to run. Come inside so we can wrap this up."

The only person that Eric didn't recognize stepped forward. "I'm not a reporter. I have business to discuss. I'll talk to you after the interview."

Eric answered the questions the best he could, which seemed to satisfy most of the reporters. Half an hour later, Eric faced the man who approached him earlier.

"My name is Larry Hollis. I'm a promoter. I attended your services yesterday and they were impressive." The man looked to be in his early forties, tall, and thin with straight, dark blonde hair. His green eyes were shielded behind wire-rimmed glasses.

"I'm not in show business," Eric said.

Hollis ignored his remarks with a smile, and pressed forward. "You underestimate yourself. What I had in mind is a convention hall in Cutler City . . . A crusade. Do you realize the importance of it all?"

"I'm not interested—even the idea scares me."

"In the future you could build another church—much larger. Your name could be a household word in a few months," He continued with emotion, "Maybe even nationwide. Don't you feel obligated to help shut-ins. and those who have not attended your church?"

The man was good, Eric thought.

"You're news!" Hollis quickly said. "Take my card, think it over and I'll call you." He put his card on the counter. "I won't press you. I can see by the expression you're getting upset . . . Just promise to think it over seriously."

"I will," Eric said. "I really have to get back to work."

"I'll contact you in a few days. Think of the people you could help, who may never get the chance to meet you."

Mr. Hollis left just as the phone rang. "Hello?"

"Eric, this is Dr. Hedwick, could you please stop by the office after closing your shop today?"

"I'll see you a little after five," Eric said. He returned to his work but his mind couldn't shut out the vision of a gigantic auditorium with many people.

"Thank you for coming," Dr. Hedwick said. Sherry had left. Evidently, Dr. Emmery as well. "Is this a private meeting?" Eric watched Dr. Hedwick as he put his hands together, his palms touching as if he was going to prayer.

He cleared his throat and tried a faint smile. "My mother is naturally very grateful to you. She's writing an editorial, trying to bring the people together for the sake of her beloved Benford." He continued, "The results of your service, while appearing successful, will obviously bring more negative reactions from other churches. You understand what I mean?"

"I do," Eric said. "I have had a man wanting to promote me for a crusade."

"I know," Dr. Hedwick said. "Probably everybody in town knows by now. You considering it?"

"No. It scares me," Eric said. "But he insisted that I take his card, and he'll get in touch with me in a few days."

"Would you consider moving to Cutler City?" Dr. Hedwick asked.

"I can't just leave my home and church, besides my business," Eric said.

"I've had a conversation with Wallace Woodstock," the doctor said carefully. "Don't look at me that way. He has asked me to pass on a very generous offer for your property."

Eric couldn't help but grin. "This wouldn't have anything to do with Wallace Woodstock running for mayor would it?"

Dr. Hedwick cleared his throat, and then added. "There have been rumors. That's beside the point. That church building of yours would never hold a much larger crowd."

"You really want me out of Benford, don't you?" Eric said.

"I have mixed emotions. Several influential, respected people think it would be best for Benford. Dr. Emmery is moving his practice to Cutler City very soon. As for my mother, she naturally respects what you've done for her. I'm afraid though, that Benford has outgrown her brand of individualism."

"That's a shame," Eric said.

"Maybe—maybe not. People are curious about you. If you're really dedicated . . ."

"What does that mean?" Eric asked.

"Your concern for people is sincere, I don't doubt that for a minute, but I believe you have changed. I think you like the idea of the publicity and the power that go with it."

"It shows, huh?" Eric said.

"Yes, you're human. Frankly—I think you've outgrown Benford."

"How much influence has Wallace Woodstock and the City Council had over you?"

Dr. Hedwick face flushed.

"I guess I got my answer," Eric said. "Good night, Dr. Hedwick. If you'll excuse me, I have a lot to think about."

Eric got home about six. Tyler was setting the table for supper.

"Another letter came from that woman who had you arrested for giving her a healing," Tyler said. "You know—the crazy one who set you up, and disrupted our church service. She's a very strange woman, and the man with her gives me the creeps! I didn't take her seriously at first, but I'm not so sure now. She swears to your destruction!"

"She has a reputation for forcing her views on everybody who disagrees with her," Eric said. "I talked to her husband before they released her. They're fanatics—but harmless."

After supper, Paul had his bath and was settled in for the night. Colleen and Evan finished their homework, and they also got ready to turn in.

"Eric, you haven't said much about this Hollis. He's got you really considering this crusade thing, hasn't he?"

"I don't know what to think, I've tried to put it out of my mind for a while," Eric said.

"Why don't you come to bed?" Tyler asked.

"I didn't realize it was so late," Eric said. "My thoughts are running away with me." He didn't realize how tired he was—even the effort of getting out of the chair seemed a strain.

"You can't let this thing tear you apart, Eric. Do you really want to be a crusader? It requires total dedication," Tyler said. "Remember—once you start—other people will control your life. You'll be swept up in a wave of public demand."

"Why do I get involved in these things that frustrate me, and make me believe that I'm letting somebody down if I don't do them?" Eric asked.

"Good question," she said. Soon he heard her gentle snoring.

"Eric, it's late. Aren't you going to work today? Your eggs are ready, and the kids already left for school." Tyler stared at Eric across the breakfast table. "The reporters have been to my folk's house. You know—background on the woman behind the man."

"I'll bet your dad appreciates that."

"Not really," Tyler said. "He's afraid of what to say. He doesn't understand your position on things. The people behind you have a right to know what you're going to do."

Eric kissed Tyler on the cheek, "I know. I'm not the only one this affects. You and the kids' lives are involved in this, too."

CHAPTER TWENTY-FOUR

The weather was unseasonably warm for the last part of March. It was after five when Eric walked down the familiar aisle, hoping Reverend Langtree would still be in his office. "I thought I heard someone," Reverend Langtree said. They shook hands.

"Eric, what a pleasure to see you. Let's have a seat. I've heard rumors about the possibility of a crusade in Cutler City."

"News travels fast," Eric said. "What's your feelings about all this?"

"I can't say," Reverend Langtree said. "Besides, it only matters how you feel about it."

"At first it panicked me," Eric said. "I confess however, later the idea of the attention and power tempted me—but it scared me more . . . ."

"I can understand. What's your family think?"

"They're on edge. The reporters make it worse. I do feel better talking to you. This church will always have a special meaning in my life."

"Have you talked with Frank?"

"Not lately. I don't think he wants any part of this."

"Time will take care of that," Reverend Langtree said. "You two used to be so close. Reporters asked about your background. I told them everything I could. I'll pray for you, Eric. Remember—I'll be around if you need to talk."

Eric finished supper and went to his church. Buck was just finishing his sweeping. "You're running a little late aren't you?" Eric said.

"Just wrappin' it up," Buck said. He put the dustpan and broom back in the closet. "Been hearing rumors you may go big time."

"Big time?" Eric questioned.

"You know—Cutler City, then no tellin' when you'd be hitting the big cities. Doesn't take long for word to get around in a town like this."

"You expect all that from one or two healing incidents that may never happen again?" Eric asked.

"If you get the right promoter," Buck countered. "It'll happen and probably much more."

"I'm not sure I follow you," Eric said

He walked over to where Eric sat. "When I was a kid, I seen all kinds of miracles all over the place! People bein' made to see, walk, and all kinds of things, night after night."

"What happened when the healing service didn't work?" Eric asked.

He looked at Eric closely "They made it work."

"You mean shills?" Eric asked.

"Well, I had an uncle who kinda worked with a group. I overheard him tell a couple one night, *You had to have somethin' goin' to bring people back.*" He hesitated a moment then continued, "This husband and wife team was the drawing card. Between being in the limelight and the money, they got swept away with it all."

"They didn't start that way?"

"Heck no. I heard 'em tell my uncle once that they believed that something would happen," Buck said. "But they couldn't be sure."

"What'd your uncle say?"

"I believe his exact words were, *when the well runs dry, you gotta prime the pump*—whatever way you can."

"I think I see what you mean," Eric said. He looked around the church at things that represented the things he believed in. The sudden silence before Buck continued was like a personal message.

"You gotta understand! They were good people who believed in themselves . . ." Buck continued, " . . . until it became too late for them to turn back."

Eric lit a Camel. "Is that the way you see me?"

"Can't rightly say—human nature being what it is. There's a lot of money involved and the promoters can't take a chance of nothin' happenin'." Buck got up to leave, then he turned back to face Eric. "I'm not implyin' nothin', understand?"

"I know." Eric put his cigarette out. "Your uncle was a promoter, huh?"

"Yeah. Him and a couple of businessmen. They exposed the couple one night," Buck said slowly. "Even as a kid, I felt sorry for 'em. I could tell the couple really hated what they were doin' and knew they had gone too far."

"The couple couldn't leave?" Eric asked.

"To do what? They had nothin'. I thought for a while there's gonna be a riot. I'm here to tell you things got rough. The people almost tore the place up. The guards sure earned their money that night," Buck said. "Course the promoters blamed the healers. The couple disappeared, and far as I know, they left the country. My uncle and his partners just looked for someone else."

Eric looked into his eyes. "They always make it work, huh?"

"Sure. People can't help looking for miracles, being's everybody's got some kinda problem or other."

"Eric," Tyler's voice called from the back door.

"I'll be there in a few minutes," Eric said. "Buck, I appreciate your telling me all of this. It'll give me a lot to think about."

"Pleasure. I gotta be goin'. Lynn's expectin' me for supper."

Eric grinned. "You two hitting if off pretty good?"

"Well . . . there's her mother, but I guess it comes with the territory. I'm sayin' good night."

"Good night, Buck."

Eric told Tyler about his conversation with Buck.

"Ironic isn't it," Tyler said with a smile. "Considering the source and the timing? I get the feeling that Buck helped you clear up your confusion . . . You're not thinking about moving because of the crusade are you?"

"No. Whatever I do will be here in Benford." The smile of relief on her face enforced his decision, just before the phone rang. Eric answered it.

"No. I'm sorry, Mr. Hollis. I know, but my decision is final. The people who want my help will have to come here. Yes, I'm sure." Tyler and the kids listened carefully to Eric's conversation before he returned to the table. "This is one time I know I'm doing the right thing," he said. He looked at their smiling faces. Evidently, they agreed.

It was the quiet time of evening after the kids were in bed.

"You look relieved," Tyler said.

"I am," Eric answered. "The fear of not being able to deliver for people, who expect so much, scares me."

"I guess it was meant to be that you had this conversation with Buck," Tyler added. "Everything fell into place at the right time."

"Yes. Those people who need help . . . I could never fake it!"

Tyler grinned. "You're an old softie."

"True," Eric countered. "Especially where you're concerned."

Next morning, Colleen and Evan were all smiles. "Guess what? Shelley's parents invited us over for supper tonight. Dad, I think you're becoming a power to be reckoned with," Evan said.

"I think Mrs. Hedwick's appearance and support had more to do with it than I did. She has such power, even when her name is mentioned."

"You too, Dad," Colleen said. "You have power, too."

"Thank you, honey

Mrs. Hedwick's editorial ran on the front page of the Benford Daily News. She called for the people of Benford to close ranks, dissolve their differences, and create the kind of community that could unite instead of separate.

"Very impressive," Tyler said that evening.

"I talked to Dr. Hedwick this afternoon. He actually seemed disappointed that I rejected the offer to move to Cutler City," Eric said.

"He's embarrassed. He's the type of man who would be."

"Is everything going to be all right?" Colleen asked. "I mean, are the people going to be kind to us again?"

"Keep your guard up, honey," Eric said. "There are still people who want me and the church out of here."

"Well, Connie and her friends seemed nicer."

"I'm happy for you. How about Glenn?"

"He's always been nice, Daddy."

Eric had just opened the shop when Mr. Woodstock stormed through the door, a newspaper in his hand. "Don't be fooled by what you read in this paper," he said.

He waved the article in Eric's face. "It sounds good, but you just don't fit—you never will."

"What bothers you is that you see some of you in me, and it bugs you," Erik said with a grin. "You're out to impress the right people. Are you really planning to run for mayor?"

Woodstock's face flushed a little. "I'm my own man. I admit I've talked to some people and the idea appeals to me. Why not?" Woodstock said. "Mayor Stevens is afraid to make a stand because of Agnes Hedwick . . . Besides he's too old."

"So you know, I've closed my Bible Study Classes through the week," Eric said.

"Not enough!" Woodstock bellowed. "You can't understand that people don't want you or your breed of church. This is a small town. Everything is reflected by the whole community."

Eric grinned. "You're even beginning to sound like a politician . . . Tell me, Mr. Woodstock—when did you lose that independence you *were* so famous for?"

His answer was the look of anger. "You never learn, do you?" He stormed out of the shop.

Mrs. Agnes Hedwick died October 27, 1959. She passed away quietly in her sleep.

Three days later, Benford held its largest funeral in years. Local businesses closed from 11:00 a.m. until after the funeral. Eric attended, ignoring the stares of Benford's prominent citizens. He saw Raymond Hedwick briefly. It was the first time he ever saw tears in his eyes.

The following day Tyler joined Eric for lunch at Rita's. The curiosity of the last several weeks had vanished. "Fame is only temporary," Tyler said. "I mean, how long do you think you should remain a celebrity?"

Rita laughed. She joined them for coffee "Eric's unique—that's for sure."

"That he is," Tyler said still smiling. "You just have to roll with his moods."

"I liked Mrs. Hedwick," Eric said. "She was strong, independent, and proud. She's one reason I decided to stick with the church. It's what she would have done. As for Wallace Woodstock—he wants to be mayor in the worse way."

"I guess he feels that could be a tribute to his life," Rita said. "I hear he's got a good chance to make it."

"You know his family?" Eric asked.

"Not really. I met his wife years ago before she passed away. Naturally, I've seen his sons in here several times." Rita stopped and asked the waitress to refill their coffee. "They used to be pretty wild," she continued. "However, I understand the eldest—Lucas—is studying Law. The other son—John—is helping run his farm."

"He's quite a character," Eric said.

"That he is," Rita added. "Just don't ever under estimate him."

"Believe me. I have no intention of doing so," Eric said.

The following Sunday, attendance at the Chapel of the Healing Light had fallen off to a few local members. The whole town of Benford still seemed to be in a state of depression.

Thanksgiving dinner was held at Karen and Frank's house. The kids were playing cards. Ted, Frank, and Eric tried to keep the kids under control while carrying on a conversation. Barry and Bruce were arguing over which was the highest hand, three of a kind, or two pair . . . while Colleen and Evan looked on in amusement.

"Just think, in another month Christmas will be here," Frank sighed. "You sure it's been a year since the last one."

Eric and Ted laughed.

"What do you think of Elvis?" Ted asked. "He's as popular today as he was when he got started."

"He'll eventually burn out, you wait and see," Frank said.

"You're wrong," Ted argued. "Look at the change in the young people. He'll always be the king."

Frank grinned. "Then there's Marilyn."

"Don't you wish?" Karen said. "I'm going to help with the dishes. It's getting late."

Later that evening, after the kids finally got to bed, Eric relaxed with Tyler on his lap. "Holding you makes it a special Thanksgiving night," he said. She laid her head on his shoulder with a sigh. A gentle snow was falling outside, which made the evening even more relaxing. She snuggled and a few minutes later fell asleep.

Later, Tyler said, "I'm sorry, I dozed off. Don't you think we should go to bed?"

"I think we should do something," Eric said.

She grinned. "Is this going to be one of those collecting nights?"

"Yes, where's your holiday spirit?"

She smiled again, "More physical than spiritual, I imagine."

Eric smiled. "Why not both?"

A few days after Thanksgiving, Tyler walked around the shop counter and kissed Eric on the cheek. "Take me to lunch," she said. "I feel like today I should be catered to."

"My pleasure, lady. Any special reason for this sudden joy?"

"It's just a nice day," she said with a big smile. Later at Rita's, Tyler wiped her mouth with a napkin and took another bite of her cheeseburger.

"How you two doing?" Rita asked.

"Great," Tyler answered quickly. "And you?"

"Better. It brightens my day to see you two looking happy. I need all the help I can get.

"I'm wound up," Tyler said. "Later this afternoon, Ted's going to drive Marie and me to Cindy's house, to see some dresses she's made. Stuart's on a construction job. You don't mind, do you Eric?"

Eric grinned. "I guess I can manage."

"You grab a sandwich until I get home. Colleen and Evan are having supper with Shelley, while Ellen watches Paul. I'll see you later." She glanced at the clock, and then winked at him. "You work hard this afternoon." She glanced at the people surrounding them, and then with a sudden look of rare mischief added, "My lover!" Tyler glanced over her shoulder and laughed. Eric looked at the people staring at him, shrugged, and finished his coffee.

Eric read the paper. The silence in the house seemed strange. He thought of turning on the television, but the rare quietness relaxed him. He sat in the big, overstuffed chair, dozing off almost immediately.

The knocking on the door shook him out of a deep sleep. He slowly got up, went to the door, and then he saw the flashing lights on the police car. It was seven-thirty. "Eric, there's been an accident," Sergeant Hullman said. "Ted, his wife, and your wife . . . They've been rushed to the hospital. Ted and Marie have slight injuries, but I'm not sure about your wife . . . ." Eric called Ellen to tell her what happened, and immediately went to the hospital

The next couple of hours, Eric waited beside Tyler's bed. She was in a coma. Marie and Ted stood beside him. "It was my fault," Ted moaned. The slight bandage over his left eye looked almost comical. Marie had her arm in a sling.

"Ted, you were drinking, weren't you?"

"The girls were busy, so I stopped in at the bar for a couple. I got carried away and . . . ."

"You're always getting carried away!" Eric yelled. "When are you going to grow up?"

Colleen and Evan entered the room. "How's Mom?" Evan asked. "Aunt Ellen told us what happened." Colleen and Evan stared at their mother in silence.

"I feel terrible!" Ted moaned. "I didn't see the other car. If there's anything I can do," Ted whispered.

"You've already done it!" Eric snapped. For the first time in his life, he felt like hitting him.

"I'm sorry, you'll have to leave the room for a few minutes," the nurse said to break the tension. Ted put his head down and slowly walked out with a tearful Marie following him.

"Accidents happen," Evan said quickly.

"She's going to be all right, Dad. I just know it," Colleen added. The three of them walked out into the corridor.

Tyler's parents entered the hospital hallway, with Ellen and Johnny right behind them. "We just heard. Is she . . . ."

"She's in a coma," Eric said. "That's all I know."

"You can go in now," the nurse said. Other than a bruise above her left eye, there was no visible sign of injury. They all sat around her bed in silence.

After a couple hours, Eric whispered, "There's nothing anyone can do."

"I guess we should go," Ellen said. "Call us if you need anything, or there's any change at all."

"Same with us," Mrs. Quinlin said. "Don't worry about the kids; they can stay with us tonight."

"I'll relieve you in the morning," Tyler's father said. "You have to keep your strength up for her and yourself." Reluctantly they all left.

The daily sounds of the hospital gave way to an occasional call over the intercom. Eric sat beside Tyler and took her hand, watching for the slightest change. "I'm here, Tyler. You gotta pull through this thing for me and the kids." He lowered his head, and prayed.

He heard the door open and Dr. Hedwick walked in the room. "We're doing everything possible," he said with his usual authoritative tone. "She's in God's hands."

"I'm scared," Eric, mumbled grasping Tyler's hand. "I'm supposed to be strong in faith, but I'm sitting here like a scared child."

"I never told you," Dr. Hedwick said, "but in some ways, I admired your strength to carry on in the face of opposition."

Eric never answered. That was the last thing he remembered before dozing off.

After Tyler's father relieved him the next morning, he left. When he got home, Colleen and Evan met him at the door. "She's the same," Eric said.

"We talked it over and prayed together last night," Evan said. "She's going to make it, Dad. I just know it."

Dad, I fixed you some breakfast," Colleen said. "We're going to the hospital. We'll see you later." Eric pushed aside his eggs. He shaved, showered, and lay across the bed, staring at the ceiling, until he drifted off to sleep. The phone rang, and Eric jumped off the bed with a feeling of panic. He picked up the receiver.

"Is Agnes there?" the voice asked.

"Who?" Eric asked with an edge in his voice.

"Isn't this the Wilson residence?"

"No, it isn't!"

"I'm sorry, I must have the wrong number," the woman said.

"Not as sorry as I am," Eric mumbled to himself. He went in the kitchen and glanced at the clock. "I should've thanked the lady for waking me," he said, "and here I am talking to myself."

He called the hospital; there was no change. Eric decided to go to the Chapel of The Healing Light. There, he lit a candle, and watched the flickering flame. "You know what's in my mind and heart," Eric said loudly. The sounds of his words echoed in the silence. "I'm asking you, Lord, to heal her—Tyler's presence keeps us going . . . She's the only remaining child of her parents."

He opened his eyes and the brilliant white light he hadn't seen for so long appeared for an instant. Eric heard the still small voice. *Have faith.* He left the church with a newfound confidence and hurried to the hospital.

When Eric entered Tyler's room, Colleen and Evan were by her bedside. "I know Mom. She's a fighter, there's no way this thing is going to beat her!"

About an hour later, Dr. Hedwick came in and nodded. He checked Tyler's chart and glanced at the three of them. "I wish I could tell you something, but there's no change."

The early afternoon hours faded into evening. It was just before six, when Karen and Frank came. "We were praying," Frank said. "Walter is taking care of the shop; he said to have faith."

"Have you got it, Eric?" Karen asked. "Faith, I mean!"

"What?" Eric asked "Yes, but it's hard to when I see her lying there, looking so helpless."

"That's when you need it the most," Karen continued. "I know you—remember? You give healings. Deep down, I don't think you really believe in yourself."

"You're really unloading on me," Eric said, "but I'll think about what you said."

"See what I mean!" Karen said. "You're always thinking. Make a commitment. For once, get your ego out of the way and maybe you'll discover what you're really supposed to do!"

Eric looked at Karen and then Frank. He put his hand on Tyler's head. "You're right, why couldn't I see that long ago?"

"Cause maybe you're human like the rest of us," Frank said with a smile.

CHAPTER TWENTY-FIVE

Eric settled back in the chair beside Tyler's bed and read a magazine for a few minutes until his eyes bothered him. Either he heard Tyler's voice or he was dreaming. He took her hand and felt the slight movement of her fingers. Her eyes opened. "Tyler," he said softly, "Tyler, can you talk to me?"

She slowly turned her head to face him. "Eric," she said softly.

He took her in his arms. "Thank God," he said.

"How long was I unconscious?"

"A couple of days."

"Are Marie and Ted all right?"

"Marie's got a sprained elbow and Ted . . . He's bruised."

"It happened so fast. I hope you're not blaming Ted—that car ran a stop sign. He pulled right out in front of us . . . Ted couldn't avoid him."

"Maybe you'd better rest a few minutes. I have calls to make," Eric said. "There're a lot of people who've been praying for you."

"I've been resting long enough and . . . ."

The door opened and Karen rushed to Tyler's bedside. "Tyler—you're conscious."

"Go ahead and make your calls Eric. We'll be fine," Karen said. "I dropped the boys off at the movies and thought I'd stop in for a few minutes."

Eric called Colleen and Evan, Tyler's parents, Ellen and Frank, and finally Marie.

"I'm so happy," Marie said. "We have been praying. Hasn't Ted shown up at the hospital?"

"No. It's my fault," Eric said. "I said some things I shouldn't have."

"Eric, he's really hurting . . . ."

"I'll find him. I'll check with you later." He saw the kids coming in the room, followed by Ellen and Johnny. "I'm gonna take off for a while," Eric said. He kissed Tyler's forehead, and said. "Turn on that smile. You have a room full of company. I've gotta find Ted."

Eric checked Smokey's. Ted was sitting at the end of the bar, staring at a shot of whiskey. Eric fought his way through the crowd. He elbowed his way to Ted and the man at the next stool. The man glared at him until the blonde-haired woman recaptured his attention.

"What's a guy like you doing in a place like this?" Eric asked.

The blonde stopped talking long enough to look their way, then said to the guy draped around her, "Did'ya hear what he said?"

"Naw baby. I was looking at you?"

"Flatterer," she said.

"Hey, there's a table, let's grab it." The guy took the blonde's hand and they disappeared in the crowd.

"Eric, I'm . . . What are you doing here?"

"What'll you have?" The bartender asked." The same thing he's having," Eric said. "Marie's worried."

"She shouldn't have called you. I haven't touched this yet."

"Your friend's right," the bartender said with an edge in his voice. "He's just been staring at it—you know—just taking up room!"

"Let's get out of this place." Eric said.

"I'm ready," Ted said. "You really surprise me. You know that?" They fought their way to the front door, through the maze of people. The mellow voice of Nat King Cole's "Mona Lisa" seemed out of place.

The fresh air was a welcome relief. "Tyler's conscious, Ted, and doing fine," Eric said. "She has a room full of people with her."

"I'm so thankful. I was going to ask you awhile ago, but I was afraid to—I felt so guilty."

"Forgive me, Ted," Eric said. "Tyler told me about the guy running the stop light."

"Forget it. I know how I'd feel if it was Marie," Ted said. "I was mentally sending Tyler a healing. I hope it helped."

"Maybe your mental healing made the difference," Eric added.

"I wish I could believe that . . . I sometimes feel my life is pointless."

Eric put his hand on Ted shoulder. "At times I think we all do. Karen unloaded on me pretty well earlier. It gave me a lot to think about."

Colleen and Evan were the only ones left in Tyler's room by the time Eric and Ted returned.

Ted kissed Tyler on the forehead and embraced her. "Marie will see you first thing in the morning," he said hurriedly. "I'm sorry it happened. I felt so . . . ."

"I'm fine," Tyler said. "The three of us were lucky. Now, if you people will take off, I want to rest. I'll see you tomorrow."

Eric smiled. "You're the boss."

"I'll remember you said that," Tyler said jokingly.

"Dad, you want anything to eat?" Colleen asked.

"Not right now. All at once, I feel exhausted. "Anything special going on with you two, the last three days?" Eric noticed Colleen motioning to Evan. She quickly went to the refrigerator and got a glass of milk.

"Why do I feel I'm missing something?" Eric asked. It was obvious that Evan was stalling. "You gonna tell me what's going on?"

He grinned. "I told Colleen I would talk to you. It seems her and Glenn want a movie date; don't laugh. It's a big deal to her."

"She's eleven years old!" Eric said. "I'll think about it. Anything else?"

"No. I'm gonna hit the sack," Evan said

Eric walked in the church, lit a candle, sat back, and let the tension of the last few days fade away. His eyes focused on the flame of the candle. A few minutes later, a purple ring formed around the flame and disappeared. "I'm gonna talk to you the only way I know. If you read my heart, you'll know how grateful we are for Tyler's healing."

The silence in the church changed to a soft, distant type of music. It was different from anything he had ever heard.

The following day, Eric went up to the hospital. Tyler's parents and the kids were there already. "I'm coming home tomorrow," Tyler said. "I just know the house will be just like I left it."

Colleen, Evan, and Tyler's parents smiled. "Well, maybe not quite," Evan said.

The door opened and a smiling Dr. Hedwick walked in the room. "What a happy looking group."

"Thanks to you, doctor," Tyler's mother said.

"To a certain extent," he replied. "From what I've heard, a lot of prayers have been answered. He looked at Tyler's chart. "Everything looks good. I'll see you later."

"Paul is staying with Marie," Eric said. "He's getting along great with the girls."

"What about you and Ted?" Tyler asked.

"I apologized," Eric said. "How in the world could anyone stay mad at Ted?"

"Impossible," Tyler agreed. "These flowers came just before you arrived," Tyler said, with a big smile. "A potted plant from a Lynn Goss and Buck Dexter."

"Talk about surprises," Eric said.

"What kind of day is it outside?" Tyler asked.

"It's beginning to look a lot like Christmas . . . ." Eric sang.

Tyler smiled and added. "Just be thankful you didn't try for a singing career!"

Eric laughed. "Amen to that. You never looked prettier," he said. He kissed her. The woman in the adjoining bed looked up from her magazine long enough to smile her approval.

"Since it's not snowing, and the sun is out, it would be a beautiful day to visit someone special at the cemetery," Tyler said.

"I think so too," Eric said. "It's been quite a while since I've talked to that special girl."

Suddenly the woman's magazine hit the floor. Her smile changed into something beyond description. Eric smiled, picked up her magazine, and handed it to her. She accepted it, and quickly pulled away. He winked at Tyler and she winked back. The woman's expression seemed frozen on her face.

Eric stood at the foot of the grave like so often before. The sounds of the surrounding countryside vanished as if they never existed. "It's strange, the things you remember, Alice. I'll never forget the expression on your face the night you came to my house, after your mother had turned off the porch light," Eric said aloud. "You were standing in the rain with the most pitiful look on your face I'd ever seen . . . I knew that moment I loved you."

He stared at the letters carved in the monument. "Do you realize I'm over thirty one years old and Colleen, our daughter is almost a teenager? She's going with a boy named Glenn. Wonder, what you'd think of that. Tyler's coming home tomorrow from the hospital. There's so much that's happened. I know you're with us in spirit." Slowly the sounds of nature returned. "'Til we meet again, Alice."

"What a pleasant surprise," Eric said, after arriving home. Both Lynn Goss and Buck Dexter stood to greet him. "Tyler and I thank you for the plant."

"It's our pleasure," Lynn said. She looked to Buck with a smile, and then her face turned a light crimson.

"We got something to tell you," Buck said. Lynn held out her left hand. There on her finger was a gold engagement ring with a small diamond in it.

"It was my grandma's ring," Buck said.

"It's beautiful," Tyler raved. "When's the big day?"

"We gotta save up some money first," Buck said, "We're thinking maybe summertime."

"Congratulations, that's great," Eric said.

"Eric, I can't come in this weekend. I got somethin' I gotta do," Buck said.

"That's okay, Buck. We'll see you Monday."

"We have to be going," Lynn said. "Glad you're doing better, Tyler."

It was a beautiful Sunday morning. Eric got up early. After an hour of exhaustive sweeping, he realized just how much help Buck really was.

"Breakfast is ready," Evan yelled. "I'll help you after I eat, it's only eight o'clock. Aren't you getting in a hurry?"

"I woke early and couldn't sleep; I'm wound up, I guess," Eric said.

"Paul, eat your oatmeal," Tyler said.

"Bugs in it?" Paul asked.

"Those are not bugs. They're raisins," she said.

Colleen came to the table yawning, with a look of forced patience. "It's early, you know," she said to no one in particular.

"I hope we got enough of everything," Eric said to Tyler, "Do you realize the healing service starts in less than an hour?"

"Relax," she said. "We've got Frank and Ted getting the basement ready. Karen and Marie are checking upstairs. Don't worry, we're covered," Tyler said.

Less than a half hour later, people started coming. "Ladies and gentlemen, I welcome you to the Chapel of the Healing Light," Eric said. The church was overflowing, familiar faces along with strangers; even Dr. Hedwick was there.

A radiant Elaine Loulder greeted people with opening messages. The sound of hymns lifted the vibration throughout the small church. "Ladies and gentlemen," she said, "On this joyous morning, we are going to have an inspiring service with the thought of pouring out blessings to all those in need."

Eric looked to the rear of the church. He saw Walter Blanchard enter the front door. Eric had talked him into saying a few words. Eric left the podium and walked up the aisle to greet him.

Suddenly, Eric saw the same woman and her companion who had caused a disturbance at his church some time ago. They quickly rose from their seats. Eric looked at them with disbelief. He saw the tormented and fanatical look in the woman's and in her companion's faces. The sudden, unbelievable, appearance of a gun in the companion's hand seemed unreal.

"*Now* Anthony, *now*! I warned you, *heathen*!" she shouted.

Eric felt the pain in his chest and fell to the floor. Everyone started screaming and scattered. Tyler, Colleen, and Evan ran toward Eric. Walter ran to call for help. The man who shot the gun and the women with him ran out the door. Karen and Marie weren't far behind, and they ran to Eric, too. Frank and Ted were in the back room, unaware of what happened until they heard a shot and people screaming . . .

"Eric never believed anything like this would happen—who would?" Karen added.

"If it hadn't been for that damn church—I mean . . ."

Eric heard screams and saw the panic on people's faces.

307

Eric tried to clear his vision. He heard voices that seemed off in the distance. He felt someone touch his arm, and heard Tyler's voice, "Eric." Her face suddenly came into focus. "Eric!" she repeated, with the look of disbelief.

"What happened . . . I?"

"Don't try to speak," Dr. Hedwick's familiar voice warned.

"I remember—expressions in their faces . . ." Eric stopped for a second, and then whispered, "How bad is it?"

"Just take it easy, Eric," Dr. Hedwick said. Eric knew from the doctor's expression he was critical. He saw the tears in Tyler's eyes. Colleen and Evan looked as if they were in shock. Eric felt Tyler take his hand.

"Everyone's all right?" he asked.

"Yes," Tyler said softly, trying to comfort him. Eric saw the look in Dr. Hedwick's eyes. He gripped Colleen's hand and pulled her close. "Listen honey, I know I've asked so much of you."

Tears clouded her big blue eyes. "Daddy," was the only thing she managed to say.

"I want you to be brave, and always remember I'll be near you . . . You must understand!" Eric said as he felt the energy flow out of his body.

Colleen gripped his hand tighter. "I'm a trooper, Daddy!" Colleen sobbed.

With strained effort Eric said, "You and Evan . . . must hold the family—together."

Tears clouded Tyler's eyes. She whispered, "Maybe you should rest a minute." It was the first time he saw tears in Evan's eyes. "Thank you for being the best part of my life," Eric whispered to Tyler.

"I love you, Eric," Tyler said, with a gnawing feeling of hopelessness.

"Tyler," Eric said slowly. "You must be the strongest . . . You have that strength!"

He saw a white light appear, and then suddenly Alice appeared, lovelier than he remembered. She reached out to him. "Alice—Alice!" he whispered.

They were the last words Eric Silkwin ever spoke.

Three days later, at eight o'clock, the morning of December 20, 1959, Tyler requested the presence of the Karlands and the Faulklands at her house. They sat around the dining room table, staring at the presence of Claude Stratman, the reporter for the Benford Daily News.

"I know this is unusual," Tyler said, "But, I've asked Mr. Stratman here for Eric's editorial and obituary. Yes, I said editorial! It's what Eric would want." The four of them stared at her.

"The funeral is less than three hours away," Frank said flatly.

"I insisted on this interview before the funeral," Tyler said.

"What about that crazy couple?" Ted asked.

"They're in jail, and closely guarded," Stratman said. "Her husband's a lawyer . . . He has expressed his sympathy."

"Big deal . . . A little late, isn't it?" Frank added.

"I agree," Claude Stratman said. "I imagine both will be sentenced to a mental institution—I would think for the rest of their lives."

"How come Ellen's not here?" Frank asked.

"She's under sedation," Tyler said.

Everyone present added their personal thoughts, feelings, and insights on the controversial life of Eric Silkwin. The emotional discussion took place for over an hour.

"I thank you all, for an in depth look at his life," Stratman said. "Eric promised me an exclusive. I had no idea it would be . . . ." The sound of his voice broke. "Naturally, as I agreed, I'll not release it until Mrs. Silkwin and my editor, Mr. Cowler approve it. I'll do the best I possibly can."

"I believe you, Mr. Stratman. Otherwise, I'd never agree to this interview," Tyler said.

"It happened so fast! People panicked and . . . ." Frank yelled. "What could anyone do? A senseless tragedy. They warned him about that couple!"

"Eric was on a quest," Ted said sadly. "I know it sounds strange . . . I've felt that for the last few years."

"What are you talking about—a *quest*?" Karen asked.

"It's a strange feeling I've always had," Ted said slowly. "It was like he was loaned out to us. I know it sounds crazy! When I worked with him and observed his healings, it was as if he were a different person, or someone else was working through him."

"We'll never know for sure," Karen added.

"What did it get him?" Frank asked.

"A feeling you and I will probably never have," Ted said passionately. "How many of us spend our lives, dedicated to something we believe in, so much that it's a part of us?" Ted asked.

Nobody commented.

"What about the church?" Mr. Stratman asked.

"It will be closed. The children and I have talked it over. I'm sure Wallace Woodstock will want the property. We are moving to my folk's house, at least for now. They love it and my folks can use the help."

"I guess that's about all I need," Stratman said. "I wish I had known him better. I appreciate your cooperation. The facts need to be clarified for Eric, his family, friends, and the endless rumors from the people of Benford itself."

"That's exactly why I wanted this—completed," Tyler said. "Reverend Langtree and Reverend Loulder will share the service."

"Somehow that doesn't seem right," Frank said. "Reverend Langtree has been the Silkwin family minister for many years." He shook his head.

"How in the hell can you get hung-up on traditional rituals at a time like this?" Ted asked. His face was pale, and he was visibly shaken. "Don't you think it would be what Eric wanted?"

Frank lowered his head.

"Tyler, you haven't said much. Is there anything you want to add?" Marie asked softly.

Tyler seemed to be numb, but in a steady voice responded. "I think Eric and I fell in love the first time we met. I almost married a man I didn't love, because of my fear and confusion about his way of life. I have a part of him—his son. I'm grateful for the time we had together and the life we shared. Our lives will never be the same without Eric."

The group stared at her with tear-filled eyes.

The church filled beyond capacity an hour before the service began. Groups of friends and the curious onlookers stood outside in the cold, brisk weather. Their faces showed the shock of this unexpected violent tragedy.

Reverend Elaine Loulder faced the grief-stricken faces of loved ones. "I have only known Eric Silkwin for a short time," Reverend Loulder said. "A very special and meaningful time. This young man, whose life knew dedication and conflict, gave of himself, the only way he knew how. He continually searched for spiritual understanding and guidance, which was so much a part of his life. He answered the call of service that had to be fulfilled." Her voice broke, "I will miss him very much."

A pale Ellen, Johnny, and daughter Elizabeth, along with loved ones filed past Eric's casket for a final farewell. Reverend Langtree ended the graveside service, with Eric's favorite—the twenty-third Psalm.

Crowds of people waited off in the distance. Among them were Dr. Emmery and Dr. Hedwick, a young man named Dexter, and strangely enough, Wallace Woodstock. Tyler and the children, along with Ellen, Johnny, Karen, and Frank greeted the mourners. Marie stood beside Ted who, after he touched the casket, sobbed openly.

Tyler stepped forward with Evan. They put their hands on the casket. "Goodbye Dad," Evan said, then sobbed, and quickly turned away.

"Goodbye darling," Tyler whispered. "Rest in peace."

She turned to Colleen and motioned her forward, and whispered. "It's your time, honey."

Colleen held four red roses. She stared at her father's casket beside her mother's grave. Colleen, with tears streaming down her face and her voice filled with emotion whispered. "I know you're together. I love you both so much. You will be in my heart forever."

In final tribute, Colleen carefully laid two of the roses on her mother's grave, and then she placed the other two roses on her father's casket, and whispered. "*Goodbye . . . Daddy.*"

CPSIA information can be obtained at www.ICGtesting.com
Printed in the USA
LVOW10s1935190815

450751LV00004B/636/P